Jana Bibi's Excellent Fortunes

Jana Bibi's
Excellent Fortunes

a novel

Betsy Woodman

A HOLT PAPERBACK   HENRY HOLT AND COMPANY   NEW YORK

Henry Holt and Company, LLC
Publishers since 1866
175 Fifth Avenue
New York, New York 10010
www.henryholt.com

Henry Holt® and ⓗ® are registered trademarks of
Henry Holt and Company, LLC.

Library of Congress Cataloging-in-Publication Data
Woodman, Betsy.
   Jana Bibi's excellent fortunes : a novel / Betsy Woodman.—1st ed.
      p.   cm.
   "A Holt Paperback."
   ISBN 978-0-8050-9349-0
   1. Fortune-tellers—Fiction.   2. Single women—Fiction.   3. Scots—
India—Fiction.   4. India—Fiction.   I. Title.
   PS3623.O666J36 2012
   813'.6—dc22   2011030598

Henry Holt books are available for special promotions and
premiums. For details contact: Director, Special Markets.

First Edition 2012

Designed by Kelly S. Too

Printed in the United States of America
1   3   5   7   9   10   8   6   4   2

To Lee

AUTHOR'S NOTE

I have set *Jana Bibi's Excellent Fortunes* in 1960 and used the place names and spellings common at that time—Bombay (now Mumbai), Madras (now Chennai), Simla (now Shimla), and Benares (now officially Varanasi, traditionally Kashi, and, today, in some contexts, Banaras).

Hamara Nagar is a fictional town; it would be somewhere in today's Uttarakhand, a state that got carved out of Uttar Pradesh in 2000 and for a while was called Uttaranchal. Terauli is also fictional.

The Indian rupee went decimal in 1957, but the characters in the book think in terms of the old system of sixteen annas to a rupee, four pice to an anna, and three pie to a pice. Similarly, both metric and British Imperial (and also various traditional Indian measures) were in use at the time of this story, hence the mix of kilometers, yards, and feet.

Recent travelers who have budgeted their trips at 40 to 50 rupees to the U.S. dollar may be puzzled by the exchange rate mentioned in the book. For many years, the rate was 4.77 to 4.79 rupees to the dollar.

Also, American readers may wonder why the boarding school students in the story are in school in July and August. With some short breaks, hill station boarding schools were—and still are—in session from February or March through November, with their long vacation in the winter months.

"Hindustani" is the blanket term for Hindi and Urdu, which at the basic spoken level are roughly the same language. Hindi is written in Devanagari script, and its formal terms derive from Sanskrit. Urdu is written in modified Arabic script, with many words of Persian or Arabic origin. Urdu, especially in modern times, is associated largely with Muslims. Polite people use the salutations appropriate to the religion of the person they're addressing.

A glossary is provided at the end of the book for terms that may be unfamiliar.

Jana Bibi's Excellent Fortunes

A New Life in an Old Place

◆ Two Letters

Mr. Ganguly perched on the wrought-iron chair and preened his emerald-green feathers. In the palace garden, a flock of wild Indian ringnecks came swooping down into the mango trees, settled and chattered and screamed at one another, reached some agreement, and took off again. The parrot turned his head briefly to look at them, without much interest. His wings were not clipped. Yet he flew only a few feet at a time, from chair to ground to table, table to chair to perch, always returning to safety.

Jana put down her teacup, took a peanut from her pocket, and held it out. Mr. Ganguly held it daintily with his claw, shelled it with his beak, and ate it.

"More," he said.

"Later. Oh, all right." She gave him another.

She heard a door close and looked up to the verandah of the palace, watched Mary's rotund figure come down the steps, the afternoon post in her hand. Most days, Jana got no letters. Who would write? Jack sent dutiful filial missives from Scotland, and friends in Bombay sent greetings on major holidays. Otherwise, people from her past stayed silent.

"Jana mem!" Mary's smile transformed her heavily pock-marked face. "Two letters! Postman was so excited, he almost fell off his bicycle." She handed over the letters and adjusted her sari. "He said it was good luck to get letters on Monday. Lord Shiva rules on Monday."

Jana smiled. Mary maintained that her family had been Christian since Saint Thomas journeyed to Madras—"in the days of old!"—but she nonetheless hedged her bets, knitting Buddhist symbols into her sweaters and shawls and celebrating Divali by putting out little oil lamps. In her room, she kept one picture of Jesus and one of Dr. Ambedkar, her fellow outcaste who had risen from his lowly status to write the constitution of India.

"Jana mem, Jack baba might be coming to visit from U.K?" Mary had seen Jack's familiar handwriting on the thin blue aerogramme.

"Perhaps," said Jana. "If only he would take a holiday from that engineering job of his."

"Engineering is good," said Mary. "But holidays are also good. And every boy also should come to see his mother."

Meanwhile, Jana was looking at the second piece of mail, a large buff envelope postmarked Allahabad, 1 June 1959. Eight months ago, Jana calculated. Still, that was not too bad, considering the number of places to which it had been forwarded. Almost everywhere she had lived in her adult life—the remote mission station in northern India, the Iranis' beach cottage in Bombay, her grandfather MacPherson's castle outside Glasgow, now owned by her son, and, finally, the nawab's palace, in the former princely state of Terauli. A doggedly determined letter, that!

She slit the envelope with a knife from the tea tray and withdrew a fat legal document and a cover letter. Mr. Ganguly, now perched on her shoulder, bent his head toward the letter as if reading it, and Mary lingered, not taking away the tea tray.

"Dear Mrs. Laird," Jana read.

It has come to our attention that you are the sole living heir of the late Ramsay Grant, whose will we probated in 1930. At that time there was one piece of property that could not be distrib-

uted, because of the terms of the lease, which only expired in 1955. Further complications regarding succession have only recently been resolved. We are now happy to inform you that you are the owner of the Jolly Grant House, No. 108 Central Bazaar, adjacent to Ramachandran's Treasure Emporium and across from Royal Tailors, Hamara Nagar, Uttar Pradesh. We assume that you are aware of the building's historic importance.

All matters related to the execution of your grandfather's will are now resolved and all property distributed. There should be no impediment to your taking possession of the building. Enclosed herewith you will find the key.

The Jolly Grant House, thought Jana. Extraordinary that it was still standing, let alone that none of Grandfather Grant's Anglo-Indian descendants had lived to take possession. A shred of memory came back to her, of a visit to Hamara Nagar in 1912, when she was ten. The family had put up at the Victoria Hotel, even though Grandfather Grant had plenty of room in the guest-house of his compound three or four miles away, then on the outskirts of town.

"You're not actually going to visit him," Jana's father had said, "and take the *children*?" And—left unsaid—expose them to *that woman*, Grandfather Grant's Indian wife?

"James, you're being so stuffy. He's almost *ninety*!" Jana's mother had answered.

That little exchange summed up the two sides of Jana's family. How many generations of them—soldiers, civil servants, engineers, architects—had worked and lived in India? Five, six? From the beginning, some—like her father—considered India a place to earn their living, while keeping away from Indians as much as possible. Stuffy folks, who insisted on boundaries, categories, and boxes. But others—like her mother—adored India and were never completely happy anywhere else. Grandfather Grant, who looked like a proper Victorian gentleman, was actually of the second sort, a throwback to the eighteenth century, when it was commonplace for a British man to have an Indian wife. He got away with his eccentricity, Jana's father always maintained, only because of his wealth.

On their way to visit the Jolly Grant House, in the spring of 1912, Jana's pony had bolted, and for several terrified minutes she'd thought she'd be thrown over the knife-edge cliff to certain death below. She remembered arriving wobbly-kneed and in tears at a large building with a lookout tower, and being comforted by an Indian woman in a soft silk sari whose skin smelled of almond cream.

She turned to Jack's aerogramme.

"Mother, you're too old to live alone," she read. "Come live in Glasgow. Isn't that where you belong? I grant you that it was noble to live as a missionary and take care of Father all those years, and I suppose that the world does need musicians, but do you need to be one of them? And aren't you tired of living from hand to mouth? What if you get sick? Remember that you'll always be an outsider there."

She had to smile. Jack had always been a little old lady. As a boy, he'd preferred reading to exploring the mission compound or climbing trees. She'd never found a lizard in *his* pocket. "Safety first" had been his motto as a six-year-old, and apparently it still was.

Now, I ask you, she said, almost aloud. Too old? Fifty-eight? And *alone*? Who was alone in India, apart from a few prayer-mumbling sadhus? The only time in her life she'd felt alone was during the six lonely years in Scotland. Grieving the sudden death of her parents, wrenched away, in 1919, from everything she'd ever known—the big white house in Allahabad, the boarding school in the hills, the sun-drenched gardens. Failing her audition to get into the Glasgow Athenaeum as a violin student, working as her grandfather MacPherson's unpaid secretary—now, *those* things had been lonely.

In contrast, going to a Himalayan hill station, with Mary and Mr. Ganguly, did not strike her as a lonely proposition. And she liked the idea of living in Grandfather Grant's house. Anyway, she'd felt for some time that her usefulness at the nawab's palace was at an end.

"Mary," said Jana, "we may have a new home." She sketched the details, knowing that Mary would like the number 108. The Ganges had 108 names; the god Krishna had played the flute for 108 milkmaids. Sure enough, Mary's eyes lit up.

"Very auspicious, Jana mem." She took the tea tray and headed back into the palace.

That night, Jana soaked in the tub in her huge bathroom, looking up at the high ceilings and wondering how she could possibly consider leaving the palace. It was so *pleasant* here. So *comfortable*. The salary was generous and the expenses almost nonexistent, so that every month she added to her savings account, a good thing after the lean years as a missionary and then as a dance musician.

But, but . . . boredom was setting in; that could not be denied. There just wasn't enough to do, now that all but one of the nawab's children had been packed off to boarding school in Switzerland. The dozen children's violins the nawab had ordered from Italy when Jana had first arrived lay silent. Gone were the days when the children would line up on the palace steps and, led by Jana, greet their father with a medley of international tunes. The night Prime Minister Nehru had come for dinner, the children had played the national anthem, "Jana Gana Mana," bringing tears to the prime minister's eyes. There wouldn't be another night like that.

She got out of the tub, wrapped herself in a Turkish towel, and dried off in the spacious dressing room. She thought she heard Mr. Ganguly calling from her bedroom and went in to see what he wanted, but he was merely going into his bedtime routine: talking to himself, settling down on his perch, closing one eye and opening it again before finally drifting off. He looked amusingly decorative and fitting against the elegant background of the room, his bright red beak and green plumage bringing out the colors in the Persian rug. She settled herself in the window seat and looked around at the huge room, with its French doors leading out to a verandah and, beyond that, the garden with the mango trees. Leave this cushiest of situations? Madness. And yet, deep down inside, she knew that the decision was already made.

Fourteen-year-old Noor, the youngest of the nawab's children, and the only remaining one to be taking violin lessons from Jana, burst into tears at the news.

"You're all leaving? Mary, too? And Mr. Ganguly?"

"But, Noor, my pet," said Jana, "you'll be leaving soon yourself. You'll love it in Switzerland, I promise. You won't think of us for a moment!"

"Promise me you'll come back during holidays," said Noor.

"I'll try," said Jana. "And you come and visit me in the hills. Get your father to buy a villa up there." It was offered as a joke, but Noor's eyes lit up.

"What's the name of the place you're going to, again?" Noor said.

"Hamara Nagar."

Noor and Jana exchanged looks, and both burst out laughing.

"That's such a silly name!" said Noor. "Our Town. *Whose* town?"

"I don't know whose it was originally," said Jana. "But soon it's going to be mine."

✧ Your Wish Is Your Fortune

"Madam! Madam!" The gnarled hand tugged at her sleeve. "Madam, I tell your future from your shadow. All truth, no lies, as God is my witness."

Mr. Ganguly, riding on Jana's shoulder, spread his wings and let out a shriek.

The fortune-teller was as ragged as the beggars waiting in the street outside the train station. A dirt-colored scrap of shawl barely covered one shoulder; a ragged *dhoti* drooped around his waist. The eyes, however, did not beg but glowed in his creased old face like two small amber beacons.

Jana looked down at her shadow, a dwarf on the scorching pavement with a feathered creature on its shoulder. What on earth could you possibly say about a person from her shadow, short at noon, lengthening at dusk, gone when it rained? Yet she could not resist any new form of fortune-telling. Palms, cards, crystal balls, tea leaves, bird flight, clouds, dice, numbers, the stars—she thought she knew about every possible way people claimed they could tell the future. Yet here was one more.

"How much?"

"As much as you want," the fortune-teller said. "Good fortune, give more; bad fortune, give less."

Jana chuckled. "Okay. Give me a fortune worth two annas."

The man frowned scornfully. "Two annas. No. Superior knowledge only for four annas. Same as chocolate bar, madam."

"*Small* chocolate bar," said Mary. She scowled at the fortune-teller with such disapproval that Jana laughed out loud. "Jana mem, come. Taxi is waiting."

"It won't take any time." Jana gestured to the man to go ahead, tell.

He planted his walking stick with a thump and got a faraway look in his eyes.

"Memsahib has a strong shadow. She will have a good future, a happy life, much money, and a good death. And her name will live forever." The man set his lips together.

"And?"

"That's all. All truth, no lies."

Mary was outraged. "That was too short for four annas. Jana mem, this man is one absolute bandit! Highway robbery he is practicing!"

The man said, "All right, I will tell one more thing. You will make a long journey across the sea. To England."

This brought another laugh from Jana and another snort from Mary. "Of course he is telling you that, Jana mem. He tells all white people that! Except if he thinks they're American; then he says they will go to America."

Jana started fishing in her handbag, then had a thought. She switched to Hindi, which made the man start in surprise, and said, "Let me ask you one thing. What do you actually *see* in the shadow? What makes one shadow different from the next?"

A look of injured dignity came over the man's face. "If I told you that, madam, then you would take my job."

"Fair enough." She gave the man a quarter-rupee coin.

"Jana mem," insisted Mary, "we have a long way to go still."

"All right," said Jana.

The man walked away, toward the crowd of passengers coming out of the railway station.

"Good luck," Jana called after him.

He turned his head. "Good luck, madam."

The taxi driver's patch over one eye and cataract filming the other did not inspire confidence. Nevertheless, the wobbly yellow letters painted on the door of his battered Morris said, "50,00,00,000 kilometres—no accidents!" Jana walked around and read what was on the other side: "Come along with me on the beautiful journey of life—you never know what will happen!"

"I hope this man can drive," Mary said grimly.

The driver's eyebrows shot up. "Madam! I am Mr. Kilometres! I am driving this road for thirty years. With my eyes closed. I used to drive miles, now I drive kilometres. Modern style. Come, kindly ascend."

There is no safety in safety, Jana reminded herself. If I'd wanted safety, I would be in Glasgow right now, Jack checking that I'd turned off the gas.

"Kindly ascend," the taxi driver repeated.

Ascending was easier said than done, since only one of the back doors of the taxi would open. Jana gestured to Mary to climb in first, which she did, gathering her sari and hoisting herself across the dusty false-leather seat. Then Jana put Mr. Ganguly in the birdcage. He looked dejected, his feathers drooping, his eyes mournful and accusing.

"You miss the palace, don't you," said Jana. All those comfortable nooks and perches, and people who brought him nuts and pieces of mango—of course he missed the palace! "Don't worry, we're going to a new home." She set the cage on the seat.

Jana watched the driver put her two tin footlockers, the wooden crate containing her harmonium, and Mary's duffel and bedroll into an already overstuffed boot. She kept her violin case with her and climbed into the cab.

They took the mountain road at breakneck speed, the taxi's horn making a whiny goose call as they went into the hairpin bends on the wrong side of the road. Jana rolled down the window and tried to breathe in fresh air instead of fumes. Every hour or so, they stopped and the driver lifted the hood and listened to the bubbling noises. Each time, Jana got out and stretched, and each time, she got a wider view of the sinuous road, the terraced fields and small villages, and far below, the plains with their snaking rivers.

By the outskirts of Hamara Nagar, Jana was dizzy and nauseated, Mary's normally dark face a chalky gray, and Mr. Ganguly silent in his cage. A barrier kept all motor vehicles from proceeding farther than the taxi depot, and there were still three miles to go to the hotel.

"Terra firma!" said Jana. "I have to walk. Mary, you can take a rickshaw if you want."

Mary, however, looked scandalized at the idea of being transported while the memsahib went on foot.

As the taxi driver unloaded their things, a crowd gathered out of nowhere. Men argued and spat streams of betel juice and grabbed for the luggage, while children crowded around the birdcage and shouted, "Hello, how are you?" The driver yelled at all of them. Struggling to concentrate in the din, Jana paid the driver and picked five porters from the press of men. Yelling triumphantly at the others to get lost, the victors strapped up and set off, incredibly fast even in bare feet. Jana kept one back to carry the birdcage, but soon, the others were out of sight.

Only five porters. Jana remembered the army of porters they had needed, when she was a child, for each April's trip to the hills. Her mother's hats alone had filled three trunks.

Now it was mid-March, not quite the tourist season in Hamara Nagar. Still, tea shops and tobacco stands were doing a brisk business. The cloth merchants sat cross-legged in their stalls, ready at the first sign of a customer to jump up and pull bolts of cloth from the horizontal rows stacked floor to ceiling. Tiny Nepalese porters trudged by under loads of charcoal, and Tibetan peddlers wheeled carts of striped textiles and turquoise-and-silver jewelry.

Jana picked up the pace, and Mary, unaccustomed to wearing tennis shoes, puffed as she tried to keep up.

"The air *is* cool," Jana said, happy to feel the breeze like peppermint on her face.

"Cold, madam," noted Mary, who said madam only when disgruntled. "Those men are making clouds." She gestured to a group of men huddled around a charcoal brazier, their breath visible in the air.

The town was very different from when Jana was ten, with no British people strolling by with parasols. The signs saying "No Indians or dogs" were gone from the main street road, the road now lined with buildings. A huge green structure claimed to house "the largest roller skating rink in all of India." Jana saw a Bharatanatyam dance school, a couple of cinemas, a camera shop. Past and present rose before her eyes like a double-exposed photograph. Was this the stretch of road where her pony had bolted?

Once truly into the English Bazaar, however, she found the landscape more familiar. At the western end of the town, she recognized the police station, the library, and the Anglican church, with its yellow roses in bloom. In the Municipal Garden, the plantings were as symmetrical and well tended as in the olden days, and the magnificent canopy of a golden rain tree shaded benches where women sat and chatted while their children played. A bronze George Everest still stood on a pedestal, peering into the distance, measuring the peaks of the Himalayas.

Finally, here was the Victoria Hotel, its circular driveway marked with white brick triangles. Jana took in her breath. It was so—so well preserved, so much the same. Even the people seemed imported from the past: the ancient *mali* watering and murmuring endearments to the pots of chrysanthemums, and the bearer in a white uniform and tufted turban standing by the entry.

By the side of the door, the porters were already waiting with Jana's luggage. She added enough baksheesh to their pay to bring smiles, picked up Mr. Ganguly's cage, and went in.

Mary followed, murmuring approval. "Old place. Very pukka."

Jana took in the antelope heads looking down reproachfully from the dark paneled walls and the stuffed tiger in the middle of the floor. There was a quirky, faded elegance to the semicircular staircase, the crisscross mullions in the windows. Would sahibs and memsahibs descend that staircase, ready for their *chota pegs*?

And then she got jolted back to 1960. Instead of a picture of a medal-laden George V behind the desk, there was Prime Minister Nehru, pensive in a white cap. And young Mr. Dass was the new breed of hotelier, clean-shaven and nattily turned out in suit and tie. He was attentive to the point of unctuousness.

"Welcome, madam. We are honored by your presence."

On writing to the hotel, Jana had asked whether birds could be accommodated, and the same Mr. Dass had answered by return post: "We are making allowances for children, well-behaved dogs, and polite birds."

"Namasté!" Mr. Ganguly, on his best behavior and fascinated by the new surroundings, had recovered his voice.

"Namasté," returned Mr. Dass, his face becoming warmer and less officious. He presented the room keys with a flourish, and briefed Jana on mealtimes, mail deliveries, and the schedule for the string band in the Vienna Room. While he was making careful entries in his ledger, she peeked into the empty ballroom, where several barefoot men were sweeping the floor. A vision came to mind of her parents waltzing, her father in white tie and tails, her mother in a gray silk dress with inserts of Belgian lace.

Mr. Dass brought her attention back to the desk. "Madam has stayed here before?"

"Once. Fifty—actually, forty-eight years ago."

"Just one minute." He disappeared into the adjoining office and reappeared with an ancient guest book. "Take a look, take a look!"

Among the entries in faded ink, Jana found her mother's elegant handwriting: "Tea was promptly at dawn, and the bearers very well trained." Jana saw her own childish signature, dated June 15, 1912. She'd written, "We had a lovely time. I hope we come here next year."

But they hadn't; they'd gone to Simla, instead.

"Madam?" Mr. Dass was asking.

"Oh, yes, what were you saying?"

"Bed tea? Do you require bed tea?"

They still had that at least, a vestige of the empire she rather liked. At her nod, he said, "Five o'clock? Six?"

"Seven?" she said hopefully.

"Of course. Oh, madam has mail." He handed her a blue aerogramme.

"Have you many guests here?" she asked.

"Not yet. But we have a busy season coming up," Mr. Dass said. "April through June—fully booked! Then, after the rains, we have the Third Annual Futurology Convention. Delegates are coming from all over the world."

"That sounds interesting. Do they make predictions?"

"They do," said Dass. "Only problem is, they make contradictory predictions. So while they're never really wrong, they're never really right."

"I can understand that," said Jana.

Jana's room was off a long verandah punctuated by planter's chairs and hanging baskets of geraniums. Bearers went back and forth with tea trays, and a young woman was delivering laundry. Jana was unpacking her clothes into an old almirah with a carved front and a spotty mirror when there was a tap on the door. It was Mary, now revived.

"Mary! Mary!" called Mr. Ganguly.

"Namasté. Bird is happy again—that's good, right, Jana mem?"

"It is good," said Jana. "How is your room, Mary?"

"No problem, Jana mem. No scorpions, no ants, no rats, no lizards. Just one cat that sleeps outside the door."

An uncharacteristically low population density, Jana thought. "Have you had any food?"

"I am going just now," said Mary. "They tell me there is a South Indian food stall in the bazaar." She smiled broadly at this unexpected find. "This town has more than you would expect, Jana mem."

Hamara Nagar Threatened

❧ *Rambir and Ramachandran Talk in the Why Not? Tea Shop*

V. K. Ramachandran, proud owner of Ramachandran's Treasure Emporium, part-time metaphysician, amateur engineer, full-time husband of the plump and beautiful Padma, and harassed father of six, poured some of his tea into his saucer to cool and then took a sip. His friend Rambir Vohra, the overworked editor of *Our Town, Our Times,* followed suit. They took tea together almost daily, at the prime table of the Why Not? Tea Shop, close to the wide-open storefront so they could see the world go by.

In their student days at Benares Hindu University, their nicknames had been Mr. Fat and Mr. Lean. "Fat" was not really fair to Ramachandran; he just happened to have a round face and a physique that his daughters described as "cuddly, Dads, so swe-e-et and cuddly." "Lean," however, did describe Rambir, who looked as if he rarely got a square meal and, when he did, immediately burned it off in worry and other excessive mental activity. Ramachandran wore an impeccable white *dhoti* and a collarless white silk shirt, topped off with a soft beige shawl. Rambir wore Western-style trousers, a blue shirt with a pointed collar, and a striped necktie.

"Has the paper been put to bed?" Ramachandran recognized Rambir's typical exhausted Friday afternoon expression.

"Not quite," said Rambir. "You know, every week it's rush rush rush. Just like in student days. Working the whole night through, finding a stupid mistake at the last minute . . . Just this morning I ended up resetting a whole page of type myself. Editor in chief, bah! Sounds important, no? But what are you? A slave, a *slave,* I tell you. This writer doesn't make his deadline, *you* quickly work to make up the time. That advertiser decides he wants twice as big an ad, *you* reorganize the page. This is the exalted world of publishing! Books, newspapers, magazines . . . you do it for love, not money. Or out of some misguided sense of public service. Because you feel the pen is mightier than the sword. That sort of thing."

"You have noble ideals—and you live by them," said Ramachandran, in a tone halfway between pity and admiration.

"Don't you think a man of my age ought to have outgrown them?"

Ramachandran gave a chuckle. "You're keeping them alive for the rest of us. But carry on, my friend. *Ad astra per aspera.* To the stars through difficulties!" Although Ramachandran wasn't keen on effort as a way of life, he liked quoting Latin expressions that exalted it.

"You tell me that every week," Rambir said. "I've had plenty of *aspera* this week. And some aspirin as well. But we're almost ready to go to print." He leaned back in his chair and let out an exaggerated breath of relief, as he did every week on reaching this point.

"Have you heard about the dam?" Ramachandran asked.

"Dam?" Rambir frowned. "What dam?"

"The government's dam."

Rambir rolled his eyes. "Which one? Bhakra Dam? You know, the government builds so many dams I can't even keep track. Don't tell me about it until next week. Government news can wait."

Ramachandran glanced quickly around the room and lowered his voice. "You might want to hear this. It will definitely be a big story at some point." He reached into a large envelope and pulled out a piece of white paper with "Confidential" written prominently across the top.

"They're planning a dam to provide drinking water all over Uttar Pradesh, even for Delhi. Talking about providing water in the dry season, irrigating the farmers' fields, making a big lake for tourists. Just the kind of thing Mr. Nehru likes."

"Why not?" Rambir was a patriotic Indian and a great fan of the prime ministers.

"Normally, I too would say, Why not?"

"But?"

"But, just read."

Rambir scanned the paper, and his eyes narrowed.

MEMO—CONFIDENTIAL

Project: Hamara Nagar Dam

Height: 245 metres

Length: 2 kilometres

Proposed location: 1 kilometre from town center

Benefits: Electricity, irrigation, drinking water, tourism.
  Largest man-made lake in the world.

Dams of comparable importance: Aswan, Hoover,
  Bhakra-Nangal

"And take a look at the description of our town," said Rama-chandran.

Rambir skimmed over a disparaging paragraph:

Second-rate hill station established during the late nine-teenth century. Of negligible importance. Some tourism, but not a fashionable destination. Level of economic activity low. Traditional trade routes from Tibet no longer in use since advent of People's Republic.

"Second-rate!" Rambir exploded.

For a moment, Ramachandran worried for the state of his friend's arteries. Perhaps breaking this news to him on a Friday, on top of the pressure of getting out the paper, had not been wise.

"And what, pray tell, do they intend to do with *us*?"

"Read on," said Ramachandran.

"Evacuation Requirements," read Rambir.

"Three boarding schools (St. Bartholomew's College—boys; St. Margaret's College—girls; Far Oaks School—mixed boys and girls, mostly foreigners) must be resited. Preferable for public relations reasons to persuade townspeople to move without use of force. Funding for project: to be decided. World Bank interested. USSR possible.

Ramachandran noticed that a muscle in Rambir's lower eyelid was twitching, something that happened when he was under pressure, as during exams in their student days and these days when on deadline.

Rambir started to hand the paper back to Ramachandran, then shook his head and read it again, as if hoping to see something different this time. "Where did you get this?"

Ramachandran looked apologetic. "My brother-in-law in the Ministry of Irrigation and Power. He thinks I should sell the Treasure Emporium and get my family out of the town before it's too late."

"But this is outrageous!" Rambir's voice rose in spite of himself. "This is our town. This is where we live. Man-made lake— you saw that, right? Biggest one in the world, they say? We'll be at the bottom of it."

"Yes," said Ramachandran gloomily. "Like the lost civilization of Atlantis."

He thought of his beloved Treasure Emporium inhabited by fishes and worms, serpents swimming between the brass stools and trays, everything else disintegrated into watery pulp.

"Just think of what they're saying." Rambir's voice was now a squeak. "Other areas might be too important to build on, but *we* are negligible. Negligible! Only they're not merely going to *neglect* us—they already do that, heaven only knows. And it's fine with me if they do. All we've ever wanted in this town was to live quietly and enjoy the views of the hills. But no, all of a sudden we're dispensable. Disposable! So they are going to do away with us. Destroy us. *Drown* us. Let me keep this memo. We'll get this story out in tomorrow's newspaper. *That* will get people up in arms."

The secret was in danger of being a secret no longer. Proprietor Joshi hovered over them. Did they want more tea, or maybe a nice samosa or some puris with special sauce? Ramachandran and Rambir shook their heads in unison.

"See," said Ramachandran, "my brother-in-law will lose his job if it gets out that he told anyone about this, and Padma will never forgive me. So discretion is in order."

Rambir said, "We can't be cowardly about this, *can we*?"

Ramachandran gave a grimace of guilt. "I think there's an alternative way," he said. "We can work on a way to protect the town without revealing how we know the plans for the dam. Why not? Work on outwitting the government. Make them decide that the dam is just not worth building."

"And how will we do that?" Rambir's eyelid was still twitching.

"We will give the rest of the world a reason for wanting us to survive. A reason for coming here. 'Not a fashionable destination'? That can be remedied."

Rambir sat back in his chair again and crossed his arms, listening.

"Our anonymity is completely undeserved," says Ramachandran. "We're all poets and philosophers here. That fellow Feroze Ali Khan, for example, who made my son Vikram's cricket uniform. He delivered it and announced, 'I have stitched high scores into every seam . . . the little sahib will shine like a sparkling star.' And guess what! Vikram batted the best game he's ever had! Then I went to that chap Powell at Sharp Eyes Vision Care. He told me, 'Better eyesight leads to better insight,' gave me an excellent eye exam, and then equally excellent specs! Here we truly live out the maxim 'Philosophy, the handmaiden of life'! Every conversation in this town gives you food for thought, doesn't it?"

"We do have history," said Rambir thoughtfully. "The Princess of Wales—later to be Queen Mary, of course—visited in 1906. She bought a carved walking stick at Garwhal Walking Sticks—and stayed at the Victoria Hotel. Rudyard Kipling, too."

"Exactly right," said Ramachandran. "And other illustrious people have been here as well. George Everest used to come here on holiday. It says so right on the plaque under his statue in the Municipal Garden."

"How about the Jolly Grant House? Didn't some strange Scottish fellow build that?"

"Must have been strange, yes," said Ramachandran. "Just the way he designed it. The tower, the outbuildings. The place is an eyesore now, though."

"Easily remedied with a coat of paint," said Rambir. "Maybe someone will buy it and spruce it up. Tourists could go up into the tower and have a beautiful view of the foothills and the plains. The thing was built around 1890!"

"Yes!" The ideas were now tumbling out of Ramachandran. "We can have that place declared a national monument."

"And your Treasure Emporium should be a national monument, too," said Rambir. "After all, it used to be the guesthouse for the Jolly Grant House. It's *very* historic—in addition to its present importance, of course."

"That's kind of you to say." Ramachandran smiled the way he did when people spoke highly of his store or of his children or of his wife.

"You know," said Rambir, "maybe we can get the Futurology Convention in the news."

"Yes," said Ramachandran. "I'm hoping that the Futurology Convention will have the status of one of the grand gatherings of mankind. Like the famous world fairs or the Kumbh Mela. I'd like to see pilgrims coming in . . . journalists . . . philosophers . . . tourists . . . every bent and inclination of humanity!"

"Why not? Doesn't having the convention *here* prove that we are a vital center for . . . a vital center, in any case."

"Yes!" Rambir's eyes shone as they used to when he was university debating club captain, and, as in those days, he veered off the subject. "A center for world peace! You know how the USA and the USSR are going to bury everyone with their atomic bombs. We must be the moral counterforce so this does not happen! World peace must start in India, right here in Hamara Nagar."

"If we become a center for world peace, that might be all the more reason they would put us at the bottom of a lake," Ramachandran pointed out. "World peace is exactly what a lot of people don't want."

But Rambir's imagination was now taking flight.

"We can get the youth involved!"

"A children's crusade?" said Ramachandran skeptically. "The last time that happened was in the thirteenth century. And you know what befell them. They starved. Drowned! Never reached their destination."

"Times have changed," said Rambir. "We have radio. We have newspapers. We can telegraph the news all over the world. I can go down to the PTT this very minute and send a story to London by telegram, and they can print it in the morning."

"Have you ever done that?" Ramachandran remembered how his friend could get carried away with his own rhetoric.

"Well, I *could* do it. Easily."

Mr. Joshi was back again, asking if they wanted anything more. It was clear that they should either drink more tea or vacate their table.

Rambir glanced at his watch. "I must get back to the press."

Ramachandran tilted his head and told Mr. Joshi to put the tea on his account.

"You know," said Ramachandran, "world peace is all very nice, but other people are working on it, sort of. United Nations and suchlike. We should offer something different. World *vision*. I am thinking thusly: Hamara Nagar—the place where the future begins."

"Doesn't the future begin everywhere?" said Rambir. "At every moment?"

"Does that disprove my point?" Ramachandran gave a triumphant smile.

⚜ Bandhu Sharma Gets Instructions from His Higher-Ups

Commissioner of Police Bandhu Sharma, having jammed his finger in the top drawer of his file cabinet, kicked the cabinet and yelled at the *chaprassi* so suddenly that the fellow jumped and knocked over the wastebasket.

"Tea! Right now!"

The *chaprassi*, who looked as if he expected his rear end to get the same treatment as the file cabinet, righted the wastebasket and was out the door in a flash.

"Secondhand finger-pinching furniture, what do you expect in a second-rate penny-pinching town!" Bandhu said out loud. He paced around his office in disgust. His gaze fell on the wooden desk with the sticky drawer, the two straight chairs with sagging cane seats. He glared at the light bulb dangling on a frayed cord from the ceiling, the craters in the cement floor. They could at least get me an up-to-date map that doesn't show India and Pakistan as one big country, he thought. Am I supposed to spend the rest of my days in this beastly little room? Three transfers I have applied for, three times I have been refused . . . what did I do in any past life to merit such a fate!

He sat down at his desk and picked up the framed family photograph. He and his wife, Manju, were in the center, Bandhu in full dress uniform, Manju seeming to shrink back into her chair. Standing were the two older boys in neat school uniforms, with expressions already echoing Bandhu's glowering stare. The third boy, the little one, was sitting on his mother's lap, dressed

in an immaculate sailor suit. Just looking at the photograph set
Bandhu off again.

"How is one to give one's family the best advantages in this
out-of-the-way hole!"

Then, noticing that the mail had come, he picked a large
manila envelope off the top of the pile and slit it open with his
brass paper knife. Curiosity temporarily calmed his bad temper,
and he perused the sheet with growing interest. By the time the
chaprassi came back with his brass tumbler of tea, Bandhu was
practically jubilant. Here, finally, was his deliverance!

"'Second-rate hill station' . . . 'negligible' . . . yes," he murmured to himself, "I quite agree with this assessment. Sometimes the fellows in the upper echelons actually get it right.
Quite right, in fact."

And the thought of the town of Hamara Nagar consigned to
the bottom of a lake twisted his face into a smile.

I won't even have to apply for a transfer, he thought. They'll
have to give one to me. Maybe Dehra Dun. Or Delhi! Oh,
Delhi . . . What was that nursery rhyme again? A cat went to
Delhi . . . *Billi gayi Dilli* . . .

And he pictured himself as a cool cat in Delhi, strolling
down the broad avenues, posing for a photograph by India Gate.

If I lived in a city, he thought, just think of what life would
be like. Cinemas, restaurants—choice upon choice! Not just two
little tea shops, one with three tables and the other with four. Not
just two cinemas that were always canceling showings because
of power failures or merely because the projectionist decided
he'd rather do something else that day. A city had things you
didn't find in Hamara Nagar. Establishments offering hospitality
to gentlemen whose wives were indisposed. Gambling houses.
Underground drinking hangouts. The existence of all these
places was good, no matter which side of the law you were on.
Either you availed yourself of their goods and services, or you
collected charges, fines, penalties, and look-the-other-way fees.
Oh, the city was the only place for a police officer of any importance to be.

Granted, there were minor income-producing opportunities of the same kind in Hamara Nagar, but really, how much could you expect to get from a handful of tinkers, tailors, and cabinet-makers?

Moreover, there wasn't even enough real crime in the town to keep a self-respecting policeman busy. The only burglar recently had been a man who disguised himself as a woman by wearing a burqa. Ha! The stupid fellow thought he could get away with it, with those hairy feet sticking out! Every now and then, the four constables cracked the heads of a few boys who drank home-made liquor and got out of hand, but all too often the policemen themselves were to be found taking a nap in the jail. In any case, there wasn't much room for prisoners, the lockup being not much more than a cowshed with a rickety door.

"I despise this town," he said aloud to the four walls.

There was a timid knock, and Bandhu looked toward the door.

"Come in!"

The door didn't open.

"Come in, I say!"

His wife, Manju, holding his youngest son, Raju, by the wrist, peered cautiously in.

"Oh God, what now?"

"I need money for the doctor," said Manju, looking as if she wanted to disappear. "Raju has been coughing."

"Well, Raju, is this true? Tell me, is it true?"

Raju said nothing.

"Don't stare at me like a baby monkey!"

Raju, struck with a fit of coughing, hid behind Manju's legs.

"You've scared him," said Manju, visibly scared herself.

"I don't understand it: he obviously understands, there's nothing wrong with his ears, there's nothing wrong with his vocal chords, but he never says a word. He used to say 'radio,' at least. Now he just points at the box."

"I'll ask Dr. Chawla again," said Manju. "Maybe he'll find something different this time."

"Different, oh yes," said Bandhu bitterly. "He'll find that the boy is now almost five instead of almost four. He'll counsel you patience and other such nonsense. The man's a quack. I don't know why you go to him."

"Last time he cured Raju's cough," said Manju.

Muttering and grumbling, Bandhu reached into his pocket and found five rupees.

"Here, give the old quack his fee, then go buy some useless potion at Abinath's."

Manju hastily bent as if to touch her husband's feet, took the five rupees, and led Raju out the door.

After they had left, Bandhu had a brief flash of guilt. If I get transferred to Delhi, he thought, I will take the boy to a first-class expert, who will do a proper diagnosis and figure out what he has—some complex or other, no doubt—and start treatment right away, and then I will have a normal son.

The Jolly Grant House

First Night in the Hotel

Dinner was the expected mulligatawny soup and mutton curry, followed by caramel flan. The Victoria Hotel, true to its boast, kept up the styles and standards of an earlier time: linen serviettes folded into the shape of swans, butter sculpted into rosebuds.

On returning to her room, Jana sat down at the dressing table, undid her braid, and ran a brush through her hair. The hazel-green eyes she saw in the mirror were clear; the olive skin relatively unwrinkled—at least in low light, she said to herself. But there were definitely more white streaks this year than last in the thick, dark mane. Lately she'd noticed advertisements in the *Illustrated Weekly of India* for hair dye—one ad promised not only to darken hair but to cool the brain, too. Kill two birds with one stone, it said. She didn't like that expression, or most expressions having to do with birds. The sayings were often negative. "Birds of a feather flock together" didn't refer to admirable people.

Now wrapped in her woolly robe, she shivered. The tiny charcoal stove in the far corner warmed only a tepid little circle.

"Are you cold?" she asked Mr. Ganguly.

The parrot looked unconcerned, although she noticed he was fluffed up and rounder than usual. A down coat you wore all the time could be a useful thing.

She got into bed, expecting chilly sheets, and was pleasantly surprised to find a hot water bottle. She opened up Jack's latest letter.

"Mum, I am considering taking up the pipes," he said. Oh my, thought Jana. Last year, golf; this year, bagpipes. He'll be 200 percent Scottish before he's through. Next thing he'll be using granny sayings: Mony a mickle maks a muckle.

Jack is bound and determined to stamp out the American side of his heritage, she thought, and also whatever mark eight childhood years in India might have made on him. He never was at ease in India. However, he now dutifully wrote, "I plan to come before too long, as soon as you're settled in your new digs. But, Mother, do think again about coming home. You'll have to sooner or later, you know."

We'll see about that, she thought, and switched off the lamp.

She dreamt she heard bagpipes, playing something that sounded like "Haste to the Wedding." She awoke briefly to the sound of the night *chokidar* thumping with his stick on the walkway to signal that he was keeping thieves away. Wide-awake now, she *was* hearing a bagpipe, and it *was* playing "Haste to the Wedding." After a while it turned into the snake dance tune from the movie *Nagin,* accompanied by syncopated drumming. I'm hearing things, she thought, and she adjusted her pillow and dropped off to sleep again. She did not wake up until the tiny tap on the door announced that the bed tea was being delivered.

Crossing the courtyard on her way to breakfast, she saw a boy, perhaps nine or ten years old, and waved him over.

"What was the noise last night?"

"Wedding, madam."

Thank goodness, she thought. I haven't gone completely around the bend.

• • •

At breakfast, she ordered rumble-tumble eggs, which arrived with triangles of toast in silver racks.

"Tea, coffee, memsahib?"

"Tea, please."

The bearer set down a round white teapot covered with a cozy, and a sugar bowl with a beaded net. He looked identical to the bearers of a half century before, in a white uniform with a maroon cummerbund.

"How long have you worked here?" she asked him, in Hindi.

His eyes lit up. "Forty years, memsahib, maybe more. Since I was a boy."

She nodded. "What year were you born?"

He shook his head apologetically. "I don't know the exact year, memsahib. Maybe 1912."

"Aha. We stayed here that year."

The bearer's face broke into a smile, his creased eyes giving him the look of an old shoe. "Many British sahibs came here in the days of old." Then his face melted into puzzlement. "Nowadays, so many new kinds of Europeans . . . Americans, Russians, Iranians . . . Japanese, also. They used to say Japanese people were our enemy. Now, honored guests."

"Everything changes."

"Last year this town got *so* many Tibetans; they came out of Tibet with the Dalai Lama. Who knows what we'll get this year?"

The man sitting at the next table had been jotting things in his notebook, occasionally consulting three guidebooks. A systematic tourist, thought Jana, but what is he going to explore? Hamara Nagar was not in any tourist guide; in fact, it was on few maps. Maybe he was planning to go over to Mussoorie, or down to Rishikesh or Hardwar.

The man was pleasant-looking, she thought, a year or two on either side of fifty, but with more pepper than salt in his hair, and the face firm and unlined. She heard him speaking Hindi to the bearers, with only the slightest trace of an American accent. The man looked up and caught her eye, gave a slight nod and smile, and went back to his notebook.

At the table beyond that, there were four young Indian men in Western clothes, clean-shaven, with precise mustaches. They were keeping the bearers hopping with demands for more toast, more tea, more jam, more porridge.

"Government wallahs," the bearer said to Jana. "They're going to build something. They go around the town with surveying equipment. Some people say they are going to build a big prison, some say a big factory. Who knows?"

The young men were arguing about catchment areas, and their conversation was full of measurements: such and such so many meters tall; outflows and inflows of so many liters per minute.

Of normal tourists, there were few, and all in couples: one German or perhaps Dutch; one French; one probably Swedish; another, American. Next month, thought Jana, the hotel will be overflowing.

They were ready to leave, both Jana and Mary swathed in mufflers that Mary had knitted for last Christmas. Jana picked up the birdcage and slung a cloth bag over her shoulder. Before they got to the gate, a small Nepalese boy in ragged khaki shorts came sprinting across the courtyard, his knobby knees pumping.

"Madam, please! Please, madam! I will carry that birdcage."

Jana hesitated.

"Madam, all birds are my friends. *Namasté, tota sahib,*" he said to the parrot. "Hello, Mr. Parrot!"

Mr. Ganguly fluffed his feathers and said, "Namasté," which seemed to settle it. Jana held out the cage to the boy, who grabbed it as if he were afraid she'd change her mind.

"Your name?" she asked.

"Tilku, madam. At your service."

They started on the road east, passing by the Municipal Garden and the Anglican church. Tilku followed closely behind, keeping up a running conversation with the bird.

Jana turned around. "Tilku, don't you go to school?"

"I went to school, madam. Two years."

"And now?"

"I am messenger boy, first-class."

She looked down at his skinny legs and dusty feet. Her own feet were cold even through wool socks and heavy walking shoes.

"Aren't your feet cold?" she said.

"No, madam. My feet are never cold. My feet have wings. I go so fast, pavement gets hot!"

That was almost believable. His smile struck sparks.

The English Bazaar seemed to Jana like a transplanted and translated Scottish village, the smells and sounds of Indian life held in the background. In the Central Bazaar, in contrast, the Western world receded and India took over. Sounds, smells, and colors were turned up full strength, and a dozen radios blared Hindi film songs.

The street narrowed; the stores became an unbroken crooked line. Everywhere, people were talking, talking, talking. In the street, in the shops. The merchants on one side of the street could even talk through their open storefronts to the merchants on the other side, and a story above, women on the balconies gossiped across the action below.

Jana's little delegation passed a small, run-down mosque, a temple flanked with fruit and flower sellers, and a Christian church of crumbling brick optimistically identifying itself as "All-Saints."

It was now about eleven A.M., and the sun washed everything in its clean, high-altitude light. On a stretch of road with no shops, just a parapet, Jana unwound her muffler and rested for a moment. Her eyes took in the great plunge of the view, the brown-and-green foothills, and beyond them the vast plain with its broad rivers. She smelled pine and distant wood smoke in the moving air.

Tilku rested the birdcage on the parapet.

"Don't drop him," said Jana.

"Never!" Tilku looked shocked.

The bird himself looked extremely interested in the scene, craning his head first one way and then another. Some boys called, *"Salaam, tota sahib,"* to him, whereupon Mr. Ganguly cried, *"Salaam! Salaam aleikum!,"* sending them into peals of laughter.

Rested, they started to walk again, and came to another line of shops. Jana noticed that the shopkeepers in this town looked prosperous, their signs freshly painted. Through their wide-open storefronts she could see their shelves packed with goods.

Inside Abinath's Apothecary, a bald man with a round face and glasses was showing an underling how to dust off the blue and purple bottles. Next came Muktinanda's Stationers and School Supplies, bulging with bottles of ink of various brands and colors, slide rules, pencil cases, and Indian and imported fountain pens. Farther on, Pahari Provisioners displayed huge tin cooking pots, electric water-heating coils, light bulbs, army blankets, and kitchen scales.

Business seemed brisk and comradely, and at the Hot Spot Tea Shop, on one side of the street, and the Why Not? Tea Shop, on the other, the customers looked happy over their samosas and tea and arguments about politics.

This town was not famous, like Simla or Mussoorie; it did not appear in the Fodor's guide or the Michelin guide; and yet, Jana liked it. It had a feeling of history, too; for centuries, Jana knew, it had been on the old trade routes from Tibet, and during both wars, it had been the site of an army intelligence office.

She was also prepared to like the people of the town. She held with her parents' view about mountain people, a positive bias not based on any particular evidence. "They're more honest than people who live at lower elevations," her father used to say. "Less caste-ridden. Less craven. They look you in the eye." Perhaps the happiness of high elevations had something to do with that.

Finally, here was the block she was looking for, although few of the stores had numbers, and those not in order. The buildings were of whitewashed stucco with corrugated metal roofs, two and sometimes three stories, with carved wooden balconies and wide-open storefronts.

First she saw Ramachandran's Treasure Emporium, which was as wide as three normal stores, with the balcony wrapped around the entire second story, like a too wide belt worn by a fat lady. On the uphill side of the street, a sign advertised "Royal Tailors, Prop. Feroze Ali Khan"; there half a dozen *darzis* worked cross-legged on the floor, the hum of their ancient sewing machines mixing with film music. Voices floated out: "How wide this hem?" "This skirt with or without pockets?"

"Aré!" There was a sudden exclamation from Mary. "Jana mem, look!"

On a terrace slightly downhill from the road, and surrounded by an ornamental waist-high wall, was a house with a six-sided tower attached to one side. Jana searched for an architectural term to describe the building, and came up short. Himalayan–Queen Anne? Indo-Scottish Nostalgic? Fanciful gables and lattices adorned the windows, and a long verandah with formal balustrade went around the front and one side of the second story. A rickety-looking staircase connected the verandah to the ground. The corrugated roof had been red, but the paint was badly faded and peeling in many places to expose bare metal. Jana peered over the wall into the courtyard, where the weeds were so thick that she could barely see the cobblestones.

Mary and Tilku stopped short. Jana stepped forward and rubbed her finger on a plaque on the wall. With difficulty, she made out the letters: "Jolly Grant House, 1890." Mr. Ganguly stretched his neck forward, then let out a squawk.

"Some nice paint," said Mary weakly. "It just needs some nice . . ."

"A *lot* of nice paint," said Jana.

Jana managed to open the rusty padlock, and they let themselves into the courtyard. Immediately, a dozen monkeys loped around from the back of the building to take up positions like defending soldiers, some on the verandah and others in front of the main door. Jana's group fled back into the street, Mr. Ganguly flapping his wings and hissing.

Jana's heart was going so fast it made her feel silly. "They're only monkeys! We can't let a few monkeys keep us out of the place."

Mary grimaced and stepped back as if to say, "You go first."

Tilku set the birdcage on the wall, picked up a pebble, and threw it in the direction of the front door. A large male monkey loped forward, picked up the pebble, and sent it sailing back.

"Go! *Jao! Allez-vous en!*" yelled Jana. Mr. Ganguly echoed her, his high-pitched parrot voice full of indignation.

The monkeys did not budge. Their large brown eyes were fixed and resolute, as if nothing could be more trivial than a few humans and a bird.

The call to Friday prayers sounded from the mosque, and the *darzis,* now in prayer caps, emerged out of Royal Tailors. But one broke away from the group and came up to Jana.

"You are having a problem, madam?" He was about twenty, handsome in a "Sheik of Araby" way, with dark eyes framed by curly eyelashes, and a neatly trimmed short beard.

"I'm the new owner of this building," Jana said. "But we're having a little trouble getting in."

"No problem," said the young man. He, too, tried throwing pebbles at the monkeys, and once again, they threw them right back.

A woman in a black burqa joined them.

"They're djinns, that's why they won't leave," she said.

"That's nonsense, they're just monkeys!" the young man said. "I know one person who can get rid of them. Don't you worry, I will tell him."

"What's your name?" said Jana.

"Moustapha."

"Any help will be very much appreciated," said Jana. "I'm staying at the Victoria Hotel. Ask for Mrs. Laird."

"And, madam, I too am at your service!" came a new voice.

Jana turned around to see an amiable-looking gentleman in an immaculate *dhoti* and an expensive-looking wool shawl holding up his hands in a gracious namasté. Then he proffered a card to Jana.

"V. K. Ramachandran, at your service."

"I'm Janet Laird," Jana said.

"We heard that the house was finally returning to its original owners," said Ramachandran. "Or, at least, to their heirs. Perhaps you know that my building was once the guesthouse."

"Ah yes, the Treasure Emporium." Ramachandran and his emporium looked as if they belonged together, the way dogs and owners sometimes looked similar. Jana smiled. She wondered if something in her own appearance resonated with the excesses and fantasies of the Jolly Grant House.

"Do let me know if I can be of any assistance when you move in," said Ramachandran.

"*If* we can move in," said Jana.

"Of course you can," said Ramachandran. "Don't think that the monkey welcome is the last word!"

"Thank you, Mr. Ramachandran."

Mr. Ganguly was stabbing at his breast with his beak.

"This bird is overtired," Jana said to Mary. "Like a five-year-old at the circus. We don't want another feather-plucking episode."

"We go back and rest now," said Mary. "That only is good sense."

"All right. Come, Tilku," said Jana.

With namastés to Ramachandran and salaams to Moustapha, the foursome made their way back to the hotel.

⌇ J Is for Jana

Back in the hotel lobby, Jana saw a door with a sign she hadn't
noticed before. "Resident SoothSayer," it said, in English letters
that were stylized to look like Devanagari script. She knocked,
listened, knocked again.

"Come in," rang out a commanding male voice. She opened
the door cautiously to find a man of about sixty years old, dressed
in a white *dhoti* and *kameez* and wrapped in a bright pink blanket. The warm, sweet smell of alcohol filled the room, which was
claustrophobia-inducing, barely big enough to hold a small
round table with two high-backed chairs. The fortune-teller was
wall-eyed, so Jana could not really tell where he was looking, but
he swayed his head slowly until one eye connected with hers.

"Please sit, madam, please sit!"

She sat, and he brought his good eye again to her face.

"Madam, I am a nomenologist. First I must know your name.
All your names, actually. Given name, married name, pet names,
nom de plume."

Jana nodded. "Yes. I was born Janet Louisa Caroline Elizabeth MacPherson. And then I married a man named William
Laird. But I've been called Jana ever since babyhood. It was a pet
name my ayah gave me. My sister, Loulou, called me Jana Bibi
when I was little, and it stuck. My classmates in boarding school
called me that, too."

"So first letter of your name is *J*, formal or informal, no?"
asked the man.

"That's right."

"*J*. Excellent! The tenth letter of the alphabet. Ten is a tidy
number. Tell me, when where you born?

"On the twenty-sixth of January." She paused. What harm
would it do to tell this man the year of her birth? "1902."

"1902! Very good, dear lady. I congratulate you. In the race of
life, many people don't make it as far as you and I have done.

And twenty-sixth of January, my, my, what an auspicious date! The Republic Day of India!"

"Yes, that always strikes me as auspicious, too," Jana said.

The soothsayer paused. "Let's think of some more significant facts. *J* . . . *J* . . . You have a son named . . . John."

He glanced away quickly, as if pulling names out of the air. "If not John, then Jack."

"That's true," said Jana.

"You will soon encounter a *jewel* . . . most probably *jade* . . . that will go with your green eyes. Maybe it will be a gift."

"That would be very nice," said Jana.

"You like to sing 'Jana Gana Mana,'" said the man.

"Yes, I do. I'm as patriotic as the next person." She loved the Rabindranath Tagore hymn that was the Indian national anthem.

"How is that, madam? Don't you sing 'God Save the Queen'?"

"I'm an Indian citizen," said Jana.

He started in surprise.

"Keep out of *jail* . . ."

"Well, of course!" said Jana.

"You play *jazz*."

"I did, a bit," she said, "in a dance band in Bombay."

"Anything you wish to ask me?" said the man.

"I have a chance to move into a building in Hamara Nagar," said Jana. "And make it my own. It's old and run-down and overrun by monkeys. What shall I do?"

"What is the name of this house, madam?"

"The Jolly Grant House," she said.

"Jolly . . . Jolly . . . Madam! Madam! Don't you see the pattern?" The man raised his eyes heavenward. "Accept what is given to you," he said. "It will bring you *joy*."

Feroze and His World

⌘ Conversation with Yusuf Baig

Feroze Ali Khan loved Friday prayers. Actually, he loved doing the prayers every day of the week, and at all five times of day. The call to prayer wafting from the mosque made him feel as if his own soul were rising to meet the sound drifting up to the skies. No matter how grumpy and tired he was, he let all thought and feeling go, and joined with his fellow believers all over the world in the swelling of praise and thanks to God. But Friday prayers were best, because they were performed with friends. The mosque was small and run-down, the minaret a plain square tower. And yet, the feeling was there.

"I feel like a small drop of water in a magnificent ocean," he said to his oldest friend, Hajji Yusuf Baig, as they were leaving the mosque and walking down the main street of the Central Bazaar.

"If you go to Mecca, you will have that feeling magnified one hundred times," said Yusuf Baig.

Feroze felt put in his place. *Of course* he would go to Mecca one day. He would make the sacred pilgrimage and dye his beard red, and be known as Hajji, just as Yusuf Baig now was. Hajji Feroze Ali Khan: that had a good sound to it. It would be fitting, too, since he was one of the most important merchants in town. One of the top three, when you came to think of it, along with

Yusuf Baig and V. K. Ramachandran. Ramachandran, being a Hindu, would of course not be interested in going to Mecca. If inclined to go on pilgrimage, he would go to Benares and bathe in the Ganges.

"You should come to Mecca next year with me. We can take the train to Bombay and then stay with my father-in-law before we get on the boat," said Yusuf Baig.

Boat. The very thought sent a wave of nausea through Feroze. As for "train," after the harrowing ride in September 1947, when he had narrowly missed being pulled off one and hacked to pieces, he could never even hear the word without feeling as if he would faint dead away.

"There are lots of train and boat accidents these days," said Feroze.

"But one should have no fear!" said Yusuf Baig. "Fear shows an absence of faith."

Feroze flinched at the criticism.

"Airplanes, too, go to Mecca, you know," said Yusuf Baig.

Airplanes. Feroze had seen few in his life. When they flew overhead, it was such an unusual event that everyone ran out in the street to look, then came back in to argue for the rest of the day about whether they were Chinese spy planes, American spy planes, or Indian planes with noble pilots protecting the motherland. In any case, the idea of being enclosed in a small metal cylinder and defying gravity above the clouds was even less appealing to Feroze than a boat trip.

"Very expensive, I would think," said Feroze.

"What is expense to a man like you or me?"

Feroze tilted his head in an ambiguous way; let Yusuf Baig think he was agreeing or disagreeing, Feroze did not want to continue this conversation.

"I will do the hajj before I die," said Feroze firmly. "I will perform that duty without fail."

Approaching Yusuf Baig's Kashmiri Palace, they decided to sit for a while on the bench at Lookout Point.

"I got a letter from my nephew in Lahore," said Yusuf Baig.

"Life is still hard for him, you know? Not much work, no school for the children. Those people who went from here, the people over there don't treat them so well. Telling them they're Indian, not real Pakistanis."

"Here they tell *us* we *should* have gone to Pakistan," said Feroze. "People say: You Muslims wanted Pakistan, why didn't you go there?" He shook his head. "Who can win? Everyone has to live somewhere. Don't you agree?"

"I do, my friend, I do. And I am glad we chose to live here, not go to Pakistan in 1947. Here we are, thirteen years later. Thirteen years older—and wiser, too, no? Business is good. The streets are quiet." Yousuf Baig looked pleased with himself and with life.

"Yes," said Feroze Ali Khan. "This place is as safe as any. It's the place we know. The place where our grandfathers established our shops. We did the right thing to stay."

They had this conversation on almost every walk, and every time came to the same reassuring conclusion.

Yusuf Baig drew his shawl around him. "I must go back to the Palace now."

"And I to my humble shop," said Feroze. He did not consider his shop humble at all, but put things in a modest way to remind Yusuf Baig that pride was a sin. Alas, subleties went over Yusuf Baig's head. Maybe the next time Yusuf Baig referred to his Kashmiri Palace as if it were a royal abode and not simply a store of rugs and shawls, Feroze would say, "And I have to go make sure that all is going well at *Royal* Tailors."

He walked down the street to his shop and looked up at his sign: "Royal Tailors: Highest-Quality Stitching from Mughal Times Until Now." Perhaps he, too, was guilty of the sin of pride. But at least it was family pride, not just personal. Why not remind people once in a while that your ancestors had been Afghan in origin, and that they had come down from Qandahar via Multan and been tailors to Akbar, the greatest emperor in history, he who had ruled Hindus and Muslims together with justice. And while one was at it, why not mention that your ancestors had also sewn for the court of the Emperor Shah Jehan, in the days when beauty reigned supreme in buildings, in jewelry, in women, in books, in paintings—and in clothes.

"*Khuda hafiz*," Yusuf Baig was saying. "God be with you."

"*Khuda hafiz*, brother."

Feroze watched the straight-backed figure of his friend go up the street, then turned and went into his shop.

At the Royal Tailors workshop, Feroze's assorted cousins were working—in their fashion. When he was not there, Feroze figured, the cousins smoked *biris,* discussed film stars, and looked at pictures of stoves, washing machines, and lawn mowers in the catalog of Sears, Roebuck and Company, which Feroze had been given by a departing missionary lady. Feroze, too, had looked at these machines, which puzzled him. How exactly would a white box wash clothes? And when he figured out the price, multiplying the dollar amount times five to get the cost in rupees, his eyebrows shot up. Three hundred dollars—fifteen hundred rupees! You could pay a *dhobi* for years and years to wash your clothes and not come up to that amount!

"In America," said Jalaluddin, the oldest cousin, "they have machines to do everything."

"Everything?" said Imran, the second oldest.

"Yes, they even make babies in machines. I saw a picture in a newspaper. It was about a hospital. There was a baby in a box with clear glass sides. They grew it in a box!"

"Boring way to make a baby," said Farid, the youngest cousin, whose wife had just made one in the normal way.

The assorted cousins rocked on their haunches and guffawed.

Now Salman was pointing at a picture in the swimsuit section of the catalog. "This one has breasts as big as melons."

"But turn the page!" said Imran, impatiently. "Look—*hers* are like water jugs! A-B-C-D cups." He made a slurping noise.

Jalaluddin pronounced authoritatively, "These women—Americans, right? All women of the night. Otherwise why would they allow themselves to be photographed like this?"

Farid and Salman started singing a lewd song.

No progress, as far as Feroze could tell, was being made on the order of girls' gym suits for the Far Oaks School. "Quiet!" He stepped between piles of cloth, into their midst. "You people know nothing. Nothing."

"But, boss," said Imran, "I went with you once to deliver the clothes. I saw the young ladies—as you call them—running around with bare arms and bare heads, screaming and laughing. When they talk to you, they look you straight in the eye. Just like this."

And he gave Feroze an exaggerated stare, causing the others to laugh some more.

"The dormitory," said Farid. "What else is it than an American brothel? You go there, you'll see the girls are kissing young men on the path. A girl kisses one boy Monday, another one Tuesday, a third one Wednesday."

"I told you to be quiet—you people know nothing, you talk to hear the sound of your own voices. *I* understand foreigners. I understood the British sahibs and memsahibs because my parents knew them and explained to me about them. *I* understand the Americans. I have known many of them. You know nothing about the young ladies."

In truth, Feroze considered the girls of the Far Oaks School with fondness, finding their antics amusing and their conversation—well, refreshing. So, you saw them walking alone, bareheaded, bare-armed, in the bazaar, without any evidence of brothers or fathers to protect them. Worrisome. But they paid their bills on time, they greeted him with smiles and little jokes. He felt—he felt *fatherly* toward them. These, his customers, were his "missahib-daughters."

And in truth, missahib-daughters were much better than that ungrateful daughter of his own who had thrown all his careful plans for her marriage in his face and run away to Bombay to lead a loose life in the cinema. Missahib-daughters never caused that kind of heartache.

Moreover, the payment he received for their clothes was not just the rupees he pocketed but the looks of pleasure on their young faces when a dress turned out as nicely as they'd hoped. In a world where hopes were often dashed, it was good to help people achieve their dreams, no matter how small. He also liked seeing the girls walking in the bazaar in the outfits he had made, proof that his life's work was useful and appreciated.

And altogether, working for the missahibs was better than working for the British memsahibs in the days of old. The girls were friendlier; they didn't seem to consider themselves completely superior, the way most of the old memsahibs had.

The girls did not always have the best taste in cloth, though. They loved that cheap plaid stuff from Madras! The color came off even in your hands as you worked, let alone in the stream when the *dhobi* washed it.

He tried to reconcile this difference of opinion when he wrote that night in his notebook. "Colors at cross-purposes, this is called a plaid! One person sees it as a cheap clashing mess. The next person sees it as beautiful. Which is right? Such are the eyes of human beings."

⌗ *Feroze Learns About Jana Bibi*

Feroze and Moustapha knelt, praised the name of God, then settled cross-legged on the floor on a mat. Zohra came with food—and smiles. Zohra's rice was perfectly cooked, never mushy; her dal was fine and tasty, with enough salt but not too much; and her cauliflower pickle gave just the right kick to the other tastes. Feroze ate lightly and drank water to clean his palate. At the end of the meal he again gave thanks to God for his good health—and for his wife. An old man like me, he congratulated himself, with a beautiful young woman like Zohra!

And if Yusuf Baig ever made any comments about Feroze's marrying a wealthy widow, well, had the Prophet (praise be upon him) done any differently? He loved Zohra, not for her money but for herself. Yusuf Baig, with his wrinkled old hag of a wife, was jealous, that was all.

As usual, Moustapha ate more than Feroze, but that was what young men did. Their engines ran at hotter temperatures, and they needed more fuel. Zohra refilled Moustapha's small dishes several times before Moustapha settled back and declared himself satisfied.

"Where were you today at midday prayers?" Feroze asked.

"Don't worry, Uncle, I said the prayers, letter-perfect. I was just not in the mosque."

"But why not?"

"I met one European memsahib in the street. She was looking at the Jolly Grant House. I said the prayers here instead."

"Offering Friday prayers with others is both meritorious and gives you a good feeling," said Feroze.

"I know, Uncle, I know. I will go with you next week."

"That's what you said last week."

"Don't *worry*, Uncle, I'll definitely come with you next week."

Feroze, although he was not completely convinced, felt better. He always felt better when Moustapha was there; Moustapha reassured him, made him believe that the future would be all right. Many times he had blessed the day long ago when Yusuf Baig had brought an orphaned infant to Feroze's door. Moustapha, too young to be aware that his own parents were dead, was no blood relative to Feroze, and yet Feroze had said yes, we will take him. "The act will bring you merit," said Yusuf Baig, but it had also brought joy and pride and love.

Zohra, who had been eating her own food off to one side, now joined in the conversation. "I, too, talked to that lady."

Feroze asked, "What did she want?"

"She has inherited the building," said Moustapha.

"To rent out?"

"No, to live in."

Feroze was dismayed. A European in this section of the bazaar? Europeans were good customers, but one living right on top of you? Why didn't this lady go to live on Maharajah's Hill, where there were several European families?

"We will have to keep our shutters closed," he said. "I don't want her seeing in."

"No, Uncle," said Moustapha. "You don't want it dark as a tomb in here, do you? The European lady isn't going to do you any harm. And her parrot is funny. It speaks Hindi. And Urdu. And English. We'll all be laughing."

Zohra gave one of her bubbling silvery laughs. "Yes, we'll all be laughing."

"Why isn't she a proper European?" Feroze asked.

"Uncle," said Moustapha, soothingly, "don't worry, this is good. We will now have something new and interesting in our part of the bazaar."

At the words "new and interesting," Zohra tipped her chin in agreement.

"Time will tell," said Feroze.

That night he wrote in his notebook: "New and interesting. Interesting for whom? Only old is gold, is it not?" Then he thought of Zohra. Not old at all, but far better than gold.

Making Herself a New Home

ᴄᵍ *Lal Bahadur Pun Offers His Services*

Jana sat on the verandah of the Victoria, trying to decide what to do next. All of a sudden, she heard a wail like a distant air-raid siren, and Mr. Ganguly went into a threat position, puffed up with his wings arched.

Gradually, she started to make out the strains of "The Jolly Beggarman" being played on the highland pipes. The sound got louder and louder, and finally, into the gates of the Victoria Hotel marched a single piper. Dogs scattered, teacups rattled, and other guests on the terrace put their fingers in their ears. Still, the man kept coming, and finally he ended in the courtyard right below where Jana was sitting. When his tune was done, he let the wind out of his pipes and saluted.

Jana looked at the man's broad Nepalese face, his wiry build, and his wide grin. A Gurkha. As a child, she'd seen whole marching bands of Gurkha pipers and drummers. But this man had gone far beyond any regimental conventions of dress. She took in his green-and-black hunting Stewart tartan, the yellow-and-fuchsia cloth slung around his bagpipe, his ruffled white shirt, and his black velvet vest glittering with gold embroidery. Incandescent white Bata sneakers and yellow-and-black argyle socks completed the costume.

"Madam! Good afternoon!"

"Good afternoon, piper sahib."

"Madam! Myself, Subedar-Major Lal Bahadur Pun!"

"Good afternoon, Subedar-Major."

"Yourself, Laird memsahib, no?" the Gurkha said.

"Yes, I am," said Jana. "How did you know that?"

"Everyone knows. Yourself, having problems with monkeys, no?"

"Yes, I've got some monkeys to deal with."

Lal Bahadur Pun drew himself up to his full height and said, "Myself, solving this problem. With warlike music. Marches and suchlike. Two hundred Scottish tunes. Plus my own compositions." The irresistible smile erupted again. "You wish to hear?"

Jana saw the other guests moving back off the verandah.

"I think later," she said. "You play very well. Where did you learn?"

"Tenth Princess Mary's Own Gurkha Rifles, madam."

"You saw a lot of service, Subedar-Major?"

"In Burma, madam. In 1944. I was taken prisoner, madam, for two years. But I did not die, madam."

"And now?"

"Pension, madam. And playing for weddings. Groom wants an excellent arrival—I lead the parade. Everyone else gets out of the way."

I'm sure of that, thought Jana.

"Madam, I am also doing pest control. If I come into your house, rats, snakes, everything will flee. Rest assured. No problem."

"And monkeys?"

"Why not?"

"I see. And your fees?"

"Fees do not matter, madam. Pay what you want."

Jana knew she would have to find out what the standard charge was and pay that. God forbid that a piper should find her a cheapskate.

"Satisfaction guaranteed," said Lal Bahadur Pun.

"Carry on, then, Subedar-Major."

• • •

The American she had seen taking notes over his guidebooks at breakfast had been listening to Jana's conversation with the piper, and now he came over, his eyes creasing in amusement.

"Kenneth Stuart-Smith." He put out his hand.

"I'm Janet Laird," said Jana.

"You sound as if you've been in India for a while."

"So do you."

Kenneth Stuart-Smith's own speech was American, but flavored with the intonation of many American missionaries she had known. How would she describe it? A lilt? An accent halfway between British and Indian? But a pleasant man, with a pleasant voice, she decided.

"I was born here," she said. "Well, not *here*. In Allahabad."

"Ah! I was born at the Landour Community Hospital. Just outside of the town of Mussoorie."

"So your parents must have been missionaries."

"They were," he said.

"And did you—follow in their footsteps?"

He thought it over. "Well . . . yes and no. I went into the diplomatic corps. Different ideology, same need for overseas adventure."

She nodded. "I went in the opposite direction. My father was a civil servant . . . and then my husband—he died many years ago—was a missionary. American, actually."

"Ah."

They compared childhoods some more. Jana's had been far more luxurious; Kenneth's family had not had indoor plumbing. But both remembered the lullabies of their Indian ayahs, a scare from a rabid dog, and the shock of being torn out of India.

Jana told Stuart-Smith about the Jolly Grant House, then asked, "Why are *you* here in Hamara Nagar?"

"I came to decide whether to put my daughter in the Far Oaks School," he said. "I can't really handle her in Delhi. We were in Paris last, and she threatens to catch a plane and go there, because she misses her friends. She's sixteen, and unfortunately, she looks old enough and sophisticated enough so that perhaps someone actually *would* believe what she says and sell her an airline ticket."

He took a battered wallet from his pocket and showed Jana the photograph of a sleek blond girl with a slightly defiant expression.

"She's lovely," said Jana. "And she sounds very enterprising."

"Oh, yes. That she is. In Paris, she once convinced a man that she was Grace of Monaco's first cousin and got herself invited to a major reception. She told us she was going to the American School of Paris prom, all decked out in a strapless gown, but really she ended up at the Belgian embassy, drinking champagne. We never would have known, except that the event got photographed for *Look* magazine."

"How old was she?"

"Fourteen. Now she at least is sensible enough to skip the champagne. She was recently diagnosed with epilepsy, and they've told her not to touch alcohol. I think she's taken the message to heart."

"You hope she has, at any rate."

"Well, yes, I certainly do! That's another reason I thought it would be better for her at the Far Oaks School than in Delhi, with the American kids all raiding their parents' liquor cabinets."

"Well, good luck," said Jana. "And drop in at the Jolly Grant House when you come to visit her."

"*Thik hai,*" said Stuart-Smith. His pronunciation and affirmative tilt of the head confirmed his long experience in India.

❀ *They Finally Get Inside the Jolly Grant House*

The next morning, Tilku arrived on the verandah just as Jana was deliberating whether to take Mr. Ganguly to the Jolly Grant House.

"He hates bagpipes. I don't want to give him a nervous breakdown."

Tilku's eyes brightened. "Never mind, madam, I will take care of him. I am one excellent ayah!" Catching a glimpse of Mary's expression, he added, "For birds, I meant! Can I open the cage?"

Jana nodded. The next moment, Mr. Ganguly was on Tilku's shoulder, nuzzling his ear.

"Don't worry, he doesn't bite," said Jana. "Unless he thinks someone is attacking."

"He will never bite me," Tilku said. "We are best friends."

"If he doesn't behave, put him back in his cage. Don't use bad language—he picks it up. And here are some groundnuts." She slung her cloth satchel over her shoulder. "Mary, are we ready?"

Mary had armed herself with a large carved walking stick, borrowed from the supply in the lobby of the Victoria. "I am prepared, Jana mem."

"So, off we go."

Way before they reached the Central Bazaar, they heard Lal Bahadur Pun playing. No wonder pipes were considered a weapon, thought Jana. She remembered one of Jack's favorite stories, that of the piper who marched unarmed on Sword Beach in the invasion of Normandy, heartening the soldiers with his rendition of "Highland Laddie." For today, it would do if Lal Bahadur Pun could merely duplicate the extermination talents of the Pied Piper of Hamelin. "Out of the houses the rats came tumbling," she murmured.

"Jana mem?" said Mary.

"A bit of poetry."

In the street in front of the Jolly Grant House, Lal Bahadur Pun was pacing, cheeks puffed up and fingers flying. Today he was in a khaki army uniform, his chest heavy with medals, a wide-brimmed hat with a strap cutting into his chin, and a curved knife and hip flask at his belt. Several monkeys took flight from the roof of the house, bounding across the wall and down an alleyway. Inside, there were still an unknown number of monkeys. Through the windows, Jana could see them skittering through the rooms, with a couple of big males poised at the top of the outdoor staircase.

Moustapha, Feroze Ali Khan, and the assorted cousins all came out of Royal Tailors, although the cousins soon put their fingers in their ears and went back inside. The portly figure of Ramachandran emerged from the Treasure Emporium, and then the stick-tall man from Muktinanda's Stationers and School Supplies, and the round-faced one from Abinath's Apothecary.

It's a carnival, thought Jana. A blooming madhouse! She glanced around at the street urchins marching and dancing to the music, and at a knot of half a dozen Nepalese charcoal carriers who were guffawing, smoking *biris,* and placing bets on the outcome of the assault.

Lal Bahadur Pun had now let the air out of his pipes and was himself taking a *biri* break.

"Morning, memsahib! Very fine morning, no?"

"It is indeed."

"First," said Lal Bahadur Pun, "I open all doors. Then I chase out monkeys." He restarted his drone and, stepping in time to the music, went up the outside staircase. The "Cock o' the North" had never sounded more purposeful, Jana thought. Within seconds, a dozen monkeys were racing out the downstairs door and around the house. In the street, boys jumped up and down for joy, and half the Nepali charcoal carriers cheered. But the monkeys dashed up the outdoor staircase, and this time the other half of the charcoal carriers cheered and clapped.

Lal Bahadur Pun winked as if to say, "It's only just begun." He went into the house again, and through the windows, Jana could see him working his way through the rooms.

"He's a very systematic man," Ramachandran observed. "It's always good to have a system."

A figure in a black burqa had been hanging back, but now came forward. "He is charming the djinns away," she said.

"I keep telling you they aren't djinns!" Moustapha said.

Lal Bahadur was now on his fifth circuit through the building. He was playing a frenzied tune Jana had never heard before—one of those personal compositions he had mentioned, no doubt. The monkeys were now clearly ready to capitulate. All of a sudden, they were scampering along the wall, babies clinging to their mother's stomachs, and the whole troop raced into the street, jumped up to one balcony, crossed a roof, and disappeared into the neighboring uphill forest.

Lal Bahadur Pun stood in front of the building, played "The Drunken Piper," and bowed to the crowd. Then he let the pipes deflate, went over to Jana, clicked his heels, and saluted.

"Memsahib," he said to Jana. "You have your building. Will you be requiring any more services today?"

"I think not. Splendid job, Subedar-Major," she said.

He saluted again, took a swig from his hip flask, and waved at his supporters among the charcoal carriers.

"Very good. Now I go to take rest before my evening engagement."

"You have your building," Lal Bahadur Pun had said. Yet *having* the building was one thing; living in it would be another. For a split second, Jana and Mary stood on the threshold, Moustapha and Ramachandran peering over their shoulders. Then they all reeled back, hit in the face by a ferocious, biting stench.

A few minutes later, Abinath came running from the apothecary with rags soaked in a pleasant floral solution. "Please, put over your noses."

Jana and Mary held up the improvised gas masks and edged cautiously into the room.

"It's a rubbish heap! A monkey rag-and-bones place!" Jana gazed despairingly at piles of clothes, pillows, jewelry, perfume bottles, calendars, walking sticks, balls of wool, knitting needles, newspapers, dolls, firecrackers, and burned-out Divali sparklers.

There were holes in the cement floor, the walls were stained and mildewed, and in the corners were piles of monkey dung.

"Let's open the windows," gasped Jana, and she picked her way across the filthy floor. The shutters to the three windows in the bay were encrusted with dirt and, even after being unlatched, would not open from the inside.

"I will go around," called Moustapha from the door. He disappeared, and they heard footsteps on the verandah on the other side of the house. After a lot of rattling, the shutters opened, and a blast of fresh air and sunshine flooded the room. Jana caught her breath. Her eye swept down to the soft greens of the valley below, to thirty-foot rhododendron trees with brilliant red blossoms. Then she looked up, to the limitless sky.

The group peered cautiously up the interior staircase. On the second floor, they discovered another large main room, plain and square, and just as filthy as the downstairs one. But it, too, had windows, which gave out on the same wide view. "My bedroom, I think," said Jana. There was a balcony, onto which Jana took a careful step. It seemed sound, so she took another.

"So far so good," she said, and went to inspect the bathroom. It turned out to be stark and empty, with a faucet sticking out of the wall, a sloping floor, and a drain in the corner.

"Lacks fixtures," pronounced Mary. "Not to worry, Jana mem. We can get a small table and a nice basin. And a tin tub for bathing. No problem."

A tiny adjoining closet held a Western-style toilet. Jana took hold of the long chain hanging down from the huge overhead water tank and pulled tentatively. Nothing happened. Mary then yanked violently several times, but also to no effect.

They trooped down two flights of stairs to find a warren of little rooms, Mary delightedly claiming the largest. Then they stepped out onto a strip of terrace held up by a retaining wall that plunged down twenty feet, and Jana felt a touch of vertigo.

"God willing the whole building doesn't slide down the hill with the next monsoon," she said.

"Every year, that's what we all say," remarked Ramachandran cheerfully. "Don't worry. I have studied engineering in my spare time. I don't see any large cracks."

They returned to the main level and inspected a gloomy little cookhouse with a hearth in the wall and a single tap from which not a drop of water could be coaxed.

"They must have drained the pipes long ago," said Ramachandran. "Monkeys don't take too many baths. Not to worry. We are absolutely modern in this town. You can get reattached. Water, electricity, everything."

"I hope so," Jana said. It was all a bit overwhelming. "I'll have to—well, get it cleaned up. And repaired. And painted." Or leave now, she said to herself, go to Scotland, live in a granny suite at Jack's, learn to knit. Her son's voice whispered in her ear: "Mother, do try to be practical."

But practical and sensible were largely in the eye of the observer, she felt, and the building already had a strange hold on her. The main room must have been where Grandfather Grant had his reception to celebrate the 1897 Diamond Jubilee of Queen Victoria, with French champagne shipped across India by camel and bullock cart and hoisted up seven thousand feet on horse and human back.

Grandfather Grant, who (after his first wife was long dead) had married his Indian lover in spite of the family's horror. Who had brought together Hindus and Muslims for little philosophical evenings, citing the inspiration of the Emperor Akbar. And who had, even more amazingly, gotten Frenchmen and Germans together to dance, laugh, and drink those bottles of champagne. The spirit of Grandfather Jolly Grant was in that house, and, of course, now the monkeys were gone.

"We haven't gone into the tower yet!" Mary said.

The tower, they discovered, could be entered from indoors or out, through an internal door connecting the main building, or an external one a few steps from the cookhouse. Had the ground floor of the tower served as the dining room? Jana wondered. Then up a staircase they climbed, to another room littered with monkey leavings, and finally, up the last flight of stairs to the top level. "Oh my goodness," said Mary, and Jana took in her breath. On not one, but all six walls, there were windows, none shuttered, and the light flooded in. Jana drank in the views, both of the street below and the distant mountains.

Something inside Jana said, Do not fight the pull of this thing. It is a gift.

Remembering William

❦ *A Conversation over Single Malt*

Back at the Victoria, Kenneth Stuart-Smith was sitting on the verandah, his feet up on the arms of a planter's chair, with a small glass of whisky at hand.

"How's the house?"

"A pigsty! Although that's insulting to pigs. But it does have potential."

"I worked in there," said Kenneth Stuart-Smith. "We used the tower for observation during the war."

"Aha! Yes, it certainly would have served."

"Join me in some Scotch? Or would your missionary background prevent you?"

"Even if it did, my ancestry wouldn't!"

A bearer who had been hovering in the background brought a small glass on a tray, and Kenneth poured the whisky.

"Ice?"

"Good heavens, no," she said. "Two drops of water."

The drink having been properly doctored, Kenneth held up his glass. "Cheers."

Jana settled back in her own chair, both exhausted and exhilarated from the day. The whisky was excellent, reminding her of the quality of drink both grandfathers used to insist on.

"What did you think of the school for your daughter?" she asked.

"I hope it will work. She's certainly not happy in Delhi. It's been an adjustment."

"Delhi has, eh?"

"Delhi . . . India . . . and the fact that her mother and I separated recently. I'm hoping that boarding school will give Sandra some friends, some structure."

"Bit dicey," said Jana. "She may love it—I always did—or she may hate it. I sent my son back to school in Scotland when he was eight. He took to it like a duck to water."

The whisky was loosening her tongue; Kenneth Stuart-Smith was a sympathetic listener, and soon she found herself deep in the story of her married life.

⤸ *Marry in Haste*

Normally, Jana would never have gone to a lecture by a missionary, but the program was about India, and William Laird, stopping over in Glasgow in transit from America, had spoken with passion about the call he had received to go there. She had gone up to him afterward, and told him of her childhood in Allahabad, and he had invited her to have tea at the Willow Tearoom.

They came in from a raw gray February afternoon, and the tearoom was warm and welcoming. William took off his jacket and put it on the back of his chair, raising an eyebrow or two from the adjoining tables. He was easily the most handsome man she had ever seen, and the strongest. Muscles practically burst through his white cotton shirt. Rough, unpolished, exuberantly healthy, he was exactly her image of an American farm boy, and, in fact, that's what he was. Before long, he was telling her the whole story of his childhood in Indiana: how blackleg

had carried off all the family's cows, how the pump kept breaking, how the mice had taken up residence in the outhouse.

She watched with amusement as he devoured a whole plate
of scones.

"And then the Children came to town," he said.

"Children?"

"Children of the Cross. They had a revival meeting. Oh, it
was swell! People were jumping and crying and pouring their
hearts out."

"Oh dear," said Jana.

"No, you should have been there! It changed my life forever.
In a flash . . . Look, here's the mission I'm going to."

He pulled a photo of a long one-story building with a
thatched roof from his pocket. Picturesque, Jana noted, but no
doubt also home to lizards and spiders and scorpions.

"I think it looks fine and dandy, don't you? They tell me
there's a well and a garden. I'm used to drawing water and weed-
ing! And I've learned some Hindi already."

He recited something vaguely resembling the Lord's Prayer,
then counted to twenty.

"Bravo," said Jana.

"Hey, you're kidding me! You know, I can hardly believe I'm
sitting here talking to a classy gal like you."

"It's—it's my pleasure," said Jana, trying not to giggle.

William turned in his chair and looked around the room. "I
wonder if they'd have any more of those biscuit things."

"Scones?"

After finishing the second plate, he walked her to her tram car.

"How about coming with me to visit my grandfather's grave?"
said William. "He came from around here. Tomorrow afternoon?"

Not knowing quite why, she agreed.

At the grave site, she was touched by the gentle way he lay
flowers in front of the tombstone.

"The flowers won't last," he said, "but maybe the thought
will reach him somewhere. I didn't know him, but my dad asked
me to do this."

"And is your father—or your father and mother—happy about your going to India?"

"Happy? No. But you might say they're proud. Proud as Punch."

Having left the flowers, they walked and walked and talked. William wanted to see the cathedral, because, he said, "we don't have old stuff like that in America." Jana was amused by William's Americanisms, touched by his innocence. She was not even aware of the cold and damp, but suddenly, as it got dark, she remembered that she'd promised to be back to go over some correspondence with her grandfather.

"I wish . . ." said William.

"Yes?"

"I wish you would come to my second lecture," he said. "It will be like the first one you went to. But perhaps you could answer questions from the audience about India."

Three days later, after the lecture, they went again to the Willow Tearoom. "That was swell of you to help out," said William. "We made a really good team, don't you think?"

"I was happy to help," said Jana.

"I hate to think of sailing from Southampton on Monday. After I've just *met* you. As a matter of fact . . ." William's very blue eyes were fixed on her. "I want to say—I've been thinking. I prayed about this, practically all night long, and I feel the Lord is guiding me. I feel . . . I mean . . . would you . . ."

He took a breath. "Would you consider marrying me and coming to India, too?"

It was preposterous. She'd known him a total of six hours spread out over five days. She could just picture her grandfather's reaction. Marry an American . . . missionary? To go to . . . India? Grandfather MacPherson resented all Americans, first for staying out of the war, then for coming in and winning it. He considered all religion "poppycock." And as for India . . . he felt it had gobbled up his son and his daughter-in-law, and he'd be damned if it would gobble up any more family members.

Why, why did she say yes? She knew very well why. If William had said, Come with me to *Africa,* or Come with me to *Indonesia,* she would not have considered it. Come with me to *India,* he'd said, and she was overwhelmed with longing. She yearned to smell the cooking flavors from the bazaar, the sandalwood perfume and coconut oil, even the oddly clean smell of burning cow dung. Her ears were hungry for the bedlam of languages, the sound of Urdu and Punjabi and Hindi, with English words popping up like currants in the pudding. And for the music of daily life—the call to prayer from the mosque, the clink of bells in the temple. The call of tea wallahs on the train platforms hawking their hot tea, *"Chai, garam chai,"* in a wonderful rhythmic chant.

She met him the next day. In the meantime, he had gone to a jewelry store and bought an engagement ring with a tiny diamond.

"May I see your hand?" he said. "Your left hand?"

He slipped the ring onto her finger, then looked hopefully into her face. "Will you? Will you?"

And, both exhilarated and terrified by the feeling that she was about to jump over a cliff, she nodded.

"Thank you," said William. "Oh, thank God that you said yes."

The doubts set in eight hours after the wedding was performed, when they were in their tiny cabin on the steamer bound for India. Having insisted that they kneel beside the berth, to pray, he launched into an interminable prayer, a veritable sermon. She was still shaky from her quick decision, from her grandfather's furious rage, from her frantic packing of one small suitcase. She opened her eyes and watched him as he prayed. The stunningly handsome face, the strong bone structure, the body radiating health and energy—all these things had swept her off her feet, and again, they reassured her. But then came the moment to get into the berth. His eye rested on the oval scar on her leg.

He frowned and grasped her shoulders.

"Your parents allowed you to be vaccinated?"

"Allowed?" said Jana. "Allowed? Why, it's absolutely necessary, especially in India. We had one almost every year." She pointed to smaller scars on her arms. "You haven't had one at all? We'll need to get them as soon as we arrive."

William's face darkened. "Allow oneself to be polluted by the discharge from the udder of a sick cow? God does not permit such a practice."

"Would you rather die of smallpox?"

"I don't believe that God has that plan for me," said William. "That would be a waste."

The argument continued, especially after the children were born. But William persisted in equating vaccination with heathen rites, speaking with revulsion of the traditional village practice.

"They think they will appease the goddess Sitala Devi by smearing pus from the pox of a sick person into a cut on the arm of a well person. Then they pour cold water over the head of that person and make offerings to the idol of Sitala under the big banyan tree outside the village."

Jana had passed the goddess every day on her evening walk, the statue of a mild young woman seated on a donkey carrying in her four hands a broom, a fan, a pot, and a bowl of water. She looked like a benevolent housekeeper.

"They are practicing a form of vaccination that has been used in India for over two hundred years," said Jana. "It's more dangerous than modern vaccination, but it definitely saves a lot of lives."

"It may save lives," said William, "but does it save *souls*?"

He continued to forbid vaccination for their children. It was one reason she wrote a penitent letter to Grandfather MacPherson, then saw seven-year-old Jack off to go live with him and attend school in Scotland. The girls, then four and three, were still at the mission. She would ship them off, too, Jana decided, soon, although it would break her heart to be without them. In the meantime, she would be diligent, keeping them away from sick people, washing, disinfecting, monitoring . . .

But then, one scorching day in May, it had happened. A young woman arrived at the mission, cradling something in the end of her sari. She uncovered the bundle to show her dying baby. It was too weak to cry, its body bubbling all over with smallpox blisters.

William bent over the child and said a prayer. When the child died, half an hour later, William told the mother to lay the body in back of the building, where they would call someone to take care of it. But no one came, the villagers being too frightened. The mother did not leave the body at the back of the building; instead she sat there holding it for a whole day. Finally, William led her off and she headed down the path to the village.

"If we catch the train to Allahabad tonight, we can have the children vaccinated tomorrow," Jana pleaded.

"No one here is going to get sick," said William. "Let us pray." Twelve days later, he had a headache and felt feverish.

With the temperature reaching 120 degrees in the shade, William burned with fever. "Am I in hell?" he whispered. It was a question Jana would ask herself in the days to come.

The mission, usually buzzing with people going about their chores, was suddenly deserted. The cook, the *dhobi,* the boy who gathered firewood, and both sweepers—the man who cleaned the floors inside and the woman who swept the gravel driveway—ran away. The mission doctor for the district came a few times, but not to William's bedside; he stood at the gate of the compound, listened to Jana's report, and gave orders.

Only the children's ayah, Mary, stayed on duty, her own pockmarked face calm and determined as she gathered firewood, boiled water and milk, fed the children, and kept them away from the sickbed. Together, Mary and Jana washed the sheets as best they could, with the small amount of water they could draw from the failing well. They emptied the chamberpots, and tried to keep themselves and William and the children clean. Meanwhile, the floors and furniture of the mission got increasingly thick with red-brown dust.

For days, William lay delirious, his entire body festering with smallpox pustules. Then, the irises of his eyes, too, erupted in blisters, and his eyelids grew so red and swollen that he was unrecognizable. Several times a day, Jana took one of the children's unused paintbrushes, dipped it in olive oil, and drew it across William's face to try to soothe the skin. She gave him a sponge bath every few hours, and sat and fanned him, to little avail; every move caused him to moan in pain. Then, on the fourteenth day, his fever broke.

"I've been spared," he whispered. "God spared me."

That evening, five-year-old Caroline complained of a headache, and the next day four-year-old Fiona, and soon their small bodies, too, were covered with blisters. Day after day their condition worsened. Jana sat next to Caroline's bed, feeding her water from an eyedropper, while Mary did the same with Fiona. The heat was searing, unbearable; birds dropped dead out of the trees, and the endless call of a brain-fever bird sounded in Jana's brain, merciless, relentless.

"Mummy . . ." Caroline whispered, holding out her hand to Jana.

"What, darling?"

"There's something in my eyes . . ."

Caroline is going to be blind, too, like William, thought Jana. If— She blocked the thought. She checked Fiona's eyes, which were not yet affected.

"Jana mem, I bathe the babas now, you sleep."

"No, Mary," she said. "You need some rest yourself."

But neither rested. On the tenth day, Caroline's hands, even under the blisters, turned a mottled blue. She's gone, thought Jana, holding up a mirror to the child's mouth. Now I must fight for Fiona. She may yet make it through. But in the afternoon, Fiona's fever again rose. The convulsions started, first violent, then dying down to a mere shudder, and as the cowbells signaled the end of the day in the nearby village, she, too, breathed her last.

☞ Mary Finds Jana at the Edge of the Well

Jana was walking, then running, she didn't really even know where. It was dusk, the path was ill-defined, her eyes were blurred by tears. The villagers were in their mud houses, the smell of cow dung–fueled fires and spices wafting on the air. She stumbled, found that she had bumped into the low, circular brick wall of a well that was no longer used. She had heard people call it the suicide well because so many women had ended their lives there for one reason or another. She sat on the wall and sobbed.

Grandfather MacPherson had been right. She had been insane to marry William, and then insane not to leave him immediately. Why hadn't she just swooped up the girls and taken them to the hospital and had the vaccinations and been done with it? But the mission had seemed so far away from anything, so quiet, so uneventful, that she'd been lulled into a false sense of security.

The final light of day was failing. She looked into the inky blackness of the well, threw a small stone into it. It made a ticking noise as it hit the bottom. No splash. She threw in another stone. You would not drown if you threw yourself down that well; you would break your neck. Or, failing that, starve slowly. Well, wasn't that what she deserved? What she wanted?

But now here was Mary, hurrying across the scrubby, dry earth.

"I sit here, too, Jana mem?"

They sat together on the brick wall, not saying anything. Jana again put her head between her hands and leaned on her knees and wept. Mary wept, too. Then she stopped, wiped her face on her sari, and spoke softly.

"Jana mem, please. Don't cry. The babas are in heaven. They are looking down and smiling at you. They are beautiful little angels."

"It was my fault," said Jana. "I could have taken them away. I could have saved them. I shouldn't have listened to William."

"Wives listen to husbands," said Mary matter-of-factly. "That is the way of things. You were caught in the middle."

She tucked her hand under Jana's elbow, pulled her away from the well. In the still baking heat of the darkness, she led her back along the dusty path.

When they got back to the mission compound, William was sitting up in a chair. The crusts had started to fall off his face, leaving it cratered and reddened, and his eyes were covered with thick, cloudy scars.

"Jana," he called. "Where are you? Where are the girls?"

She came and sat next to him. "William, I'm here."

"And the girls?"

"The girls are gone."

"God took them?" There was shock and disbelief in his voice. Jana didn't answer.

"I can't believe it," William said. He closed his sightless eyes and clasped his blistered hands in his lap. "Did God want them so badly? Did God want them more than we did?"

The tears were running down his face.

"Jana, are you still here? Are you going to stay?"

In that moment, she felt that he was giving her a chance, even permission to leave, as if she could say, "No, I'm leaving" with a clear conscience.

"I'm staying, William," she said.

❧ Blind William Continues as a Missionary

She did not get the disease herself. She looked at the scars on both thighs and both upper arms and did not know whether to bless or curse the vaccinations she had gotten growing up. Though the immunity was usually thought to fade, in her case,

it seemed, the annual twirl of the needle during her younger
years had saved her, even after a goodly period of time. But saved
her for what?

William talked the elders into letting them stay at the mission; he could still preach the word of God, he said, and now
that he was immune to smallpox, he could go into villages no
matter whether the disease was circulating or not. That he had
been spared was truly proof that God wanted him to continue in
the work.

With the scar tissue covering his formerly clear blue eyes, he
decided that blindness was a blessing. He swore that he could see
the face of God, more brilliant than any mortal sight. "All things
work together for good for those who love God," he said several
times a day.

That was why, he said, he could even give thanks for the
death of the girls, their instant ascension to heaven. He said he
saw them playing on a velvety stretch of green lawn, and running
among cosmos flowers that were taller than they were.

"They are forever young and forever happy," he told Jana.

Moreover, he had had a dream in which God had told him
that he must live and die in this very place.

When he was able, he walked with a cane around the compound, then up the lane to the village and back, requiring always
that Jana be with him to ward off pye-dogs and look ahead on
the path for snakes and scorpions.

For twelve more years she served as William's eyes, rising
before William, making sure all his belongings were in the right
place, positioning the shaving cream and brush and bowl precisely where he could reach them. Increasingly, he would allow
only her to minister to him, no one else. He didn't allow the
local barber to come, so she cut his hair. No one else could trim
his fingernails. No one else could lance a boil, or put a baking
powder paste on his prickly heat rash.

Not that William complained or was a particularly difficult
patient. For every favor or service rendered, he said, "God bless
you for your kindness." And during the hot months, he insisted

that he didn't mind the heat. Rather, he said, it was a reminder of the fires of hell, which he fully expected to avoid in the afterlife.

One such hot morning, William mentioned—uncharacteristically, but without belaboring the point—that he was feeling tired. In the middle of his sermon, he pitched forward onto the pulpit, one hand clutching his other arm. He raised himself briefly, sweat beading on his pockmarked face, and turned his eyes to the ceiling. "Praise . . ." he said, and then fell backward. The men in the congregation—only four left by then—sprang from the mat on the floor. By the time they carried him to his stringed cot, he was dead.

Kenneth Stuart-Smith shook his head. "You stayed. At times it was hell, and you still stayed."

Jana sighed and shrugged. "For better or for worse . . . And it wasn't *all* hell. There were things I loved about the village."

"And about your husband."

"Obviously."

"And then?"

"Oh, several years in Bombay and, after that, a few more in a little princely state called Terauli. Teaching music, mostly." She was exhausted. In any case, she'd already told too much to this almost total stranger. That sometimes happened, in hotels, on trains . . . sometimes stories just wanted to come out.

"And your son?"

"He stayed in Scotland. He got on famously with my grandfather—that was my dad's dad, not the Jolly one—and ended up inheriting the drafty old castle. It's just a big house, really. I visited there; he came to India a couple of times."

By now, she was thoroughly talked out. She didn't tell Kenneth Stuart-Smith what she had done after William's death. About her time in Bombay, playing in dance bands, living in a friend's beach house, taking up with unsuitable men, making up for the puritanical years at the mission. And after that, the quiet years as a violin tutor at the nawab's palace, perhaps the sanest period of her life.

"You've let me chatter on and on!"

"Not to worry," said Kenneth Stuart-Smith. "As a bona fide mish kid, I can understand. Although my parents were *giving* vaccinations, not preventing them."

"Far more enlightened," said Jana. *If only.* If only William had been *that* sort of missionary! She caught herself. No looking back. No if onlys allowed!

Moving In

◆ *The Jolly Grant House Gets Cleaned Up*

The next day, they started on the cleanup of the Jolly Grant House. Or at least Jana tried to start. Her stomach turned at the stench, but she steeled herself to get right on the job. She spied an Indian broom in the corner, a long, soft bunch of sticks bound together with a bit of string. She picked it up and gave a swipe to the mess on the floor, succeeding only in raising a cloud of dust which tickled her noise.

"No, *madam*," Mary said firmly, and grabbed the broom. Jana stared at her.

"*Madam*. You don't do this."

"But . . ."

"No. If you are doing this work, I am finding other work. It is a matter of—honor."

Jana doubted that Mary would really quit, after all those decades of service—at the mission, in Bombay, at the nawab's palace. Still, she was not going to risk it. Mary, who had taught herself to cook and read and write a little English while in Jana's employ, would be all too valuable an addition to somebody else's household.

"Very well. But we're going to need people to help."

"I will organize," Mary said firmly.

"But you're just as new in town as I am," said Jana.

"Not to worry, Jana mem," said Mary, still resolute, but with a gentler tone. "I know how to do this."

"Somehow," Jana wrote to Jack, "she's found an army of sweepers and is driving them like a drill sergeant. And my neighbor Ramachandran sent down eight carpenters, half a dozen painters, and a mason. I've never seen things happen this fast in India before. I really can't believe it! But there seems to be something about the reputation of the house. The Hindus in town have become convinced that it's a meritorious act to be in on the cleaning—Ramachandran's wife's astrologer may have had a hand in that. The Muslims are happy we got rid of the monkeys, which some say were malicious spirits. The Christians are happy to add Mary to their tiny number."

Jana walked around the house, watching a workman climb a flimsy scaffolding and slap a coat of yellow color wash onto the front of the building. Above him, another workman was painting the balcony a dark brown. The man below yelled at the man above to stop dripping paint on him. Jana stepped out of the way to avoid the drops herself. She went around to the back of the house, where a mason was mending the stone parapet. The man hunkered over his task, banging at a stone with a mallet, and Jana was soon driven off by the dust and the noise.

She went back to the Victoria and settled on the verandah to look at the newspaper. Within minutes, a modest man in a *dhoti* and a heavy homespun jacket was standing in front of her, politely clearing his throat.

"They say memsahib needs a blacksmith. For the parrot," said the man.

Mary had obviously been at work again, moving things forward with relentless energy.

"They say you need a good cage, not just a carrying cage. A big one. Not a little carton."

They say, thought Jana. "That's right," she said. "The bird is about sixteen inches from head to tail. More than half the length is in his tail. We don't want him constantly banging those feathers against something."

"Tail of course needs space," said the man.

"Shall we draw a picture?" Jana suggested. She grabbed a piece of notepaper from her bag and sketched her ideas for a birdcage on it. Or, rather, a bird palace.

"I see," said the man. "We put one bay here? Staircase? Some swings and ladders?"

"You have the idea," said Jana. "Exactly."

The project barreled along of its own accord. Jana eyed the bay window in the sitting room and pictured built-in seating, and the next day a carpenter was banging the boards into place. With Mary, she went up to Pahari Provisioners to buy a tin bathtub, and while there she also picked up an electric hot plate with two burners and a tiny refrigerator that ran on kerosene. She commissioned a platform bed for herself and bought the new *charpoy* Mary had requested. "Try lying down on it," Jana said, and was relieved to find that the sturdy wooden frame and taut webbing held Mary's bulk without as much as a creak.

Jana had settled down to have tea and a samosa at the Why Not? Tea Shop when her soon-to-be neighbor Ramachandran arrived, saying namasté from the entry and then coming over to her table.

"Please join me?" Jana said.

Ramachandran wagged his head politely and sat down.

"And how is the renovation coming?"

"Astonishingly well," said Jana. "The wind seems to be at our backs. I must thank you for recommending all those workmen."

"Oh, no need to thank me. I wish to see our quarter spruced up! My wife, Padma, also is very eager to see things beautified. In fact"—he paused while Mr. Joshi brought his tea and an éclair—"she would like to make sure that your building is properly blessed before you move in."

"What would be entailed in that?"

"Oh, not to worry. Her pundit—the family priest—our

astrologer—could take care of it. And what day do you plan to move in?"

"May first," said Jana.

"No, no, no." Ramachandran pulled a long face. "May first is not a good day. That's a Sunday. Do it on Monday. That will bring much better luck."

"I've already told Mr. Dass I'm moving out . . ."

"Mr. Dass should know that Monday is the more auspicious day."

"I think he's already promised the room to someone else . . ."

Ramachandran's brows knit. "All right, I have the solution. You spend the night in the Jolly Grant House on Sunday, as if you were temporary guests. But then you carry your luggage back out to the street on Monday, and we'll have a proper opening."

Jana sat back in her chair. "That's a good solution."

"You just have to define things correctly," said Ramachandran. "Monday, May second will be your official move-in day. I'm hopeful that the spirits in your house will agree."

"Spirits? Not ghosts, surely."

"Nothing ominous," said Ramachandran. "Perhaps I should have said memories, or ethos, or zeitgeist or some such. All buildings, I have observed, have a leftover *something* from the people who have lived there. Schools are *full* of spirits, for lack of a better word. Old students roam the halls. Glass closets full of athletic shields with names of past stars taunt the current students, saying, Can you beat us? Just try, you younger generation."

Ramachandran swirled his tea in his cup and continued.

"Hotels definitely have traces of past guests. Take your Victoria Hotel. In the kitchen they still say, 'Make the tea good enough for Queen Mary.'

"In addition," he went on, "a house *itself* has its own soul, independent of the people who have lived there. Some houses are friendly—they embrace you lovingly. Others are hostile— you have to propitiate them. Otherwise lamp fixtures fall on your heads, pipes burst, railings give way . . ."

"I believe that the Jolly Grant House has a jolly *good* spirit," said Jana. "My grandfather had a lot of—charisma, I believe the word is. I think there's still some of him in there."

"Ah! Jolly Grant, jolly good! Yes, of course." Ramachandran bit into a second éclair and spurted whipped cream onto his immaculate shawl. "Bother. Padma will scold." But he returned to the matter at hand. "The house hasn't had very good occupants lately, with all those monkeys. But once you are in, the house will smile. The Central Bazaar will smile. I just feel that."

Conversation with Ramachandran put one in a metaphysical mood. Would the house really embrace her, Jana wondered as she walked back to the hotel. Or would this be, as her son, Jack, kept warning, a silly act of self-indulgence? Either way, it was too late to turn back.

◄ Move-In Day

On Sunday, May 1, 1960, Jana paid her bill.

"Mrs. Laird, we will miss you," said Mr. Dass, who had long ago shed his veneer of officiousness with her, and gotten into the habit of telling her about his heart palpitations and other concerns.

"You'll probably have my son as a guest here before long," she said. "I haven't a proper guest room for him yet."

"You send him here, he will get first-class service!"

"I have no doubt of that. Namasté, Mr. Dass."

The relentless grapevine of the ayahs and bearers and sweepers had ensured that word of Laird memsahib's impending move had made its way throughout the town.

"Madam is shifting?" Tilku had said, his face crumpling. "My friend Mr. Ganguly is shifting, too?"

"We are," said Jana gently. "But you can come visit us. And I'll visit you, too."

"Visits not as good as living here."

"I'm sorry, Tilku. That's the way of hotels. People don't stay forever."

The old bearer who had made sure he always waited on her in the dining room also came to Jana's verandah to pay his respects, with many namastés and an offering of a single marigold.

"Thank you," said Jana. "I will come often and eat here. When I need a touch of elegance." Which may be fairly often, she thought.

Now the same five men who had carried her luggage from the taxi stand on the day of her arrival appeared in the hotel court-yard to move her to the Jolly Grant House. They loaded each other up, adjusted their tumplines, and started trudging out the gate. Jana was about to hand the birdcage to the last man when Tilku came running up.

"Madam! I carry the bird!" He glared at the porter.

"*Jao!* Get out of here!" The man raised his hand.

"But, madam! I am this bird's friend! I carry the cage!"

"Madam has hired *me*," the man replied adamantly. "Leave."

Tilku's small face twisted with fury, and Mr. Ganguly let out several indignant screeches.

"Wait," said Jana to the porter. "Give him the cage. You can carry some other things."

She handed him the bag of items she had accumulated during her stay at the Victoria: a few books, a Tibetan hat, some stationery. Mary added her knitting bag.

"All right? You're off."

The man, smiling broadly at the featherweight load he had compared to the others, hurried out the gate.

"Okay, Tilku, one last time, let's go. Mr. Ganguly, don't make a scene."

How many times in the last few weeks had they walked from the Victoria Hotel to the Jolly Grant House? Jana wondered. The twists and turns of the town had begun to feel very familiar. And now, here she was, at the newly painted gate of her very own house, with the brass plaque on the wall brightly reflecting the sunshine. In the courtyard, the porters were waiting, the luggage still on their backs.

As Jana was about to open the front door to the house, Mary reminded her of Ramachandran's advice about the move-in date. "Jana mem, I'm thinking we shouldn't unpack today. Not if we have to move in officially tomorrow. So maybe we should have the men put the bags just inside the door."

"I don't think unpacking will do any harm," said Jana. "We'll do it in an unofficial way. Ramachandran merely said to move the luggage out to the street tomorrow, he didn't say it had to be full." Turning to the porter who had her footlocker, she said, "Please take that to the second floor," and she opened the door.

Mary thought it over. "I will unpack *most* of my duffel bag, but not absolutely all."

The porters entered the house first, and the stairs resounded with their footsteps as they took the luggage upstairs and down.

"Come, Tilku," said Jana. "We'll take Mr. Ganguly to his new house." She went into the large main room, Tilku following with the carrying cage.

The main room was largely empty except for the built-in window seats, a round table, and the new birdcage. That, however, was a work of art, a bird mansion, with decorative swirls over the gate, and alcoves, swings, and ladders.

"Let's see if he likes it," Jana said. She took the parrot on her hand and let him into the cage. He climbed one of the ladders, hopped onto the swing, and promptly did a 360-degree turn.

"He likes his house," said Tilku. "Madam, I like *this* house, too."

"Yes, so do I, Tilku." She dug into her purse for a tip. She thought of the number of times Tilku had stayed with Mr. Ganguly when she was out on errands, and the times he had carried her bundles. "Tilku, I'm going to miss you. You've helped me a lot. I'm very grateful. My stay at the Victoria wouldn't have been half as nice without you."

Tilku shook his head at the rupees she held out.

"Please take some payment," she said.

He burst into sobs. "Madam is my mother and my father! This bird is my brother! Madam, please. Please, can I stay here? So much room downstairs. Mary said she didn't mind."

"She did, eh?"

"Yes, she said those are servants' quarters, in a proper household they should be filled up. Not all empty and echoing."

"Mary," Jana called downstairs.

Mary came puffing up the stairs.

"Jana mem?"

"Did you tell Tilku he could stay?"

"I said *if* Jana mem says yes, I say yes."

Tilku pleaded. "I will deliver messages. Do whatever work you want in the house. Don't worry about salary!"

I think there's been some coaching here, thought Jana, looking at Mary's innocent expression. That was the same appeal Mary had made when she'd arrived at the mission and pronounced herself ayah for Jana's three small children. Well, it often seemed to happen that way. When she was growing up, the most successful head bearer their family had ever had was one who'd arrived out of the blue. Sometimes you hired servants, and sometimes they adopted you.

"Jana mem, what harm is it if Tilku stays here?" said Mary. "I will supervise. Such a small boy, he doesn't eat much."

Yes, and he should eat more, thought Jana, looking at Tilku's small wrists and skinny arms. I wonder if he has worms.

"Madam, I will clean the birdcage," Tilku said. "Just ask Mr. Ganguly." He opened the door to the cage and let the bird step up onto his hand. Mr. Ganguly made a kissing noise.

"See, he gives me a kiss," said Tilku. "He will cry if I go."

Jana sighed. "All right, Tilku, go get your things from the Victoria."

"I brought everything with me, madam."

He reached into his pocket and drew out a comb.

"That's all?"

Tilku waggled his head. "I am ready to stay." His tearstained face lit up with a dazzling smile.

The rest of the day did not go completely as planned, either. The electric hot plate did not work, and there was neither wood nor charcoal to make a fire in the hearth. The water pressure in the bathroom was feeble; the kitchen tap yielded a poisonous-looking orange trickle. Mary announced that she was taking Tilku to find food in the bazaar, and finally Jana went up to Kwality and ordered a ham banjo, not knowing what to expect, but finding the round fried sandwich that came deliciously hot and salty.

When Mary and Tilku had said good night, Jana went upstairs. Her bedroom was spare, with only the platform bed and an almirah to put her pathetic clothes in. There were no curtains on the windows yet. She realized she was homesick for the Victoria Hotel, where everything was established and running as it had for a hundred years. She decided not to think about things too much, to have a nice hot bath and go to bed.

In the bathroom, the bare sloping floor made her think of a game she and her sister had played as children. They would make the bathroom floor slippery with soap, then push off from the wall with their legs and slide on their bare bottoms across the room.

She smiled at the memory as she dragged the tin tub under the tap, filled it with water, and plugged in the heating coil. Within minutes, she heard fizzing noises and saw bubbles around the coil. Absentmindedly, she tested the water with her finger, and received a stinging electric shock.

She let the water heat a little more, and this time she carefully pulled the heater plug from the wall before dipping her toe into the water. Once in the tub, if she slumped down far enough to get wet up to her armpits, her knees had to stick up in the air. Still, it was a victory, of sorts. A hot bath.

After the bath, she tipped the tub so that the water went down the drain. Out of the corner of her eye, she caught a glimpse of a

small coiled piece of rope in the corner, then realized it was a
tiny snake. She edged out of the bathroom. Lal Bahadur Pun can
get rid of it tomorrow, she thought. A bit of wire mesh over the
drain would also be in order.

She did not sleep well. Early in the evening, the bazaar noises
kept her awake—loud conversations, singing, even some music.
Then, when things quieted down, she heard owls hooting, and
something scampering across the tin roof. What now! More
monkeys? Rats? She had just dozed off, gratefully, when the pre-
dawn call from the neighboring mosque drifted into her dreams.

"The time for prayer has come. Prayer is better than sleep." She
was a child again in the great white mansion in Allahabad, hearing the call from another mosque. Then she was in the mission
compound, hearing cowbells clinking and William singing a
hymn. Finally, it was 108 Central Bazaar, Hamara Nagar, U.P.,
Monday, May 2, 1960; the sun was up, and she was truly awake.
The voice drifting up from the kitchen was Mary's, singing a
garbled version of "When Morning Gilds the Skies."

She wrapped herself in a woolly robe and went downstairs, to
where Mr. Ganguly was already eating a piece of banana.

"Where did you get that?" she asked.

And here was Mary coming in from the cookhouse with a
tray of tea, fried eggs, toast, and marmalade.

"How did you do *that*?" Jana asked.

"Egg wallah came. Bread wallah came. Charcoal wallah
came. Six o'clock this morning."

Jana was flooded with gratitude. "They waited until our official move-in day," she said.

"Yes," said Mary. "Also, Moustapha from across the street
fixed the electrical connection so the hot plate works. And we
found the valve to turn on the water in the kitchen."

"All that just this morning?"

"Jana mem, some people get up early," said Mary pointedly.

"Thank goodness," said Jana.

• • •

Padma Ramachandran's astrologer had set eleven o'clock in the morning as the auspicious move-in time, and fifteen minutes before that, Lal Bahadur Pun started piping in the street. Jana and Mary managed to get the trunk and duffel bag out in front of the gate, and Tilku brought out Mr. Ganguly in his carrying cage, the parrot screeching in protest at the bagpipe's sound. Jana padlocked the gate, and they all stood there as if just deposited by a taxi. Within minutes, they'd drawn a crowd: Feroze Ali Khan and the assorted cousins, as well as Moustapha and Zohra, in her burqa; Ramachandran and his wife, Padma, and their six children, dressed in their best, all carrying garlands of marigolds. Lal Bahadur Pun let his pipes die down, and Mr. Ganguly stopped complaining.

Precisely as the All-Saints Church bell struck eleven, the pundit arrived, followed by half a dozen small boys carrying pots and flowers and incense. When he gave the order, Jana turned the key in the new padlock, and the crowd pressed into the freshly weeded courtyard. The little boys put bowls of rice and water and flowers on the doorstep, and the pundit recited long strings of names, occasionally tinkling a little bell. Another bell sounded from the courtyard, Mr. Ganguly's polite imitation. Jana suppressed a chuckle. When the pundit sprinkled water on the sill and proclaimed the house habitable, there was clapping all around, and Ramachandran's family practically buried Jana in marigolds.

Not ten minutes after the ceremony, Lal Bahadur Pun came forward, clicked his heels, and saluted. "Madam, have you engaged a *chokidar*?"

"I don't really think I need one," Jana said.

"Madam!" Lal Bahadur Pun's eyes grew stern. "*Everybody* needs a *chokidar*. Who will guard your house at night? And don't hire just anyone. You see my *kukri*?" He drew the broad, curved knife out of the sheath hanging from his waist. "One swipe!" He demonstrated a quick swish. "One swipe! Heads—off!" He made such a ferocious face that she drew back, but then he grinned so happily that she had to laugh.

"Madam! No payment! Just lodging! Not to worry."

She drew a deep breath. "Very well, I won't worry."

He saluted and clicked his heels again. "Madam will sleep soundly!"

And, in fact, that night she did, much better than the previous night. The one brief time she awoke, she heard Lal Bahadur Pun in the courtyard, clearing his throat and stamping his stick.

In the morning, after breakfast, Jana saw a wizened old man sweeping the broad front step of the building.

"Mary," she asked. "Mary, who is that man?"

"Oh, that is Munar," Mary said. "He's our new sweeper. He's a good old man. He came late last night to offer his services. Jana mem was sleeping. He is willing to exchange services for sleeping downstairs on a good mat. And one–two meals a day. He makes no trouble. I asked in the quarter."

Munar looked over, gave a namasté, and bestowed on Jana a benign smile, showing a toothless mouth with red gums. His eyes, too, were red, but, thought Jana, that could be from the dust.

"Are you sure he doesn't smoke hashish?" she said.

Mary shrugged noncommittally. "Not excessively, Jana mem. Where are you going to get a sweeper who doesn't smoke hashish?"

Jana paused. Where indeed?

"All right, Mary."

"Very good, Jana mem."

◦ৡ *Money Worries*

Jana stared first at her bankbook and then at Mary's grocery account book. The money Jana had saved at the nawab's was fast evaporating. The small income from Grandfather MacPherson's legacy was not going to be enough to live on, even in India, even with Mary's unsurpassed bargaining talents getting the best prices on everything from chickens to firewood. The people living in her house providing services "for free" still weren't cheap. Lal Bahadur Pun ate an astonishing amount, and old Munar, skinny as he looked, tucked away respectable quantities of rice and dal. As for Tilku—well, she couldn't sit by and do nothing while she had a ten-year-old in her house, running around barefoot and probably needing to be treated for worms. She'd have to send him for a checkup and shots and get him some socks and shoes at Bata and buy him some decent clothes. And really, the idea that two years of school was enough for that child . . . what was his future going to be?

As for the house—despite all the work she'd already had done, it still cried out for more. Would the roof hold up during the monsoons? And the retaining wall? A proper bathtub would be nice. Her mind floated back to the enormous bathroom she'd had at the nawab's. Those were the luxury days, she said to herself, then quickly stamped out the thought. You were *bored,* she reminded herself sternly, and rejected the idea that it might be wonderful to have a little boredom right now.

She put down the account books, took a swallow of tea, and picked up the local English-language newspaper, *Our Town, Our Times.* Quite an interesting paper for a small town, she had found. Always an international story or two. "An American spy plane," she read, "has been shot down over the USSR and Soviet Premier Khrushchev is demanding an apology from American President Dwight David Eisenhower." The editor, Rambir Vohra, thought that President Eisenhower should issue one.

Jana glanced at the local news, the philatelist's column, the jokes, and the crossword puzzle. Her horoscope made her nod: "Financial matters preoccupy you, but don't despair. Careful planning will stand you in good stead. Are you exploiting all your talents?"

I must get some students, she thought. I could hold lessons in the tower; that would be pleasant.

Grabbing some scrap paper, she quickly drafted a letter announcing her availability as a violin tutor, then copied it three times on good stationery, once for each of the boarding schools in the area. She also made up an advertisement for the newspaper: "Violin Teacher. Adults and Children. Reasonable Rates."

She briefly considered whether she could teach in the style she'd seen at some concerts in Bombay, seated on the floor with the violin sloping down and the scroll resting on her foot. Best not to attempt it, she decided, and instead inserted "European-Style" in the ad.

Then, with Mr. Ganguly on her shoulder, she walked down to the postal, telegraph, and telephone office. "Good work," said Mr. Ganguly as the clerk thumped his stamp down on the envelopes. They proceded from there to Aaj Kal Printing Press, where she could hear machines clacking in the back room.

"So you're Mrs. Laird," said the editor, a thin, frazzled-looking, but nonetheless courteous man. "My friend Mr. Ramachandran of the Treasure Emporium told me about you. And this is . . . ?"

"Mr. Ganguly."

"Hello, hello!" said the bird.

Jana held out her advertisement. "Might this go in the next edition?"

Rambir took it in at a glance. "Oh, violin lessons, how nice! I've heard strains of music coming from the tower; it sounded lovely."

"You're very kind," said Jana.

Rambir was now counting the words of the ad. "Mrs. Laird." He looked up. "The rate for an advertisement is a rupee for a dozen words. You've got nine words. Would you like to put in three more?"

Jana tried to come up with some phrases. "Amaze Your Friends?" "Everyone Has Talent?" "Music Cures All?"

Rambir said, "How about 'Don't Be Shy'? I know of people who would like to take music lessons but they're too bashful. Afraid of making fools of themselves. They just need a little encouragement."

"That might work," said Jana. "I like the sentiment. Let's try it."

The next week brought three polite letters from the boarding schools, all professing to be honored at the receipt of her letter, but all regretting that their music departments were at that moment fully staffed. However, they would keep her credentials on file and notify her speedily should an opening occur.

Music teachers come and go, she thought; it shouldn't be too long before something pops up. As for the advertisement, it drew a few favorable comments from her neighbors, flattering but inconsequential. Ramachandran said that he had always been fascinated by the violin, but his wife, Padma, you see, wanted the girls to learn singing, and his sons were more interested in cricket and Meccano sets than in music. Abinath and Muktinanda and even Mr. Joshi said that they enjoyed the sounds of Jana's playing drifting down the street and that they would direct interested people her way. But the days went by and the interested people failed to appear.

"All right," she said, "while I'm waiting for something to turn up, I'll work on old Ian's tunes."

During the six years after Jana's parents died and her grandfather MacPherson had summoned her back to Scotland, the only bright spot had been learning fiddle tunes from old Ian the butler. One night late, she had heard music coming from the pantry, and there was Ian, his sleeves rolled up, turning out one tune after another. "The Ale Is Dear," "Corn Rigs," "My Love She's But a Lassie Yet."

Jana was still smarting from the failed violin audition at the Glasgow Athenaeum. When she had received the notice, her grandfather had made her feel even more unworthy, saying, "Your music training in India must have left a lot to be desired." But Ian had been kind. "Not to fret," he said. "Playing classical music isn't all there is, Miss Janet. You can play for people to dance to. You can play for your own amusement."

He taught her tunes whose composers were long forgotten. "That's what traditional is, Miss Janet . . . way back in time, *somebody* made up those tunes. It's just that people got careless and didn't keep in mind who they were." He also had a few books, and they went through them, picking out dance music of J. Scott Skinner and Nathaniel Gow and Niel Gow. "The strathspey's a noble kind of tune," said Ian. "The snaps give it spice, but it's easy and nice to dance to—dignified, you might say." Of his favorite composer, William Marshall, he said pointedly, "*He* was a butler, too." Ian himself had composed many tunes, which he taught to Jana by ear and said he would write down one day.

That day had never come, and now Jana vowed to get them down. She got Rambir to print her some staff paper. She bought a quill pen at Muktinanda's, as well as some black ink. And then she began. It was not easy; she found herself straining to pull those tunes up from her memory—humming, playing a few notes, writing down a bar or two, playing them again. Mr. Ganguly liked to help in this activity, imitating the phrases from his perch next to the table.

The room, happily, turned out to be perfect for this work. With the smooth walls and ceiling, the acoustics were lively, and the music seemed to sparkle. The bay window let in plenty of light, and when Jana got tired or lost her concentration, she merely had to look out at the sweep of the hills to feel refreshed.

She figured out the ending of the nice little reel she was working on and drew in the final bar. Then she looked up at Mr. Ganguly. "See if you like this one." She took up her violin and played the tune through twice, adding ornaments at liberty.

This time, the bird seemed unimpressed. She wasn't surprised; he liked jigs best. So she played "A Hundred Pipers," one of the first tunes she'd learned from Ian, and at the first bar, the parrot started dancing on his perch.

When she was done, he called, "More!"

"Oh, all right. Shall we have 'Mr. Ganguly's Jig,' otherwise known as 'Miss Margaret Brown's Favorite'?"

That one, too, always made him dance, and even whistle along. When she had finished playing, he said, "Good bird."

"Thanks for the compliment," she said. "You're a good bird, too."

Suddenly Mr. Ganguly was on the alert. "Hello! Hello! Namasté," he called.

Mary appeared and announced, "One woman and small boy are here, Jana mem. She says she wants to talk to you."

"Well, tell them to come in," said Jana.

The tiny woman keeping the end of her sari over her head was so self-effacing, Jana was afraid that if she spoke too loud, it might blow the woman off her feet. And the little boy of four or five looked delicate, too, but beautiful, with luminous dark eyes and neatly combed curls.

"Hello, my dear," Jana said, and the child hid behind his mother's legs.

"Come! Come!" said Mr. Ganguly, and the boy peeked out and smiled.

"I think he likes the bird," said Jana. "May I ask your name?"

"I am Manju," said the woman, almost too softly to hear.

"What's your name?" Mr. Ganguly asked the little boy.

The boy blushed and looked at the floor while his mother waited with an expression half anxious, half hopeful.

"Your name?" the parrot asked.

"His name is Raju," said Manju. "And he is—shy. And that's why we're here. I saw your advertisement, which said, 'Don't be shy,' and I thought . . . maybe if Raju could learn some music he wouldn't be shy. And maybe he would . . ."

"He would . . . ?" Jana leaned forward to hear Manju better.

"He would talk. But . . . but don't tell anyone. My husband wouldn't like it. I will have to take some rupees out of the food money for lessons."

How could she possibly charge this woman any lesson fees? Jana asked herself. "How do you know that the child likes music?"

"He dances to the radio," said Manju. "And he always stops outside your gate to listen."

"Have you got a child's violin?"

Manju shook her head.

"Any other instrument?"

"I have an old harmonium. My husband doesn't like the sound of it."

"Hm. Well, let's think about this. I know—let's go up to the tower for a moment."

She led them up into the tower. Raju looked delighted, going from one window to the next, pointing at the views. Meanwhile, Jana took out the harmonium on which she had played hymns at the mission. She sat cross-legged on the carpet and patted the spot next to her. "Raju, let's see if you can reach the bellows." Raju sat down, and Manju did too, at a slight distance from the instrument.

His little hand could reach just far enough to pull the bellows toward him.

"That's very good!" She changed to Hindi, and both mother and son's faces lit up. "A little more . . . now see if you can press these keys."

The boy pressed the keys far more firmly than she would have expected. When the notes sounded, he gave a little gasp and smiled proudly. Manju leaned forward, as if waiting for a word from his mouth.

"Bravo, Raju. *Shabash!*" said Jana. She turned to Manju. "Bring him back next week and I'll show him a few more notes."

"And, madam—fees?"

"No charge for today," said Jana. "After this—one rupee. No, eight annas. We'll start him off with a half lesson at a time."

She could just see her son, Jack, rolling his eyes. *Eight annas for a lesson. Really, mother.* Well, she'd charge a more normal fee of ten rupees to those who looked as if they could afford it. If they ever walked through her door, of course.

The Work of Royal Tailors

◦§ *The Cousins Mess Up the Tumbling Uniforms*

The assorted cousins were cross-legged on the floor with the old Singer sewing machines humming. On one side of the shop, the pile of unhemmed uniforms for the boys' tumbling team at the Far Oaks School was getting smaller; on the other, the hemmed pile was getting larger. All seemed to be going smoothly. But shortly after Feroze Ali Khan entered, there was a wail from the corner.

"You took my trousers!" Imran said.

"You took mine!" Jalaluddin insisted.

"What's happening?" Feroze felt a flash of irritation. Why was there always one drama or another with these fellows? You gave them a job out of family duty and then they made a mess of things.

"He took my trousers with the forty-inch inseam and made one leg thirty-five!"

Imran held up the lopsided trousers and glared at Jalaluddin. Feroze's impulse was to give them each a good clack on the side of the head.

Moustapha came over and said, "Listen, you fellows, get this sorted out. Uncle, please come and look at this sketch for the choir robes."

He pulled Feroze out into the wide storefront opening and made him sit and calm down. "Uncle, not to worry—those boys always get confused, but in the end, they do things right."

Feroze smiled at Moustapha's use of "boys," since the cousins were all several years older than Moustapha himself.

"See, the choir robes are simple and only three lengths—short, medium, and long. This will be an easy order to fill."

Feroze nodded. It was easy to get riled up with his cousin workers, but Moustapha seemed to know how to put things right. That was a comfort to Feroze. When I am in the grave, he thought, at least Moustapha will be running the business and keeping everything precisely in order. It was hard to find someone who was good with details and yet could soothe people when their tempers flared. But that was Moustapha, sometimes mature beyond his years. Not always, Feroze thought, remembering Moustapha's occasional temper and his cinema habit. How to keep the boy from this useless thing called cinema, Feroze had not figured out. In any case, with family, you have to take the bad with the good.

"Uniforms aren't as easy as you might think," said Moustapha.

And I have built my business on uniforms, thought Feroze. Army uniforms during the war; now school uniforms of all types. Sports uniforms, band uniforms, Girl Guide and Boy Scout uniforms.

He went back into the shop and settled himself in the chair of the single table-model sewing machine in the room. Feroze had not yet let anyone but Moustapha use this machine. After a lifetime of sitting on the floor, it still seemed odd to Feroze to sit in a chair and use a foot pedal, but it was definitely easier on the knees. Perhaps he would replace his other machines gradually, although then it might be harder to impose discipline on his cousin employees. If everyone was at your height, staring you in the face when they were working, they might get even more obstreperous than they were now.

He had written in his notebook the night before: "Being the owner, the boss, the father and mother to many—is this good fortune? Or is it a burden one must accept? Take a look at a coin from both sides."

He pulled a 1943 two-anna coin from his pocket. Not so many of these left, he thought, especially as the government had brought in this new money, one hundred paise to a rupee. He granted that this was a good thing; one hundred could be divided many different ways. But he still thought in terms of sixteen annas. And he liked the two-anna coin, the rounded corners and the square shape. On one side, there was a portrait and the words "George VI King Emperor"; on the other, it just said, "2 annas." Two sides of one coin—a king on one, a humble numeral on the other. That was life.

Bandhu Sharma Gets a New Uniform

The afternoon had worn on without incident, unless one counted Jalaluddin using brown thread on black trousers and Moustapha having to run down to Fab-Fab to get a few more yards of the black cotton for the tumbling uniforms. Feroze was looking forward to going home and seeing Zohra's beautiful young face and eating Zohra's excellent dal and chapattis and pickle and then forgetting the cares of the world in Zohra's beautiful body.

"Uncle, you are in a good mood," said Moustapha.

"I give thanks to God for all my blessings," said Feroze.

But a shadow fell across the door of the shop, and Feroze's feeling of thankfulness instantly disappeared. Bandhu Sharma.

"*Salaam aleikum*, Feroze Ali Khan," said Bandhu.

Feroze hated it when Bandhu was polite and used the Urdu greeting. He knew perfectly well that Bandhu did not favor Muslims, and it was galling to have Bandhu put on a show of being a civilized person. And Feroze knew that Bandhu knew it was galling.

"Namasté, Commissioner sahib," Feroze said, forcing himself to respond as Hindus would greet one another. His throat tightened. Feroze did not like policemen. When his house had caught fire during the riots of 1947, the police had stood by smirking, until there was nothing but ashes and rubble on the ground.

"Feroze Ali Khan, you charge regulation prices for police uniforms, no?" Bandhu held out a piece of paper with "Hamara Nagar Central Police Department" on the letterhead and a typed price list below.

"Of course, Commissioner sahib, I always charge a fair price," said Feroze. He skimmed the list. Shirt, long pants, half-pants—all had absurdly low prices, below the cost of the cloth it would take to make them, prices invented by Bandhu and given this look of legitimacy! Bandhu was like one of those leeches that came out during the monsoon and latched onto your leg and had a nice big meal of your blood before you even noticed it.

"I need a new summer uniform," said Bandhu. "You have my measurements from last time."

Feroze gave a halfhearted tilt of his head. "It is an honor to take the Commissioner sahib's business," he said, hoping he wouldn't choke.

Bandhu looked as if he had gained weight since last time. Feroze would guess at the new measurements and make the garments a little big on purpose; after the fitting he would fine-tune the seams and put in tucks where necessary.

"Bring it to the police station Tuesday for fitting," said Bandhu.

Moustapha was smirking.

"Something wrong?" Bandhu leaned forward to peer into Moustapha's face.

"Nothing wrong, Commissioner sahib," said Moustapha.

Feroze did not like the feeling of Moustapha and Bandhu face-to-face; it was like two dogs circling, making growling noises in their throats. Best to get Moustapha out of there.

"Go to Fab-Fab and get the cloth for the Commissioner sahib's uniform!" Feroze spoke more loudly than necessary, making Moustapha jump.

"But, Uncle, I just got back from Fab-Fab."

Feroze's eyes flashed.

"That was before the Commissioner sahib arrived. Go now, so we can start on his uniform right away—immediately, *ekdum*, right now!"

"Of course." Moustapha gave an obviously insincere smile and slid out the door.

"Anything else, Commissioner sahib?" Feroze said.

"Your occupancy permit," said Bandhu.

"Occupancy permit?" asked Feroze in dismay.

"It is past the expiration date," said Bandhu. "I am giving you a generous grace period. Occupancy permit in my office by Monday noon, and all is forgiven. One minute late, and a stiff fine will be imposed." He paused. "I am also giving you the opportunity to contribute to a good cause."

Feroze felt the hair on the back of his neck stand up.

"I am collecting for the Homeland Purity Society—very worthy cause, supports widows and orphans and lepers and flood relief."

The cousins were all listening now, waiting to hear how Feroze would handle this request to give to a society whose motto was "Hindustan for Hindus."

"I give alms regularly," said Feroze with dignity. "I give alms to the Muslim girls' orphanage and to the poor who gather outside the mosque."

"One more worthy cause will only add to your merit," said Bandhu.

Silently, Feroze drew a ten-rupee note from his pocket and handed it to Bandhu, who examined it as if it might be counterfeit.

"I accept your contribution," said Bandhu. "Unlike with garments, the size is not really important." He gave an unpleasant hoot of laughter at his own joke. "It's the thought that counts, of course."

"*Khuda hafiz,* Commissioner sahib," said Feroze, and brought one hand to his forehead in a salaam.

"Good-bye, Feroze Ali Khan," said Bandhu.

After he left, the cousins exploded, half in anger, half in laughter.

"Make the uniform with the old measurements," said Imran.

"Yes, maybe even smaller," said Jalaluddin.

"Then he'll walk like this," said Farid, mimicking someone with half-pants too tight in the crotch.

"Quiet!" Feroze shouted. "Finish the tumbling uniforms! You want to work overtime? You want to work late into the night?"

The cousins fell silent. Avoiding looking at one another, they each grabbed a pair of trousers and started hemming.

Having gotten his employees back to work, Feroze went over and leaned against the frame of his wide storefront. On the other side of the street, he saw the Gurkha bagpiper coming out the gate in his plaid skirt and mismatched shawl. Not pleasing colors, Feroze thought. Then came a box wallah into the courtyard, and Feroze watched as the man spread his wares out on a cloth, and the European lady's Madrassi ayah bought what looked like a packet of needles and some thread. The little Nepali boy went out the gate, taking the bird for a ride. Those people were very much settling in. About this, and about many things in life, Feroze had mixed emotions. On the one hand, he had not liked the monkeys and looking across at a ramshackle mess of a building. On the other hand, it always took him a long time to decide whether he liked someone or not. Zohra and Moustapha were already talking about how *they* liked the European lady and her bird. They met her in the street; she chattered away to them in Hindustani. As if she'd lived in this country all her life!

"She has," Moustapha had reported.

"Why didn't she go to England in 1947?" Feroze asked, disbelieving.

"She didn't want to," Moustapha said. "She likes it better here."

✑ *Feroze Buys a New Notebook*

After coping with the annoyance of the tumbling uniforms and Bandhu's visit, Feroze went for a walk to calm his mind. Passing Muktinanda's Stationers and School Supplies, he remembered that he had only one page left in his current notebook. He used half of his notebook for his business, writing down each customer's measurements and what they owed. But at night, he turned the notebook over and, starting from the other end, wrote down his thoughts in Urdu.

At Muktinanda's, a bunch of students from St. Bart's College were clustered at the counter, and Feroze had to wait. The young Indian sahibs were buying cricket magazines. "*Playfair Cricket*, please," they asked and "*Cricketer*?" and "Have you got the new *Wisden Almanack*?" Feroze eyed their gray flannel trousers, navy blazers, white shirts, and ties with maroon and navy stripes. He hoped to find puckered seams. Alas, there were none. Another *darzi* in town had the St. Bart's account, and Feroze wondered how stable that situation was. What if Feroze suddenly got that account! It made his head swim. The profits would be quite fantastic, he thought. He felt a faint surge of greed, then quickly stamped it out—greed was a sin, and the resultant overwork would only lead to misery. He didn't want to expand his shop, and it was bad enough getting his cousins to do an honest day's work, let alone men from outside the family.

The students had interrupted Muktinanda's weekly reorganizing, and when they left, Muktinanda pointed to the pile of new supplies on the counter.

"Feroze Ali Khan sahib, take a look at all these new things! Pencils, pens, protractors, slide rules, small magnifying glasses, rulers, India-rubber erasers, square-lined notebooks, stencil cards for tracing letters and numbers!"

"My friend, why have you ordered so much?"

"Convention, brother, preparing for convention."

"Convention? What convention?"

"Futurology Convention at the Victoria Hotel. People coming to make predictions. Economists, astrologers, geographers, political scientists. All sorts of people."

"What nonsense is this?" Feroze asked. "Only Allah knows the future."

"They don't *know* the future, they just want to *talk* about the future," said Muktinanda. "And they will need ink and pens and notebooks, to keep track of their arguments and resolutions. Like you with your accounts and your thoughts, Feroze sahib. Well, what can I do for you?"

"Again, I need a notebook. Same as you sold me last time."

"Square notebook with square-ruled pages, right?"

"Right."

Feroze waited patiently while Muktinanda found the right category of notebook.

"What color cover?"

"Black," said Feroze.

"Oh my goodness, I am sorry. The students bought up all the black notebooks. I can only give you green."

Feroze felt disappointed. All those years he had been a faithful purchaser of black notebooks, and now this man could not give him what he wanted.

"Would you like to wait until I get some more notebooks in?" Muktinanda asked.

"How long will that be?"

"Hard to tell. It depends on when I make the order. Then on how fast the postman walks down to the post office, and when the man puts the letters on the truck to Dehra Dun. Then—"

"Please, no need to make this recitation," said Feroze. "I will buy a green one."

"Now," said Muktinanda, "may I sell you a new fountain pen?"

"Why new? What's wrong with my old one?"

"Just look," said Muktinanda. "This kind has small cartridges. You unscrew the barrel of the pen and drop in the cartridge. For customers who keep up with the times."

"How much are the cartridges?"

"One rupee for a box of ten."

"How much is a bottle of ink?"

"Seventy-five naye paise."

"Then you get more for your money in the bottle," said Feroze.

"Granted, but what if you got ink on your fingers and then on a customer's dress? The cost would be a lot more than a box of ink cartridges. I'm thinking that bottled ink is going to go out of style. Like quill pens."

It was the same argument that Moustapha kept pressing on him: new is better than old. Uncle, you should trade in the floor models of the sewing machines for some table models. But if Feroze got table models, he pointed out, he'd have to buy chairs. One expense always led to another.

"Of course, you could buy a ballpoint pen," said Muktinanda. "But I myself think they will be a passing fad. Blobs and gobs all over the page. You write such nice flowing Urdu, you need nice flowing ink."

"Tell you what," said Feroze. "I will think about the cartridges. I don't have to buy ink yet, but next time I come in, I will reconsider this whole matter. Today, it's just the notebook."

"Very good, you have made the right choice." Muktinanda always said that, Feroze had noticed. One said that to customers, even if one was appalled. You had to console the customer for parting with his money and giving it to you.

"Feroze sahib, has the Commissioner sahib come to your workshop to collect your occupancy fee yet?"

Feroze felt the squeezing sensation in his stomach that he always did when the policeman's name was mentioned. "He has come."

"And?"

"He tried to tell me that my occupancy permit is overdue. This is nonsense. Every year he moves the date up a little. So really we are paying more and more. First for twelve months, then for eleven months and three weeks, then for eleven months,

two weeks. Compressing a year as if he were the imam announcing the date of Ramadan."

"Yes, Mr. Bandhu Sharma, I think, considers himself the priest
of the municipal administration calendar! And he will time our
offerings accordingly."

Muktinanda and Feroze Ali Kahn shook their heads in a little
synchronous ballet, sympathizing with each other, bound in
agreement with distrust of their common enemy.

"Guess what that man told me this time!"

"I cannot guess," Feroze said.

"He said my newspaper-and-magazine rack is too large. That
it is exceeding regulations, sitting there on the top step of the
entry to my shop. Then he tells me I am lucky: he will give me
an extension of time to come up with the cash. I am completely
exasperated."

"I, too, Muktinanda sahib."

"We can't have Bandhu Sharma perpetually sucking the life
out of us, can we?"

"No, we certainly can't, but what can we do? Well, good
afternoon, brother. I am on my way."

"Good health to you."

"And to you."

"And to your good wife."

"And to yours."

ꙮ *More Irritants*

The radio blasted a film song, "My Shoes Are Japanese." That
tune! It was a veritable worm that burrowed into one's ear. Moustapha had changed the setting on the radio again! Feroze always
tuned it to All India Radio to listen to the Urdu ghazals, and
Moustapha would turn it right back to Radio Ceylon and listen
to *Binaca Geet Mala,* with its countdown of pop tunes. Feroze

spun the dial, listened without interest to a report about millet prices, and clicked off the radio.

Something was up. The cousins were being fawning and polite—always a bad sign. What's more, *all* of them were being fawning and polite at the same time. What did they want now? An advance in pay? Time off? Help with school fees?

"*Huzoor,*" they were saying. "*Malik.*" Your Presence. Ruler. Friend of the poor. This was excessive, and delivered, he was sure, tongue in cheek.

"*Huzoor,* families should stick together, shouldn't they?"

Well, of course, he said, wondering what trap he was being led into.

"Even if borders come between them, no?"

"Out with it," Feroze said. "Tell me what you want."

"Uncle Faiz Ali Faiz in Lahore . . . We just got the letter. . . ."

What they wanted was for *all* four cousins to take off at the same time and go to Pakistan for Uncle Faiz Ali Faiz's son's wedding.

"Just two weeks," said Jalaluddin. "In October and November."

"But maybe three weeks is necessary," said Imran. "Or four. If we must wait in line for our visas in New Delhi. They say that takes a long time. And the form is so long and difficult that you have to hire someone to fill it out for you."

"Oh, never mind, that will all get sorted out," said Salman.

"Boss, you come, too. We'll take up practically a whole compartment on the train."

The one thing he was definitely not going to do was travel in a train. What was wrong with these younger people? Granted, Feroze did not talk to them about his own ordeal in 1947, but hadn't they seen the photographs of people packed into the compartments of the trains, clinging to the roofs, their belongings tied up in bundles, old people, children, women on the verge of giving birth? People caught on the wrong side of the new border, Hindus fleeing for India, Muslims for Pakistan, both desperate to reach safety. Then the screech of brakes, the shouting, the screams of people seeing their loved ones hacked to death before their eyes, begging for mercy from the attackers. That could happen again, thought Feroze, so why take the chance and get on a train?

The cousins all fell silent, waiting for his response.

"If all four of you go," Feroze said, "who will keep the shop open and the business going? You all aren't responsible for such things; you don't even think of what's entailed. No. I can't go."

"But we can go, right?"

How could he refuse others the pleasure of a family wedding?

"You may go," he said.

All four broke into cheers.

"Enough!" said Feroze. "If you're going to take off later, you must work double hard now."

"Oh, double hard and triple hard, not to worry, boss!"

As if that wasn't bad enough, Moustapha came in with the hesitant look that *he* wore when about to make a special request.

"Uncle," Moustapha said, "can I take the rest of the afternoon off?"

"Why? Cinema again?"

Moustapha's expression confirmed Feroze's suspicion.

"Uncle, I am getting free admission. That would be bad to waste, wouldn't it? And I have finished my stitching."

"Let me see your work," Feroze said.

He examined a salwar and a skirt and a man's high-necked coat. They were up to standard, Feroze decided. He could afford to give the boy a few hours off.

Moustapha flashed his famous smile. "Uncle, you are the *best* uncle. That's what I tell everybody."

That night Feroze wrote in his notebook: "The best uncle, the best employer. Just as long as you give them what they want. Flattery is a poison food, all too easy to eat."

The next day, Feroze understood why Moustapha had gotten into the cinema for free.

"How many days a week?" Feroze said, not quite believing his ears.

"Every day."

"*Every* day. *Every* day you will be going to this so-called work?"

"After stitching is over, Uncle! I will never miss a day of work here, I promise you. But after stitching is over, I will be on duty at the evening show."

Cinema. It had taken over India, infecting people like a fungus growing on toenails. His own daughter, Rania, running away to be in films. His own wife, Zohra, wanting to *buy* a movie theater. And now Moustapha getting a job as an usher at the Bharat Mata.

"How much money are they paying you?" Feroze asked.

"Not too much." Moustapha was a truthful young man, as young men went, but Feroze's suspicions were aroused, and he pressed the question.

"How much is not too much?"

"Well, actually, they're not paying anything, Uncle. But giving us free passes so we can let members of our families go to the films. You, too, could go, Uncle."

I could go. What impertinence.

At that moment, the lights flickered and went out. Looking down the street, Feroze realized that his was the only shop affected.

"Uncle, I can fix that," said Moustapha quickly. He disappeared out the door, and Feroze saw him standing on a footstool and doing something to the power line. The lights came back on, and the cousins cheered again.

"Well, Uncle," said Moustapha. "Is it all right for me to do that small ushering work?"

What did the Europeans say? Tit for tat? "All right," said Feroze. "*If* you do your sewing on time."

That night Feroze wrote in his notebook: "Life comes and hits you with first one thing. And then a second. And then yet a

third. Who would voluntarily be an archery target for others?
An uncle and an employer, that's who."

And then the late-night call to prayer sounded from the
mosque. Feroze put away the notebook and took out his prayer
rug. After saying the prayers, he rolled up the rug, and both his
back and his spirit felt soothed.

❦ Feroze Sees His Handiwork in Action

The next Saturday, Feroze tried to get Moustapha to go with him
to the May festival at the Far Oaks School.

"Uncle, don't you have enough to do?"

If I'd spoken to my father like that, Feroze thought, he would
have given me a cuff. But he explained as patiently as possible:
"Think of an artist wanting to see his paintings in a gallery. Or
a cook peeking into the banquet room to see who's eating what.
When you work, you want to see the results. Why don't you
come, too? Just to make your uncle happy."

In fact, Moustapha *did* like making Feroze happy, and not
just out of gratitude for Feroze's having rescued him from desti-
tution as an infant. School fees, clothes, medicines, shoes, a job,
a roof over his head—those things didn't appear from thin air,
but Moustapha's feeling toward Feroze was not only a matter of
cupboard love.

"All right, Uncle, I'll come."

They made their way through the crowd in the bazaar. On this
May weekend, the tourists were out in force, euphoric from the
mountain air and from having escaped the scorching heat of
the plains. German hikers with backpacks strode by on muscular legs; American visitors in plaid jackets chewed gum and took
photographs. Indian tourists, Feroze noted, now outnumbered
the foreigners. Thirteen years after independence, the older
people still looked surprised that this was now their own coun-

try, while the younger ones, to all appearances, had always owned it.

Moustapha and Feroze made their way through the Upper Bazaar, where the shops were smaller and poorer than those of the Central Bazaar, some no bigger than six feet square. When they came out onto the open road to the Far Oaks School, they had a good view of the plains, shimmering with heat below, and of the sky, enormous over the brown-and-purple lower ridges. Feroze was grateful for a long view on which to stretch his eyes, tired these days from the close work of stitching.

Moustapha sang a film song about a girl whose red shawl was blowing in the wind.

"Uncle," he said, "have I ever told you I have a feeling that my kismet is good?"

"Not more than ten times."

"You will be proud of me one day," Moustapha said.

"I already am," said Feroze, instantly feeling foolish for having let a sentimental thing like that slip out.

At the school, a mountaineering demonstration was drawing a crowd. Feroze craned his neck to see a figure inching his way up the fortresslike gray walls, helped by a system of ropes. It was Bernard sahib, the physics teacher, for whom he had made a special hiking vest.

Climbing a wall like a spider seemed foolishness to Feroze. When Bernard sahib finally tumbled into a window on the fourth floor of the building, Feroze breathed out in relief.

"Come," he said to Moustapha. "Let's go to see my skirts dancing."

Folded and ready to deliver, the skirts had made a pleasing rainbow-colored pile, but Feroze wanted to see them in action. With Moustapha, he followed students, parents, and townspeople up a ramp to a courtyard, where a line of girls in pastel skirts stood ready to dance. Some waved to him, and he smiled back and salaamed. When the girls skipped and starting threading the Maypole, the skirts flared out and bounced over ruffled petticoats. His skirts were dancing! Dancing like flowers in the wind.

Next came a tumbling demonstration, and Feroze was relieved that the tumbling uniforms held up under such strenuous activity, and that there were no uneven pant lengths.

Moustapha was getting bored. "Have you seen enough, Uncle?"

They set off for home. Feroze was in a good mood but tired. Moustapha had to pull him out of the way of a mule train, on a place where the road was narrow and still not repaired from last year's monsoon.

"They should mend that," said Feroze. "A stitch in time saves nine."

Police Chief Bandhu on the Warpath

"Uh-oh. What's the problem?" said Jana.

Mr. Ganguly was craning his head toward the front hall.

"What do you hear?"

The bird did not answer but continued to listen, as if to say, "Be quiet. I'm identifying who's coming."

Then there was a sharp knock that made them jump. Jana hurried to the front door and opened it to find a large man on the sill. Everything about him was intimidating and precise: the pencil mustache, the starched khaki uniform, the official-looking hat with gleaming metal badge. Behind him was a smaller man carrying a clipboard, a satchel, and, even though the rains were nowhere in sight, a black umbrella.

"Police," said the large man. "Making official rounds."

"Good morning, er, Inspector?" she said.

"Bandhu Sharma. Police *Commissioner*," said the man. "You are Mrs. Laird, is it not?"

"Yes, Commissioner, I am."

"I am here to register your household."

Jana paused for just a moment, then asked, "Would you like to come into the sitting room?"

Bandhu Sharma followed her into the big main room, his eye taking in the birdcage, the newly painted walls, and the freshly washed windows. Mr. Ganguly was puffed up, shifting from one leg to the other on his perch.

"Would you like to sit down, Commissioner? May we bring you some tea?"

"Not necessary." He turned to his assistant and said, "Take notes." Then he turned back to Jana. "Mrs. Laird. What was your husband's name?"

"William . . . William Laird. He's been dead for many years."

"My condolences," said Bandhu brusquely. "Next. What was the late Mr. Laird's nationality?"

"He was American."

"His occupation?"

"He was a missionary."

Bandhu grimaced and he muttered something to his assistant. Then he resumed questioning Jana: "So if Mr. Laird is no longer with us, who is the head of the household?"

"I am," said Jana.

"Other occupants?"

"Well . . . there's my ayah, Mary."

"Her place of origin?"

"Madras."

"I see. And the other members of this household."

"There's also Lal Bahadur Pun, the piper," said Jana.

"Oh yes. That nuisance."

Jana felt like saying, "On the contrary! He gets *rid* of nuisances." Instead she said, "There's also Munar, the sweeper."

"A ne'er-do-well! We keep an eye on him!"

If they already know who's here and what they do, thought Jana, why do they have to come ask? Chilled, she continued her recitation: "We also have young Tilku."

"And what does he do?"

"He's a messenger boy."

"Origin?"

"He . . . he came from the Victoria Hotel."

"Mrs. Laird, don't try to make jokes with me."

"I'm sorry, I don't know where he was born. I don't think he does, either."

The assistant scribbled furiously on the clipboard. Mr. Ganguly was getting restless on his perch, raising his wings and eyeing Bandhu suspiciously. "That's an aggressive creature," said Bandhu.

"We haven't seen any aggressive behavior," Jana said, as mildly as she could. But she coaxed the parrot onto her arm, murmuring, "Here, Mr. Ganguly, time for a little rest," and put him back in his cage. Bandhu's bluster became more pronounced.

"May I see your visa, Mrs. Laird?"

"I'm sorry, what visa, Commissioner?"

"Tourist visa, student visa," Bandhu said impatiently. "Whatever kind of visa you have. What is the purpose of your visit?"

"My visit?"

"Your stay here."

"Well—just to live."

The frown line between Bandhu's eyes deepened. "When did you arrive in India?"

"When did I . . . actually, I was born here. On the twenty-sixth of January, 1902. I grew up here. Then I went to Scotland for a few years. I came back with my husband in February 1925."

"May I see your papers, please," he said impatiently. "Passport, deed to this house. Come now, Mrs. Laird, you know perfectly well that all foreigners must have all their papers in order."

"I'll—I'll go get them, Commissioner. I'll be right back."

She went upstairs, opened the almirah, and took out her Indian passport and the deed to the building. When she got back downstairs, she found that Mr. Ganguly had turned his back on Bandhu.

"Your bird is quite rude," said Bandhu.

"He feels anxious," said Jana. "Here are my papers, Commissioner."

Bandhu's frown line reappeared.

"But, Mrs. Laird, this is an Indian passport."

"Yes," she said.

"That would mean you are an Indian citizen."

"Yes."

Bandhu opened the passport, inspected each page, one by one. Few of the visa pages were filled in, as Jana had made only a couple of trips to Scotland and a short holiday to the Maldive Islands.

"You don't travel much, Mrs. Laird," he said.

"That's true, Commissioner. I prefer not to," she said.

Bandhu looked exasperated at the lack of interesting material he was getting.

"Your occupation, Mrs. Laird."

"I'm a . . . a fiddler."

"A what? A fiddler is a thief, no? A cheater? That's a strange thing to admit."

"I'm sorry. I spoke informally. A violinist. And violin tutor."

"Aha. 'Tutor,'" he told his assistant to write, his mouth curved with scorn. "That's what lots of unemployed people put as their occupation, even if they have no students. How many students do you have?"

She took a breath. "Oh. Er—no violin students, at the moment."

"As I thought."

"I'm also doing some music transcriptions. To be published in Scotland, eventually. I hope."

"That doesn't sound like much of an occupation," said Bandhu. "Publish, wublish. Every person scribbling on a piece of paper says it's going to be for publication." His attention had turned to the house deed. "This is a historic site; it really should be taken over by the government of India."

"I agree that it's historic," said Jana. "And I see my role more as a trustee . . . or steward. I intend to take good care of it."

"Most foreigners don't feel that way," said Bandhu. "Especially your kinsmen, Mrs. Laird. They robbed the country blind and then they ran out in undignified haste, leaving chaos in their wake. People of your ilk, madam, can't even imagine what suffering they caused. Don't even know the meaning of the word 'suffering,' for that matter."

"Of my ilk?"

"Imperialists, Mrs. Laird. Can you deny, Mrs. Laird, that because you were British, you got the best of this country and never gave anything back?"

Jana bit her lip.

"Your papers will have to be authenticated, Mrs. Laird. Forgery is a growing problem in this country."

Mr. Ganguly, on increasing alert, gave a sudden shriek, making both Bandhu and Jana jump.

"*Badmash!*" the bird screamed. "*Badmash!*"

"Who is your bird calling a scoundrel?" Bandhu asked.

"He must see some boys out the window," said Jana hurriedly.

"Mind he doesn't become a nuisance in the quarter," said Bandhu.

"No, of course not, Commissioner. May I ask when I may have my papers back?"

"When I have finished with them." He handed both the title and the passport to his assistant. "Don't assume that you can stay in this building forever, Mrs. Laird." He turned on his heel and left the room, and his assistant scurried after him.

Jana let herself down onto the window seat. Suddenly she heard a noise from the corner, a loud belch, something the children in the palace had taught Mr. Ganguly to do.

"Yes," she said. "That's what I thought, too."

She was shaken by Bandhu Sharma's visit, though, perhaps because of the grain of truth in his accusation. She couldn't deny that she'd had a fairy-tale childhood, living off the fat of the land, just as he'd said, all because her father had been one of the top members of the civil service. She thought of the flowing lawns, the brilliant flower gardens at the big house in Allahabad. Yes, her parents had hosted balls in that house, with seven-course dinners. Yes, she'd ridden in carriages with four matched horses, and later in shiny new autos. There'd always been more household servants than she could count.

But never known the meaning of suffering? Not suffered when her older brother was killed in the Great War? And, barely a week after the end of that Great War, not suffered when both her parents succumbed to influenza within days, coughing their lungs up? When she had to leave the abundant sunshine and everything she'd ever known to go back to the cold and damp of Scotland? And not suffered after the death of her two daughters?

What an outrageous man, making assumptions about her and strutting in here with his bullying ways. Everyone else in town had been so welcoming, she had started to think of Hamara Nagar as her lucky town, and the Jolly Grant House as her lucky house. Moreover, that shadow-reading fortune-teller at the train station and that nomenology fellow at the Victoria Hotel—hadn't they both said everything was going to be tickety-boo? Not using that exact expression, of course, although perhaps they both should have; it was rather a good one. Tickety-boo, she'd read somewhere, very possibly came from the Hindi *"thik hai,"* it's fine.

Of course, fortune-tellers *had* to err on the tickety-boo side. Jana slumped into the window seat, worn out from the encounter with Bandhu. The magnificent view, which she usually found friendly, looked implacable to her today. All those sullen lumps of mountains sitting there not saying a word.

Mary arrived with a tray full of lunch—vegetable curry and chapattis, and a pot of tea covered by a cozy—which she put on the table.

"Jana mem is looking pulled down," she said. "No need! Worrying is no good. Here, taking lunch. Drinking tea." Mary coaxed her the same way she used to coax Jana's children—bossy, but always loving. *Come, babas, drinking milk. One sip. Now one more. Very good, Jack baba. Very good, Caroline. Fiona, now you, you try to catch up with the big babas.* Now she said, "Not to fret, Jana mem."

"All right, I won't. Thank you, Mary. You're right, of course."

"Of course!" said Mary. "Why not?"

⚡ Bandhu Everywhere

Once Jana had met Bandhu, it was like learning about a new disease—suddenly you heard about lots of people who had it. Bandhu seemed to be everywhere, harassing the merchants, giving orders to his underling, throwing his considerable weight around.

The day after his visit to the Jolly Grant House, Jana went up to the Why Not? Tea Shop, where she found Ramachandran and Rambir engaged in their daily discussion. The radio was again playing "My Shoes Are Japanese," and people were chattering happily. But then Bandhu came in like an ill wind, his clipboard-toting assistant in his wake. Mr. Ganguly, on Jana's shoulder, spread his wings, hitting her in the ear.

"Steady on," she murmured to the bird.

"Hello, R and R!" Bandhu stood over Ramachandran and Rambir's table. Ramachandran forced his round face into an unconvincing smile, but Rambir looked unamused and gave a barely perceptible nod of greeting.

"I call you fellows R and R because you're always having rest and recreation!" Bandhu laughed loudly at his own joke. He sat at the table next to them, while Jana moved closer to the door.

"No need to run off, Mrs. Laird!" said Bandhu. "Makes you look as if you're evading the law." He laughed evilly. "Eh, Mr. Joshi, my friend. What have you got to eat today?"

Mr. Joshi put a plate of *laddus* on Bandhu's table. "Add it to my bill," Bandhu said. He leaned toward Ramachandran and Rambir. "By the way. Have I asked you for a contribution to the Homeland Purity Society?"

"Oh yes," they both said together.

"But I think that was last year, was it not? I'll be around to collect again. Unless you want to give right now. You graduates of Benares Hindu University, I'm sure you support the advance of Hindu civilization."

Ramachandran's head gesture was open to interpretation, but Rambir, either disinclined or unable to conceal his annoyance, looked downright irked.

Bandhu fixed Rambir with his gaze. "Mr. Vohra, I thought your opinion piece in the paper on government irrigation projects was a bit harsh. Freedom of the press is all very well, but it's unpatriotic of you to deny irrigation to the masses."

"I merely pointed out a few drawbacks to placing government dams in unsuitable places. Such as earthquake zones." Rambir glared over the rims of his spectacles at Bandhu. "And mentioned that many defenseless villagers will have to move against their will."

"This is what they call bleeding-heart politics," said Bandhu. "Sooner or later you must live in the real world."

Mr. Joshi brought another plate of sweets.

"Mr. Joshi here will be happy to make a contribution to the HPS, won't you?" said Bandhu.

"Yes, of course," Mr. Joshi said unhappily.

Jana slipped out the door.

After leaving the Why Not?, Jana went to pick up some almond hand cream at Abinath's Apothecary. Abinath, his round bald head shining, seemed very busy relabeling the glass-fronted cabinets. At Jana's "Hello, Mr. Abinath," he jumped and turned around to face her.

"I'm sorry I startled you," she said.

"I was merely reorganizing. Medicines go in and out of favor," he told Jana. "A few years ago, everyone had migraine and tension headaches, so I put the headache medicine right behind the counter. After that, bunions and athlete's foot bothered people, so I put remedies for those close to hand. Best foot forward, so to speak."

"What maladies are making the rounds now, Mr. Abinath?"

"The principal malady," he answered, lowering his voice, "is

Bandhu. At least, that is what I myself am suffering from. He told me I must file a local pharmaceutical efficacy certification. What nonsense. He invented that."

"And what is the remedy?"

"The remedy, Mrs. Laird, is bribery. I had to give him lots of free samples before he would go away."

"So what did you give him?" Jana asked.

"Mostly hemorrhoid cream," Abinath said. "But also head-ache pills and some very expensive preparations for vitality and vigor. I think he takes too many of those."

"Mr. Abinath." Gazing at the vanishing cream, Jana said, "Could you give Bandhu a potion that would make him disappear?"

Abinath smiled at the joke. "Oh, I wish I had such a potion, Mrs. Laird. Now, what can I do for you today? Some of that almond cream, no?"

"You read my mind," said Jana.

She had barely handed him the payment when she sensed someone in the doorway. Mr. Abinath glanced over her shoulder and raised one eyebrow, and Jana turned to see Bandhu Sharma coming in the door, his assistant three steps behind with his clip-board and anxious look. Jana muttered a perfunctory namasté to Bandhu and moved quickly down the doorstep to the street, where she could not help stopping to listen and discreetly observe what was going on inside.

"Mr. Abinath," said Bandhu, with no pretense of a polite greet-ing, "I've come to check your import license." Bandhu looked self-congratulatory at having invented yet another bureaucratic requirement.

"Import?" said Abinath hurriedly. "Sir, I get everything from local suppliers."

"But what about your *superjuice*?"

"Sir?"

"Your potion made from caterpillar fungus?"

"Sir, I get that from old Doma the trader."

"Old Doma, as you call her, is a Tibetan. If you're getting the

caterpillars from her, you're importing." He turned to his assistant. "Write out an import regulation violation!"

While the assistant was filling out the form, Bandhu put his
elbow on the counter and leaned toward Abinath's face. "You've
been doing this illegal importing for a long time, haven't you?
How about those lipsticks?" He pointed.

With a sigh, Abinath lifted a carton of American lipsticks down
from the shelf. "These I got from a supplier in Dehra Dun," he said.

"Ah, now, but he shouldn't have had them, should he?"
Bandhu tucked the box of lipsticks under his arm.

By now the assistant had finished writing out the complaint.
He handed it to Bandhu, who waved it in the air and then put it
down on the counter.

"You have until tomorrow to pay the fine." He turned on one
heel and went back into the street.

Abinath looked at the form in disgust. "One hundred rupees.
That man drinks blood."

◦ᧁ Raju's Dad

Jana woke up the next morning thinking of Bandhu. What an
odious man, she decided as she went about her day. Making a
great show of performing his duty, using government jargon,
intimidating people by carrying his stick.

"Mary," she said, "does Bandhu have a family?"

Mary wiped her hands on her sari. "He has a wife. I saw her
buying cooking oil in Pahari Provisioners. He has three children; two go to school. The youngest is about this big." She held
her palm about waist-high. "The little one doesn't go to school.
People say he is simpleminded. They hear Bandhu yelling at him."

Jana sighed. Cruelty was everywhere in this world. "Does
Bandhu ever laugh?"

"I don't know if he laughs because something is funny," said

Mary. "I think he laughs when someone slips on a banana peel. That kind of thing he laughs at."

"Unpleasant," said Jana.

She turned to her music transcription, becoming so absorbed that the morning hours flew by. She had a sandwich on the terrace for lunch, came back in, worked on another tune. When her fingers were aching as much as her head, she put the work away for the day.

"Want to take a walk?" she asked Mr. Ganguly.

"Jana mem zindabad!" He climbed up onto her shoulder.

In the street, Jana saw Feroze and Muktinanda closing down their shops. Abinath was still going strong, as the people whose headaches or toothaches had tightened in on them over the course of the day came rushing into his shop for relief. Jana waved, and Abinath did a namasté from behind his counter.

In the Municipal Garden, Jana sat on a bench in the far corner and let Mr. Ganguly hop and splash in the birdbath. Suddenly, she went on the alert. Just outside the garden was a man in a starched uniform, walking with a familiar toe-out stride. Undeniably Bandhu—but this man had a child on his shoulders. A beautiful curly-headed boy . . . Oh dear, thought Jana with a shock of recognition. It was little Raju. She ducked behind the rain tree, where she could observe them without being seen.

Bandhu and Raju entered the garden and went to the children's playground, where Raju rode on the spinning platform while Bandu turned it, telling Raju to hold on tight. Was Raju laughing? Could Bandhu have been *smiling* as he made the platform go faster and faster? Jana couldn't tell for sure. After Raju had had a good long ride, Bandhu hoisted him back onto his shoulders and turned to leave. But Raju, having caught a glimpse of Mr. Ganguly, squirmed around, holding his arms out toward the bird. From the birdbath, Mr. Ganguly leaned his own body toward Raju and raised one wing, as if waving hello.

Bandhu said something sharp and bounced Raju back into place on his shoulders, and the two went out the gate and disappeared from view.

Mary Spreads Rumors

Mary came with the account book and her latest completed knitting project.

"Egg wallah asked for high prices, Jana mem, but I said we would only buy at regular price that everyone else pays."

"Well done, Mary. And what's this work of art?"

It was a pullover with intricate cables and a dizzying variety of designs in green, blue, yellow, purple, and red.

"I got old knitted things from the *kabariwalla* and pulled out all the wool," said Mary proudly. "I used all pieces, long and short."

"That was very thrifty of you," said Jana.

"It's for Tilku," Mary explained. "Next I make one for Lal Bahadur Pun. To go with his tartan."

Was there a trace of a blush on Mary's face? But Mary met Jana's questioning look with a serene gaze.

"Has Tilku tried on the pullover?" Jana asked.

"I am calling him right now!" Mary leaned out the window and let out a piercing "Tilku!"

The patter of small bare feet announced his arrival.

"Stand still!" said Mary, and she pulled the sweater over his head. Tilku looked in the mirror; his face lit up, and Jana mentally took back any reservations she'd had about the sweater. Quiet good taste wasn't everything.

Tilku raised his arms and wiggled his hips. "People will see me in the bazaar and they will say, Look, there is a big bird flying by to deliver a message."

From his perch, Mr. Ganguly flapped his approval. "Beautiful! Marvelous!"

"Good bird," said Tilku.

Meanwhile, Jana noticed that the new wool sweater was at odds with Tilku's ragged cotton shorts and bare feet. "Tilku, you need new half-pants. Those are falling apart. Feroze or Moustapha can make you some new ones. And where are the socks and shoes I got you at Bata's?"

Tilku said, as if it were self-evident, "Saving for special occasions."

"They are to wear now," said Jana. "We'll worry about special occasions later."

"Oh, Jana mem," Mary broke in. "Maybe Munar needs one uniform, too? We don't want him looking *jungli*. Pukka household needs pukka staff."

Jana weighed her shrinking bank balance against the needs of her growing household and Mary's increasing standard of respectability.

"Send Munar up to Royal Tailors to be measured, too," Jana said.

If you acquire a household, Jana found, sooner or later you are required to have it photographed. Slim young Ajit Singh from H. S. Singh & Sons Photographers arrived on her doorstep, loaded down with equipment, and offered to give a "small small" price on a group photo. Five rupees?

When she went to pick up the photo, she liked it so much that she had it enlarged to a full-page size, and had an extra one made to send to Jack.

"Jack, dear," she wrote, "here I am alone in the Himalayas."

In the photo, they were all standing in front of the plaque of the Jolly Grant House: Jana in a salwar kameez with her hair in braids, Lal Bahadur Pun in mismatched tartans and smiling a huge smile, Mary round-faced and implacable, Munar in a new khaki shirt and trousers, squinting into the sun, and Tilku in a kaleidoscopic pullover, standing tall with Mr. Ganguly on his shoulder.

⌘ Mary Talks to Lal Bahadur Pun

Jana was not an intentional or a habitual eavesdropper, but Mary and Lal Bahadur Pun's voices were drifting up from the kitchen terrace, and she couldn't help looking down at them from the tower. Lal Bahadur Pun was mending a tear in the tartan cover to his bagpipes, and Mary was knitting a new sweater, this one promising to be even gaudier than the last.

"Business is good, Lal Bahadur Pun?" Mary asked.

"Very good. You heard? Monkeys invaded the skating rink."

"They were skating?"

"No, no! But they invaded the snack bar and made off with all the potato chips."

"*Aré!*" Mary managed to sound amazed, amused, and impressed at the same time.

"So the manager called me in complete distress."

"Complete distress, of course."

"So I went and piped the fellows down the street. They took up residence behind the PTT!"

"My goodness," said Mary.

"Yes. The postmaster called me. He, too, in complete distress."

"Naturally," said Mary.

"But I piped those rascally creatures way off into the woods. Now they really won't bother anyone."

"Very good," said Mary. "And you have collected fees."

"Both customers have paid in full. And one gave a bonus of potato chips and the other of postage stamps."

"Excellent!"

"And how is your life, ayah-ji?"

"Oh, very good. Except that one always has to walk up and down, down and up, this is a good town to live in."

"Jana memsahib plays music a lot," said Lal Bahadur Pun. "I also know some of the tunes she plays. Good Scottish tunes, just like I learned in the regiment. And I hear the bird whistling them, too."

"Oh, the bird is very intelligent. Actually, he knows more than a bird should know."

"Yes?"

"I think he might be an avatar of a deity. Vishnu, perhaps. Or maybe Jesus. He is a very religious bird."

"What religion?" said Lal Bahadur Pun.

"*All* religions—that is the thing. When he hears the church bells ringing, he says, 'God bless you.' When he hears the call to prayer from the mosque, he says, *'Allahu akbar.'* When he sees Mrs. Ramachandran's Brahman astrologer go by, he says *'Ram ram.'*"

"My goodness! *Bapré bap!*" said Lal Bahadur Pun.

"Also he is very polite. He knows to say *'Namasté-ji'* to Ramachandran and other Hindus and *'Salaam aleikum'* to Moustapha and Feroze and other Muslims. Some humans don't do as well!"

"What about atheists?" said Lal Bahadur Pun.

"Ah—no problem. He becomes a patriot and says *'Jai Hind.'* Victory to India! He's a bird for all," said Mary.

"Most certainly. A bird for all," said Lal Bahadur Pun.

Jana, smiling in the window above, thought suddenly of Bandhu.

"A bird for *almost* all," she said to herself.

❧ *Jana Gets Her Eyes Examined*

The conversation she'd overheard between Lal Bahadur Pun and
Mary came back to Jana the next day, as she was sitting in the
chair at Sharp Eyes Vision Care. She squinted into the machine
while Mr. Powell rotated and clicked the lenses, asking "Better or
worse?"

"Better, I think. Perhaps I ought to see that again."

"Of course." Mr. Powell did things at a reassuring old-fashioned
pace. He was reassuring in appearance, too: an Anglo-Indian of
gentlemanly mien, wearing a high-collared white coat and tidy
black eyeglasses.

"Do you fit yourself for spectacles?" she asked.

He laughed. "No, that would be like playing tennis on both
sides of the net."

He finished the exam and moved the machine away.

"Very healthy," he said. "No signs of glaucoma or all those
other annoying things. I congratulate you."

"Oh, good," said Jana. One more positive thing she could
report to her son.

"Shall we look at frames, Mrs. Laird?"

He led her into the annex of his office, and Jana was impressed
with the range of eyeglasses, imported and domestic, and also
by the microscopes, telescopes, binoculars, spyglasses, and other
expensive optical wares. She picked out a pair of tortoiseshell
frames and studied herself in the mirror.

"With your good bone structure, those are quite dramatic,"
said Mr. Powell.

"You think so?"

"Oh yes, indeed."

"All right, I'll take them."

"Good choice," said Mr. Powell.

She paused over the telescopes.

"You might be interested in one I made myself," said Mr.
Powell. "Actually, why don't you take it as a loan for a while?"

"That's kind of you," said Jana.

Mr. Powell wrapped the telescope in tissue paper and put it in a cardboard box. "Well, Mrs. Laird, I'll send a note down to you when the specs are ready."

"Thank you," said Jana. "In the meantime, I'll send in my ayah; I noticed she was squinting."

"Ah yes. Actually, I've met your ayah. A sturdy-looking woman from Madras?"

"That's the one."

"We spoke after Sunday service at All-Saints. She told me all about your arrival, and having to chase out the monkeys. Quite a saga! And quite a household, with the psychic parrot and all."

Jana laughed. "Yes, that was definitely Mary. The bird is very lively and talkative, but I'm not sure I'd go as far as to credit him with psychic powers."

"Animals can seem that way," said Mr. Powell. "My dogs can definitely read my mind. They pick up on smells and sounds . . . and, well, vibrations, don't you think?"

"Of course," said Jana.

"I've often marveled at how superior animals can be to human beings. Take a three-month-old kitten. Does it need bathing and changing? And what could be more awe-inspiring than a bird winging its way across the sky? Did you know, Mrs. Laird, that crows distinguish one human from another? Do *we* distinguish one *crow* from another?"

"We don't much, do we," she agreed.

"They just seem to have better powers of observation than we do."

"Well, Mr. Ganguly—my parrot—is certainly a good judge of character. I've never disagreed with him yet on his appraisal of a person."

"Perhaps he and I shall make each other's acquaintance one day," said Mr. Powell.

"That would be a pleasure," Jana said.

Zohra Reports a Conversation with Mary to Feroze

It was evening time, when the day's work could be rewarded. Feroze looked approvingly at the dishes Zohra set down on the mat. Rice, dal, and some good radish and onion relishes.

"The monkeys are gone," Zohra reported.

"Well, of course they're gone!" said Moustapha. "The Gurkha scared them away."

"First they went to the skating rink and then they went to the post office," said Zohra. "One tried to come back to the Jolly Grant House and the parrot told it to go away. In monkey language! I tell you the monkeys are djinns, and the parrot is a djinn, too. Only the monkeys are bad djinns and the parrot is a good djinn."

"Nonsense," said Moustapha. "He's good, but he's not a *djinn*."

Zohra stood firm. "Mary the ayah told me the bird has special powers."

Feroze said, "When were you talking to the ayah?"

"Oh, just now and then, in the street. Mary also says Mrs. Laird, too, has special powers. Mrs. Laird says, 'I just have this feeling that a letter from my son will come today.' And then up comes the postman to the door and hands over the letters, and sure enough, there is one with that picture of the queen on it."

"So she writes a letter, she gets an answer," said Feroze. "What magic is there in that?"

"All I know," said Moustapha, "is that she is a kind lady. Nicer than most Europeans."

"Her ayah told me she *is* Indian," said Zohra.

"No," said Feroze. "Not possible."

"Yes, she was born in Allahabad and has an Indian passport. And you know, her skin is not quite as pale as most Europeans'."

"Why was she born in Allahabad?" asked Feroze.

"Because that's where her mother was at the time," Zohra said matter-of-factly.

"Well, she's here and there is nothing to do but accept the fact. And she has brought some business," Feroze said.

"Oh?"

"I am making her a cape so that the bird can ride without . . . without harming her clothes." Feroze wrinkled his nose; he himself would never allow a bird to ride on his shoulder.

Zohra and Moustapha laughed. "That's a good idea."

"She is a strange memsahib," Feroze said. "With a strange household."

"But good for this quarter, I think," said Zohra. "I am going to take her some sweets. Maybe she needs a friend."

Feroze felt uneasy. "You can pay a short call," he said, "but only out of politeness. Europeans mostly stick to Europeans."

"I, too, will call on her," said Moustapha.

"Why?"

"Why not?" said Moustapha.

"Because . . . because you'll bother her. She probably likes to be left alone with her parrot."

"Hm," said Moustapha. "That's not something I would want."

"Nor I," said Zohra.

Sometimes Feroze felt as if his wife and his nephew were joining forces against him. Of course, they were nearer in age to each other than to him, so maybe that was unavoidable. Still, it didn't seem quite right.

He turned once again to the topic of their new neighbor. "A woman should not be living there alone without a husband. Why doesn't she have a husband?"

"He died," Zohra said. "The ayah told me."

"Then why doesn't she get another one? Instead of living like some Hindu widow?" said Feroze.

"You could take her on as a wife, Uncle." Moustapha laughed uproariously at his own joke, although Zohra, rolling her eyes, didn't seem very amused. "You can afford two wives," persisted Moustapha. "I think this is a very good plan, don't you?"

"What nonsense," said Feroze.

"The man who built that building supposedly had an Indian

wife. . . . I forget what they say she was, Parsi or Christian or something."

"That's different," said Feroze.

"Why is it so different?" Moustapha asked.

Feroze shook his head. Moustapha did not need such an obvious thing explained! He is just baiting me, Feroze thought.

In his notebook that night, he wrote, "Patience is always required in family matters. And in every other matter, too, actually."

·❧ *Zohra Pays a Call on Jana*

There was a tap and a polite call from the doorway. Jana opened the door to find a figure in a burqa, holding a bundle. It was Feroze's wife, Zohra, delivering the shoulder cape Jana had commissioned for taking Mr. Ganguly on walks.

"Come in," said Jana. "Please wait a moment." She went to get money. When she returned, Zohra, instead of leaving after a quick salaam, had thrown back the head flap of her burqa. Jana started in astonishment. She had wondered what kind of face would be under that veil. Someone Feroze's own age, perhaps fifty-five? Instead, here was a fresh-faced woman, not much older than thirty, with expertly lined brown eyes and velvety skin. She wore gold earrings set with rubies and a matching necklace. She would not have been out of place in the palace where Jana had spent those years tutoring the nawab's children in the violin.

"*Begum sahiba*," Jana said, addressing her as she had addressed the nawab's wives. "Will you stop for tea?"

Zohra took another package out of her robes. "That is very kind. I don't need tea right now. But I have brought you some sweets."

"Please, please take tea. We will have it in the tower."

Once in the tower, Zohra took off her whole robe, revealing a green silk sari. Jana caught a whiff of musky perfume.

Mary brought the tea, and her eyes widened. "Salaam, memsahib," she said to Zohra.

"These sweets look so nice!" Jana exclaimed, unwrapping the package Zohra had brought.

"Made with my own hands," said Zohra, and Jana glanced down at manicured pink fingernails. "And here is the famous parrot," Zohra added delightedly.

"*Adab!*" Mr. Ganguly was on his best behavior, making his most formal bow.

"He speaks very purely and politely." Zohra gave a silvery little laugh. She herself spoke a more formal Urdu than the normal bazaar Hindustani, and Jana suddenly felt that her own use of the language was sloppy and unrefined.

"He speaks politely only to people he likes," Jana said.

Zohra looked around the room, went to the window, and peeked through Mr. Powell's telescope.

"Beautiful!" she said. "Inspiring!"

She declined to eat the sweets she had brought but drank the tea delicately, as if she had been in a British drawing room. Jana asked, courteously, "How is your husband's health? And Moustapha's? Is everything going well at your house?"

Zohra smiled and tipped her head to say yes.

"Tell me about your life," said Jana. "Where are you from?"

"Oh," said Zohra, "I was born in Lahore. But then I had to go to my first husband's place outside Amritsar. Then we came to this town. In 1947, all my family was on the Pakistan side; I was the only one on this side."

"And . . . do you have any children, *begum sahiba*?" Jana asked.

"Sorrowfully, no. My first husband was too old and floppy. And now? Well, there is always hope."

"Your first husband died?"

"Yes, Mrs. Laird, he died a few years ago of smallpox."

Jana grimaced and waited for Zohra to go on.

"I was the only one who went into the room to take care of him."

"And how did you dare do that?" Jana asked.

Zohra pushed up her sleeve and showed a couple of long vaccination scars. "I had this done several times; my father insisted. My husband didn't want one for himself. He said it was a plot to sterilize Muslim men."

Jana took in her breath. "My husband got that same disease. Only he said vaccination was blasphemy. He didn't die immediately; he lived for twelve years afterward, completely blind. I had to be his eyes. He would not walk anywhere without me by his side."

Zohra's eyebrows shot up in horror. "Oh, Mrs. Laird. You had practice in being a saint. My husband at least passed on and left me a good inheritance."

"And your good present husband?"

"He saw me taking care of my first husband, and he was kind to me during that time. So we developed a friendship."

"Aha." Jana smiled. "Tell me more. Do you have brothers and sisters?"

"Yes," said Zohra. "I have two brothers and two sisters living. But we have lost touch."

"But Feroze Ali Khan has such a big family—cousins and the like? Don't they have wives? Are they company for you?"

"They're jealous," Zohra said darkly. "They say, She can read and write, she has money from her first husband, she puts on airs. I tried to make friends—I still try. I always speak nicely to them, play with their children . . . to no avail. They think their husbands are all falling in love with me."

They probably are, thought Jana.

"I used to write letters to my big sister in Lahore. But then she died. And the other two don't write well, and letter writers are so expensive. So now they don't bother anymore."

She flicked her pink-nailed fingers in a dismissive gesture.

"You and I can be sisters now," said Jana.

Zohra smiled, and Jana saw she had two deep dimples, which instantly made Jana smile back.

"Okay, it's settled, we are sisters," said Zohra. "You are my big sister. I will call you *didi*. Now tell me about your children."

"My son is in Scotland," Jana said.

"Why doesn't he come to visit? Or why don't you go to live there?"

"I like this better."

"Ha!" said Zohra. "I thought that must be it."

"But he checks up on me, like a granny. He'll be here before too long."

"Good. A son should visit his mother. As much as possible. Especially if he is the only one! No daughters?"

"I had two daughters," said Jana, "but they, too, died of smallpox."

Zohra let out a sympathetic breath and shook her head. "A terrible thing." She patted Jana gently on the arm, her face more knowledgeable than her years. They sat in silence for a moment.

"Well, *didi*, I must go." Zohra rose.

She had barely put on her burqa when Mary came puffing up the tower stairs. "Jana mem! Tilku is here, and he is completely wild. He can't stop crying."

Now Tilku, too, tumbled into the room, choking and sobbing and wiping his runny nose with his hand. Mr. Ganguly drew his head up and started caterwauling, too.

"Quiet, quiet." Jana wiped at the boy's face with her handkerchief, until Tilku was finally able to gasp out his story.

"Abinath sahib asked me to run down from the apothecary to the police station and deliver his certification report. So I went down there. The *chaprassi* said, Wait here in the waiting room. There was one small bench in the waiting room and six people were already trying to sit on it. I went and stood against the wall. After a while, I realized I could hear what was going on in Commissioner sahib's office.

"Jana mem, Commissioner sahib was very angry. He was shouting, grumbling, calling the *chaprassi* an idiot. Then I heard ring ring, and Commissioner sahib said, 'Hello?' He talked in a different tone of voice—very polite and respectful. After a while, he was laughing."

The tears started once again down Tilku's face. "And then I figured it out." He gave a sob. "Madam! They are going to drown us."

"Who is going to drown us?" Jana asked.

"Police or government or someone. Commissioner sahib said that we—all of us in the Central Bazaar—are going to be in the *catchment* area. We are going to be fish, and they are going to catch us."

Jana turned to Mary. "Have you heard anything like this?"

Mary shook her head vigorously. "I only heard that government wallahs were making measurements, and I saw a couple of them in the street. Someone told me it was for a new road."

"Did you know about this, Zohra?"

Zohra shook her head. "I will ask the men. They may have heard about something."

Jana showed Zohra to the front door, then returned to the now quiet tower room. Mr. Ganguly cocked his head questioningly.

"I hope we're not out of the frying pan, into the fire," Jana said.

The bird, alerted by her ominous tone, raised his wings in a threat position.

"You're right," said Jana, trying to sound confident. "We don't just roll over and accept this state of affairs."

But she went to bed that night uneasy, and didn't sleep until early morning, and then not for long.

Jana Gets a New Career

The Why Not? Tea Shop rang with its usual cheerful noise, and Ramachandran and Rambir sat down at their table overlooking the street. Mr. Joshi brought over a plate of potato patties with coriander sauce.

"Specialty of the day!" he said.

Ramachandran tried one, nodded, and tried another. Rambir nibbled on his more slowly.

"It's an honor, you know, Rambir." Ramachandran poured his tea into his saucer and took a long, noisy gulp. "Dealing with dignitaries, all that. The letter came, and I said to Padma, They want me to be the liaison for the town. For the Futurology Convention! Padma said to me, Who but you could possibly do it?"

"We will have to put our best foot forward as a town," said Rambir. "Put up welcoming signs. Provide amusements and amenities."

"Oh yes," said Ramachandran. "But you know, there's a problem. The town is *quiet*."

Quiet, they both realized at the same moment, was not literally true, as in the next moment Mr. Joshi turned up the Why Not?'s radio to drown out the competing radio of the Hot Spot, across the street. And a moment later, the wail of bagpipes sounded as Lal Bahadur Pun passed on the street, on his way to driving rats out of Pahari Provisioners.

"I didn't mean *quiet* quiet," said Ramachandran. "I meant *uneventful* quiet. Oh, I say—look. Look there in the street. Do you see what I see? What are those men doing?"

A man was setting up a tripod just below the Jolly Grant House. Having settled it on a level space, he then waved and started talking into a walkie-talkie. Ramachandran looked upward to the slope above Royal Tailors, where a small figure in white trousers and shirt was standing in front of another tripod, waving back.

"These are the government surveyors," Rambir said darkly. "Already taking measurements for the dam."

"Actually, I was hoping that whole business would disappear."

"No," said Rambir. "I talked to the milk wallah this morning. He comes in from his village, five miles away. Already the government chaps have been there, counting the number of houses, taking names. The milk wallah was so upset! He recently had to shift once for a government project, and now he thinks he's going to be shifted again, to some place worse, on land nobody wants. Development this, development that, he said, but in the end, it's always development for somebody else."

"Oh dear me," said Ramachandran.

"We've got to stop wringing our hands and start acting," Rambir said. "Is anyone from the government coming to the Futurology Convention?"

"The wife of the minister of irrigation is opening the proceedings!"

"Well, that could be useful," said Rambir.

"Oh, absolutely. We must show her that here in the mountains, we offer hospitality. We treat all guests with the utmost respect. Guest is God!"

"Well, one bit of progress has been made," said Rambir. "The Jolly Grant House looks very nice. I understand you helped get it repaired."

"Oh, I recommended some workmen," said Ramachandran

modestly. He dipped another potato patty into the sauce. "How about getting the Scottish lady involved in the rescue of our town? I have a good idea."

Rambir listened. At university, Ramachandran's good ideas had mainly involved attracting the attention of girls, and they'd rarely worked out, such as when the two young men had sneaked into the girls' dormitory dressed as workmen and been thrown out the door, onto the grass. As Ramachandran talked, Rambir's expression grew more and more skeptical.

"But," concluded Ramachandran, "there's no harm to it, and nothing ventured, nothing gained! *Qui audet adipiscitur!* He who dares, wins!"

"Would she even consider doing it, though?" said Rambir.

"I think she has an adventurous spirit. And some imagination. And whimsy."

"Perhaps you're right," said Rambir. "All right, let's put it to her."

A Proposition to Jana

Jana woke up with a headache, thinking of what Tilku had told her about the government dam. The idea of relocating again was appalling to her. Moreover, once Jack heard of this new problem, he would put his foot down, hard. She could just imagine the lecture he would deliver: "Mother! Of all the places you've chosen to live, this takes the cake!"

And what about the other members of her odd little household, now settled in and so happy? Mary was delightedly finding new people to gossip with. Tilku bragged about how many messages he delivered every day. Old Munar did about one hour of sweeping a morning, then sat in the sun and smoked his Mangalore Ganesh *biris*. Lal Bahadur Pun was expanding his bagpipe repertoire, adapting Jana's violin tunes and adding his own Nepali flavor. We're all just people living funny little lives, she thought. Wasn't a democratic government supposed to let you do just that?

And we aren't the only ones who've roosted here after having disrupted lives, Jana mused. Zohra, first a teenage bride torn from her family to go to her first husband, then separated from her sisters by a line drawn down a map in 1947. Feroze, losing everything he had in the riots of that same time—shop, house, sewing machines. Rambir, Jana had learned, after having been tossed out by his family for marrying below his caste, had made a new life in this place where he could hold his head up in public. Ramachandran, after giving up hope of getting an easy government job in his native Kerala, had left the comfort of South India and family to collect and nurture and find people who would adopt his treasures.

These people had conquered their disappointments and put together new lives for themselves. And now they were going to have the waters of a river diverted over them? Why not just turn a fire hose on us all, she thought.

She worked distractedly on old Ian's tunes, ruined a couple of pieces of score paper with stupid mistakes, then decided to run over to the Why Not? and have a bite before going on. She got there to find Ramachandran and Rambir on their third plate of Mr. Joshi's potato patties.

"Mrs. Laird, please join us," said Ramachandran. "We were just talking about you."

"Nothing bad, I hope," said Jana as Mr. Joshi swooped down and quickly put tea in front of her.

"Oh, not bad about *you*, dear lady. But there *are* bad things on the horizon. You know that the future of the town is in jeopardy."

"I've heard," said Jana. "The dam."

"Yes, the dam. Did you know that we are probably going to be right in the catchment area?"

"So it's true? Young Tilku heard something to that effect and was in complete hysterics."

"Unfortunately, yes."

"Is it settled, then?" said Jana.

"It will be settled unless we can *un*settle it," said Ramachandran. "And here's our idea. We will persuade people that this town is too valuable to be submerged under water. We will put the town on the map and in the tourist guides. And—we think you can help us in that."

"Oh?"

"For starters, you might allow tourists to visit the Jolly Grant House—go up in the tower and see the view."

Having expected a more important request, Jana was taken aback by this innocent suggestion. "That's easy. I can do that. But it seems like a small thing. After all, good views in this part of the world are two a penny."

"But wait, we have some other ideas, too. Mrs. Laird, have you heard about the convention?"

Jana nodded. "At the Victoria. In October."

"Yes, that's the one," said Rambir. "Ramachandran here is the chairman of the local welcoming committee. I am the vice chairman."

"And the other committee members?"

"None at the moment," said Ramachandran. "We are hoping that *you* will agree to serve."

"What are the duties?" Jana asked.

"A few short meetings," said Ramachandran. "Don't worry—they will be *short* short. We have to spread the word among the merchants to open not only their shops to the delegates but their hearts, too."

Jana, although a little uneasy, was flattered by the invitation. An offer to become an essential part of the town—that was a compliment, she felt, to someone who had barely moved in.

"The committee part seems easy enough to me," she said, "and I am honored by your invitation."

"So, you accept?" Ramachandran's eyebrows went up, whether in surprise or delight, Jana was not sure.

"I do accept."

"Oh, excellent, excellent!" said both men at once. Then they fell silent and looked at each other as if to say, "You ask her. No—you."

Ramachandran took a long, noisy sip of tea and said, "We have a third idea. It has to do with something we could have used before, dam or no dam. But it's doubly important now. You know, Mrs. Laird, it's incredible, but we're probably one of the few towns in India that don't have a full quotient of . . ."

The clatter of teacups momentarily drowned out what he was saying. Jana leaned forward to hear.

"Of fortune-tellers. There's one little South Indian woman who reads coffee grounds, one mad holy man who reads clouds, and a retired barrister who reads the flight of birds. But people really don't like them all that much. They're lacking in—personality. Charm. What's that marvelous word? Charisma!"

"But surely there are plenty of astrologers?" said Jana. "How about your wife's pundit, who blessed my house when I moved in?"

"Oh," said Ramachandran. "He's terribly overworked, drawing up horoscopes for babies right and left. There are so many babies!"

Jana asked, "What about that fellow at the Victoria Hotel who tells your fortune from the first letter of your name?"

Ramachandran said, "You didn't know? They fired him. He was unreliable. He'd tell them he would appear on Tuesday, and then he wouldn't show up until Thursday. He'd blame it on the stars. My diagnosis was: hangover. Anyway, young Dass at the hotel told him to pack up his incense and his posters and go home."

"That's a pity," said Jana. "Granted, he was a bit odd. But I felt he had a gift of sorts."

Rambir, who had been listening quietly, jumped into the conversation, saying, "Speaking of gifts—"

Ramachandran interrupted: "We understand that you are prescient."

"That I'm what?"

"Prescient. That you can predict the future. That you can see things other people can't see. Know things other people can't know."

"With all respect, may I ask where you got this idea?"

"My wife, Padma, told me," said Ramachandran. "She heard it from our ayah. That's where she gets most of her news about the town."

Aha, the ayah network.

"Well," said Rambir, "are you?"

"No, not at all," said Jana. "I mean, I have hunches; everyone does. Occasionally I'll have a dream that seems to point to a direction I should take. But nothing out of the ordinary. And I'm suspicious of people who say they can see the future. So many are just plain delusional. Especially economists and other university types."

"We don't want anyone dry and dull like that!" Ramachandran looked appalled at the very suggestion.

"Rambir, what do you think?" Jana asked. "Is another fortune-teller what this town needs? I mean, you seem to be a man of science and rationality. Just last week you wrote in the paper about eliminating superstition and moving without fear into the modern world."

Rambir, looking uncomfortable, gave a slow oscillation of his head. "It's complicated," he said. "On principle, of course I stand with science—reason, statistics, all that. But sometimes one must adapt one's principles to circumstance. And you know, fortune-tellers—soothsayers of all types—certainly can coexist very comfortably with science. When it comes to figuring out individual lives, that is."

Ramachandran, his eyes burning anew, said, "Yes! Just take my own life, for example. I was down and out. I mean, *discouraged*. At that point, I already had three children to support, and Padma was very annoyed at my lack of success. A palmist told me that I hadn't yet found my true calling—but not to despair! I would find buried treasure. Treasure, he said, most emphatically! At the time, I took it as a metaphor. Yet the very next week, I learned that the Treasure Emporium was for sale. Coincidence? Perhaps. But it was just the right prediction for me; it came along at the right time!"

"But could I in good faith make predictions?" said Jana. "I can't tell you what's going to happen next week."

"Okay, let's phrase this a different way," said Rambir. "Let's not talk about your being able to predict the future; let's talk about your helping to *save* the future. To *make* the future. Let's just picture it. You set up a fortune-telling salon on the ground floor of the Jolly Grant House. Tourists come in. You tell them something to make them feel optimistic, and also to associate that feeling of optimism with the setting, this town, this spot in the mountains."

"I set up a fortune-telling salon in my sitting room?"

Rambir looked apologetic. "I know. It's a lot to ask. But better to have it as a fortune-telling salon than to have it underwater."

"And you see me telling fortunes. Reading cards and palms and the like?"

"And having your *parrot* tell fortunes, too," said Ramachandran. "Word is out that your parrot is quite special."

Mr. Joshi brought a plate of walnut fudge. Jana took a sip of tea and cut off a small bit of fudge with a knife and fork, then tasted it. A world without Mr. Joshi's walnut fudge would be impoverished, she thought.

"Well—who would come into the salon?"

"Tourists," said Rambir.

"Yes, people looking for fun," said Ramachandran. "On holiday."

Rambir said, "I'll get things off to a good start by putting a story about you in the newspaper. And I can print up a flyer for the Victoria Hotel. They can put a copy in every room!"

Ramachandran rushed on enthusiastically: "We can find some beautiful furnishings for a salon right in the Treasure Emporium! Well, how about it, Mrs. Laird?"

She shook her head. "I think of fortune-telling as a parlor trick. My mother used to read palms at dinner parties, when people had

had too much to drink. I did that myself, once, at a fancy-dress ball at the palace where I was a violin tutor."

Rambir's eyebrows went up.

"Not *drink* too much, read a few palms," Jana clarified.

"Okay, we have palmistry," said Ramachandran. "What about cards?"

"You're grasping at straws," said Jana. "But . . ."

A couple of memories came to mind, and she laughed.

"I used to play at reading cards, dressed in my mother's old ball gowns. I'd tell my sister, Loulou, what we were going to have for dinner that night. She was gullible enough to believe I knew by magic, not because I'd heard the cook giving orders to the scullery boy."

"It doesn't matter where information comes from!" Ramachandran said. "It only matters what you do with it."

"Well, I got into trouble for reading cards once. In boarding school. We were being silly, after lights-out, having a secret feast in my room. I dealt a girl the queen of spades and told her it symbolized the house matron, and that she—the matron, that is—was an evil queen and was coming to give the girl a demerit. The girl told on me! The house matron scolded me for lies, nonsense, and sacrilege. I got a demerit for each of those things and was gated for two weeks."

"Never mind that," said Ramachandran. "No one is going to punish you for this. Here are the essential facts: Your mother read palms. It was passed down by family tradition, and you've been practicing it since you were a young girl. You had early experience at reading cards, too. Those things are *credentials*. Rambir, put all that in the newspaper."

"Wait, wait, wait," said Jana.

But Ramachandran rushed on: "I'll find furnishings in the Treasure Emporium that will set the mood."

Jana looked at Rambir, the more sensible of the two friends. Yet he was wiggling his eyebrows in a most encouraging manner.

"It still seems a bit mad," she said.

"Mrs. Laird," said Ramachandran, "the thing with madness

is, it often works much better than method. And when method
fails, madness is absolutely essential."

"May I think it over for a day or two?"

"Of course! Completely prudent of you; we understand
entirely," said Ramachandran.

She took another piece of walnut fudge and washed it down
with tea.

"And," she said, "I'll have to consult my parrot on this, since
he will definitely be part of the project."

"Of course!" boomed Ramachandran. "Rambir, make sure
you put the parrot in the newspaper story, too."

Jana went home and thought over the bizarre proposal. At the
very worst, she decided, it would be a form of entertainment. Of
storytelling. And perhaps she could even be useful to someone.

One could use props—cards, crystal balls, dice—to set the
mood. But basically, fortune-telling would be a chance to sit quietly with a person, focusing on that person's hopes, their dreams,
their fears. Listening. Sometimes that was all people wanted.
Sometimes it was all they *needed,* to set themselves on the right
course. Because really, she thought, the truth usually lay with
the person's intuition. The fortune-teller's job was to pull out
what that intuition was. What harm could there be in that?

She went up to the tower of the Jolly Grant House and looked
out over the premonsoon landscape. Below, the plain shim-
mered with dust, parched and beige. Up in the tower, she heard
the noise from the bazaar as if it were coming from a huge distance. She leaned over the windowsill, and saw Mary sitting on
the terrace below peeling potatoes, and Tilku, who was happily
puffing on a *biri* with old Munar.

That boy should not be smoking, she thought, and the next
moment, she heard Mary roundly chewing him out on the subject, to no noticeable effect. Jana called down, "Tilku! You're too
young to smoke! It's a filthy habit."

Tilku looked up and shot a dazzling smile in her direction. "Madam, I am a clean boy. Not to worry!"

Jana shook her head and stepped back into the room.

"Well, what do you think, Mr. Ganguly? Shall we go into a new business?"

"Jana Bibi zindabad!"

Long live Jana Bibi. All right, she would be a fortune-teller, if it would help save the town and her new home.

Ramachandran was over at the Jolly Grant House the next afternoon. He declined tea and toast, having just come from the Why Not? "And," he added, "my daughters are telling me I should do a little slimming."

"One's children do start telling one what to do. All out of love, of course," said Jana.

"Oh yes," agreed Ramachandran benevolently. "All out of love."

"How is Padma?"

"Very well, thank you. In fact, never better. She's always cheerful when . . . well, she's very cheerful these days."

Already informed through the ayah network, Jana mentally filled in the blanks: when she's in the family way. "And how are Asha and Bimla?"

"They, too, are well."

"And Vikram?"

"Happy as can be, for one who is failing in school."

Jana went through the names of Ramachandran's family to the best of her ability, and then he asked after the health of everyone in her household.

Then they settled in the bay window seat, against a panorama of fair-weather clouds scudding by. Bright mountain light flooded the room. Mr. Ganguly was happily picking the strands out of a knot of jute rope.

"I've been thinking about a sign for the fortune-telling salon," Ramachandran said. "What are you going to call it?"

"I'm thinking Excellent Fortunes," Jana said.

"Mrs. Laird's Excellent Fortunes?"

Jana pulled a face. "That's rather boring, wouldn't you say?"

From his cage, Mr. Ganguly gave a squawk.

"Excuse me, Mr. Ramachandran, let me just get the bird out of the cage. He hears us talking and wants to be part of the action."

She carried the parrot to his perch by the table, and he cried out his usual way of saying thank you. "Jana Bibi zindabad! Long live Jana Bibi."

"What did he say?" asked Ramachandran. "Who is Jana Bibi?"

"Oh, that's me," said Jana. "When my sister and I played fortunes as children, she called me Jana Bibi. . . . Then I happened to mention that to the children at the palace where I taught, and they started calling me that, and the parrot picked it up."

"It has a ring to it," said Ramachandran. "Wait. Jana Bibi's Excellent Fortunes. That's it! We can get the sign painter who did the sign for the Treasure Emporium to quickly make one up for you."

Jana hesitated. Ramachandran's own sign was—well, *busier* than she would have wanted for herself. Way too many symbols and promises.

"Something simple should do," she said.

"But you need some pictorial interest," he said. "A swastika, for example, is an auspicious symbol."

Jana was taken aback. "Surely not."

"It's an ancient Sanskrit symbol. And used by Buddhists as well. It has been found in all sorts of archaeological sites, from the Indus Valley to China and northern Europe."

"Yes, but don't you think its more recent history is a problem?" Jana said. "Let's find something neutral."

Only what symbol wouldn't cause trouble? Crosses were too Christian; a crescent and star, too Muslim. Buddhist symbols, Jana thought, were possibly less contentious. Conch shells, pairs of fishes happily swimming together, and lotus flowers seemed unlikely to give offense.

"Bells," said Ramachandran. "They purify the environment."

All the while, Mr. Ganguly was flapping his wings.

"I think your symbol should be the parrot," said Ramachandran. "No one seems to have bad associations with the bird. A nice painting came into the emporium just the other day: the Hindu god of love, Kamadeva, riding on his parrot. People look at such a painting and think they are going to be lucky in love. Right, Mr. Ganguly?"

"I love you," said Mr. Ganguly, cocking his head dreamily.

"And the parrot is the sign of purity and truth, too. Not to mention wisdom and crafty thinking. Think of the parrot in the *Tutinama*!"

"*Tutinama*?" said Jana.

"A lovely fourteenth-century illustrated Persian manuscript! I wish I had one to sell. What a story. A wealthy merchant goes off and leaves his wife with a mynah and a parrot to watch over her. Both birds are good talkers. The wife wants to engage in all sorts of mischief with a lover! The mynah tells her not to, and the wife wrings its neck. So much for truth telling! So the parrot takes his turn at guarding the wife. He cleverly tells her fifty-two stories—so her attention is distracted and she doesn't fall into adulterous ways. But the parrot doesn't risk its own life in the process. Now, that's a clever bird!"

"That's just the ticket, Mr. Ramachandran," said Jana. "I think you've solved our problem. The sign can have a small green symbol of a parrot in the corner. What do you think, Mr. Ganguly?" She lightly scratched the parrot's head.

"Jana Bibi zindabad!"

Palmistry

"Mary," said Jana, "let me see your palm."

"Palm, Jana mem?"

"For practicing," Jana said, pointing to a stack of books and articles on palmistry.

Mary put her hand out, and Jana chuckled, remembering her one foray into palm reading. It had been at the nawab's palace, and the nawab was throwing one of his house parties. Jana had told a shy stenographer and an even shyer passport clerk from the British High Commission that they were on the verge of romance, and a month later, the pair had been married. That bit of matchmaking via palmistry had been fun, although the bountiful champagne at the party might have had something to do with the results, too.

"I'm brushing up," Jana now told Mary. She read aloud from an article she'd clipped from a film magazine: " 'Your history,' it says " 'is written in your hands. Take the marriage line below the little finger. A long marriage will show a deep, distinct crease. A marriage line sloping toward the heart line means the death of your spouse.' "

She'd been married to William for twenty-two years, and, of course, he *had* died, but where was her marriage line? She held her hand up to the window and twisted it around as far as she could. Mr. Ganguly peered down from his perch and twisted his head, too.

"Jana mem?" said Mary.

"I'm trying to find my marriage line. I don't seem to have one. Have you got one?" She took Mary's hand again. It was small but strong, and rough as burlap, the palm a mass of creases. Mary, Jana saw, had three distinct marriage lines on the left hand. The right hand was the same.

"Mary, your hands say you had *three* husbands!"

Mary pulled her hands away. "One scoundrel was enough. Any more would have finished me off."

Jana consulted the magazine article again. "Take a look at the thumb," it said. "A long, strong thumb denotes a strong will."

She held up Mary's palm against her own and compared the thumbs. Both looked good and strong to her, but Mary's perhaps had the edge.

"You have a good strong will, Mary."

"Of course, Jana mem, I had to have a strong will. Or I would be back in my village. Or dead."

Of course, thought Jana. Anyone who had escaped from cleaning cesspits and drains with her bare hands, who had hitchhiked across half a subcontinent to throw a violent husband off the scent, who had not gotten raped or kidnapped in the process, anyone like that had a strong will and a quick mind, as well. She called to mind the image of Mary arriving at the mission and announcing that, henceforth, she would be Jana's ayah, and of Mary sitting with young Jack in her lap, the two of them learning to read English from the same primers.

"Yes, Mary," she said, "you have a good strong will."

As for the other lines, she couldn't see that the lines on her own palm or on Mary's matched up well with the diagrams in Cheiro's guide or Mrs. Dale's book or the magazine article. I obviously need a much larger sample, she thought.

"How about your palm, my zygodactylous friend?" she said to Mr. Ganguly. "Shake hands?"

He put up his right claw to shake.

"If I knew which one was the thumb, I'd say you had a strong will, too."

She looked at another page in Mrs. Dale's book. "'The mount of the moon . . .'" She pushed down on the fleshy part at the base of her thumb. Was it very large and full? If so, it denoted caprice and lunacy.

Caprice and lunacy? Well, why not? In the appropriate dose, of course.

Shopping at the Emporium

In the Musical Instruments section of the Treasure Emporium, a young European man was trying out a sitar, while another thumped on a set of tablas. A hint of incense and cloves hung about the place, and the woven hemp carpet had a grassy smell. Jana felt a little dizzy from the sights, smells, and sounds. With Mr. Ganguly on her shoulder, she threaded her way through the maze of tables and shelves.

Atmosphere, Jana thought; how do we create an appealing atmosphere for fortune-telling? In her dorm room at school, she had covered a trunk with a paisley cloth and lit a candle. At the nawab's party, it was easy: the halls and arcades and nooks looked like something out of the Arabian nights anyway, and massive amounts of champagne had put the guests in a believing mood.

Dozing in one corner of the emporium was Ramachandran's old aunt Putli, on duty because, as Ramachandran had told Jana, "there is nothing else she can do, given her memory and her eyesight." Ramachandran's twin sixteen-year-old daughters, in matching salwar kameez and with braids to their waists, came running over with big smiles and namastés. Jana could never tell which one was Asha and which one was Bimla.

"Dad told us about the shop!" said one of them. "It's a smashing idea! Ripping! We'll help you choose some good decorations."

"You've got a lot in here!" Jana said.

"Every curiosity known to man," proclaimed the sign on the wall. Jana's eye swept over a blur of hookahs, brass finger bowls, wine goblets, decanters, paperweights, and a pair of bookends in the shape of bare-breasted mermaids.

Ramachandran himself came out from the back room to greet her. "Mrs. Laird! Jana Bibi of the Excellent Fortunes. Let's see which objects volunteer for service."

"Volunteer?"

"Why, yes. Objects have souls, some stronger and more opinionated than others. We'll just see which ones wish to be part of Jana Bibi's Excellent Fortunes and rescue the beautiful Himalayan town of Hamara Nagar.

"By the way, I thought you should know that Padma's astrologer vets all the items that come into here. Nothing inauspicious allowed! Of course, he hasn't seen the things in the back room. I have trunks of things, to be ruled on at a later date. Sometimes cleaning out is difficult, isn't it?"

Asha and Bimla nodded vigorously at that.

"Girls," said Ramachandran, "Mrs. Laird is looking for a combination of comfort and mystery. A bit of magic. I look for magic, all the time. That's why I bought this place, to tell you the truth. Every day something magical comes in."

"And, hopefully, goes out!" said the girls.

"My daughters show no respect," said Ramachandran, which prompted both Asha and Bimla to give him a hug.

"Does this call out to you?" Asha (or was it Bimla?) held up a statue of a gnome playing the violin. "We hear you playing in the evening. It always sounds so nice."

"He's a sweet little creature, isn't he?" said Bimla. (Or was it Asha?)

Jana shuddered but tried to keep a polite look on her face. "He *is* sweet," she said, "but I don't think he's *quite* right. A bit too cartoonish for my tastes."

"Something more modern?" Ramachandran pointed out a statue of Saint Francis of Assisi. The saint's face was stretched out and melancholy, the birds on his arm shaped like paper airplanes.

"A bit—abstract. But you're on the right track. Saint Francis would be kindly."

The girls looked around. "Here's one!" they cried together. "He surely wants to come home with you."

This Saint Francis was a friendly one, not too modern, not too religious. "All right," Jana said, warming to the task. "Let's see if Mr. Ganguly can stand on his shoulder."

She brought the parrot close to the statue, and he stepped onto its head.

"A useful perch," said Ramachandran.

"Here's something really nice." Asha (it turned out) held up a small painting in the Mughal style of ladies feeding parrots.

"That speaks to me," said Jana.

"This mirror? With such a nicely carved frame?" said Rama-chandran.

"Very nice," said Jana.

"We'll get the minions to carry your purchases over to your house," announced Ramachandran, summoning his quartet of young men, who at the moment were unoccupied.

"Oh, Jana mem has so many items!" Mary's eyes grew wider and wider as a procession of Ramachandran's minions filed into the sitting room. They carried Kashmiri ottomans, a brass tray, and a sideboard of rosewood with ivory inlays of Krishna playing the flute and the shepherdesses dancing. There was a pair of painted Rajasthani peacocks, which Mr. Ganguly had initially vetoed with an alarmed screech, but finally accepted.

"Very good, memsahib!" Lal Bahadur Pun particularly liked the table mounted on a carved elephant with painstakingly real-istic wrinkles and pores.

"It's taking shape," Jana said, as Lal Bahadur Pun drove nails into the walls and hung the pictures.

In addition to books on fortune-telling and birds, Jana had come home from the Treasure Emporium with a crystal ball, a set of tarot cards, Freud's *Interpretation of Dreams,* and, not for-getting Mary's complaints about the kitchen, a potato masher and a toaster with sides that flipped out.

Mary was ecstatic over the potato masher and the toaster. "Excellent shopping, truly excellent, Jana mem!"

"Thank you," said Jana. "That certainly was one of my most successful excursions."

That night she was exhausted. She drew her bath, forgot not to put her fingers in the water, and gave herself a shock.

"Try not to be so stupid," she told herself.

She soaked in the tub, looking at the lizards on the wall and thinking that she still needed to buy some cushions for the win-dow seat downstairs. All in good time. Once in bed, she flipped through Dr. Freud's book. There were a lot of long words and long sentences, and after a few minutes she dozed off and the book flopped forward, waking her up. After that happened a couple more times, she put it on the bedside table and turned off the light.

✑ Dreams

Jana awoke with a start. In a nightmare, she'd been playing in her dance band in Bombay, enjoying the warmth and darkness of the room, sensing the dancers responding to the music. Then, suddenly, there were no dancers, and the room was closing in on her. There was one little escape route through a window, but someone was boarding it up. The sliver of daylight shrank, disappeared. Bandhu Sharma was pounding on the door, saying, "Open up, madam, open up! You are in violation of the rules!"

She threw off the covers, panting in relief. Oh, thank goodness, just a dream! But what had she read last night? That dreams were the fulfillment of *wishes*? Why would anyone want to be trapped alone in a room being boarded up like a packing crate? Who would want Bandhu Sharma to come knocking?

She carried Dr. Freud's book over to the kitchen building, where Mary already had the tea made. Jana sliced two pieces of bread and put them in the newly acquired toaster.

"You have to watch carefully or the toast will burn," Mary warned.

"I can do that," Jana said. She sat down next to the toaster and started flipping through the book, looking for a mention of a policeman. The egg wallah arrived, Mary went to the back door, and suddenly there was the smell of burning toast.

"Oh, Jana mem!" said Mary. "I will do toast. And eggs. You go sit somewhere else."

Chastised, Jana went out onto the terrace.

While Mary was scrambling eggs and making a new round of

toast, Jana read about the policeman dream. A woman whose hus-band was a policeman dreamt she was in a forest, not so different from the forests surrounding Hamara Nagar, with a road leading from a church to a mountaintop. Sounds like here, thought Jana. And in the dream was a *policeman* with a cloak. According to Dr. Freud, just about everything in the dream had to do with sex: climbing a mountain, going to a chapel, entering a dense forest. Was *Bandhu* a—sex symbol?

Mary came out with the eggs and toast.

"Mary," said Jana. How to put this? she wondered. "Do you think of Bandhu as—attractive to women?"

Mary spluttered. "That man? He'd be lucky if a mule liked him."

"As I thought," said Jana. She read on, the passage explaining that a policeman with a cloak represented a demon and that, furthermore, a cloaked demon was of phallic significance.

"Do you think he's like a demon?" she asked.

"Definitely like a demon," said Mary and went back inside.

Dr. Freud and Mary agreed, which improved Jana's opinion of Dr. Freud. Her mind drifted back to the village where she had been a missionary. On the outskirts, there had been a shrine with a lingam, the divine phallic symbol, at which the village women left offerings. Dr. Freud would have been completely at home in village India, Jana concluded.

In the meantime, she hoped she would not dream any more of Bandhu. It was bad enough having to cope with him in real life.

✃ *Cards*

She did not want to fall too far behind on the transcription proj-ect, so that morning she got a nice strathspey down on the page, with the dotted rhythms pretty much as she remembered old

Ian playing them. Having done her quota, she cleared the table in the salon and picked up the tarot cards. She cut and shuffled, Mr. Ganguly hopping up and down with excitement. Then she spread a few cards on the table and studied them.

Some throat clearing made her look up; Mary was holding up the laundry list and two unfamiliar pillowcases.

"Jana mem, that *dhobi* has taken our good linen and given us these two ugly-looking things."

"He'll sort it out next week," said Jana.

"And I think his wife must have worn my petticoat. . . . She is a fat woman, and see, here it's split at the seam. I'm going to tell him we'll get a new *dhobi* if he doesn't bring our things back properly."

Jana did not want to concentrate on laundry problems just then. "Mary," she said, "I have to practice doing cards. Would you mind helping me?"

"Jana mem?"

"You will pretend to be the tourist who comes off the street into the salon of Jana Bibi's Excellent Fortunes. You will have a question to ask, and I will try to answer it, using the cards."

"But, Jana mem, I must go to the vegetable wallah."

"Didn't he come this morning?"

"Yes, but I forgot to buy cauliflower for supper tonight."

"Cauliflower can wait. Come sit at the table."

Mary sat at the table, adjusting her sari.

"We'll spread the cards in a great crescent," said Jana. "Let's look at your present situation."

Mary started to get interested in spite of herself, but when Jana turned over the first card, Mary's face darkened. The card featured two beggars, one on crutches; they cut forlorn figures as they made their way through the snow.

"This is *myself,* madam? All bent over and sad? This looks like bad luck. I don't like looking at this card at all." Mary shuddered and shook her head so vehemently that a hairpin fell out.

"All right, let's try another." Jana turned over the Fool.

"This is a young English sahib, is it not?" Mary said. "He is mountain climbing. Those young Europeans go back into the mountains with no purpose whatsoever except to wear out their shoes. What's this to do with me?"

"It's your *past*," said Jana. "It says so in the book. It must be young Master Jack, whom you took care of so nicely until he went away to school."

"Oh." Mary shook her head in an ambiguous way, perhaps agreeing, perhaps not. "But Jack sahib—does he like mountain climbing?"

"The occasional ramble, I suppose," said Jana. "All right, let's continue. What does your future hold?"

She turned over a card labeled "The Star," and Mary dissolved into a fit of giggles.

"What's so funny?"

"Jana mem, this is a naked lady! She has no clothes on! Why is that?"

"I don't know," said Jana. "It's because she's—a symbol, I guess."

"She must be Eve in the Garden of Eden," said Mary. "But they should have put a fig leaf on her private parts."

"Well, they didn't," said Jana.

"Jana mem, I can take a fountain pen and draw in some fig leaves."

"No, no," said Jana. "This is—artwork. Statues at Khajuraho don't have fig leaves."

"Maybe," said Mary. "But, Jana mem, if you have cards with naked ladies, ruffians will come into your store, just wanting to look at dirty pictures. And after they've looked at the dirty pictures, what do you think they will do to you and me? I will take these cards and fix them up."

"No, Mary, the artist who made these cards had some significance in mind. Don't worry! If ruffians come into my shop, I will set Mr. Ganguly on them. Right, Mr. Ganguly?"

The bird gave a vigorous flap of his wings.

✑ *Feroze Makes Jana a Fortune-Telling Outfit*

Jana stood staring into the almirah, wondering what on earth she could wear to be a convincing fortune-teller. She saw a couple of wool pullovers, a few skirts and trousers, and some salwar kameez for the warm weather. Useless. But in the back of the almirah, there was a length of green-and-gold silk that her mother had owned. After her parents' death, Jana had taken the sari back to Scotland with her and then, packing to return to India with William, had thrown it into the suitcase. The sari was more than forty years old but still lustrous and soft.

Jana went downstairs and called, "Tilku? Tilku!"

The patter of small bare feet sounded in the hall, and Tilku arrived, breathless and smiling.

"Memsahib?"

"Would you please go ask Feroze Ali Khan if he can come this afternoon?"

"I am flying," said Tilku, and he took off.

That afternoon, Feroze arrived with his Sears, Roebuck and Company catalog and his notebook under one arm.

"*Salaam aleikum,* Feroze Ali Khan sahib."

"*W'aleikum salaam,* memsahib."

"How is your health?"

"My health is fine, thanks be to God."

"And the health of your good wife?"

"She, too, has the blessing of good health, Allah be praised."

The inquiries into health proceeded through the various members of both households, and then they got down to business.

"Feroze Ali Khan, I wish you to make a piece of clothing for me. Only you have the skills to do that."

"Memsahib will please tell me her wishes. Does memsahib wish to copy a piece of her clothing?"

Jana shuddered. "No, no, nothing I already have would be suitable. It has to be more glamorous than an ordinary dress. Something that will impress the tourists."

"Memsahib?"

"I'll be having a fortune-telling salon in my main room. As part of the effort to make Hamara Nagar a bigger destination for people. So it will go in the guidebooks. So we can show the outside world that we should continue to exist." Her Hindi vocabulary was strained to the limit explaining these things, and at first Feroze looked puzzled, but then he nodded.

"So we need something with flair," said Jana. "Like something for the theater."

"Dancing costume, memsahib?"

"More like—oh, say, a wedding costume."

"Memsahib is getting married?" Feroze's eyes widened.

"No, no, no . . . pretend . . . like in films."

The word "films" made Feroze frown. "Surely memsahib is not acting in a film?"

"No, no, I'm not going to. . . . What would they wear . . ." She had a sudden burst of inspiration. "In the days of Shah Jehan?"

"Ah! In the days of old . . ." A dreamy look came over Feroze's face, and Jana knew she had struck the right chord.

"In the days of old," said Feroze, "all was sumptuous wealth and beauty and jewels. Veils with gold embroidery. Layers of filmy material that swirled and rustled when people walked."

The man has an artist's eye, Jana said to herself.

Feroze went on: "Ribbons of gold braid. Ropes of pearls. Belts with stripes of gold and violet and green. Yes, I know what they wore in the days of old! I have a good picture of that. In my head. Memsahib, not to worry. I can make you a costume worthy of the Mughals."

"Might you draw me a little sketch?" Jana asked, and she took a clean piece of staff paper off the table where she had been working.

With his face screwed up in concentration, Feroze drew a rough sketch. It was a full-skirted dress worn over a set of pantaloons, with a flowing shawl for the head.

"My drawing is not so good," he apologized. "I am a *darzi*,

not a painter. This looks plain. But made of fine silk, with bro-
cade and ornaments—all will be beautiful. My wife does very
nice embroidery. She can embroider some flowers and vines . . .
anything memsahib's heart desires."

"That sounds lovely," Jana said.

"Shoes!" Feroze looked pointedly at Jana's sensible brogues.
"Memsahib must have proper shoes. Memsahib must get the
mochi to make slippers with curved-up toes. Not all heavy and
plain like those shoes."

"Of course!"

He stopped suddenly. "In the days of old, they wore *very* expensive costumes. But these are modern times. I will give memsahib
a small price. And—another thing. Memsahib will have to wear
lots of jewelry. Can't be just—plain."

Jana was amused by Feroze's implied criticism of her normal
workaday appearance, the rough wool skirt and pullover and
total lack of jewelry. "I'll see what Mr. Ramachandran has in the
Treasure Emporium," she said.

"Memsahib has no jewelry of her own?"

"Not much, Feroze Ali Khan sahib," she said. "Just my old
wedding ring. Which I can no longer get on my ring finger."

Feroze shook his head. "Time goes by, memsahib."

"It does," she agreed. "Which reminds me: how long do you
think it will take you to make this costume?"

"Memsahib, I will cut this one carefully and stitch it slowly.
And as soon as it is finished, I will bring it over here."

Feeling put in her place, Jana nodded.

"I'm sure it's going to be beautiful," she said.

"*Inshallah,*" said Feroze.

"Of course," she said.

·◦§ *Jana Gets Jewelry from Ramachandran*

With Mr. Ganguly on her shoulder, Jana went up to Ramachandran's, where they were having a busy day. Old Aunt Putli was making out receipts at the cashier's desk, and the minions were running around like miniature whirlwinds, wrapping purchases, bringing things out from the storeroom for customers and taking them back.

Spotting Jana, Ramachandran stopped scolding the minions and weaved his way across the room. "Mrs. Laird, how is our project going?"

"Very well, I think, Mr. Ramachandran. Feroze Ali Khan is making me a special outfit."

"Ah yes, the philosopher-tailor. You can count on him to stitch excellent fortune into every seam. That's very good."

"And the *mochi* seemed quite excited about making dainty slippers after all those hiking boots for the students. The neighborhood seems to be quite caught up in this project."

"As they should be," said Ramachandran. "It's going to affect our survival. We've got to impress the higher-ups with the idea that we are precious jewels—something unique and not merely peons to be drowned by one of the government's gigantic dams. Sacrifices on the altar of national development."

"Now you are talking like Rambir," said Jana.

"Oh yes, speaking of Rambir. He is going to put a large announcement in the newspaper about the opening of your shop."

"Very good," said Jana. "I came to choose jewelry for the costume. What have you got in your back room?"

Ramachandran yelled to the minions, who whirled into the back room and came out with a tin trunk.

"Oh!" Ramachandran looked taken aback by the size of the trunk. "I'd forgotten all about that."

They put the trunk down on the floor in the corner, Ramachandran unlocked the padlock, and everyone crouched down to look inside. An incomprehensible muddle greeted them: necklaces with no clasps, earrings without their mates, broken lockets, pendants with no chains, tiaras with missing gems, mismatched ankle bells.

Ramachandran ordered a sheet to be brought over, and the minions turned the entire stock of jewelry onto it. Mr. Ganguly looked down from Jana's shoulder and seemed prepared to lunge right into the pile of glittering, interesting objects. He flapped his way off her shoulder and seized a necklace in his beak. It had dozens of small green stones and a huge green pendant hanging from it.

"No wonder," said Jana. "Green is his favorite color." A memory of the Victoria Hotel's banished nomenologist flitted through her head. Jade will be lucky, he'd said. These stones definitely weren't jade, though; they looked more like sea glass.

"That should certainly be usable for your costume," said Ramachandran.

Having picked out the key piece, Jana added earrings, some strings of pearls to lay on the part of her hair, several finger rings, and ornate bangles. When they had finished making their selections, Ramachandran had the minions scoop back the remaining jewels, and then he locked up the trunk.

"What do I owe you, Mr. Ramachandran?"

"Oh, these things are of little value," he said. "All paste. Accept them with my compliments. After all, it's for the cause."

⋰ Feroze Works on the Costume

The opportunity to make something truly royal-looking comes along seldom—if ever—in a person's life. When Feroze made clothes for weddings, he reserved every bit of the operation for himself, not letting the assorted cousins touch a thing. So it was now. He looked at the green-and-gold silk Mrs. Laird had given him. He would prepare thoroughly before cutting such a thing! He made a pattern from paper, planning carefully where he would put the darts and how wide the seams would be. He went himself to Fab-Fab and looked at trim, then talked the owner into giving him some samples, which he took back to Jana for approval. There were to be no zippers or buttons in this garment, just soft frog closures and a couple of ties.

He thought for a while about his new neighbor. He still did not entirely approve of her. Zohra and Moustapha spent far too much time over at her house. It was disruptive! He'd call for Zohra or for Moustapha, and there would be silence. What kind of a state of affairs was that?

Also, she had so many Hindu friends. She was always drinking tea in the Why Not? Tea Shop with Ramachandran and Rambir. For all he knew, she might be friends with that odious Bandhu; although that seemed unlikely, since Bandhu, to Feroze's knowledge, *had* no friends.

But then there were positive things. Mrs. Laird was a good customer. He'd made curtains for her house, salwar kameez for her to wear, even a cloth cover for the bird's cage. She was courteous, she spoke to him with the correct Urdu greetings, she obviously knew about the customs of ordinary people. She was not like the tourists who just wanted to know "how much" and "when will it be finished." On balance, he decided, she was quite a lot more good than bad.

He was carefully fitting the gussets into the dress part of the special costume for Mrs. Laird when, glancing out through the storefront, he saw one of Ramachandran's minions up on a ladder, putting a sign above the entrance to the Jolly Grant House.

"Jana Bibi's Excellent Fortunes," spelled out Feroze. Jana Bibi— sounds like a high-class Persian lady, he thought. He decided to work on the costume with all possible speed.

As Feroze and Moustapha ate their evening meal, the topic of Mrs. Laird came up, as it always seemed to. Zohra, having brought a second round of cauliflower to the men, also threw in her opinion.

"It's amusing," Zohra said. "This is giving our quarter something different, don't you think? Out of the ordinary. How many small hill stations have a European lady fortune-teller?"

"None that I know of," said Feroze. "And there's a reason for that. It's not natural."

"Uncle," said Moustapha. "She's good for the quarter. Remember when you used to say that the Jolly Grant House was an eyesore, and depressing because no one lived there? You can't say that now. Now more tourists will come, and *everyone* will get more business. Besides, you are providing her costume. You, too, have already benefited."

Feroze felt a twinge of guilt, as if he were in league with the devil.

"Not to worry," said Zohra, who sometimes seemed to read Feroze's mind. "Nothing bad will happen."

"Something good might even happen," said Moustapha. "They might put the dam somewhere else."

"Dam?" said Feroze.

"Uncle, don't you know what everyone is talking about? Even Mrs. Laird's messenger boy knows about this. The town is going to disappear from the face of the earth, Uncle."

"But—so many shops? So many buildings?"

"Uncle, what do you and Yusuf Baig talk about when you're taking your walks? Don't you ever pay attention to what's going on *today*?"

Zohra muttered, "Yusuf Baig only talks about how many times he has made the hajj," and Moustapha flicked his eyes heavenward.

"So, tell me!" Feroze said.

As he heard about the rumors, his heart sank. Once you had stood the test of one catastrophe, why would God send another catastrophe to test you again? Had Feroze not earned the right to live peacefully and quietly, and deliver the best tailoring to all customers, Muslim and Hindu and Christian alike?

That night, he poised his pen above his notebook. Usually he liked to write things that sounded like proverbs. Thoughts on work, human nature. But this time, he wrote an uncustomary reference to his fears: "The *Angrezi* lady has put a sign up above her house. 'Excellent Fortunes,' it says. I am afraid. I know that fortunes aren't always excellent. Moustapha says we are to be swept away by a dam. I feel quite quite ignorant."

He put the book away, heard the late-night call to prayer sounding from the mosque, and unrolled his prayer rug. When the prayer was done, he felt some of his tangle of worry starting to loosen. The bazaar was quiet. Moustapha was off somewhere unknown with his friends.

Zohra had unrolled the bedding on the low string cots and had let down her hair. It hung to her waist, black and lovely.

"Tired?" she said. "Let me rub your ankles."

Feroze lowered himself to the cot, feeling the twinges in his knees and back. "Do you really think we will have to leave this place?" he asked.

"I hope not," she said.

"I, too, hope not." The simple statement conveyed much less than he was feeling. No, his heart cried out, I don't want to leave everything I've built. The shop, with its smooth, solid floor; the six Singer sewing machines, all in good working order; the regular business. And the good neighbors, Hindu and Sikh though they were, and even the European Mrs. Laird. When he thought that he might lose all this and have to build his life anew, an enormous weariness came over him.

There was a long pause, during which Zohra rubbed Feroze's ankles. "If we have to leave," she said, "then at least we will leave together."

He put his finger under her chin and tipped her face toward him, and he felt a wave of gratitude flood through him. As long as he had Zohra, Allah had given him happiness that he could take with him, no matter where, no matter why.

✑ *Jana Writes to Jack*

Jana put a new cartridge into her fountain pen. She had just written the morning's date on an aerogramme when Mary came into the salon with the account book.

Jana scanned the payments to the wallahs—egg, milk, bread, meat, charcoal—all in Mary's painstaking numerals. "That looks in order, Mary. Well done."

"Thank you, Jana mem. Writing to *chota* sahib?"

Yes, she was writing to the "little sahib," as Mary had always called Jack.

Mary crossed her arms. "Why doesn't he come live here with us?"

"He's too busy in Scotland," Jana said. "Being a successful engineer and a professional Scot."

"Professional?"

"Oh, I'm just making a joke. Not very funny."

"I wish he would come," said Mary. "He was such a sweet little boy—golden curls, blue eyes, white white skin. Looked like he was dipped in milk."

"His hair is brown now. His eyes are still blue, however."

"I will send him one card, also," said Mary. "Just now, I am running and getting it."

She disappeared and came back with a postcard showing the Central Bazaar, the Jolly Grant House plainly sticking up in view. The laboriously written message was "Jack sahib, come to see your mother and myself in Hamara Nagar. Best regards, your faithful ayah, Mary Thomas."

"Very nice, Mary. I'll take that to the PTT later today."

Jana turned back to her own letter: "Jack, dear, I'm settling in and you're *not* to worry about my being alone or not being accepted by the community. I've made friends with a lovely woman across the street, and I'm giving weekly harmonium lessons to the *sweetest* little boy."

She did not say, "His dreadful father is the police commissioner, and he had better not find out about these lessons or there will be all hell to pay." No need to cause Jack anxiety. She resumed writing: "Young Moustapha, whom I told you about, comes almost daily to chat. He's good fun and has decided opinions."

She searched for a while for something Jack would like to hear about. She wrote, "I'm making good progress on old Ian's tune transcriptions. So original and yet so delightfully within our Scottish tradition."

She had not yet used up every bit of the aerogramme, which seemed like a waste. She sucked on the end of the fountain pen, wondering how to break the news of the fortune-telling project in a way that wouldn't make Jack think she had lost her mind.

"The local merchants are trying to make the town more attractive to the outside world," she wrote. "I'm helping out a bit. I'll be allowing people into the tower."

Well, that's what they did in the stately homes in England, didn't they? Nothing too outlandish about that.

"And I'll be running a sort of advice service. Mostly to make people feel optimistic. Do visit in October. After the rains—say, around the 15th. That would be lovely. Mary wants to see her *chota* sahib."

Hurriedly, she finished, signing herself "Your loving mother," and sealed up the aerogramme before she could make any changes.

In Business

❦ Mrs. Paniwalla

On the opening day of her salon, Jana stood in front of the mirror in the fortune-telling dress Feroze had made. He's really outdone himself, she thought. The skirt fell gracefully over the perfectly fitting pantaloons, and the bodice was beautifully cut, with gussets and darts that one didn't often find in clothes made by a small-town tailor. Zohra's exquisite embroidery set off the neckline and the sleeves.

"Well, Mary, what do you think?"

Mary never dispensed approval until all the details were in place, and now she pursed her lips. "Jana mem needs help with hairdressing." As she used to do with Caroline and Fiona in the mission days, she took the comb and made a perfect part. Then she made some feeder braids on each side and worked them into the main braids, which she gathered in an intricate arrangement at the back of Jana's head.

"Almost perfect," said Mary, "except where is . . . ?"

"Oh, the jewelry!" Jana exclaimed, remembering. She got the box of costume jewelry Ramachandran had given her and laid a string of paste pearls and glass rubies on the part of her hair, with a pendant resting in the middle of her forehead. The necklace with the emerald-green stones went on next, and then several rings and bracelets.

"Jana mem is the queen of the fortune-tellers!" said Mary.

"Why, thank you," said Jana.

Jana Bibi's first customer was a lady in a shot-gold Benares silk sari, way too formal for a day in the bazaar. The gold bangles on her arms tinkled an expensive little song, and her earlobes sagged with the weight of ruby earrings in the shape of peacocks. From the doorway, Jana saw her progressing up the street, making stops at the Kashmiri Palace, Nanda Lal Goldsmith, and Janki Dass Silversmith. After each stop, the three little boys in her wake were carrying yet more brown paper parcels. Jana went back inside to find Mary placing the last of several vases of flowers around the salon.

"I think we are ready for business, Jana mem."

"Good work, Mary."

Suddenly, Mr. Ganguly went into raptures. "Beautiful, marvelous! Come in! Sit down!" He fluffed himself up, flapped his wings, and repeated, "Come in! Sit down!" And there was the expensive-looking lady with the peacock earrings, glancing around with a benign and wondering expression on her plump face.

"Hello, hello. You are Mrs. Jana Bibi, are you not? Oh, I do love birds," she said. "You've got a lovely one, haven't you?"

She peered at Mr. Ganguly, then at the artwork on the walls, the textiles, and Mary's flower arrangements.

"What a simply beautiful salon!"

"You're kind to say so," said Jana.

"I am Mrs. J. K. Paniwalla, president of the International Futurology Alliance—science and intuition united for a more idyllic world. I'm in town to check on the preparations for our annual conference. And, of course, I'm tucking in a little shopping as well."

"Welcome, welcome, Mrs. Paniwalla. Please, have a seat, make yourself comfortable. May we get you some tea?"

"Oh, no," said the lady. "I've just had some."

"But please," said Jana. "A little tea will be refreshing." With her eyebrows, she telegraphed a signal to Mary, who disappeared into the cookhouse.

Mrs. Paniwalla settled at the table, adjusted her sari, and beamed magnanimously. "I do love this little town. And I've always told my husband, if only it had a high-class fortune-teller catering to really—well, *tony* people, if you know what I mean. . . . If only it had such a salon, it would be practically perfect."

"And your husband?" Jana asked.

"Oh, he's in Delhi. Can't get him out of that ministry office! He's *wedded* to his work. He's the minister of irrigation. You've heard of him, I'm sure. J. K. Paniwalla. And there's so much going on these days, with hydroelectric dams and whatnot. Pandit Nehru is charging ahead with development."

On hearing the word "dam," Jana instantly went on the alert. Was this lady friend or foe? Was her being here simply a coincidence? She listened carefully as the woman went on.

"I too, of course, am all for development. But sometimes it clashes with historic preservation. This town, for example. What could be more perfect, with the historic buildings and the Municipal Garden and the paths and the views?"

"I *quite* agree with you," Jana said.

"Hubby and I argue about this all the time. I'm for views; he's for progress. Actually, he and I argue about everything—in a friendly way, of course. I love birds; he hates birds. I love cinema; he hates cinema. However, I always win him over to my point of view. Right now, all he cares about are dams. Dam nonsense, I call it! And the worst thing is that he wants to put one right here. Practically where we're sitting!"

"I know that," Jana started to say, but checked herself.

Mary came back with a tray fully loaded with tea and cheese straws.

"How *lovely*," Mrs. Paniwalla cooed.

Jana poured Mrs. Paniwalla a cup, added milk, and poised the tongs over the sugar bowl. "How many lumps?"

"Two . . . well, thank you, three. I shouldn't, but I'm such an addict of nice sweet tea. Life is hardly worth living without it, isn't it? Now, about the town. Couldn't someone come up with a prediction that would turn people against the dam? Such as: it will burst and flood half the state?"

My goodness, thought Jana. This is too good to be true. A made-to-order ally! And yet—could Mrs. Paniwalla be trusted? She seemed so willful.

Meanwhile, Mrs. Paniwalla had grabbed the pack of tarot cards and was riffling through them. "I'm sure we can coax a good prediction out of these," she said. She rejected several cards, then found several picturing a river. One showed a bound and blindfolded woman, another a disconsolate man with some over-turned cups. Jana felt that someone had grabbed the reins of the horse she was riding.

"So, my dear, what do you predict from these?"

Jana thought quickly. "The river—will have its revenge."

"I couldn't have put it better myself," said Mrs. Paniwalla.

Mr. Ganguly cocked his head at a sage angle.

"See, he's so intelligent," said Mrs. Paniwalla. "He knows what we're talking about. Sixteen inches of wisdom in emerald feathers. Aren't you a good bird?"

"I love you!" burst out Mr. Ganguly. "Beautiful! Marvelous!"

"How swe-e-e-t . . ."

Mrs. Paniwalla had a second cup of tea and several more cheese straws.

"Well, my dear, I must be off," she announced. "I'll see you again in October."

"Good-bye, Mrs. Paniwalla."

"Oh, you must call me Chickie. Everyone does."

After Mrs. Paniwalla had gone, Jana ran up to Ramachandran's, where she found him adding books to his Rare Book Corner. The whole story of Mrs. Paniwalla tumbled out. "I can't even believe it," said Jana. "Doesn't this seem to you like a bull's-eye on the first shot?"

"I would definitely classify it as an auspicious start," said Ramachandran.

"Do you think she really has much influence over her husband?"

"Wives *do*," said Ramachandran. "I wouldn't be surprised."

"I'd hate to think our fate hinges on the power struggle in some minister's marriage."

"Stranger things have happened," Ramachandran said. "You know, like Roman history turning on Cleopatra's nose."

"I suppose," said Jana. "But . . . when one reads cards, should one really allow the customer to seize the deck and divine whatever they want?"

"They'll hear what they want to hear, anyway," said Ramachandran. "This was just an extreme example. Just remember: the customer is always right. I think you did splendidly!"

"Beginner's luck, I'd say. But thank you, Ramachandran. We'll see what tomorrow brings."

⋅ᴄᵮ *The Japanese Couple*

The next morning, Jana hummed as she braided her hair, applied eye makeup, and put on the green necklace she'd picked out of Ramachandran's box of costume jewelry. She stood on her bedroom balcony for a moment, looking down at the tourists already going by, some on horseback, some on foot to late breakfasts at the Why Not? and the Hot Spot. The season was in full swing, with even more tourists than the day before. She went downstairs with a light step.

"We're going to have another good day," she told Mr. Ganguly. He, however, was in one of his moods.

"Get up on the wrong side of the perch, did we?"

He turned his back on her and pecked at a piece of rope.

"All right, be that way."

She took out the tarot deck, floated some rose petals in a bowl, and arranged the cushions on the window seat. Then she sat and waited.

"Walk," Mr. Ganguly said in an annoyed tone of voice.

"We'll walk later," she said. "Be patient. Here, come on out."

She had just let him step up onto her hand and put him on the standing perch by the table when she heard footsteps in the front hall. It was a Japanese couple of about fifty years of age, the man's neck strung with a camera and a pair of binoculars, the woman dressed in a tidy gray skirt and jacket and carrying a trim square pocketbook. Husband and wife each gave a polite little bow, smiled and said "Good morning," then smiled and bowed again. Jana, too, bowed, and so did Mr. Ganguly, his interest diverted from the piece of rope.

"We noticed your sign," said the husband. "So we decided to come in."

"Thank you," Jana said. "I am honored."

Mr. Ganguly piped up with a "Hello!" and the couple bowed to him, too.

"We would like our cards read," said the husband. "Together, if we may. It is our wedding anniversary. Number thirty."

"Congratulations," Jana said, "that's a wonderful thing. Please sit down here."

"Thank you," said both husband and wife. They sat, the husband placing his camera and binoculars on the table, and the wife tidily lining up her handbag. Both seemed subdued to Jana. She looked from one to the other.

"Have you a particular concern?"

The couple exchanged glances.

"We are wondering," the woman said, "if we will ever have grandchildren. Our daughter has been married for many years, but nothing has happened. Perhaps . . . we wanted to know if there's still hope?"

"Aha." Jana felt that she was in over her head. This was more a question for a doctor, she thought, but she spread the cards out. Mr. Ganguly hopped from his perch onto the table and watched carefully. Jana glanced up and saw the Japanese couple looking trustingly into her face. She placed a half dozen cards facedown on the table and turned one over. The picture was of a frowning devil sitting on a block to which a young couple were chained. The Japanese couple paled.

"It's an *oni*," the wife whispered. "And it's captured a young couple. That must be our daughter and her husband. They have acquired horns." She clapped her hand over her mouth and noiselessly started to cry.

Mr. Ganguly put his head forward, listened carefully, and made no sound.

"No, please don't worry," Jana begged the couple. "I do believe they're going to be all right. The devil card is—it just means there's a bad thing in their past. I'm sure their future will have nothing to do with being chained by a devil. Let me quickly turn over another card."

This time, it was the man who gave a gasp.

"People falling out of a burning tower . . ." he said.

Again Jana searched desperately for a happy meaning. "An old order was destroyed, but a new one took its place."

"Yes," said the husband. "We know that."

There was a long silence, and the man spoke again.

"We have seen too many burning buildings in our life. You see, we lived a few miles from Nagasaki. When the bomb fell, our building fell down from the shock waves."

"Oh, I am sorry," said Jana, feeling a lump rise to her throat.

"We could have been inside, but we weren't. We survived, and our ten-year-old daughter survived. Now she is twenty-five, a good age to have babies. But will she? We don't know. Many people died or got sick from radiation. . . . These two cards taken together seem like bad omens to me."

Jana looked at the stricken couple. She thought of the day, fifteen years ago, when she'd heard about the destruction of Hiroshima and Nagasaki. It had meant that the war was over, and she'd been flooded with relief and happiness that Jack— barely eighteen, just commissioned—didn't have to go to the

Pacific. The war had ended for them. But it was not over yet for this couple.

The wife had not said a word since the picture of the *oni*. The husband put his arm around her shoulders.

"Come, we must go."

Jana rose to follow them, to apologize, to take everything back, but they were already in the hallway. She heard the door close. Drained and shaken, she put the cards back in the sideboard.

At the Why Not? Tea Shop again, Jana looked despairingly at Ramachandran.

"Yesterday this project seemed so easy, but today was terrible. What if I do more harm than good? Those people were so trusting, so hurt . . . they needed hope so much. And what did I do? Revived old nightmares. I made them feel worse. A *lot* worse."

Mr. Joshi, seeing her distress, hurried over with tea and samosas.

Ramachandran heaved a sigh.

"We must live and learn. You had the good kind of beginner's luck on the first day and the bad kind on the second day."

"The problem is," said Jana, "you just don't know what experiences in the person's past are going to be called up by the images on the cards."

Ramachandran took a noisy swig of his tea, adjusted his shawl, and thought it over.

"You could use the parrot more," he said. "Let *him* pick a card, and then always have something good to say, no matter what. Use a pack of Hindu gods. I'm sure you can get a brand-new one at Muktinanda's. And stick to the happier gods. Could you not have several of Ganesh? Remover of obstacles? God of opportunity? Your bird picks up Ganesh, you tell the customer he will succeed at his new venture! Or Lakshmi, goddess of wealth. Who doesn't love Lakshmi? The bird chooses Lakshmi, you predict that riches are on the way!"

"In other words, you're saying I should stack the deck."

"Why not?"

"All right," said Jana. "I'll leave out demons and devils. Who needs to be reminded of destruction?"

"That's the ticket!"

"There would still be room for individual variation," said Jana thoughtfully. "Say Saraswati comes up. To a student, I'd say, 'Study hard and you will pass your exams.' To a musician, 'Practice hard and you will be chosen at the audition.' To a writer, 'Never go a day without turning out a line.'"

"All very good advice," said Ramachandran. "Now you just go home and play your fiddle and have a nice rest. And tomorrow start in with a bright new attitude. Accentuate the positive!"

Jana smiled. Ramachandran's optimism, though couched in different vocabulary, reminded her of Mary's. She asked herself if it was a typically South Indian trait, then thought of Lal Bahadur Pun's habitual cheery confidence. *He* came from the other end of the subcontinent. I'll keep my chin up, she resolved.

The Schoolgirls

Girls, girls, girls. One group went by and then another, like little subflocks of birds in a major seasonal migration. Jana watched the parade from her gate. She smiled at half a dozen Indian schoolgirls in the St. Margaret's College uniform, navy pinafore dresses over white blouses, and they smiled back, Ramachandran's daughters Asha and Bimla among them. Then came some European and American girls from the Far Oaks School, each dressed in a different color, with the wind catching their dirndl skirts to reveal touches of ruffled crinoline. Frilly carnations came to Jana's mind, and perhaps to Mr. Ganguly's, too; perched on Jana's shoulder, he called, "Beautiful! Marvelous!" like a Kashmiri flower vendor touting his wares.

One pair coming out of Keram Chand's Fabulous Fabrics caught Jana's eye and her ear with their American accents: a tiny girl with short black curls and a tall blond one with a new leather pocketbook slung over her shoulder. They carried brown paper packages. She watched them approach Royal Tailors, then saw Moustapha welcome them in with a salaam.

Jana had gone back into the salon and was changing Mr. Ganguly's water when she heard voices at her door.

"Roo, this is so stupid."

"Sandra, it's just for *fun*. Come on, it won't take long."

And there they were. The curly-haired sprite bounced over the sill, shot Jana a sparkling smile, and said, "Hi!" She examined the carved elephant table, the Rajasthani peacocks, the view out the window, and Mr. Ganguly, then executed a pirouette. "I *love love love* this place!"

The blond one stood and watched, oozing superiority or something else. Boredom? Loneliness? Where had Jana seen this girl? All of a sudden, she remembered the picture in Kenneth Stuart-Smith's wallet. His daughter, who had crashed the party at the Belgian embassy in Paris.

"*I'm* going to have my fortune told," curly-haired Roo said to Jana. "And Sandra might, too."

"Maybe," said Sandra flatly.

"Very well, girls," Jana said. "Let's sit down at the table. My bird will chose a card for you."

"What kind of bird is it?" Sandra asked.

"He's an Indian ring-necked parakeet."

"That's interesting." Sandra's expression became less haughty. "He doesn't *look* like a parakeet. We had a parakeet once. A little bitty yellow thing. Your bird's a lot bigger."

"There are lots of kinds of parakeets," said Jana. "They're true parrots, however. The Latin name for this one is *Psittacula krameri manillensis*."

"Will he ride on my finger?" asked Roo.

"Offer him your hand," said Jana.

Roo held out her hand, and Mr. Ganguly stepped up onto it and made kissing sounds.

"He loves me!"

"Do you want him to tell your fortune?"

"Sure. You'll tell me a good fortune, won't you?" Roo made kissing noises back at the bird. Then she sat as quietly as she seemed able to, and Jana dealt the cards slowly.

"Choose me a good one!" said Roo.

Mr. Ganguly picked up a card with his beak and handed it to Roo: a picture of a handsome blue-skinned Rama and a fair, wide-eyed Sita.

"Romance is in the offing," said Jana.

"Really?" Roo's face lit up.

"Roo, you're so gullible." Sandra turned to Jana. "If Roo gets a boyfriend, this means he'll have blue skin, right?"

"Come on, Sandra, don't be a wet blanket!" Roo said. "If I get a boyfriend, he's not going to have blue skin! But he's going to be tall, dark, and handsome. With curly hair."

"You've done some thinking about this," Jana said.

"Yes, I have," said Roo.

Roo didn't appear to be the kind of customer who needed a lot of bucking up. Maybe telling her to put on the brakes was more to the point. Still, Jana went on, saying, "Someone will soon catch your fancy," and Roo held up crossed fingers.

"Stay calm and cool, and you may catch *his*."

"Calm and cool," Roo groaned. "Okay. I'll *try*."

Working hard not to laugh, Jana turned to Sandra.

"And you, my dear? Would you like Mr. Ganguly to pick you a card?"

"Oh, all right."

Mr. Ganguly picked up a card picturing the elephant-headed Ganesh.

"Well, gee. A fat guy with an elephant's head. What's *he* going to do for me?"

"Oh, plenty," said Jana. "Ganesh . . . a favorite all over India.

Remover of obstacles, god of opportunity. He's also the god of writers, by the way. Do you write?"

"Not really. I do crossword puzzles. Does that count?"

"I suppose. Mr. Ganguly likes them. He ate a couple of them just the other day."

That drew an unexpected laugh, transforming Sandra's face.

"So, you girls are students at Far Oaks?"

"Yup," said Roo.

"How did you know that?" said Sandra. "Oh well, I guess it's obvious."

Jana smiled. "How is school?"

"It's great!" said Roo. "We have class parties and slumber parties and hikes and all sorts of stuff. I'm going out for cheerleading. It's just like being in the States, sort of."

"It is *not* like being in the States," said Sandra. "The food stinks, there are a million rules, there's never enough hot water in the showers, there are rats in the dorm. The toilet paper is so stiff that a guy typed his Scripture homework on it! And there are all these corny traditions that you have to follow, whether you like them or not. Like the school song and the school pledge and, oh, I don't know. *Marching* competitions! Marching! Around the sports field! Spare me!"

"Sandra, you're just a spoilsport."

"But, Roo, really, all that stuff is so *juvenile*."

"It's *fun*!" Roo turned to Jana and grinned. "We just got material to have roommate dresses made!"

"Ah yes, roommate dresses." Jana remembered that craze from her own boarding school days. "And what do your parents do in India?"

"My dad's in the embassy," said Sandra. "He goes to a lot of receptions and cocktail parties and stuff. Something to do with fighting communism. How do *I* know what he does? All I know is that I'm supposed to be a little ambassador."

"Oh yeah, mine says that, too," said Roo.

"And what are the duties of a little ambassador?" Jana asked.

"Oh, be prim and proper. Don't start World War III by chewing gum in public. Smile and shake hands. Don't be loud. Stuff like that," said Sandra.

"And what do your parents do, Roo?"

"My dad goes out into the countryside and tries to get farmers to use new seeds."

"Aha. And your mothers?"

"My mom's the president of the American Women's Club in Delhi. They put on luncheons and hear lectures and soak up culture." Roo rolled her eyes. "Sometimes they go visit leper colonies."

"That's gross," said Sandra.

"My mom says it's uplifting."

"And *your* mother?" Jana asked Sandra.

Sandra shook her head and looked out the window. "She's in the States." Jana remembered too late Kenneth Stuart-Smith's mention of his divorce.

Roo suddenly looked at her watch. "Yikes! Sandra, we have to get back or we'll be late!"

Sandra shrugged, but Roo insisted. "We'll get demerits. You don't want to be gated, do you?"

Sandra rolled her eyes. "Okay, I guess you're right."

Sandra and Roo each put a rupee in the bowl, and Jana said, "Thank you, girls. Come again and chat and have tea."

"All right. See you later!" Roo pointed one toe out and bowed deeply from the waist.

"Au revoir!" squawked Mr. Ganguly.

"Au revoir," said Sandra.

By Saturday, word about the salon had traveled along the Far Oaks School grapevine. Roo and Sandra came in again, Roo to report that her fortune had come true, and that Douglas Benedict had walked her home and taken her to the Friday night movie in the auditorium.

"And they held hands," said Sandra.

"Oh, shut up, Sandra," said Roo.

"Shut up!" squawked Mr. Ganguly.

"Please be careful," said Jana. "He repeats things if he hears them said with a lot of energy."

"Oh, sorry," said Roo. She mouthed, "Sandra, shut up!"

"So what's new in the dorm?"

"Oh, nothing. The Dragon's on the prowl. Maggie O'Reilly told us she had this foolproof method of telling when she was coming around after lights-out. You put sugar from the dining room down on the hall floor, and then it goes *crunch crunch crunch* under your shoes. But the problem was that she and her roommate were laughing so hard that the Dragon caught them anyway and gave them two demerits—one for talking and one for the sugar."

Sandra said, "Another thing: the Dragon set her watch five minutes ahead so that she can give you a demerit for signing in late even when you aren't late!"

"Sounds like you should set your own watches to hers. What's her real name?"

"Miss Durgin," said Roo. "Her hair looks like she's always wearing rollers!"

Jana smiled. So they had an evil queen, too. Every boarding school had to have one, she supposed.

Later in the day there was a stream of other Far Oaks students: the much-demerited Maggie O'Reilly, buxom and cheerful; her roommate, Laurel, cool and amused-looking; Qudsia, from an aristocratic Muslim family; Winifred, whose clothes screamed "mission box"; and Beryl, who looked like the track star she was. After a while, Jana lost track of the names. She kept hearing a lot, too, about the boys of the school: Koko Irani, whose father owned a good chunk of Bombay; Douglas Benedict, Roo's true love for this week; Jerry Miller, the one who had turned in his Bible homework on school toilet paper. The only boy who came in to consult Jana was Tenzin, a Tibetan who wore brand-new American clothes. Both his English and his Hindi were poor, and he was afraid he would fail his exams and lose his scholarship to Far Oaks. Could she give him any European magic? "All I can tell you," Jana said, "is to study twice as hard. That's about the only magic that works in school."

ᴄᵇ Bandhu Says Jana Needs a Permit

Bandhu Sharma was in the salon, shadowed by an anxious *chaprassi* carrying a sheaf of documents.

"Madam," Bandhu said smugly, "I'm afraid you are in violation of another local regulation." He turned to the *chaprassi*. "Form one!"

Jana looked at the thick, oversized document. "Permit to own a performing animal," it said. There were numerous copies to fill out, the top one buff-colored, the others blue, pink, white, and gray.

"Performing animal?" said Jana. "This bird is my pet. He's a member of the family."

Bandhu gave a knowing sneer. "That's what the circus families say about their children who are in violation of the child labor laws."

Mr. Ganguly raised his wings in a threat position.

"See," said Bandhu Sharma, "he is performing. Doing a dance, to all appearances. And we have been led to understand that he tells fortunes."

He turned to the *chaprassi*. "Form two!" With obvious relish, Bandhu handed Jana a second thick sheaf of paper.

"Here is a form for medical examination of a performing animal. To be administered at the veterinary clinic of your choice, madam."

"But he's a very healthy bird," said Jana.

Bandhu took a long look at Mr. Ganguly, whose pupils were now dilating and contracting.

"Rules are rules," said Bandhu. "Mind you, have these filled out within forty-eight hours and delivered to the police station, with the license fees. In cash."

He turned to the *chaprassi*. "Onward!"

Jana watched Bandhu's broad, muscular form and the *chaprassi*'s slight one go out the door.

"*Badmash!*" shrieked Mr. Ganguly.

"Mind your language," murmured Jana, not knowing whether Bandhu had heard.

❦ *The Dragon Comes In*

The woman matched Roo's description so perfectly that there was no doubt who she was. The black hair was streaked with gray, with one tight sausage curl on either side, as if she'd forgotten to take out her rollers. The dark, dense eyebrows almost met, and the woman had a penetrating X-ray gaze that of course would be able to see if you had been breaking the rules, even if you'd broken them the day before. She wore a heavy brown cable-knit sweater, a pleated olive-green skirt, brown wool socks, and saddle shoes.

"So you're the fortune-teller. My name is Geraldine Durgin."

"Do sit down, Miss Durgin." Jana gestured to the bay window.

Miss Durgin shook her head. "What I have to say won't take long. It is quite simply this: we can't have the students patronizing pagan establishments in the bazaar. So you will not be seeing students from the Far Oaks School in your shop from now on."

"But—"

"I'm sorry; we have lots of high-spirited young people who are highly suggestible. We can't afford to let them associate with just anyone. I have brought you a copy of the school rules."

She handed Jana a booklet in a buff-colored cover. "Kindly make yourself familiar with these rules and do not aid and abet students who want to break them."

With that, she turned on her heel and left the shop.

Why, how preposterous, Jana thought. She thumbed through the booklet, noting the do's and do not's. Approved chaperones . . . decorous dress . . . no dancing, card playing, gambling, smoking, drinking—well, no surprises there. Things hadn't changed very much in the boarding school world since Jana had been a student during the Great War. Then, stapled to the back of the booklet, she found an addendum, dated the previous week.

"In the bazaar," it declared, "students shall not patronize establishments injurious to their morality, mental or physical health, or contrary to the high principles of the school. These include, but are not limited to, bars, breweries, pool halls, dance halls, houses of ill repute, and fortune-telling salons."

"They've lumped me with brothels!"

Rambir and Ramachandran looked at Jana and then at each other, and burst out laughing.

"It's all very well for you to laugh! But so far, the fortune-telling salon is a matter of one step forward, two steps back. I've had a complaint from the Japanese embassy, paid two hundred rupees in Bandhu's phony license fees, and been banned by the Far Oaks School."

The Why Not? Tea Shop was more crowded than usual today; Jana and Rambir and Ramachandran had been pushed over to a table in the corner. The four government engineers who had been staying at the Victoria on Jana's arrival were sitting at the best table, with maps and graph paper stacked up on a chair beside them.

Jana motioned with her head toward them.

"Look. They're back. And this time they were measuring my back wall! They came down the alley without so much as a by-your-leave! They scared Mary half out of her wits. She was having her breakfast in the sun and suddenly here were all these men talking about sluice gates and tunnels. And they were making jokes about how in the future you'd need masks and snorkels to see this building."

"The enemy is among us." Ramachandran popped a whole *laddu* into his mouth and was temporarily unable to speak.

"And pretty soon the monsoon will start and we'll have no tourists," Rambir said gloomily.

"We've still got the fall tourist season," said Ramachandran, when he had finished the *laddu*.

"The Futurology Convention has just *got* to make a splash," said Rambir.

"Don't use expressions having to do with water," said Ramachandran. "They dampen my spirits."

"It's not a laughing matter!" said Rambir.

"I know, I know," said Ramachandran. "All right, we'll keep up the effort even during the monsoon. Rambir, you will write your editorial pieces, with passion! Mrs. Laird, you will practice your soothsaying skills on townspeople while the tourists are gone. Don't worry. We *will* prevail."

Roo and Moustapha

✐ Roo Crashes into Moustapha's Life

Feroze was irritated. Why was life sending him such irritating things? Maybe to test him and make him develop patience, as fasting on Ramadan was supposed to do. Maybe to make him stop asking the very question of why! Why was why, that was all. Because was because.

Here was this girl, all topsy-turvy. The little curly-haired one who had ordered the cheerleading uniform. One minute he was quietly running the sewing machine; the next moment there were shrieks and yells and the sound of rickshaw wheels rolling by on the pavement, and the curly-haired girl sprawled on the floor of the shop, the contents of her handbag spilled beside her. Lipstick, hairbrush, photographs, wallet, this, that, and the other thing.

Now she was going into waves of apologies and thank-yous to Moustapha, who was standing and looking like some film hero, all proud and modest at the same time.

"You saved my life!" said the curly-haired girl. "I didn't hear it coming until it was right on me. Golly! Oh, I'm so sorry to make a mess here and bother you guys and everything."

Feroze got up from his sewing machine and went over. "Not to worry, missahib, no harm done. But best to keep an eye out for rickshaws in the bazaar."

"They go so fast downhill!"

"Yes, they do. That is why you must keep your eyes open."

"I will, I will."

Again, the girl was paying all sorts of attention to Moustapha, and telling him he was so fast and strong to grab her out of the way.

"Enough, enough," muttered Feroze under his breath.

"It's not a problem," Moustapha said. "I am happy to help."

Yes, please run in front of a rickshaw anytime, Feroze filled in silently. My nephew will be all too happy to be a hero. Just like in a film.

Feroze and Moustapha Do a Fitting at the Girls' Dormitory

The noise of record players issued from the rooms of the girls' dormitory. Feroze undid the bundle of finished clothes and handed the little dress with the short skirt to Roo Wiley.

"Yay! You finished it!" She ran to her room and was back in the front hall in a minute. She twirled, and the skirt stuck straight out around her waist, showing the matching bloomers beneath.

Moustapha's eyes traveled to the muscled little legs. Feroze had to decide whether to box Moustapha's ears or pretend he didn't notice.

"Mind your own business," he muttered to Moustapha.

"Uncle, helping you *is* my business."

"Act correctly, then."

"*Hi*, Moustapha!" Miss Roo Wiley was not making it easy for Moustapha to act correctly. She looked him straight in the eye and gave a huge smile. "How do you like my cheerleading uniform?"

"Very nice." Feroze noticed that one of Moustapha's eyebrows was twitching.

"Want to see a cheer?"

"Of course, Miss Wiley."

"Okay, clear some space." She waved them back, then took a few steps forward and leaped into the air, arms thrust backward. "Fight, team, fight!"

"This is a fighting uniform, Miss Wiley?" said Moustapha.

"No, it's for *cheerleading*. It's to make the team play harder. The basketball team. Or the baseball team."

"I see," Moustapha said.

Feroze wasn't sure that Moustapha had seen anything other than Roo's legs.

"Come to a basketball game and you'll see," said Roo. "I'm actually not a *real* cheerleader, I'm a substitute cheerleader. But next year I really want to make the squad."

Moustapha turned inquiringly to Feroze for translation.

Feroze wasn't quite sure what Roo's ambition was. But he did know that cheerleading involved an amalgamation of acrobatics, dancing, and drilling the troops of an army with the loudest voice possible.

"Missahib will be jumping as high as the roof in this dress," Feroze said.

Roo went into squeals of laughter.

"I'll try! Thank you so much! I love the uniform! I wish I could wear it to school."

Moustapha was in equal parts mystified and enchanted, his eyes wide.

When Feroze sat with his notebook that night, he was at a loss for what to write. Finally he made a stab at it: "Young American women. Good at heart—they mean no harm. But my goodness. What *do* they mean?"

❦ Roo's Hindi Class Goes to the Movies at the Bharat Mata

Zohra came across the street to get Jana, and they both walked down to the Bharat Mata, bearing their free tickets from Moustapha in their hands. The film was *Mother India*. Zohra had seen it twice already, Jana, never, but she'd heard some details about it from Mary.

"And the husband loses his—" Mary had started.

"Don't! Don't tell me." Jana had stopped her. "I'll see it for myself."

Zohra now said, "I wouldn't want to be like that village woman in the film. That is a very hard life. I think it's much better to live in a town, as we do. With electricity. And tap water!"

The crowd outside the Bharat Mata was studying the posters. Jana saw groups of young men, some well dressed, others in such rags that she wondered how they could possibly afford a movie ticket. There were Indian schoolgirls in tight clusters and a couple of families. Jana was thinking that hers was the only white face in the crowd when she saw Roo and a dozen other Far Oaks students, accompanied by a young Indian woman in a sari.

Roo's field trip! She had mentioned earlier that she was trying to get their Hindi teacher to take them to the movies.

"Hi, Jana Bibi! Hi!" Roo waved wildly.

The doors to the cinema finally opened, and they all filed in, Zohra and Jana going ahead with their free passes.

"Your seats are in the balcony," said Moustapha. "Not near the ruffians downstairs. Uncle would never allow his wife to sit near those hooligans."

A few minutes after Jana and Zohra had settled in, Roo's Hindi class filed into the seats just in front of them. Roo was systematically flirting with first one boy and then another in the class. But when she saw Moustapha she gave a little cry.

"Moustapha! Do *you* work here? I thought you were a tailor."

Moustapha looked both uncomfortable—as if he wished she would hush—and proud.

"I do this work, too," he said.

"Wow, that's so neat. So you get to see all the movies you want."

"Yes," said Moustapha. "Well, Miss Wiley, I hope you and your friends like the film." He moved off to seat other customers.

"I don't see the yellow-haired girl," Zohra said to Jana.

Jana leaned forward and lightly tapped Roo's shoulder. "Where's Sandra?"

Roo said, "Oh, she doesn't take Hindi. She doesn't think it's worth the effort. She doesn't like anything Indian. She went somewhere with her dad. He came up from Delhi to see her and give her a pep talk."

The lights went down. There was a newsreel, and a cartoon, and then they were immersed in the story of a humble woman who struggled and worked and was on the verge of losing everything.

◦𝒸ℱ A Different Kind of Spy

"He's a CIA spy, I tell you," said Moustapha. He had tried out the harmonium, pronounced it "very harmonious," and was proceeding to give Jana his opinions on the flow of traffic through the bazaar.

"Who do you think is a spy?"

"Princess Grace's father."

"Princess Grace?"

"Sandra Stuart-Smith's. Zohra thinks she looks like Princess Grace of Monaco. And my uncle, too, thinks she is some sort of aristocrat. Of course, that suits him. Royal Tailors and all that, you know."

"She—Sandra—has a certain air to her," Jana said. "But I don't know about her dad being a spy. If you really were a spy, would you go around ostentatiously looking as if you were collecting information?"

"Double bluff," said Moustapha. "Americans are everywhere you look. Some of them have to be spies."

"I think he's just one of those conscientious travelers who keep a travel diary. Who knows, maybe he's a poet or something. Jotting down verses."

Moustapha obviously thought that was a far-fetched hypothesis. He got up off the floor and went over to the telescope. "May I look through?"

"Of course."

"*Wah!*" He stepped back in amazement. "You can see everything from here."

"Yes," said Jana. "You can see a lot, can't you." She suddenly remembered Kenneth Stuart-Smith talking about using the tower for intelligence gathering during the war. Yet she decided not to fuel Moustapha's suspicions with this piece of information. In any case, he was turning to leave.

"I have to go and stitch," said Moustapha. "Big order of marching uniforms."

"Well, do come again. That instrument needs playing."

"Thank you, Jana Auntie. I can call you Jana Auntie?" he asked anxiously.

"Of course. I would be honored. Zohra calls me *didi*, after all."

"Okay. Salaam, Jana Auntie."

"Salaam to you too, Moustapha."

Late that afternoon, Jana went to answer the front door. There was a runner from the Victoria Hotel, holding a tallish box wrapped in brown paper. "From Stuart-Smith sahib," he said.

Jana peeled a bit of the paper off. Johnnie Walker Black Label. Good heavens! Even bought duty-free, how much must it have cost? She unfolded the little note tucked into the box: "With many thanks for your kindness to Sandra. She says you're the only one she can talk to. Very truly yours, Kenneth Stuart-Smith."

If the man was a spy, Jana decided, he was a very generous one. And one with good taste in whisky.

⌘ Feroze Makes Arrangements

Jana was now finding Feroze distinctly less standoffish than he had been at the beginning. In fact, he could even turn chatty, as on this morning, when he brought over the bedroom curtains he had made for her.

"How is your health, Feroze Ali Khan sahib?" Jana said.

"By the grace of God, I am well. And yourself?"

"I, too, am well, God be thanked," said Jana. "And your good wife?"

"She, too, is well, all thanks to God."

She paid for the curtains, but Feroze showed no signs of leaving; rather, he hesitated, as if considering whether to bring up a difficult subject.

"Laird memsahib, you have a son in U.K., correct?" he said.

"Yes, that's right, Feroze sahib."

"Your son is married, right?"

"No, he isn't, Feroze sahib."

"But how old is he?"

"Let me see—Jack is thirty-four."

"So old! Why so old and not married?"

"That's something you'd have to ask him," said Jana. "I think the girls of Glasgow are trying to put that right."

"He needs a wife," Feroze said firmly. "But I suppose it is hard for you to arrange such a thing, alone, here, at a distance. And no man in the family. No uncles? No brothers?"

"Afraid not," said Jana. "Yes, Jack is going to have to fend for himself. But I don't think he'd take much direction from me, anyway."

Feroze shook his head. "I know, this is the way of Europeans. It is curious. Parents know best, isn't it? How can someone with no experience of life make an important decision like choosing a spouse?"

As the conversation turned into a more personal one than they usually had, Jana was puzzled and intrigued. Then Feroze said, "Moustapha, too, is old to be unmarried."

"Is that so? How old is he?" Jana said.

"Twenty last month."

"I see."

"But luckily, I have just now arranged his marriage."

Jana had heard nothing of this from Moustapha, who had been there the day before, playing the harmonium and giving Jana an earful of opinions on films, singers, politicians, the superiority of electric over manual sewing machines, and the like. She said cautiously, "Congratulations are in order, Feroze Ali Khan sahib. Where have you found a girl?"

"Dehra Dun," said Feroze. "Actually, Yusuf Baig found her. She comes from a reliable, God-fearing family. There aren't many such families left; so many went to Pakistan in 1947."

"And when will this happen?" asked Jana.

"Soon, soon!" Feroze said happily.

"And Moustapha? He likes your choice?"

"He doesn't know yet!"

"He doesn't know?"

"No, I wanted to make sure everything was in order so I wouldn't be telling him one thing one day and another the next. As you English say, I wanted to be sure that the cat was in the bag. And—I must request one thing."

"Yes?"

"Please don't tell this to Moustapha just yet. I will tell him when the time comes. You know, with Moustapha, he's touchy. He gets a lot of ideas from cinema. About falling in love, that kind of thing. Left to his own devices, he'd marry a foreigner! Or a Hindu! Or he'd want to go to Bombay and try to find a film star. Films have put impossible ideas in his head. So this is a risky situation."

"But wait—how about you, Feroze Ali Khan sahib? Didn't you yourself choose Zohra?"

She thought she saw a flush spread across his face.

"That was different," he said hurriedly. "Completely different. My first wife was dead; Zohra was the wife of a friend who was dying. I saw how attentive she was to him in his last days. That is the mark of a good woman, I thought. My friend had so much money and no other heirs, so she stood to inherit a lot. Another woman might have given him a tiny push over the edge, you know? Maybe forget the medicine, something like that. But oh, no. Zohra gave him every minute of her time, every breath of her life until his dying day. He said to me, When I am gone, will you marry my wife? I said, Of course. So I did that. Not just to fulfill the wish of a dying friend—also because I saw what a good wife she would be."

"So," said Jana mischievously, "you might call this a love match." (With a bit of money thrown in, she thought.)

Feroze did not merely color; he blushed to his ears.

"But highly sensible," Jana hurried to add. "Who could criticize? She has brought you happiness."

"That is true," said Feroze with an expression of wonder. "That is true."

"Might Moustapha do well if he went looking for a woman as fine as Zohra?"

"There is none," Feroze said quickly. "Besides, all of Moustapha's friends are in good health, so nobody's wife is about to come loose. Anyway, we have found him an excellent bride!"

·✑ *Zohra Doesn't Like the Arrangements*

Zohra came up to the tower room, shed her burqa, and dropped into a chair with a sigh.

"It won't work," said Zohra. "I know that young woman. She's pretty, all right. But she's not very bright. She will irritate Moustapha. He'll yell at her. Or hit her. What's the good of that? Also, her family is very . . . old-fashioned. Just the kind of family Yusuf Baig would come up with."

"Well, are there any other choices?"

Zohra thought it over. "Not so many. My husband thinks he's done well to come up with a girl, any girl. But sometimes just because you are relieved that a problem is solved, that doesn't mean that it is really solved." She laughed. "I have an idea. You should tell Moustapha his fortune and say to avoid a short girl from Dehra Dun."

"I think that would be meddling, don't you?"

"Meddling can be very good," said Zohra. "Meddling is acceptable if it's for a good cause."

Zohra dipped one of Mary's sugar cookies into her tea. Her mind had turned to another problem.

"My husband . . ." she said, and then looked embarrassed.

Jana said sympathetically, "He's just trying to do his duty with Moustapha."

"Not that thing, something else. I'm starting to wonder whether *I* will ever have . . . a child to carry on his name."

"How long have you and Feroze been married?" Jana asked cautiously.

"Two years, *didi*. I am beginning to worry. They always say it is the woman's fault. My first husband's family said it was my fault even though that man was too old to do *anything*! And now all my new relatives are gossiping and saying it is my fault and that my husband should not have married me. *Didi*, do you have some medicine to give me babies? I've been to Abinath's and consulted him in strictest privacy and taken half a dozen of his medicines."

"And?"

"And they're nice medicines and they taste good, but still nothing!"

"You could go to the mission hospital and have a doctor check and make sure all is well."

Zohra looked horrified. "A doctor sahib?"

"There's a lady doctor, I think."

Zohra thought it over.

"But expensive, isn't it?"

"I doubt it," said Jana. "In any case, you are not a poor woman. What else is more important to spend your money on? Go find out; then if you are okay, we'll know it's your husband who needs the medicine."

Zohra looked uncomfortable. "Then I would have to tell him that I went to the mission hospital. And that something is wrong with him."

"Let's cross that bridge when we come to it," Jana said.

"In the meantime," said Zohra, "can you read my cards? Or can the bird read my cards?"

Mr. Ganguly perked up and did a twirl on his perch.

"He says yes, he'd be delighted to read," said Jana. She took out her deck of Hindu gods.

"Don't tell my husband you used those Hindu cards on me," said Zohra.

"Don't worry," said Jana. "Nothing leaves this room. It's my hard-and-fast rule."

She spread the cards, and Mr. Ganguly picked Nandi, the bull.

"Aha, a symbol of fertility," said Jana. "He guards the palace of Lord Shiva."

"Fertility for Hindu women, maybe," said Zohra. "We have to keep this quiet."

"Not to worry," said Jana. "But why not go to the community hospital and talk to the lady doctor anyway?"

"All right," said Zohra.

❧ *Jana Tells Moustapha's Cards*

Late the next afternoon, on his way to his ushering job, Moustapha dropped in and said, with barely a word of greeting, "Please
do my cards."

"Certainly. What would you like to know?"

"I want to know when I will become a playback singer. For
films."

"You wish to become—a playback singer?"

"I will become nothing else," said Moustapha.

"Sing me something."

Moustapha sang a few scraps of "My Shoes Are Japanese." He
could certainly sing *that,* but so could half the bazaar. Hardly a
day passed when she didn't hear someone singing it.

"Something a little more soulful?" she suggested.

He thought for a moment, then sang the beginning to "Oh
Guardian of the World." Not bad, Jana thought; there's something there, a self-assurance and mellowness beyond the young
man's age. With a lesson or two, he might really develop his talent. But to sing for the films, to be the voice behind the handsome faces of the heroes?

Jana spread the Hindu gods and goddesses faceup on the
table before Mr. Ganguly.

"Name?" Mr. Ganguly said to Moustapha.

"Moustapha Ahmed Khan."

"Name?" the parrot squawked again.

"I *told* you."

"Maybe he's asking you for a stage name," said Jana. "You
know what I'm talking about. Dilip Kumar was born Yusuf Khan;
Johnny Walker was Badruddin Jamaluddin Kazi."

"They changed their names," said Moustapha. "I don't like
that. If you are not trying to hide something, why would you
change your name? I refuse to take a Hindu name or an English
name. I will keep my own, just as Mohammed Rafi did. Muslims
don't have to change their names to succeed in film. Or come

from a big film family, either. Mohammed Rafi used to have to work in his brother's *barbershop.* His father didn't want him to be a singer."

"Very well." Jana turned to the parrot. "This is Moustapha Ahmed Khan and he is asking your opinion on when he will be a playback singer."

Mr. Ganguly flapped his wings. "Moustapha zindabad!"

"Yes, I agree, long live Moustapha. But pick his card, please."

Mr. Ganguly craned his neck. After making a show of walking back and forth around the cards, he finally picked up the goddess Saraswati and presented it to Moustapha with a bow. On the card, the goddess of music, learning, and the arts plucked serenely on her *veena,* with her peacock in the background.

"Bravo," said Jana. "He's chosen success in the arts as your fortune."

Moustapha leaned toward Jana with an urgent look on his face. "But I want to know when. *When,* Mr. Ganguly?"

"Now!" shrieked the parrot. "Now, now, now!"

"Good bird," said Moustapha. "Give me a kiss." He let the bird onto his hand, then touched its beak with his mouth. "My future . . . begins with this very moment."

"How about the rest of your life. Marriage and so forth— don't you want to ask about that?"

"No, no," said Moustapha. "I don't have time right now for marriage."

"But . . . your family would want . . . ?"

"Certainly," said Moustapha. "They've got this ignorant little girl from Dehra Dun picked out for me."

"How did you know that?" said Jana.

"Easy—Yusuf Baig's daughter's husband's brother told me. Everyone in that family knows. I'm not supposed to know."

"But you do know . . . and what now?"

"I just say no," said Moustapha. "No, no, and no."

"And?"

"And then I leave."

"Won't that be a blow to your uncle?"

Moustapha shrugged, but his face twisted.

"I think Zohra might put in a word for you," said Jana, then noticed a blush spreading across Moustapha's face. Aha, she thought. Zohra is closer to Moustapha's age than to Feroze's. Yes, of course, it would be only natural for Moustapha to fall under Zohra's spell—who wouldn't? And Feroze may even see this; hence his haste to marry off Moustapha.

"Oh, all right, do some more cards," said Moustapha.

"Let's switch from the Hindu cards to plain playing cards," said Jana, and she went and got another deck from the sideboard. She shuffled and had Moustapha pull a card.

"Good! Nine of hearts—the wish card." She clapped her hands. "Your wish, no matter what, will come true."

"Thank you, Jana Auntie," said Moustapha.

A Change of Season

♪ Raju's Music Lesson

Manju brought Raju for another music lesson, and at first Jana was nervous, having visions of Bandhu bursting in on them. But, settled on the floor in front of the harmonium, with Manju watching from a chair in the corner, Jana lost all other thoughts and worries and focused on the small, elfin-looking person beside her. *Educo,* she had learned long ago in Latin class: "I teach, I educate." But it also meant "I bring out." She set herself to work, not on stuffing something into Raju's curly head but on bringing a message from his soul out of his sweet little fingers.

She played a fragment of a scale—just three notes. Raju imitated her very quickly and assuredly, then gave her an inquiring look. This time she did a run of five notes, and he played that, too. Then, without waiting for direction, he played a few notes of his own, a suggestion of a tune. The phrase sounded in the room, and they both looked up at Mr. Ganguly, who sang it yet again and announced, "Good bird."

"He could mean you," said Jana, "or he could be congratulating himself. Would you like to hold him?"

Raju said nothing but held out an arm, and Jana transferred Mr. Ganguly to it. Mr. Ganguly gently flapped his wings, making alarm flash over Raju's face.

"Don't worry, he's just getting comfortable," said Jana.

She had the strong feeling that there was something on the tip of the boy's tongue, maybe even a torrent of conversation, and that it wouldn't take much to bring it out.

"*Nam kya hai?* Name? Name?" the parrot asked the boy, but Raju was silent.

"He won't talk," said Manju. "His father gets so angry at me; he thinks it's my fault."

"His father should know better," said Jana sternly.

"No, don't say that. He's a good father—my other two children will tell you that straight off. He always helps them with their homework and goes to school functions, everything. But he can't do anything with Raju. Raju just stands and stares at him with those eyes."

"You've taken him to a doctor?"

"Oh, old Dr. Chawla just says wait and see, not to worry. My husband gets so angry when I tell him that. I don't know what to do. They say in the bazaar that you have special gifts. And the bird, too. Do you know what to do when a child doesn't talk?"

Jana looked at Raju. In her opinion, his eyes spoke more eloquently than most people did with floods of words. "I'll talk when I'm ready, and not before," they were saying.

Manju went on: "If he doesn't talk, he can't go to school. There we'll be, with this mute child. Can't you read his cards or something and tell me what to do? Or look at his palm?"

Jana took the boy's hand in hers. It was trusting and cool and relaxed, a normal child's hand.

"You know," she said to Manju, "perhaps Dr. Chawla is right. Perhaps there is nothing to do but wait."

She kissed the little hand. Mr. Ganguly made his kissing noise, too, and once again, Jana thought the words were about to burst out of Raju. But all he gave back was the tiniest flicker of a smile.

·◌ The Monsoon Season

At the end of June, the monsoon rains came rolling in as if in a
B-grade Hollywood movie. For days, clouds boiled up from the
valley, and then all of a sudden came a huge *crack!* and pitch-
forks of lightning stabbed down from the sky.

At the beginning, Jana liked the monsoon because it brought
things to life. Not just mold and mildew but wonderful things,
too—lacy green ferns that covered the oak trees and tiny purple
orchids that pushed out between the stones of the retaining walls.
She liked the mists that floated up the hillside, and even was
amused by the sound of beetles rattling against the windowpanes.

By the end of July, however, the novelty had worn off. The
cheerful holiday crowds of May and June gave way to workaday
local people scurrying by with black umbrellas. Dampness stained
the walls of the Jolly Grant House. After all that painting and
cleaning, thought Jana, it will all have to be done again. And then
next year, too.

"Thirty inches of rain in July," Mary announced.

And six or eight weeks to go, thought Jana grimly.

The postman came, not to deliver anything but to apologize:
the road to Dehra Dun was out, and the post could not get
through.

On Saturday morning, the newspaper wallah came. Because
of the mail failure, he did not have the selection of newspapers
he usually offered—old copies of the Scotsman or the *Glasgow
Herald,* occasionally *Le Monde,* often the overseas edition of the
New York Herald Tribune. This time, he didn't even have the *Times
of India* or the *Hindustan Times.* He did have the latest edition of
Rambir's *Our Town, Our Times,* however. Jana bought that and
took it up to the top of the tower, the only room in the house
where there was enough natural light to read by.

"Homes and shops flooded," she read. "Major roads and
bridges washed out. Crews have been valiantly clearing the roads,
hoping to keep one step ahead of the rains."

That was an optimistic hope, Jana thought. Crews might work valiantly, but they would always be one step *behind* the rains. On the road that led from the town to the Far Oaks School, she'd seen the men working in pairs, one guiding a shovel into the pile of rock and mud, the other pulling on the rope attached to the shovel.

Editor Rambir then went on to regional news: "The rivers are overflowing their banks, and the villagers are seeing their fields underwater. Mother Nature sometimes acts like the wicked stepmother in 'Cinderella.' And lest you think you can tame and bully Mother Nature, the proposed uber-Dam will only make everything worse. Where we now have floods, if the dam breaks, we will have inundations of biblical proportions."

The first page also had one of Rambir's think pieces about the future of technology. "Should India get television?" he asked. "An experimental station is even now transmitting for forty-five minutes a week in Delhi! Used correctly, what a wonderful educational medium TV would be! Science and literature for the masses. But right now, a television set is beyond anyone but a Tata or a Birla. This is the problem with progress. So few people share in it."

Jana turned the page. Her eye caught her own name and the photograph of her household standing outside the Jolly Grant House. "Our very own celebrity! Destined to spruce up the attractions of our Central Business District. Do stop in and get her perspective on *your* life."

Central Business District. Too grand a name for their little bazaar, and now, in the rainy season, sprucing it up seemed only a remote possibility. She looked out the window at the quarter. Water squirted off the corrugated roofs, ran down the gutters like rampaging little rivers, and turned the street glistening black. The Nepali charcoal carriers trudged by, their loads partially covered by ragged tarps, water trickling down their faces and arms. From alcoves and eaves, monkeys peered out disconsolately, and a dripping cow edged its way into a vegetable stall.

Looking out in the other direction, toward the hills, Jana saw a misty landscape of gray, green, and white. The clouds billowed up between the town and the Far Oaks School, revealing here and there a corner of a red roof. The valley had disappeared, for all she knew, not merely from view but from the very earth. They were floating in a town in the clouds.

"*Pani,*" observed Mr. Ganguly.

"Yes, there is a lot of water out there," Jana said. She took a bite of scone spread with Pahari Provisioners' best plum jam, thankful that she had stocked up.

"Walk!" said Mr. Ganguly.

"All right," said Jana. "Let me just finish the newspaper. And this scone."

Having polished off the last crumb, she put on her rubber boots and raincoat, attached the bird cape, settled Mr. Ganguly on her shoulder, and took her umbrella out of the stand.

Outside, the rain had let up, so that walking, if wet and sometimes slippery, was still a relief from being cooped up inside. She breathed in the cool, moist air and set off on one of her standard walks, a turn up to the English Bazaar and back. The Victoria Hotel looked quiet. Lights were on in the dining room, but no one was walking in the courtyard. She swung by the Municipal Garden, where the fountain was overflowing and the statue of George Everest glistening wet, making the surveyor look more like a disconsolate mariner.

Mr. Ganguly let out a purring sound.

"Oh, yes," said Jana. "You want the birdbath."

She let him down onto the rim of the birdbath, then watched as he dipped his head, lowered his chest into the water, and raised it. Having finished his bath, he did a dance of sheer joy, flapping his wings and shaking off the water in a circle of drops.

"He enjoys life," said a voice. Mr. Powell the optometrist, a closed umbrella in hand, was letting his two dachshunds chase each other around the park.

"As do your dogs," said Jana.

"Yes," said Mr. Powell, "they have fun in a simpler and more joyous way than most humans do. Their pleasures seem more reliable. All you have to do is say the word 'walk' and they're wiggling from head to toe. How are the new specs, by the way?"

"They're very helpful, thank you, Mr. Powell. I can read the small print in Rambir's newspaper now."

"That's good when the news is good, I suppose."

They chatted while Mr. Ganguly watched the two dogs, occasionally letting out his own high-pitched version of a bark. Then Mr. Powell continued his walk, and Jana let Mr. Ganguly climb onto her shoulder again and turned back toward the Central Bazaar. The rain started again, Mr. Ganguly noticing it before she did, and ordering her, with a squeak of "*pani!*" to put her umbrella up.

At the apothecary, Abinath was rearranging the various containers that were catching drips from the ceiling.

"Mind the puddles on the floor," he said to Jana. "What can I do for you?"

"Some of your special almond hand cream," she answered.

Abinath wiped the moisture off the glass cabinet and reached in for a small purple jar.

"Last jar, just for you."

The one bare light bulb hanging in his store cast odd shadows and made things look dingy and depressing. Mr. Abinath himself looked uncharacteristically frazzled, lines wrinkling his broad forehead.

"It's like this every year," Abinath said. "Everyone is excited at the first rain. Then, after a few days, they begin to feel oppressed." He rubbed his forehead.

"Are you all right, Mr. Abinath?"

"Bit of a headache, Mrs. Laird," he said, "and I don't have the ingredients to mix up my special headache medicine. Traders haven't come in for several days."

"I see," said Jana.

"I'll make do with aspirin," he said gloomily.

Jana gave him a sympathetic "Oh dear" and shook her head. "Mr. Abinath, I will see you later." She paid for the hand cream and continued on her way home; once there, she left the open umbrella to drip onto the salon floor.

Mary came in with a sour expression.

"Jana mem, that *dhobi* came, but didn't bring any clothes. Shortage of charcoal. The sheets and towels hang in the drying shed day after day, but with no heat, they don't dry."

Jana went up to the tower room, took out her violin, tuned it, played a few notes, retuned it, played a few more notes, and tuned it again.

"Hopeless!"

The harmonium, too, was on strike, the keys sticking when she tried to play.

Jana felt her own spirits sagging. How could one live in this clammy, damp shower bath! It was like being twenty thousand leagues under the sea! So let the government come and build the dam. Why not?

Then she made herself remember that she always felt, in Mary's words, "pulled down" at mid-monsoon, and that it *would* pass.

⁂ *Sandra Complains to Jana*

Sandra tumbled in, alone and petulant, startling Jana and making Mr. Ganguly flutter in surprise. The girl waved her open umbrella, sending a shower of drops across the room. "Where shall I put this?"

"In the front hall. In the stand." Jana was annoyed both by the interruption of her music transcription and by the girl's total lack of umbrella etiquette. Plus, there was that matter of the Far Oaks ban on brothels and fortune-tellers.

"You're not supposed to be here," she said, not making much effort to keep the testiness out of her voice.

"Oh, yeah, maybe," said Sandra. "But I was going stir-crazy. The rain will drive me out of my mind! And I thought it would be safer today than Saturday. That's when the Dragon trolls around the bazaar, spying on us. Anyway, what do I care? If I get in trouble, my dad will just have to come and take me out."

"You may not like that as much as you think, you know," said Jana. "I doubt it's much fun being expelled. And you have to do a lot of explaining at the next place you go to."

"Aw, so what."

Without being invited, Sandra sat down at the table.

"So, what's going on?" said Jana.

"Same old crap!"

"Crap!" Mr. Ganguly echoed. "Crap! Crap! Crap!"

"Oh damn, I'm sorry," said Sandra. "I forgot."

"It's an uphill task keeping a parrot's language clean," said Jana. "He can swear in six languages. Please don't say *m-e-r-d-e*, or he'll repeat that, too."

"Okay," said Sandra.

What was troubling the girl? Sandra pressed her lips together and appeared to be willing back tears that might escape at any moment. Seeing the girl's distress softened Jana's irritation.

"What's wrong?" she said, more gently.

"Oh, nothing," Sandra said. "I mean, I just don't want to be here."

"So where would you rather be?"

"In Paris. I really liked it there. I liked going on the metro. And eating pastries. And speaking French. I was *used* to it. Then all the stuff with my mom and dad came up. And then we got transferred to Delhi. My dad was *supposed* to be an ambassador—I forget where to, Syria or something, and then the State Department decided to send him to India. You just have to go where they send you. And kids have no choice, anyway."

"Sometimes adults don't have very good choices, either," Jana said.

Sandra paused and considered this idea.

"Maybe not. Oh well, don't tell anyone I came in here, okay?"

"I thought you wanted to get caught."

Sandra grimaced and shook her head. "Oh, I just don't know." Again the tears threatened to spill over, and again Sandra seemed to pull them back inside.

"The school is so stupid!" said Sandra. "I miss the American School in Paris. And my friends. I just don't have any here."

"Not Roo?"

"Oh, Roo. She's all right, I guess, but so juvenile! And she goes on and on about how everything is so neat in India."

Finding Roo's attitude close to her own, Jana said nothing. Sandra was now on to another topic.

"You can't imagine the food. The only thing worse than the food is the jokes about it! You go to dinner and there's shepherd's pie and someone always says, 'Grade B shepherds!' And for dessert if there's tapioca, at least three people will say, 'Fish eyes!'"

Jana Bibi was now laughing in spite of herself. "It doesn't sound as if things have changed much. We had exactly the same jokes in boarding school."

"And they played this really dumb trick on me in the dining room."

"Let me see: they told you to ask for a big *chumma*—a kiss— instead of a big *chammach*—a spoon?"

At the word "kiss," Mr. Ganguly went into his kissing noises.

"How did you know?" said Sandra.

"I regret to say that I played that trick myself on a poor unsuspecting classmate."

"So stupid!" said Sandra.

"If it's any consolation, I now wish I hadn't. The girl was homesick, and the last thing she needed was to be laughed at."

Mary came with her sugar cookies and *nimbu pani*. "Oh wow!" Sandra said. "Thanks!" She munched three cookies in a row and washed them down with the lemonade, which temporarily improved her spirits.

"Did you *like* school?" said Sandra.

Jana paused, then let out a long sigh. "Actually, I did. Most of it."

"When were you there?"

"From 1914 to 1918."

Sandra looked at her in disbelief. "Holy cow! That was the *First* World War. We learned about that in history."

"Yes, my parents thought it too dangerous to send me back to Scotland to school, which they would have done in normal times."

"I didn't think—I didn't think you were that old. I mean, I'm sorry."

"No offense taken," said Jana. "It's not that bad, you know. In fact, it's easier in some ways than being young."

Sandra considered and rejected that remote possibility.

"My mattress is lumpy."

Oh good heavens, thought Jana. The princess and the pea. "You could have the mattress-fluffer man come and fluff it up."

"Really? That's so weird."

Mr. Ganguly broke in now, whistling a few bars of "The Atholl Highlanders."

"He's telling me to get back to work on some music," said Jana.

Sandra rose to go. She slung her expensive handbag over her shoulder and took her umbrella out of the stand, then turned suddenly and asked, "You're Scotch, right?"

"I am a Scot by birth," corrected Jana. " 'Scotch' applies more to the whisky. But I'm an Indian citizen."

Sandra looked utterly disbelieving.

"You are? *Why?*"

"Why? It's my home. I live here," said Jana.

"Do you *like* it?"

"Of course. I love it, actually."

"Jeez," said Sandra.

Her horrified expression was so extreme that Jana couldn't help laughing. "Everyone's got to live somewhere."

In the days to come, Jana saw Sandra several times in the bazaar. Once, the girl was heading into the Europa Cinema with two young men, one with a beard and wearing a turban, the other clean-shaven. The three were speaking French. Another time, Sandra was heading into the Victoria Hotel, at the hour of the weekly tea dance.

She really *is* determined to get expelled, Jana thought.

⌁ *Feroze Fits Sandra for Marching Trousers*

Feroze and Moustapha tried to keep their bundles of clothes and fabric dry under umbrellas. A rickshaw passed, the top pulled up over the customers, the rickshaw pullers slanting into the rain with water pouring down their faces.

"Next time maybe we'll take a rickshaw." Feroze had been talking about this idea for a long time.

"How about *now*?" Moustapha said.

"Oh, we are more than halfway there. Just a little more patience."

"Uncle, that's your motto! *Just have a little more patience, please.*"

They passed through the Central Bazaar and climbed the steep street of the Upper Bazaar, then walked along the dirt road to the Far Oaks School. There, they went up the steps to the back entrance, which gave onto a hallway. Feroze could see several missahibs in the adjoining dining room, still having their coffee and breakfast. Others were already lined up in the hall, with fabric in hand or clothes to be altered. Miss Sandra Stuart-Smith, unsmiling, was the first in line. Feroze found her page in his notebook.

"Miss Ess-Sandra Ess-Stuart Ess-Smith," he said to her. "High-class name, right?"

"I don't know," said Sandra. "I never really thought about it."

"The matching roommate dresses for you and Miss Roo were satisfactory?"

"Yes, thank you," said Sandra. "We wore them to school the other day. Like twins."

Feroze smiled.

"Now we have to have these dumb marching uniforms made."

Feroze already knew something about the uniforms for the Far Oaks School intramural marching competition. He had assigned to Imran and Jalaluddin and Ali the job of making the exact same trousers for other girls.

"The pants are stupid," said Sandra, "but we're all required to have them."

"Oh, missahib," Feroze said, "that is the nature of uniforms. They must be made so many people can wear them; they can't be very special."

"But I bought better cloth," said Sandra. "See? Not cheap flimsy stuff—nice heavy cloth."

Feroze fingered the cloth and tipped his chin appreciatively. Yes, this was quality that did not scream about itself.

"I'm wondering if you could put an extra pocket in these pants?" Sandra said. "It won't show, but it would be more useful."

"Of course," said Feroze. "Extra pocket, no problem. Good idea, missahib. We will put quality on the inside, even if the outside must be plain."

"We had to learn this speech in English class," said Miss Stuart-Smith. " 'Costly thy habit as thy purse can buy.' It means you should buy top quality. If you can."

"Of course!" said Feroze. "Missahib knows. A few extra rupees spent on quality is never cause for regret."

The next evening, over their dinner, Moustapha said to Feroze, "I saw Miss Stuart-Smith running about today."

Zohra, arriving from the kitchen with more spinach and *paneer,* said, "I, too, saw her! I said to myself, there goes Princess Grace again. I'm thinking she'll marry some European prince."

"Yes, then we'll see newsreels of her wedding. Those of us who go to the cinema will see, at any rate," Moustapha said pointedly.

"It would be good to see a newsreel of Miss Stuart-Smith's wedding, wouldn't it?" Zohra said.

"If we bought the Bharat Mata Cinema, we could show the newsreel as often as we wanted," said Moustapha, and Zohra gave a peel of laughter. Feroze made no response. "Uncle, maybe you will make the wedding dress. Then you really would *have* to go to the cinema and see the newsreel."

"If that happens," said Feroze, "then I will go to the cinema."

Jack's Visit

Mr. Kilometres Delivers a Passenger

When the road to Dehra Dun was repaired and the post *did* get through, it carried a couple of letters from Jack. The first said that he planned to visit in August. "I know, Mother, you told me the weather would *not* be ideal. But that's when I've got leave."

The second letter had been posted a week later, and on reading it Jana did a double take.

"Mary! Jack baba is coming *tomorrow*."

Mary was wiggling her head in delight. "Very good, Jana mem! I will make him my Madrassi specialties."

If memory served from Jack's previous visits to India, Jana's meat-potato-and-two-veg son would abandon even his Scottish thrift to avoid Mary's Madrassi specialties. He was one of those travelers who, upon arrival, instantly look for things that will make them feel at home.

"He'll take most of his meals down at the Victoria," said Jana. Seeing Mary's face fall, she quickly added, "But we'll give him lovely teas here. He loves your cakes. And we can get some tinned Scottish beef and shortbread from Pahari Provisioners."

The next day, there was a break in the rains. Though gray-and-white mists still swirled up from the ravines, the sky allowed thin streaks of blue to break through. The whole household walked down to the taxi stand to greet Jack. When Lal Bahadur Pun spied the taxi hurtling forward on a twist of road half a mile below, he started up his bagpipes. Mary and Tilku held garlands of marigolds, and Tilku, who was wearing his new Bata tennis shoes, could not keep still.

It's only been five months, thought Jana, since I arrived on that very road . . . and, was it possible, in that very taxi? It *was*, with Mr. Kilometres himself at the wheel. Jack, his face graygreen, carefully tested the ground as he got out.

Mr. Kilometres sprang from the driver's seat, and Jana noticed that he had a new plaid eye patch and that the uncovered eye was now clear. He must have had cataract surgery, she thought, and probably drives all the more wildly because of it.

"Madam," Mr. Kilometres cried in triumphant delight, "I have delivered your son to you! And once again, I have made this run without accident."

"We came close, though," said Jack grimly.

Jana had a flash of memory of Jack, as a little boy, gratefully getting down off a pony. "It's *lovely* to see you, darling."

"It's lovely to see you, Mother."

"Did you get *any* sleep on the plane?"

"Not much."

"Poor darling, your eyes *are* red!"

By now, Lal Bahadur Pun was on the fourth variation of a tune of his own composition, the name of which, he had told Jana, was "A Gurkha Piper's Welcome to Mr. Jack Laird on his Arrival in the Hills." Mary stepped forward and garlanded Jack, then put her palms together. Tears streamed down her cheeks. "Jack baba has come! Tilku, come here!"

Jack, realizing that Tilku was too short to garland him directly, bent forward and let Tilku drape him in marigolds.

"Namasté, sahib! Namasté!"

"Can you walk, darling?" said Jana. "We can get a rickshaw, you know."

"Of course I can walk, Mother."

They made their way back to the Central Bazaar, a procession of barefoot boys growing behind them, while merchants leaned out of their stalls and said namasté and salaam. When they reached the Treasure Emporium, Ramachandran and Asha and Bimla emerged, each with yet another garland of marigolds, and Jack let himself be welcomed again. Soon they were standing in front of the Jolly Grant House, right by the sign for Jana Bibi's Excellent Fortunes.

"Mother," said Jack weakly, "what's this sign for?"

"I'll explain later," said Jana.

They stepped inside. A volley of "Hello hello hello!" greeted them from the birdcage, and Jana let Mr. Ganguly out onto her arm.

"Kiss please," said Mr. Ganguly.

"Maybe when we know each other better," said Jack.

"Jack baba wants tea?" Mary asked hopefully. "And my cake?"

"I don't really need . . ." Jack began. Then, seeing Mary's face fall, he added, "That would be . . . lovely, Mary. Just a small piece, please."

"And one nice cup of hot tea," said Mary, firmly.

After Mary's tea, Jack revived sufficiently for Jana to lead him on an inspection of the house. In the tower, she stood proudly as he took in the 360-degree view of the hills and the town and peered through the telescope.

"You *have* got good views," Jack said. "I'll grant you that."

He inspected the stairs, indoors and out, the wiring, the kitchen hot plate, and the light fixtures. He flushed the toilets and ran the water. He found a cracked windowpane and said he would replace it himself while he was there. Outside, on the lower level, he looked skeptically at the terrace and the retaining walls.

"Does your engineer's eye detect any problem?" Jana said.

"There's a problem every two feet! Mum, it's all held up by magic!"

"Perhaps that's what Grandfather Jolly built it with. There had to be *some* magic mixed into the mortar."

"The whole *town* looks as if it's held up by magic," said Jack. "Buildings clinging to the hillside with no discernible support . . . I suppose your house isn't any worse than any of the others."

"Better, I think," said Jana. "And it's stood the test of time."

"I prefer more of a margin of safety. For *you*, Mother, that is."

"I know. You do worry." She gave him a quick hug. "But really, it's all quite, quite all right."

She was relieved that Jack, in his sleep-deprived state, forgot to grill her about the meaning of her sign, and instead staggered off to check in at the Victoria. But later that night, when they were dining at the hotel, he remembered.

"Oh, and by the by, what does the sign above your front door mean?"

"Oh, yes, that. That's—part of the stratagem."

"Stratagem?"

"For saving the town. You see, the town is under attack. Now, don't look so hopeful! The government wants to build a huge dam, and we'll be right at the bottom of the catchment area. *If* they succeed. But we believe we can turn things around. Get public opinion on the side of the town. Get some support in high places."

"It's a dreadful place for a dam," said Jack. "I've built a few of those, and I can't think of a worse place. You're right in the Central Himalayan Seismic Gap. If a dam burst, you can't imagine the chaos it would cause, all the way down to the plains."

"I wish you'd write a letter to the editor of our weekly newspaper, saying all that."

Jack looked uneasy at suddenly finding himself taking one of his mother's positions. He paused and gestured to the bearer to bring more water, then held up the glass suspiciously.

"Do you suppose this water is adequately boiled, Mother?"

"Of course it is. I eat here all the time."

"But you've got years of immunities built up."

"So it would be a pity to waste them by leaving India, wouldn't it. Now that I'm adapted, I might as well stay."

Jack gave a grudging laugh.

"Still, Mother. Now tell me what 'Jana Bibi's Excellent Fortunes' means. Jana *Bibi*?"

"A pet name the ayah and Loulou used to call me."

"Sounds like a Kashmiri flower seller to me."

"Not at all; 'Bibi' has rather an aristocratic ring to it."

Jack looked unconvinced. "And 'Excellent Fortunes'? That's what you've renamed the house? 'The Jolly Grant House' wasn't good enough?"

"It's—it's the name of my fortune-telling salon." She sat back and waited for his reaction. "Part of the effort to increase tourist attractions," she added.

"You're going to tell fortunes."

"Yes. Why not?"

"Mother, what do you mean, 'Why not?' Like some itinerant Gypsy?" He leaned forward and imitated the voice of an old woman. "Come, my pretty, cross my palm with silver."

"Most of the silver that crosses my palm will go toward printing costs and so forth for Rambir—our local editor—to keep the cause alive. It's for the good of the town."

"But doesn't fortune-telling strike you as . . . vulgar?"

Jana sighed.

"Not really. A little different, that's all."

"Mother, it's bizarre beyond description."

Dear Jack, just like Jana's father: quiet, proper, coloring within the lines. Jack was definitely a MacPherson. Whereas she, like Grandfather Grant, was definitely more of a Grant—or at least that was what the family always said.

Jack went on, still distressed. "It just strikes me as—daft. The music thing you did in Bombay was bad enough, and working at that nawab fellow's palace . . . but now *this*."

"Jack, I'm not doing anything illegal, or dangerous. Just providing some harmless . . . entertainment."

"All right, for the sake of argument, let's say that telling fortunes is the most appropriate and constructive thing you could do. But telling fortunes *in India*? Isn't that like being a French cook in Paris? Or singing opera in Milan? Or acting in films in Hollywood? Aren't you bringing coals to Newcastle?"

"If coals are what Newcastle needs . . ."

"But how do you expect to hold your own against people who have been doing this all their lives?" Jack's face reddened. "You can't compete, you know."

"It's not a competition," said Jana. "It's a cooperative effort with the merchants of the town to add to the attractions, give a lively, optimistic feel to this part of the town, impart variety to the Central Bazaar. . . . Of course, there are astrologers in town, but they'll continue happily on their way, casting horoscopes for the orthodox Hindu babies . . . I wouldn't think of competing with them for a moment. The Tibetan soothsayers will tell the Tibetan peddlers when to start on their journeys. Palmists will read and recite folks' past, present, and future. But those people aren't concerned with saving the town."

"Nor should you be, Mother. You should be concerned with getting out of it."

Another version of that conversation took place the next day, in Jana's tower room. With a good night's sleep under his belt, Jack attacked the question with renewed energy.

"What is it you *want*, Mum?"

She considered. "The first thing: to live in a beautiful place, with a view."

"There are no views in Scotland?"

"Of *course* there are views in Scotland. But does any view compare to this one?"

"It's nice, I grant you."

"It's more than nice. It's inspiring."

"I still maintain that we have plenty of inspiring views at home."

"All right, I'll give you that. What do I want? The second thing: to live somewhere that captures my imagination. It's got to have that extra something. . . . And this place does."

"But don't you feel . . . out of place?"

"On the contrary. I feel completely *in* place. . . . I'm part of the town . . . part of this quarter . . . this bazaar. This little corner of the earth has always had immigrants and wayfarers, refugees from here and there. I'm not the slightest bit out of place or odd here. I fit right in. How would I fit in back in Glasgow?"

"Perfectly nicely," said Jack. "You could join musical societies. The RSPCA. You'd find plenty of old Indian hands. You could eat curry with them and trade stories about life in the *mofussil*. About dressing for dinner in the bush and how the tiger made off with your dog."

"All very well for fossils," said Jana. "But I'm trying to acquire a few more stories to tell so I'll have some good ones when my fossildom arrives."

Jack shook his head. "No matter what, Mum, you can't stay here forever."

"No one can stay anywhere forever."

Mr. Ganguly was following the conversation closely, bringing his head up when Jack did, lifting a leg when Jack lifted his hand. When Jack's voice rose, Mr. Ganguly puffed up his feathers and flapped his wings.

"That bird gets on my nerves," said Jack.

"*Ullu ka baccha!*" said Mr. Ganguly.

Jack searched his memory for the meaning of the phrase, then burst into laughter.

"*Ullu ka baccha!* Son of an owl . . . of course. That's rich! Having a parrot call you an owl. I wonder if he thinks I look like one."

"May I remind you that 'son of an owl' is not a compliment."

"I don't think you have to remind me of that, Mother."

By now the parrot's pupils were dilating and contracting, and a red ring showed around his eyes. Jana murmured to him, "Mr. Ganguly, please calm down. It's only Jack. He's not going to harm me."

The rain was beating down heavily, but it seemed pointless to stay in the house arguing about where she should live.

"Come, let's take a walk," said Jana. "I'll introduce you to my neighbors."

Royal Tailors was the first stop. Jack received such a chorus of *adabs* and salaams that it seemed to blow him off balance.

"Jana Auntie's son!" Moustapha said.

Jack looked at his mother hard, as if making sure that she was indeed Jana Auntie. Jana said, "Moustapha is very knowledgeable about things in the film world. He moonlights as an usher at the Bharat Mata Cinema and gives me free passes."

"Very kind of you," said Jack to Moustapha.

Feroze had come forward now from the back of the shop. He made a formal and elegant gesture of welcome, bringing one hand toward his forehead.

"*Adab,* Mr. Laird, sahib, welcome. This is—great honor."

"Thank you," said Jack. "Er . . . it's a great honor for me, too."

Feroze turned and muttered a few sentences to the cousins, and Imran went into the back room and returned with something made of green fabric. Feroze unfolded it and handed it to Jack.

"One waistcoat, sir. As memory of us."

"But really, you shouldn't have . . ."

"Please, please. When you go home to Scotland, you can wear this and remember your mother's quarter in Hamara Nagar!"

Jana murmured, "Put it on," and Jack took off his raincoat and jacket, put the waistcoat on, and waited for the reaction.

"Very nice," said Jana.

The cousins and Moustapha and Feroze were all smiling

broadly. Feroze said to Jack, "Any stitching you need, come to us! Even mending. We will do mending free of charge. Anything for Laird memsahib's son."

They made their way up the street, each under a big black umbrella, Jack picking his way carefully across the occasional pile of wet dung and stepping back into the closest storefront when a mule train went by.

"Abinath's Apothecary," said Jack. "That sounds like something out of the Middle Ages."

"You're thinking of alchemy," said Jana.

They stepped up into the store, avoiding the puddles on the floor.

"Mrs. Laird!" Abinath cried.

"Mr. Abinath, this is my son."

"Oh, so delighted, so delighted! How are you finding the climate? The altitude? Being in a new place can affect one's digestion, of course. And sleeping? You are sleeping yet? Or still all turned around from traveling? Any ailment you have, you just tell me."

In the course of the conversation that ensued, Abinath extracted from Jack the information that Jack suffered from migraines.

"I, too, am suffering!" said Abinath. "Oh, we are prisoners of our pain, are we not? Here, you take some of my own special headache medicine. I just got the ingredients in and made a new batch. Try it out. No charge for Mrs. Laird's son."

At Muktinanda's Stationers and School Supplies, Jack's eyes lit up at the selection of British cricket magazines, and he reached for one at the top of the pile.

"Your mother is the patron saint of the neighborhood," said Muktinanda to Jack. "No, don't take that magazine; it got too battered in shipping. Take this nice clean one."

On the steps going out of Muktinanda's, Jana asked, "One more visit? Or have you had enough of a welcome for one day?"

Jack's dazed face was answer enough, and they sloshed back

to the Jolly Grant House with their arms full of tangible evidence of the neighborhood's goodwill.

The next day, the rain had tapered off, and Jack seemed to have recovered enough to go back into the welcoming fray. They went next door to the Treasure Emporium, and Ramachandran wiggled his head back and forth with such energy that Jana was afraid it might fall off.

"Mr. Laird! Hail the conquering hero comes!"

Old Aunt Putli echoed, "The conquering hero!" The minions all namastéd and smiled, and one skittered off and returned with tea. Asha and Bimla, just back from school, parked their satchels in the back room and came running up to be introduced.

"Oh, Mr. Laird!" cried Ramachandran. "Your mother is the cornerstone of our development strategy! She is going to save us from the bureaucrats and the bulldozers. But we were all worried about her."

"You were?" said Jack, immediately on the alert.

"Well, not really about *her,* more about *you.* Doesn't she have any family? people were asking. I mean, we knew she had family . . . but you seemed so far away in Scotland. . . . Never mind! We are glad to see you! We hope you stay a good long time!"

Jana had warned Jack that he might get a barrage of questions, but even she was a little startled by how curious the Ramachandrans all were about him.

"How old are you?" said Ramachandran.

"I'm—thirty-four," said Jack.

"And no wife?" said Ramachandran. "You must get married, soon. Maybe we can find you a girl right here!"

"Where did you do your studies?" Asha asked.

"Edinb—"

Bimla interrupted. "What level of degree did you obtain: fail, pass, what class?"

"Engineering . . . first—"

"First!" said Asha. "You must be so *brainy.*"

"And you must be earning so much money, right?" said Rama-chandran.

"What does your house look like?" Bimla asked.

"It's a . . . well, it's rather a drafty old place—"

"A castle!" Ramachandran said triumphantly. "I know you live in a castle."

"Do you have a refrigerator?" asked Asha.

"Actually—"

"Shortwave radio? Gramophone?"

Jana realized that Jack was again being overwhelmed. She quickly said, "Mr. Ramachandran, you and my son have a lot in common. Maybe you can get together and take a walk around and talk about engineering."

"That's an excellent idea, Mrs. Laird!" Ramachandran beamed. "Rain or shine, I will take you anywhere you want to go! We could go right now, in fact."

"That's very kind of you," said Jack.

Jack, Jana was sure, would rather go back to the Jolly Grant House and sit alone with an old issue of the *Scotsman*. But Rama-chandran insisted, "Come, come!" and Jack let himself be led off to be further welcomed and introduced.

ᴄᐟ A Box from the Treasure Emporium

Over the course of the two-week visit, Jack fared better than Jana would have predicted. On several days, he hiked back into the hills, returning drenched and with several leeches stuck to his calves, but having satisfied his curiosity about local geologi-cal peculiarities. On other days, he discussed engineering with Ramachandran and optics with Mr. Powell, whom he had met in the Municipal Garden. He also won the heart of Lal Bahadur Pun by asking for tips on bagpipe ornaments. Jana looked on, amused and relieved. Obviously her son was less of an introvert than she'd thought. He just needed to get to know people one by one, and at his own pace.

Mary did not abandon her wish to feed him her Madrassi specialties, and he finally consented to eat one of her curries.

"It's actually better than I remembered," he said, despite the sweat beading on his forehead.

"You're a good sport, darling," Jana said. "She utterly adores you." She finished Jack's plate for him, and when Mary returned from the cook house and saw the empty dishes, she was ecstatic.

"Jack baba has eaten well," she said, just as if he were four years old again. "I know what good foods to give him."

"Well done," said Jack. "Mary, your cooking is—indescribable."

On the last day of Jack's visit, one of the minions came down from the Treasure Emporium with a note and a metal box secured by a rusted padlock. Jana made out wobbly white letters on the black metal: "Major Ramsay Grant, Jolly Grant House, Hamara Nagar, Uttar Pradesh."

"A box that belonged to Great-grandfather Jolly," said Jack. "That's rather interesting."

Jana unfolded the note and read, in Ramachandran's precise, upright handwriting: "Mrs. Laird, we haven't gotten to the bottom layer of the storeroom, but we did unearth this. It must have belonged to your family. I regret, there is no key."

Jack shook the box; there was a rustling noise.

"Tilku," called Jana. "Do run over to Royal Tailors and borrow a screwdriver, there's a good lad."

On Tilku's return, Jana and Jack settled at the table in the salon with the box, and Jack removed the hasp and opened the lid, revealing several packets of letters tied up with thin blue ribbon.

Jack held one packet of letters to his nose. "Insecticide?"

Jana took a cautious sniff. "Mothballs." She carefully slid a letter out of its yellowing envelope and held it up to the light. There were several pages, the last one signed, "Your affectionate sister." Jana admired the stately handwriting, perfectly regular even on unlined paper.

"September 1, 1892," Jana said. She read the first page and smiled. "It's begging Grandfather Jolly to come back to England before he dies of some terrible disease or gets killed off by a bear or falls over the cliff! I guess he wasn't afraid of any of those things."

She looked at a second one and read aloud: "'Ramsay, you really can't bring that woman home with you.'"

"I wonder why he even kept the letters," Jack said, "when they obviously said things he didn't want to hear, let alone heed. Come home, Jolly, but don't bring your wife!"

"He had a sense of history, it seems," Jana said.

"Maybe he was just a pack rat and never threw anything away."

Jana picked up a piece of pasteboard illustrated with garlands and crowns. "Here's a menu! Queen Victoria's Diamond Jubilee dinner at the Victoria Hotel, in 1897. Good heavens, seven courses . . . how could you eat soup, fish, veal, glazed duck, saddle of mutton, vegetable pilaf, and pastries all in a single meal?"

Jack was now sorting the letters by postmark date. Jana had a memory of Jack at seven sorting his stamp collection on the verandah table at the mission, shortly before being shipped off to Scotland. The same calm concentration, the same careful gestures. She felt a rush of grief, of longing for that little boy, and for his two little sisters in their graves on the plains of northern India. She drove back the lump in her throat. In the meantime, Jack had made another discovery.

"Oh my word!"

"What?"

"Here's a letter from *you* . . . December 12, 1911. 'Dear Grandfather Jolly, today we went to watch the King being crowned Emperor of India. It was lots of fun. I liked watching the camel corps . . .'"

Jana looked at the childish handwriting, a tiny voice from one of the different worlds she had lived in.

Jack handed her another. "February 17, 1911."

Jana read aloud: "'Dear Grandfather Jolly, this letter is going by air! Not by passenger pigeon—by a real aeroplane.'"

"Here's one from your sister, Loulou, on the same subject," said Jack. "And one from your mother!"

"I do remember some excitement about air letters," said Jana. "People were saying 'dawn of a new era.'"

"New eras seem to dawn with relentless regularity." Jack continued to sort the letters. "Well, we've certainly got some family history here. What would you like to do with these? I can take them back to Glasgow and have someone type them up so they'll be easier to read. In duplicate, if you wish. We can put the originals in the family archives."

Jana thought it over. "And you can mail me the carbons?"

"Of course."

"That sounds sensible," she said.

She went to bed with a feeling of impending farewell, reminded of another departure, twenty-five years earlier, when they'd sent Jack off to his great-grandfather MacPherson. That decision saved his life, she reminded herself, and now that air travel was commonplace, no parting was as bad as in the old days. Still, Scotland seemed so far away. Maybe she *should* reconsider, go there and live a sensible, conventional life. Maybe Jack even *needed* her. She rejected that possibility, however. Jack was obviously getting along very competently at home. Maybe when he made a sensible marriage to a sensible wife and they had sensible babies there would be a role for—a sensible grandmother?

Or . . . Her mind wandered as she drifted off to sleep. If not a sensible grandmother, one of those eccentric ones that were much more fun. One who took the grandchildren for rides in taxis just so they could sit in the jump seats.

In the morning, they stood at the taxi depot. Lal Bahadur Pun looked vulnerable without his pipes, and Tilku and Mary were disconsolate.

"Jack baba," said Mary, "we are feeling very pulled down. Next time, you come for a longer visit."

Jana was not sure whether Jack's slight smile signified agreement, affection for them, or relief at escaping. Maybe all three, she concluded. And also happiness that he was to ride to Dehra Dun in a taxi he'd booked through the Victoria. Not Mr. Kilometres.

"Dass assured me that the car would be a brand-new Hindustan. With working brakes," Jack said.

"Yes, yes," said Mary. "I know that car. And the driver. Not to worry, very reliable man."

But where was he? The taxi stand was empty. Jack looked at his watch.

As on the day he had arrived, the rains had paused, giving them a view of the serpentlike road below and the mist wafting up through the gorges.

"Mother," said Jack, "why don't you come to Glasgow for Christmas. We can do all sorts of traditional things. India's not the only place with tradition, you know."

"Yes, I know," said Jana gently.

"I can introduce you to people. You'd have a lovely time. I promise. Give it some thought."

She loved the way he said that. Calm, rational Jack.

He looked at his watch again. "I don't understand this. Dass seems so reliable. If I miss my train, I'll miss my plane."

The gooselike honk of a horn sounded. They all looked down, and there was a battered motorcar, barreling around the curves. A few minutes later, Mr. Kilometres jumped out of his taxi.

"Hello, Mr. Laird! So happy to report for service again! That young driver you ordered—he got stuck in Dehra Dun. Transmission gone! He is sending me instead to save the day."

"But . . ." Jack's face was a study.

Mr. Kilometres said firmly, "That young man—I taught him everything he knows. But those new vehicles can't compare to trusty old ones. Hop in, Mr. Laird, hop in!"

Jack took a deep breath. "Well," he said to Jana, "he got us up here; I suppose he can get me down."

Jana gave him a long hug. "You'll be all right," she said firmly, praying that that was true.

"Namasté, sahib, safe journey," cried Lal Bahadur Pun, Mary, and Tilku, in chorus.

"Namasté," said Jack, "and *shukriya*."

Preparations for the Talent Show

⌁ *Roo Gets a Bharatanatyam Costume*

On Saturday morning, Roo Wiley popped into Royal Tailors. Feroze saw Moustapha's face perk up, and the assorted cousins put down their sewing and looked up, too.

"I have to have a Bharatanatyam costume. Like this. And here's the material to make it with." Roo held out a picture from the *Illustrated Weekly of India* and a multicolored silk sari.

"Nice costume," Feroze said. Bharatanatyam might have originated in Hindu temples, but he was willing to fashion such an interesting garment even if it had been designed by the devil himself. The pleated fan that opened up when a dancer did a deep knee bend—he was sure he could stitch that to perfection. And he analyzed the tight bodice and gathered pants, the little apron that hugged the dancer's bottom and hips.

Moustapha came over from the corner and peered over Feroze's shoulder at the picture. "I can make this costume for Miss Wiley."

Feroze turned and gave him a stern look. "I will do this one myself."

"Oh, let Moustapha do it! He did such a good job on my cheerleading uniform." Roo gave Moustapha a cheery grin.

"Uncle, not to worry," said Moustapha. "This will get done perfectly."

Feroze was annoyed by the solicitous look Moustapha was giving Roo and by the continued rapt silence of the cousins. Who was the proprietor of this shop, anyway? Where was respect from the younger generation? Certainly Moustapha had the skills to do the costume—hadn't Feroze taught him well? But it was up to Feroze to give the assignment. "We will see," he said.

Moustapha and Roo exchanged what Feroze felt were all too intimate glances.

"It's for a talent show," said Roo. "At school. I'm going to do the opening number."

"Number?" Feroze waited for clarification.

"I'm on first! It's a short dance, but it's got to be perfect."

"Don't worry, Miss Wiley, it *will* be perfect," said Moustapha. "Costume and all."

When Roo was gone, Feroze stared at the magazine clipping she had left behind. The picture was small and blurry, so he took out a magnifying glass from the cupboard and examined it more carefully. He tried to count the pleats, but the dancer's posture hid some of them. He glanced up and saw Moustapha looking at him.

"Uncle, making that costume will be hard on your eyes."

"No problem," said Feroze. "You help Imran and Ali with the marching uniforms."

At Moustapha's disappointed expression, Feroze relented. Perhaps I will let Moustapha help with the dancing dress, he thought. He is the best tailor in the shop, after me. Giving him something interesting to do may take his mind off films and singing and all that frivolous stuff.

"Moustapha!"

"*Ji?*"

"You can do the pleats on this costume."

Moustapha signaled vigorous assent. "Okay, Uncle."

Later in the afternoon, Feroze turned around and Moustapha was not in the shop. He went out into the street and finally spied

Moustapha outside Muktinanda's Stationers and School Supplies, paging through the movie magazines in the rack. Moustapha returned with a nonchalant air.

"What are you trying to do?" scolded Feroze. "Here we have so much work and you're loitering outside Muktinanda's looking at trash!"

"Not trash, Uncle. I was studying the pictures of film stars in dance postures. Seeing how long the pleated aprons are. Now I have a better idea of how to do the costume."

Feroze let out a long breath.

"Just research, Uncle! You have to find things out so you can do a good job."

A few days later, they went over to the Far Oaks School to do the fitting of Roo's costume. On the way, Moustapha sang a scrap of a song from the movie *Chhalia* (The Con Man). *Aré*, Feroze thought. If the hero of a film is a cheat, this tells you what we are coming to. "Hindu, Muslim, Sikh, Christian, I give you all my salaam," sang Moustapha.

"Enough salaam," muttered Feroze.

As always, when they arrived, the girls were streaming out of breakfast, Roo the first in line.

"Did I hear you singing?" she said to Moustapha.

"I was—a little," he said.

"Sing some more."

Feroze was frowning at him to be quiet, but Moustapha sang a verse from the same song.

"Very good!" cried Roo. She took her costume, and shortly she returned in it, the effect marred only by her bedroom slippers with fluffy pink pompoms.

"Look!" She did a deep knee bend, and the pleats fanned out perfectly.

"I sewed that part of the costume," Moustapha said.

"It's beautiful!" Roo said. "I'll tell everyone you did it. Oh, I just had an idea. Would you sing for the talent show? You'd be really good."

Feroze heard Moustapha stammering, "That would be an honor . . ." and saw Roo Wiley doing some Bharatanatyam head and hand motions. The thought "Wait, I did not give permission" flitted through his head.

Roo turned to Feroze. "You should come to the talent show. It's free. There will be lots of different acts. I'm on the committee that's organizing it. Bring your wife, and anyone else. You don't have to get tickets. Just come."

"Very kind, missahib," mumbled Feroze.

On the way home, Moustapha was quiet. He's a good boy, thought Feroze. I am lucky to have him as my nephew, even with all his modern ideas. One day, I'll turn over the shop to him, and sit in the sun and have conversation and take my ease. But in the immediate future, I still have some work to do with this boy. He still needs direction. Energy of youth, he has that; wisdom of age, I must try to impart.

Moustapha Practices

It was sundown, evening prayers had been completed, and the bazaar fell into a quiet time before the evening rush. From the salon, Jana could hear Moustapha practicing in the tower, accompanying himself on the harmonium. The strains of film songs wafted down the stairs, some bouncy and mischievous, some melancholy. Jana marveled at how much Moustapha was teaching himself, picking up the basics of harmonium playing just by experimenting. He had a good sense of rhythm and phrasing, and an accurate ear.

"His voice is very good," Mary pronounced, "like dark, sweet liquid."

Moustapha was now singing "O Guardian of the World." Jana Bibi had heard the master Mohammed Rafi sing this song on the radio. It was different in sound but not so different in feeling from the Highland laments she had learned from old Ian the butler. What did Moustapha, with his unlined brow, know of sorrows? Yet the way he sang the song captured a feeling of longing and made a shiver go down her spine.

He came down the stairs, hands in his pockets, looking happy and relaxed and not the slightest bit sorrowful.

"Moustapha," she teased, "I think you are going to be the next Mohammed Rafi."

"No one can be like Rafi sahib." Moustapha grinned, obviously wanting to be contradicted.

"New talent always has to push up to replace the last. It's a law of nature." Jana watched Moustapha absorb this idea. "You are a songbird. It is your nature to sing, and it would be a crime against nature if you didn't."

Mary agreed. "Do you want some rice and dal?" she asked him. "Tea?"

Moustapha declined. "I will eat with my uncle." He gave a polite salaam to both women and slipped back across the street.

"He is very determined," Mary said. "He will succeed."

Jana nodded, and felt a twinge of something she was ashamed to acknowledge as envy. When she had been that age, she had been so full of doubt and fear that it had crowded out any determination she might have had. I made mountains out of mole-hills, she thought. One bad audition and you don't just give up—but she had, she reflected, remembering the mortifying day almost forty years earlier at the Glasgow Athenaeum. Moustapha had the will to overcome more than one bad experience, she felt.

In any case, Moustapha was almost too ignorant to be fearful. He had one example he wanted to follow—Mohammed Rafi—but he did not know that there would be competition, and he thought the only obstacle in his path was his uncle.

· · ·

Moustapha came back from the talent show rehearsal around eight o'clock one night, excited, punchy, laughing. Jana settled him in for tea and listened.

"Roo Wiley was running the whole thing," said Moustapha. "She was giving orders to everyone, even the boys! Like a sheepdog herding sheep bigger than herself. That is what some American girls are like."

"Did she give orders to you?"

"Oh, only to say it was my turn. She likes me very much. She told me my singing was fantastic."

Jana nodded.

"So I told her that her dancing was fantastic. Then she invited me to go to the cast party. At first I was confused. I asked, What caste? Americans have castes? Then she explained that the cast are the people who perform."

Moustapha finished his tea. "What time is it? *Aré,* I have to be at the Bharat Mata at nine to do my ushering shift!"

"You're not tired?" Jana said.

"Of course not," said Moustapha. "Why would I be tired?"

"Will Feroze come hear you sing?" said Jana.

"He says not. But he will change his mind and come, just watch. If for nothing else, to see the stage curtains in the auditorium. Big, heavy, brown velvet things. He made them; he won't be able to resist going to see them in action!"

Jana laughed. Moustapha knew Feroze very well.

"That hall can hold five hundred people. To think, five hundred people will hear me perform."

"Just a beginning," said Jana. "Just a beginning."

The Town Gears Up for the Futurologists

✑ Jana Delivers Two Flyers

It was barely light. From her bedroom, Jana heard the jingle of mule bells announce the milk wallah. Not much later, the crunch on the gravel told her that the bread and vegetable wallahs had arrived. She heard Mary demanding the juiciest tomatoes and the crispest radishes. Jana turned over and went back to sleep, ignoring her perpetual New Year's resolution to be an earlier riser. It was eight o'clock when another voice floated up from the courtyard. Rambir. What could he possibly be here for? Jana hurried into her clothes and went down to the salon.

"Good morning, Mrs. Laird." Rambir had dark circles under his bloodshot eyes, his shirt was rumpled, and he looked even skinnier than usual. Nonetheless, he was triumphant. He held out a large flyer printed on yellow paper.

"Have you been up all night?"

"I couldn't help it," said Rambir. "The paper had to be put to bed, and then the talent show programs for the Far Oaks School had to be printed, and the exam schedules for St. Margaret's and St. Bart's. None of these things could wait!"

"Your wife will scold."

"Oh, Ritu, she is just as bad, with all her classroom preparations and such. Always burning the midnight oil!"

"You don't want to end up in adjacent beds in the hospital," Jana said.

"Not to worry," said Rambir. "But take a look, tell me what you think."

Jana read the flyer aloud.

ESTEEMED DELEGATES TO THE
THIRD ANNUAL FUTUROLOGY CONVENTION

Hamara Nagar Welcomes You

Ramachandran's Treasure Emporium:
Pop In and Shop

Abinath's Apothecary:
Make Your Headaches a Thing of the Past

Royal Tailors:
Overnight Tailoring for Lifelong Satisfaction

Muktinanda's Stationers and School Supplies:
Necessary Now and Forever

Why Not? Tea Shop:
Eat with Us, Repeat with Us

Jana Bibi's Excellent Fortunes:
Start the Future Today

The whole thing was bordered with little cartoon pictures of the different merchants.

"What a wit you have, Rambir!" Jana was amused to see herself with an enormous bird on her shoulder, proportionally three times the size of Mr. Ganguly.

"I tried to be pithy," Rambir said.

"You succeeded very well."

"Oh," said Rambir, "there's also this little notice about the Far Oaks School Talent Show. A little curly-haired girl asked me if I'd print up a batch. I asked if I could hold out some for the Victoria. 'See tomorrow's talent today,' it says."

"We can ask Mr. Dass to put one of each in every room in the Victoria," said Jana. "And extras in the lobby."

"Could your boy Tilku run them over?"

"I'll take them myself," said Jana. "I need the walk."

When Rambir had gone, she settled down to a breakfast of Mary's fried eggs, toast and guava jam, and a couple of cups of strong tea. Then, with Mr. Ganguly on her shoulder, she headed over to the Victoria.

The last of the rains had disappeared, and the October sun spread its light across the distant ridges, the renewed forests, and the red metal roofs of the town. Corners and alleys that had been dark and damp for weeks opened up, cheerful again. Across town, merchants put out posters announcing special bargains and hung streamers across their storefronts.

The Bharat Mata was advertising a gala showing of *Mughal-E-Azam* (The Greatest of the Moghuls), and the Europa was showing *Anastasia*. From the Bharat Mata's signboard, Dilip Kumar and Madhubala stared across the street at Yul Brynner, Helen Hayes, and Ingrid Bergman, who stared back undaunted.

At the Victoria Hotel, workers were running back and forth with stepladders, yelling at one another and trying to hang green, white, and saffron bunting on the walls and gate. Mr. Dass hovered and fretted.

"Oh, Mrs. Laird! You see how we are in a tizzy! I fear for my heart!" He placed a hand across his chest.

Mr. Ganguly, from Jana's shoulder, called, "Hello, hello! *Kya bat hai?* What's this?" turning his head to the right and the left to follow the action. Gradually, and seemingly despite everyone's best efforts, the bunting was positioned in place.

"It looks beautiful," Jana said. "How is your heart, Mr. Dass?"

"Symptoms are subsiding." Dass cast a glance over the flyers. "Very good, Mrs. Laird; we'll see that the delegates get them."

"Is everything else in order?" Jana asked.

"I *hope* so, Mrs. Laird! I've had people painting and cleaning for a month. And putting in supplies! Extra tea and coffee, extra sugar, rice, extra chutney, jam . . . What if we run out of anything essential?"

"You do have a lot of responsibility, don't you, Mr. Dass?" Jana said soothingly. "Now, you're not to worry. Everything will go absolutely swimmingly." She remembered Bandhu and the dam and wished she hadn't used that expression. "I mean to say, it will all be a great success, mark my words."

"Pray!" said Dass.

On the way home, she made a detour through the Municipal Garden. She watched a monkey snatch a banana from a picnicking couple, and smiled at a dozen schoolgirls playing hopscotch and skipping rope. In their singsong rhymes, she thought she heard them saying something about Bandhu. Mr. Ganguly listened intently. He loved picking up words from children. As they left the park, he straightened himself on her shoulder and called out, "Bandhu is a robber! Bandhu is a thief!" The little girls clutched one another with laughter and waved back at him.

Jana knew that the best way to discourage unwanted language from the parrot was to say nothing, but a chuckle slipped out, and he repeated the cry.

Speak of the devil, she said to herself, for coming out of the police station, heading right toward them, was Bandhu, his assistant trotting meekly behind him.

"Bandhu is a robber! Bandhu is a thief."

Jana stopped, picked the bird off her shoulder, and held him close, under her jacket. As usual when wrapped in cloth, he did not struggle, but she felt his tiny heart beating against her hand.

She walked right past Bandhu, giving him a polite namasté and nod. When they were out of the policeman's earshot, she let the parrot back on her shoulder again.

"*Merde*," said Mr. Ganguly.

"That's very rude," said Jana sharply, which made him say it again.

She continued down the street, past the Aaj Kal Printing Press, where the loud clacking noises announced that Rambir

was on his way to meeting another deadline; past the Giant
Rink, where strains of "Green Door" emerged from an actual
green door, along with the roar of roller skates; and past the two
cinemas, which were disgorging audiences from the afternoon
showings.

A short distance farther, she met Moustapha, on his way to
deliver a bundle of completed clothes to a customer.

"*Salaam aleikum,* Jana Auntie," he called.

"*W'aleikum salaam,*" she called back.

All these things felt familiar and comfortable. In what other
town on earth would a young man call out "Jana Auntie" to her?
And she felt good about the Futurology Convention, Mr. Dass's
fussing to the contrary. The patriotic bunting on the gates had
set a cheerful jaunty tone. The town was ready.

Once at home, she fed Mr. Ganguly, then went across to the
kitchen building. Mary had left a note: "Jana Mem. After Heating
Soup, Turn Hot Plate Off. Don't Forget. And Don't Burn Toast."
Jana considered eating the soup cold but gave in and flicked the
switch. After several moments of stirring, she did indeed turn
off the hot plate. Then she made toast, keeping her eyes fixed on
the rack, and spread it with some tinned Australian butter. Dinner achieved without burning anything or shorting out the electricity! She congratulated herself.

⁕ Opening Day at the Convention

The ballroom at the Victoria was buzzing with people fueled by
strong coffee and tea. Mr. Dass showed Jana and Ramachandran
to their seats at the head table, where their name cards said,
"Official Futurologist, Hamara Nagar" and "V. K. Ramachandran,
Chairman of the Welcoming Committee." In the center, Jana

noted, was the seat for Mrs. J. K. Paniwalla, "President of the Third Annual Futurology Convention."

At one side of the room, Rambir fussed with a tape recorder and hooked up wires. He also had a large pad of paper and a dozen pencils handy—"just in case," he'd told Jana.

Meanwhile, the delegates, who had been forming and re-forming little knots of conversation, started settling into their chairs. An African dignitary in a robe of purple, orange, and brown took his seat next to a flock of nuns in black habits. Professorial-looking men with thinning hair peered over their eyeglasses, a statistician did calculations on the back of an envelope, and around him flowed a half dozen Buddhist monks in saffron robes. All the while, Ajit Singh of H. S. Singh & Sons Photographers ran about and snapped pictures, his flash bulbs popping and crackling.

Jana was going over her welcoming statement when there was a rustle in the doorway. Heads turned as Mrs. Paniwalla, in a dazzling pink, gold, and peach sari, made her entrance. On reaching the head table, she came over and kissed the air on either side of Jana's head.

"My dear! How are you? And how is your brilliant little bird? Once the convention is well under way, I'll have to come down to your place in the bazaar and we will *chat!*"

Jana felt a touch of unease; somehow Mrs. Paniwalla didn't seem as benign as she had when she'd come into the salon earlier in the year. But Jana pushed that thought back in her mind and returned the smile. Mrs. Paniwalla sat down in her place of honor, coughed, and spoke into the microphone:

"Ladies and gentlemen! Welcome to the Third Annual Futurology Convention. All of us have seen huge changes in our lives. We have seen empires rise and fall. Beloved leaders assas-sinated. Freedom come to many! But what lies ahead? How do we chart the future? Ladies and gentlemen, we must rely on our knowledge—on our reason—but also on our hopes, our dreams, our faith, and our *intuition!* Ladies and gentlemen, I declare the convention open! And now a welcome from our local welcoming committee!"

She sat down and beamed at the applauding audience.

Next, Ramachandran stood up, leaned forward until he was practically kissing the microphone, and began:

"Ladies and gentlemen. You are here for a noble purpose: to look into the misty veils of the future without fear and with all the tools at your disposal. Sages and savants of all times have tried to do the same. You are dealing with things that do not exist yet—no tedious twice-told tales for you! All will be fresh, all will be new!

"Marcus Aurelius Antoninus said, 'Never let the future disturb you.' And Seneca said that the mind that is anxious about the future is miserable," Ramachandran noted. He proceeded with quotes from Shakespeare, Goethe, and the Bhagavad Gita. The nuns and monks listened politely; the professors jotted down notes, perhaps preparing rebuttals, and Jana noticed that Mrs. Paniwalla's eyelids were starting to close. So she was relieved when Ramachandran reached his final point, which was the welcome he was supposed to be making.

"Distinguished guests," he said, "the townspeople of Hamara Nagar are thrilled to have you in our midst. Perhaps you did not know that in this town we are fighting not only for a brilliant future but for survival itself. There are those who would like to wipe us out—destroying all traces of our past, ruining the lives of those who live in the present, and making the future impossible. We appeal to you to get to know our town. Come talk to our merchants. Each and every one of us has fashioned ourselves a unique life here, and we wish to share our talents, our products, and our happiness with you. Perhaps you'll find a treasure at the Treasure Emporium! But in any case, we hope that you will always treasure your visit. And spread the word!"

Ramachandran sat down to spirited—and relieved—clapping.

"And now," said Mrs. Paniwalla, "I'm happy to introduce our resident soothsayer, Mrs. Jana Bibi, of Jana Bibi's Excellent Fortunes."

Jana stood and started speaking into the microphone, startled at how her voice popped out of it and expanded into the room. It gave her an odd feeling of pleasure and power, and she could see why people persisted in long speeches even after their audiences had fallen asleep.

"Dear delegates," she said, "you are here to talk about the future of the world. No small task, and I know you will do it well. But sometimes, one needs to step back, look away for a moment from the panorama, and savor the cameo of one's own life. Here in Hamara Nagar, we are small, and we think that it is important to pay attention to small things as well as to large things.

"Walk down to the Central Bazaar. We can offer you a new garment for a special occasion, a remedy for a nagging ailment, a notebook in which to record your otherwise fleeting thoughts. A snack, a treasure, a fortune told—for all their smallness, each is no less important in the making of an afternoon, and an afternoon in the making of a life. I wish you all the most excellent of fortunes."

A burst of applause rewarded Jana for her talk, and the morning's speeches proceeded. A geographer told the audience that pretty soon, all the countries of the Western Hemisphere would be under the government of the United States, and that all of Europe and Asia would be in the Soviet Union. A telephone specialist said that soon there would be so many phone wires overhead that birds would get trapped and that the buzzing would be so loud that no one would hear the messages. And a climate specialist warned that if a nuclear war broke out, the earth would fall into a deep chill and all civilization would be wiped out.

On her return, Jana found Tilku and Lal Bahadur Pun on the back terrace, both smoking *biris*.

"Subedar-Major!" Jana exclaimed. "You're setting a bad example for that child. He's way too young to smoke! And it must be bad for *your* wind, too!"

"Oh, don't worry, madam, it does no harm. We are just

relaxing," said Lal Bahadur Pun. "We've been working so hard. Yesterday I played *so* many welcome marches every time a bunch of delegates arrived at the taxi station."

"And I worked hard, too," Tilku said. "I ran back and forth from the Victoria a hundred times. I wore out my shoes!" He showed her where the sole to one of his Bata shoes had fallen off.

Jana sighed. "We'll buy you some new ones."

Tilku bubbled on: "One futurologist wanted a reservation at Kwality; another wanted to find out if Bata had size forty; another wanted a notebook and blotting paper from Muktinanda's . . . one errand after another!"

"I think this futurology is an excellent thing," said Lal Bahadur Pun. "If nothing else, it brings us more work in the present."

"Yes, that is one good thing," Jana said, and went into the house.

It was late afternoon when Rambir stopped by, on his way from the convention. His eyes glowed in his bony face.

"I sent off a telegram to the *Times of India* and the *Hindustan Times*," he said. "Here, look at the carbon."

"Under the leadership of Mrs. J. K. Paniwalla," Jana read, "the delegates passed a number of resolutions pointing mankind in the direction of unity, harmony, and creativity. During the day, the various experts reported on amazing progress. We fully expect that before this turbulent twentieth century is out, mankind will have reached the moon, conquered cancer, eliminated poverty, and turned this planet into a veritable paradise."

"Inspiring sentiments," Jana said. "And fast work on your part, Rambir."

"What's even better," said Rambir, "is that Mrs. Paniwalla is delighted. I overheard her telling someone that Hamara Nagar is her favorite hill station, and that she's going to talk her husband into buying a property here."

"That's marvelous!" said Jana. "That's just what we wanted!"

"Yes, the minister of irrigation is not going to put a dam on top of his own house!"

"Bravo, Rambir, we're making progress."

"Touch wood, Mrs. Laird."

ᴄᴚ The Second Day of the Convention

Jana woke on the second day of the convention feeling optimistic about the way things had gone the day before. She said hello to the lizard on the bathroom wall, drew her bath, and heated it without giving herself an electric shock.

She had a quiet and productive morning, getting two of old Ian's waltzes down on paper, although Mr. Ganguly kept screeching, as he didn't like waltzes anywhere near as much as jigs.

"You can't come to the Why Not? with me if you make that much noise," Jana said firmly. But just to put him in a good mood, she played "Miss MacPherson Grant's Jig" and "Craigellachie Lasses," which earned her a "Good bird." When she went over to the Why Not? to meet Ramachandran for elevenses, Mr. Ganguly was riding on her shoulder.

At the Why Not?, Jana saw the African dignitary and several of the bespectacled professors from the convention, all sampling the day's special, listed on the blackboard as "Green Revolution Chapattis."

"Green chapattis?" said Jana. "Made with spinach, perhaps?"

"No, no, Mrs. Laird." Mr. Joshi put a plate of them in front of her. "Green *Revolution* chapattis—made with high-yield wheat from the Punjab. The grain of the future. But we're wrapping them around some old-fashioned whipped cream and brown sugar syrup."

"My favorite breakfast when I was five years old," said Jana.

"And mine, too," said Ramachandran.

Provided with tea and this forward-looking yet nostalgia-inducing snack, Ramachandran and Jana congratulated themselves on how well the opening day of the convention had gone.

"Your welcome was very warm and eloquent," said Jana.

Ramachandran brought his plate up to his chest to avoid dribbling whipped cream on his clean wool shawl.

"Yours too, Mrs. Laird! And people seemed very receptive to the charms of our town. I've seen several in the bazaar today, all enjoying themselves. I saw some old duffers buying canes at Garwhal Walking Sticks, and some, shall we say, young duffers going by with tennis rackets."

Mr. Joshi came over to refill the sugar bowl and threw in his two bits. "I had several conventioneers for breakfast," he said.

"Did they taste good?" Ramachandran put another lump of sugar in his tea and glanced impishly at Mr. Joshi.

"Oh ho ho . . ." Mr. Joshi laughed politely.

"The main question is," said Jana, "did they look *happy* to you? Enthusiastic?"

"Oh my, yes. Raving about the clean air and the views and the exhilaration of being at high altitude."

"Keep up the good work!" Ramachandran said.

Jana still felt good that afternoon. A convention delegate in a three-piece suit dropped by and identified himself as an astrologer to heads of state. To make sure I'm not competition, Jana thought; but apparently a quick look around put his mind to rest. A pair of the Buddhist monks came, delivered their sincere wishes for peace to her and to all sentient beings, refused tea, and went on. Then, around five P.M., a commotion in the courtyard brought Jana to the front door. There, in yet another splendid sari—this time silver and turquoise—was Mrs. Paniwalla.

"Welcome, welcome," said Jana. "You're just in time for tea in the tower."

Mrs. Paniwalla got a bit out of breath on the stairs, but once they were in the tower room, she could not contain her enthusiasm. "Oh my dear! This room is my very own fantasy." Noticing the telescope, she walked over to the window. "Do you mind if I take a peek?"

"Of course not, Mrs. Paniwalla," said Jana.

"Chickie," Mrs. Paniwalla reminded her. "Do call me Chickie." She twirled a knob on the telescope. "Our eyes are quite different, aren't they? There, that's better. Oh! It just makes you feel as if you *own* the landscape, doesn't it? I can see the *leaves* on the trees on the opposite hillside. And the boys running around the track down at the school . . . the mules coming in on the road. Oh, what I would do to be able to look at this view every day!"

Mary clattered in with the tea tray.

"Tea, Mrs. Pa—" said Jana. "I mean . . . Chickie."

"You haven't any whisky, have you?" Mrs. Paniwalla said. "I thought, being a Scot and all that . . ."

Jana went quickly to the low cabinet beneath one window and pulled out the bottle of Scotch Kenneth Stuart-Smith had given her and two small glasses. She poured a tot for Mrs. Paniwalla, then poured herself one, too.

"Quite delicious!" said Mrs. Paniwalla, her features already relaxing. "Oh, it's so lovely here! Sitting in this tower, looking out over the hills and at the plain below. I've been telling my husband that this is *exactly* what I want. Darling, I said, put that silly dam fifty miles farther back into the hills."

"Or perhaps not build it at all?" Jana suggested.

"Oh, development will have to happen somewhere or other," said Mrs. Paniwalla with a dismissive wave. "With all the people who are going to make money on it, you just can't stop it. But— for the future of *this* place, I see a return to the past."

She pointed to the ancient photograph Jana had put on the table. "The Jolly Grant House *as it was*. No dreadful little bazaar crowding around it and ruining the impression of a wonderful English country home. *Darzis'* shops and tea shops and apothecaries—we'll move all those out of sight. Poof! They're gone! It will be a model restoration project. You said you wanted tourists? That's fine, too. We'll buy up the schools and make *those* into lovely luxury hotels."

Jana's head began swimming, partly from the whisky and partly from a vision of Mrs. Paniwalla sweeping through the town with a giant broom, tossing the shops and merchants over the cliff.

"Fortunately," said Mrs. Paniwalla, "there are some progressive elements in this town. They have a modern fellow in the police department; my husband and I think highly of him."

"Of . . . of Commissioner Bandhu Sharma?" said Jana weakly.

"Yes, he'd like to clean out the town, get rid of the riffraff and the subversive elements. . . . He's in favor of the dam, of course, but if we offered him a different vision, I'm sure he would agree with that. My dear," said Mrs. Paniwalla suddenly, "how much did you say you wanted for this building?"

Jana's hand trembled as she put down her whisky glass. "I don't remember saying it was for sale."

"Oh. I heard that it was. Money's no object." Mrs. Paniwalla smiled serenely. "Just name your price."

Jana said quickly, "It's an old building. When you come right down to it, it's not really very comfortable. And not big enough for entertaining, really. There are no guest bedrooms. The original guesthouse is now Ramachandran's Treasure Emporium."

Mrs. Paniwalla flashed her very white teeth. "We'll buy that, too!"

"But Ramachandran—"

"Oh, I've done my research. He's in debt up to his ears; he'll give up that place in a flash."

The word "research," so calculating and severe, sent a chill down Jana's back. *Would* Ramachandran sell out so easily? Was he really in such trouble? Of course, he did have seven mouths to feed, soon to be eight. No, Jana mentally corrected herself, *nine*, including his own, which required a lot of feeding in itself. And Aunt Putli, that made ten! Oh, and you also had to count the minions and the ayah and the cook and . . .

"But . . . but, Mrs. Chickiewalla . . ." she stammered, "I mean . . . Mrs. Paniwalla . . . the other merchants of the quarter . . . they're very well established. Rooted, you might say. I don't think they'll want to leave."

Mrs. Paniwalla shrugged. "They may not want to. We often have to do things we don't want to do."

"As for me," Jana continued, "I just got here. I've got an old family tie to this building. I really couldn't possibly sell."

Mrs. Paniwalla gave a vague and benevolent gesture. "Ah well, let it be for the moment. . . . I don't mind if I do—just a drop more." She held out her glass.

"She finished all the whisky!" Mary observed when Mrs. Paniwalla had weaved down the staircase and out the door.

"And I think she wants to finish us, too," said Jana.

The next morning, Jana's head throbbed; she hadn't slept well and Mr. Ganguly, too, was subdued. He ignored the pieces of banana she put in his dish and didn't even say namasté.

"All right, then, have yourself a nice little sulk," Jana said.

"Jana mem is very tired." Mary put the tea tray on the table in the bay window. "Very pulled down. Here, here is good strong tea. I am bringing rumble-tumble eggs just now."

" 'Rumble-tumble' describes my life as well as the eggs," Jana said.

"No, no." Mary pointed to the view. Over the purple ridges, the wide sky was startlingly blue, about as problem-free as a sky could be. Close to the house, the dahlias were in bloom, great showy blossoms against a backdrop of green. "Everything is going to go completely well."

"You sound like a character in a film," Jana said.

However, the tea and the rumble-tumble eggs made her feel a lot more ready to face things. She scribbled notes to Ramachandran and Rambir and gave them to Tilku to deliver.

"Memsahib," said Tilku, "I run like the wind." He darted out the door, his multicolored pullover a flash of color.

Jana went out to the courtyard, where old Munar was sweeping with a traditional broom. He gave her a namasté and a red-gummed smile. *He* seemed perfectly happy and not at all worried about the future of the town or anything else, so why should she be? She heard the footsteps of the postman at the gate, took the envelope he drew out of his satchel. Another letter from Jack.

"Mother," he'd written, "I've had an unexpected whirl of social activity. I'm still sorting the correspondence and am going soon to take the postage stamps for appraisal. I'll report to you without further delay, I promise."

As requested, Ramachandran and Rambir showed up in the late afternoon to discuss their progress. Jana led them into the salon, where they settled around the table in the bay, Rambir accompanied by his inevitable notebook. Jana noticed idly that Ramachandran was wearing orange argyle socks with his sandals. It seemed a bit of a lapse from his normally classical neutral color scheme.

Mr. Ganguly had recovered from his morning sulk, and greeted Ramachandran and Rambir with not only a namasté, but also a volley of "Hello hello hello beautiful marvelous."

"I thought it would be better to talk here." Jana said. "At the Why Not? our business is everyone else's as well."

"Quite right," said Ramachandran. "You said in your note that you were worried about something."

"Yes," said Jana. "I thought Mrs. Paniwalla would be an ally, since she loves the town so much. And I get the impression that she *has* convinced her husband to put the dam elsewhere. Or will soon. But . . . maybe she likes the town *too* much. She wants to buy our buildings"—she nodded at Ramachandran—"and then tear down all the shops in the Central Bazaar."

Ramachandran looked shaken. "Oh, my word. She . . . she wants to buy us out?"

Jana studied his face, not sure how to interpret the widening of his eyes. Was Mrs. Paniwalla *right*? Would Ramachandran sell out at a moment's notice? Rambir's expression, however, was unambiguous. He resolutely set his bony jaw.

"We're not going anywhere," he said. "They are not going to divide and conquer. Let us keep our heads. Panic serves us no good whatsoever. I give you my word: I will absolutely not sell, and I will redouble my efforts to give the town good publicity. Ramachandran, do you stand with me?"

Ramachandran seemed to be struggling with considerable inner conflict, but he finally drew a deep breath and said, "I stand!"

Jana summoned up Mary's type of optimism. "Rambir, you are absolutely right. Panic serves no end. Tomorrow we may indeed have a burst of good news. I, too, stand with you."

On the last day of the conference, Jana met Kenneth Stuart-Smith at Kwality for lunch.

"Sweet-and-sour pork," said Kenneth to the waiter.

"Ham banjo." She turned to Kenneth. "I know, it's what the kids all eat. I love them, too. How were yesterday's speeches at the Victoria?"

"Well, we had your optometrist, Mr. Powell. He was brilliant," said Kenneth. "He said that in the future there would be huge telescopes allowing us to see deep into outer space. And tiny cameras that would see inside the human body. Such a quiet, unassuming man! He gave us an overview that included Galileo and Newton and people you've never even heard of. We were all stunned at his erudition."

"And your own speech?"

"I spoke on cycles in human history. Former enemies become allies, and vice versa, in an almost biological cycle. Twenty years ago, France and Germany were killing each other; now they are trading and exchanging students. The United States and China were pals, and the big enemy was Japan. Now it's the opposite."

"And the moral of the story?"

"How 'Love your enemy' isn't just a religious platitude but

makes sense, because in a few years he's going to be your friend
and trading partner anyway. It got a standing ovation from the
delegates. Those themes of reconciliation play well with Indian
audiences. I only hope I don't get fired from the State Department for heresy."

"Hope you do or hope you don't?"

"Hope I don't, of course. I've got mouths to feed."

ᴄᵇ *Moustapha Sings*

Feroze sat forward in his seat in the front row of the balcony. He
had not been in the Far Oaks auditorium since the day when
they hung the heavy brown velvet curtains he had made. At that
time, his purpose had been to make sure that the hems were
even. How long had it been? Long before the last world war, he
was sure, but time flew by so fast and played such tricks with
one's memory.

The auditorium was rustling, a pleasant, warm noise that
meant that people were happy and anticipating a good evening.
Below, Feroze could see many girls he knew—his missahib-
daughter customers—some chatting with boys, others in little
clusters, whispering and giggling. He smiled each time he recognized a dress or a skirt he had made, not always worn by the girl
for whom he had made it. Missahibs borrowed each other's
clothes a lot, no harm to it. He spotted Miss Sandra Stuart-Smith
in the audience, sitting companionably with her father, and
Miss Roo Wiley peeking out from behind the stage curtain.

Several teachers, too, he recognized. Old Miss Orley, for
whom he had made a burgundy wool suit every year or two for
the last thirty years, and Mr. Luc Bernard, the mountaineer,
there with his pregnant wife and two children.

Moustapha had left the house early, dressed in a clean white
salwar kurta and the patchwork red vest and matching hat he

had made himself. Feroze pictured him backstage, lightly finger-
ing the keys to the harmonium as he went over his song.

Feroze was pleasantly aware of the faint musky perfume of
Zohra, at his elbow. She seemed delighted to be at the show as
she chatted with Jana Bibi, commenting on the high ceiling, the
tall windows, and the rows of seating. That afternoon, after
some discussion, she had persuaded Feroze that in that audience, with all the Americans and other foreigners, she would be
less conspicuous without the black burqa than with it. The com-
promise was that she was still totally swathed, her head covered
by a pale pink shawl. "In any case," she had said, "no one will be
looking at me. They will all be looking at the stage!"

If one had a beautiful, modern young wife, Feroze said to
himself, one had to give a little here and there.

Zohra nudged him and gestured with her eyebrows at a group
of people sitting near them in the balcony. "Futurologists," she
whispered. A strange lot, Feroze thought, those people who had
been staying at the Victoria all week.

The lights dimmed; the brown velvet curtains swished slowly
apart; and the show began. Miss Roo Wiley was the opening
number, with a traditional Bharatanatyam introductory dance.
Feroze was on the alert, judging how the pleats spread when Roo
did her deep knee bends. The dance and the garment both succeeded. Zohra whispered to him, "Good costume," and Feroze
relaxed back into his seat.

Then came a skit in which the students lampooned the teachers, old Miss Orley and Mr. Bernard included. Such disrespect,
thought Feroze, but to his surprise, Miss Orley and Mr. Bernard
laughed right along with the rest of the crowd. After that there was
some European music that Feroze found hard to understand,
although he did approve of the choir robes his workers had made
for the students.

Finally, when Feroze felt one of his feet going to sleep and his
back aching from the hard wooden seat, it was Moustapha's
turn. A young white man dressed in black carried out a mat, and
another carried out Jana Bibi's harmonium and set it down in

the middle of a spotlight. A burst of applause announced Moustapha, his red vest a splash of color as he crossed the stage. Feroze, butterflies tickling his stomach, clapped along with the rest.

Then, to his surprise, out came Miss Roo Wiley. She carried a pair of tablas and settled down next to the harmonium, to an outbreak of applause from her classmates.

There was silence again. Moustapha, still standing, took a deep breath and said, "This song . . . is for my uncle."

A lump sprang to Feroze's throat. The image of a small orphan boy came to his mind, a boy crying, not understanding why he would never see his parents again, why he could never go back to his own house. He was not even Feroze's real nephew, and yet it had taken no time for him to become the joy of Feroze's heart. He and Rania, Feroze's only living child at that point, had become friends. But Rania had betrayed Feroze, and Moustapha, though not his flesh and blood, never had.

Moustapha sat cross-legged, gave the harmonium a few squeezes, and began. Out came the haunting introduction, the notes that asked a plaintive question. Then, with Miss Roo Wiley starting up the tabla accompaniment, Moustapha launched into the rhythmic body of the song.

Feroze felt a tear trickle down one cheek. At his elbow, there was a nudge from Zohra, and out of the corner of his eye, he saw her dabbing at her own face with the end of her shawl. Feroze had heard the song before, coming from Jana's tower so often during the last few weeks. But it had always been in pieces, against the background of Mr. Ganguly's competitive squawking, the bazaar noises, sometimes even Lal Bahadur Pun's bagpipes. Now he was hearing the song as it was meant to be heard.

When Moustapha finished, there was silence, then clapping and cheers, and someone started a chant of "Encore!" Moustapha stood, bowed, and left the stage, followed by Miss Roo Wiley. The demands for an encore continued, and finally Moustapha reappeared, alone, and sat down again. He made a false start on the harmonium, struck his forehead, and grinned at the audience. Everyone broke into laughter, and Feroze, too, found himself laughing. Then Moustapha began a song about how difficult and heartless the city of Bombay was. The sentiment may have been hard, but the tune was irresistibly jaunty, and within a few bars the audience was singing along and clapping.

When he finished the last line, "This is Bombay, my love!" the futurologists in the balcony were the first to stand, and then Feroze realized that everyone else was standing, too. Moustapha bowed, waved to the audience, and went off the stage, and the curtains swished shut.

After the show, the performers stood in the hall, shaking hands with all the well-wishers. From the edge of the circle of people around Moustapha, Feroze saw one of the futurologists hand Moustapha a card, and the two exchanging salaams. Moustapha was flushed, his red vest partly unbuttoned; he was talking animatedly in a mixture of Urdu and English, laughing, punch-drunk. Feroze finally managed to push into the inner circle, where he felt Moustapha's arms wrap around him in a bear hug.

"Did you like the show, Uncle? Did you like it?"

"Your song was best," said Feroze, not caring who heard or what other performer might be offended.

He made his way back to the bazaar, saying nothing as Zohra and Jana discussed every item on the program. It wasn't until they had gotten home that he realized that Miss Roo Wiley had been nowhere in sight after the show. The other thing he dimly sensed, while his heart was still full of pride for Moustapha, was that this was the beginning of an end. All those things Moustapha had been saying for months about going to Bombay, singing in films, all those things that had seemed far-fetched before . . . they might just come true.

The Day After

✧ *A Disappearance*

Jana sat in her bay window, reading *Our Town, Our Times* and enjoying Mary's poached eggs. The exhausting week was over. Now they could all get back to something resembling normal, she thought. Mr. Ganguly also seemed quietly content, first exercising his wings, then whistling something that sounded like "My Shoes Are Japanese."

She had barely started her second cup of tea when she heard a frenzied knock on the door, and without waiting for anyone to let her in, Zohra swept into the room and threw her burqa on the chair.

"Moustapha's in jail!"

"What?"

"Yes. He got into some sort of fight last night, after the show, with some of his usher friends. Bandhu's men picked them up. The other boys' fathers went to the jail and got *their* sons out by making contributions to the Homeland Purity Society, but Bandhu didn't even let *us* know he had Moustapha. Mr. Joshi of the Why Not? told us! My husband's gone down to the police station just now."

"But why did Moustapha get into a fight?"

"I have no idea. You saw him same time as I did—laughing

and happy, everyone congratulating him. . . . We started worrying around midnight, when he didn't come in. My husband thought maybe he'd done something stupid like try to sneak into the girls' dorm at the Far Oaks School. I said, 'Don't worry, he'll be with his friends,' so finally we went to sleep. But this morning, he *still* wasn't there."

"I'll send a note to the dorm to see if Roo Wiley knows anything," Jana said.

"When you learn something, *didi*, please tell me immediately!"

"Of course. Now, don't worry. This will all get sorted, I promise you."

The schoolgirl scrawl from Roo, however, did nothing to set Jana's mind at ease. "I didn't see Moustapha after the show," Roo wrote. "Douglas Benedict took me to the cast party and then walked me back to the dorm. Moustapha wasn't even at the party! We told him to come. I don't know where he went. Your harmonium is still backstage, by the way."

Zohra was back in the afternoon, with news of how Feroze had gone down to the police station.

"He sat for six hours! Six hours! At the end, the *chaprassi* told him, 'Sorry, Commissioner sahib is not available for the rest of the day.' And no one else had the authority to let a prisoner out. There was no one there even to take baksheesh! What kind of a police station is that? Worse than corrupt, I tell you." Zohra looked thoroughly disgusted.

"So now what can we do?" Jana said.

"I'm going to Yusuf Baig to see if he has any ideas. Also, can't you ask that American embassy man—Miss Sandra's father—if he can help?"

"I think he's on his way back to Delhi," said Jana.

"Ramachandran?"

"Away for one of his son's cricket matches."

"Rambir? Mr. Dass?"

"I'll try them," Jana said.

Zohra put on her burqa and hurried out the door, leaving Jana to write notes to Rambir and Mr. Dass and dispatch them via Tilku.

"Bring the answers back as quickly as you can," she said.

"Memsahib," said Tilku reproachfully. "When am I not doing that?"

Bandhu Delivers an Eviction Notice

Tilku returned in an hour with notes from Rambir and Mr. Dass, but, although they said that they would keep their ears open, neither offered any helpful information. Then, at five o'clock, there was a sharp rap on the front door. Mr. Ganguly, alert on his perch, puffed himself up and lifted a claw as if to pounce. Mary and Jana looked at each other. "I'll open it," Mary said.

A moment later, Bandhu Sharma was in the salon, with his *chaprassi* behind him.

"Good afternoon, Commissioner," Jana said.

Bandhu gave a curt nod. "Mrs. Laird."

"Will you sit down?"

"That won't be necessary."

"Have you come about . . . young Moustapha?"

"Which Moustapha?"

"Feroze Ali Khan's nephew."

"Oh, that ruffian. No. Mrs. Laird, I am here to deliver your notice to vacate this building." He held out an official-looking certificate.

"*Vacate?*" Jana felt her stomach plummeting.

"Yes. This building is being taken over by the government."

"May . . . may I ask why?"

"It is needed, madam, to use as a control tower for engineering purposes."

Jana stared at Bandhu. His face was utterly still, the mustache straight and even, with just a gleam of satisfaction in his eyes.

"Engineering purposes?" whispered Jana.

"Yes, Mrs. Laird. Surveying headquarters."

"For the dam? I was under the impression that it was going to be placed elsewhere."

"Madam, it's not for you to ask where the dam will be placed. At the end of a fortnight, if you have not left, armed guards will assist you to evacuate the building."

Jana's legs were trembling now. "Commissioner, how can you do this? This is my home. I have the title to it. My papers are in order. I am an Indian citizen."

"Eminent domain, madam. It's only done for the common good."

By now, Mr. Ganguly was swaying and hissing on his perch.

"If my department can assist you to move, don't hesitate to call on us. Just send your small boy down with a note and we'll be there in no time flat."

"But wait a minute," Jana cried. "You can't do this!"

"I'm afraid I can," said Bandhu. "In fact, I must. I have received orders to do this. I extend my condolences to your household, but I have no choice."

"*No!*" Mr. Ganguly's shriek was eardrum-piercing. The parrot was now vigorously flapping his wings and straining toward Bandhu.

"And I advise you to put your bird back in his cage."

Bandhu took one step toward Jana. And then—it happened so quickly that Jana hardly knew how—Mr. Ganguly flew the few feet toward Bandhu, landed on his shoulder, bit down sharply on his ear, and returned to Jana's shoulder. "*Badmash!*" The parrot shrieked. "*Badmash!*"

In disbelief, Bandhu raised his hand to his ear. He looked down at the blood dripping onto his clean, starched uniform.

"Mrs. Laird." Bandhu's voice was ominously controlled. "You will put that bird in a cage and follow me to the police station, immediately! Otherwise, I will be obliged to dispatch him with my club." He turned to the *chaprassi* and said, "You may put the handcuffs on Mrs. Laird."

"Mary, please get the carrying cage from the storeroom," said Jana, her heart pounding.

✑ In the Pokey

The door to the lockup swung shut behind her. Jana looked around a dim, dingy room where the only light came from the small windows high up near the ceiling. Propped up in the corner, a dejected Moustapha was sitting cross-legged on the bare floor. He was still wearing the clothes he had performed in, but the white salwar and kurta were now stained and dirty, with some dried blood on one sleeve.

Mr. Ganguly let out a screech. "Moustapha! Salaam! *Adab!*"

Moustapha leapt to his feet. "Jana Auntie! What are you doing here? You came to get me out?"

"I wish that were true," said Jana. "Bandhu's locked me up, too."

"What happened?"

"Mr. Ganguly bit Bandhu," said Jana.

In spite of himself, Moustapha gave a choked laugh, which made Jana half laugh, too, but only for a second; then she shook her head.

"Does my uncle know I'm here?" Moustapha asked.

"Yes, last I heard, he was trying to get you out. But you know how Bandhu enjoys playing with him—like a cat with a mouse."

Moustapha made a disgusted face.

"Can't somebody else help? How about that embassy man who always takes notes? Sandra Stuart-Smith's father."

"If Mary can find him. She's the only one who knows at the moment where we are."

"Mary will rescue us," Moustapha said.

They were quiet for a while. Mr. Ganguly looked small and hunched up, not touching the little dish of rice and dal that Mary had slipped into the carrying cage.

"We all need water," said Jana.

Moustapha went to the door and called out the little barred window. "Guard! We need water! For ourselves and for the bird. Did you know that the bird here is an avatar of Vishnu? You can't let him die for lack of water."

He came back and joined Jana, who was now sitting on the floor herself, her back against the wall.

"It's *cold* in here," she said.

"Wait till you've been here a whole night and a whole day," said Moustapha.

"We'll get out," Jana assured him.

"And when we do," said Moustapha, "I'm on my way to Bombay. One of the futurologists was the music director of Dreamistan Studios! He gave me his card. Bandhu took it away from me, but I had already memorized the name. And the address. I've been saying it to myself over and over so I won't forget."

"You sang superbly last night," Jana said. "Things are so utterly mad! One minute everyone's patting you on the back, and the next minute you're in jail. How did that happen? Why didn't you just go to the cast party and then go home and go to bed? Roo Wiley told me she'd invited you."

Moustapha's nostrils flared.

"That slut."

"What do you mean? She's just a little girl, Moustapha."

"Just a little typical American girl."

"So what do you know about Americans?"

"I see lots, in magazines and films and all. No morals, no standards. I was led astray because she was so friendly. 'Oh, Moustapha, you have such a good voice!'" He imitated Roo's animated way of talking. "And then playing music with me, on the stage! Making me think she was completely in love with me.

"Then, afterward . . . I went to get the harmonium backstage, and there she was. Kissing that boy who carried the harmonium out to the stage. I could have killed him. But instead I went and punched someone else in the bazaar."

"Well, that wasn't very bright of you."

Moustapha let out a deep breath. "I know. I should have stayed and punched the real culprit."

Around nine o'clock, there was a click of the padlock, and a new guard let himself in the door. A tall, well-built Sikh, he cut a striking figure in his starched uniform, with a badge fixed to his khaki turban. He held a tiffin carrier of food and a thermos, two tin plates and cups, and a couple of blankets.

"Your ayah sent this," he said, cautiously friendly in tone. He gestured toward Mr. Ganguly. "This is the bird everyone is talking about? Can he tell my fortune?"

"Not without cards," said Jana. "But he might talk to you. Tell him hello."

"Hello!"

"*Sat Sri Akal!*" Mr. Ganguly gave the proper Sikh greeting— God is truth—and the guard's face broke into a delighted smile.

"You may take him on your arm if you like," said Jana. "Here . . ." She opened the door to the cage, and the man held out his arm.

"I will tell my wife," the guard said. "I will say, I held the famous parrot!"

"I wonder why the Commissioner bothered to put Mr. Ganguly in *here*," said Jana. "Why didn't he just throw him into the pot and eat him for stew?"

"He knows," said the guard.

"Knows what," said Jana.

"Knows the reputation the bird has. So he's being a little cautious."

Mr. Ganguly flapped his wings.

"It's very nice to feel a small creature like that on one's arm," said the guard. "It's like holding a child, so small and trusting. Thank you, madam."

He returned Mr. Ganguly to Jana.

"Come back soon," said the parrot, as the guard let himself out the lockup room door and clicked the padlock shut.

"We might as well eat." Jana gave one of the tin plates to Moustapha and ladled out some rice and dal from the tiffin carrier. Then she unscrewed the cup of the thermos bottle and found a note from Mary.

"Jana mem, not to worry," it said.

Bandhu Under Siege

❧ The Demonstration

Feroze had just finished his noontime prayer and rolled up his prayer rug when Zohra came into the room. Her burqa was on over her clothes, but the face piece was pulled back.

"I have been talking to Mary," she said. "She has been spreading the word. We are going to tell Bandhu what we think of him. We must stand up for your nephew—and for my sister Jana Bibi!"

Feroze had never seen his wife's face set in such a resolute expression. He had heard about Razia Sultana, a lady warrior who had ruled Delhi in the days of old. Was Zohra perhaps descended from such martial stock?

"We are taking direct action," she said. "Come, we will march. Together."

Feroze drew a deep breath. There would be a crowd. He feared and distrusted crowds—anything could happen; one minute everything would be peaceful, and the next minute buildings would be burning down or policemen would be charging forward with their sticks. Yet how could he look like a coward in front of his wife?

He put on his best high-collared coat and squared his astrakhan hat firmly on his head.

"I am ready," he said, as a blast of bagpipe music came from the street.

As they stepped out the door, Feroze and Zohra bumped into Mary, who was carrying a large sign that said, "Free Jana Bibi!," and Tilku, whose placard said, "Free Moustapha!" Old Munar the sweeper limped along after them, and his sign said, "Free Mr. Ganguly." As they made their way down the street, they were joined by Abinath and Muktinanda. Then, as fast as his portly frame would allow, came Ramachandran, flanked by his twin daughters, and Rambir with a tape recorder and notebook in hand.

They marched toward the English Bazaar. Once in the square in front of the police station, Feroze saw that there was already a crowd: the bearers and housemaids and messenger boys from the Victoria, Roo Wiley and her friends from the Far Oaks School, the ushers from the Bharat Mata.

"What is happening?" a rickshaw puller asked Feroze.

"They are telling Bandhu what they think of him."

"Aré! Come over here, you people," the man called to several more rickshaw pullers, who left their vehicles on the edge of the square and came running. "Down with Bandhu and his regulations and his fines," one said. "We piss on his police station!"

Next to arrive were a couple dozen Tibetan peddlers. "We'll wheel our carts where we want to," they cried. Road crew workers and Nepalese charcoal carriers were next, waving flags and yelling, "Down with tyrants! Free the prisoners!"

Next, to Feroze's amazement, came Ramachandran's wife's astrologer, carrying an incense holder, with a number of small boys following behind him, all intoning religious chants with their eyes closed.

The town madman ambled over, his eyes lighting up at the shouting and commotion, and he joined in, yelling something incomprehensible and waving his arms. The cows abandoned the tomatoes at the vegetable stands and joined the crowd, their moos blending with Lal Bahadur Pun's bagpipes, and stray dogs barked frantically. An army of monkeys skittered across the roofs and, brown eyes glaring, started throwing pebbles at the police station.

Manju and Raju

Inside the lockup, Jana could hear shouts coming from somewhere in town.

"What's going on?" she asked the surly guard who had replaced the amiable Sikh.

"Ruffians protesting higher prices," he said.

Another hour went by; the surly man finished his shift, and the Sikh was back, bringing food from Mr. Joshi at the Why Not?

Jana unwrapped the package to find a huge supply of samosas, *pakoras,* and potato *parathas.* "Take," she said to Moustapha, and she also held the package out to the guard. She fed Mr. Ganguly some pieces of *paratha,* then ate one herself.

They had just finished this unexpected little feast when a rap came on the door, and the guard went over and peered through the grate. He paused, then opened the door to let in a little boy in a sailor suit, straining forward and dragging his mother behind.

"Don't tell anyone we came!" said Manju. "Raju pulled me here."

Raju ran over to Jana and Mr. Ganguly and held out his arm, and Mr. Ganguly stepped up onto the tiny wrist, flapped his wings, and said, "Namasté!" A smile spread across Raju's face, and he looked up at his mother.

"He likes it when people greet him, too," said Jana, but Raju shut his lips in a firm line.

"We can only stay one minute," said Manju. "I don't want this guard to lose his job."

Meanwhile, Mr. Ganguly was asking Raju, "What's your name? Your name? Your name?"

Still Raju said nothing.

"Maybe he should go back in his cage," said Jana, and she took Mr. Ganguly onto her own arm. A disappointed look came over Raju's face.

"Your name?" said the parrot again.

"Come, Raju," said Manju. "We have to go home now."

The shouting outside continued, but the lockup seemed a little bubble of silence as Raju struggled with something. Finally, he took a deep breath and said, in a barely audible voice, "Raju."

"Your name?" repeated Mr. Ganguly.

"Raju." The voice was a little louder this time, and again, the parrot asked the same question. This time "Raju!" came out very loud, with a note of triumph. "My name is Raju."

"Raju zindabad," said the parrot.

Manju was transfixed. She looked at Mr. Ganguly, and at Jana, and then, tears streaming, she ran over and bent and scooped up Raju and covered his face with kisses. "I love you, Raju, my beautiful boy! Say something more. Say something more for your mother."

"Mummy-ji! Mummy-ji! I love you, too!"

"The bird has worked a miracle," Manju sobbed. "And my husband says he's going to bring it home and that I have to kill it and cook it."

"No! No!" shouted Raju.

Jana turned to the Sikh policeman. "Can you perhaps smuggle the bird out and hide him somewhere for a while?"

After a moment of hesitation, the policeman said, "Yes, I will do that."

Together, Manju and Raju let out a cry of "Thank you!" But their thanks were cut short by the sound of footsteps, and then the door burst open, startling everyone. Jana held Mr. Ganguly closer to her, and could feel the bird's heart beating furiously. Bandhu was among them, stick in hand.

"What are you doing here!" he bellowed at Manju and Raju.

Raju dived behind his mother, sobbing.

"I brought the child," Manju said, "because I thought—"

"What did you think? It's not your business to think!"

Manju seemed to be reaching a decision. She took a deep breath and drew herself up to her full height, her lower lip trembling. She looked Bandhu straight in the eye. "Very well. Not *thinking*. I brought him because I *knew* the bird would make him talk!"

Mr. Ganguly, now in the threat position, screamed, "Go away! Go away!"

"Mrs. Laird," said Bandhu, "you won't use my son to save your malicious and dangerous pet. Hand him over to the guard at once!"

But no one moved, everyone frozen in a strange little tableau. Then, quietly, Raju unwrapped his arms from Manju's waist and went over to his father.

"Papa-ji."

From outside, the sounds of shouting and chanting were growing louder. Bandhu started, his eyes wide with disbelief.

"Papa-ji," said Raju, "that bird is my friend."

Jana stared at Bandhu. Were those *tears* springing to his eyes? As everyone in the room held their breath, Bandhu, his arms out, took a step toward Raju.

"Raju? My son . . ."

"Papa-ji, the bird is my friend. Don't hurt my friend. Please don't hurt my friend."

"You spoke?" Bandhu said. "You are speaking?" He turned to Manju. "Did you hear him?" And then to Raju again, "What did you say?"

"I said, don't hurt my friend."

Bandhu's voice dropped to a whisper. "I won't, then."

The next moment Raju was running toward his father and Bandhu was lifting him up, and both were laughing and crying at the same time.

"Mrs. Laird," said Bandhu, "kindly hand the bird over to my son. Manju and Raju, follow me."

The guard opened the door again, and Bandhu gestured to Manju and Raju to go out. Raju, his face a mixture of happiness and bewilderment, turned to look back at the prisoners. There was a sudden flutter of green, and before Jana knew what was happening, Mr. Ganguly had flown out the door, into the late-afternoon light.

Over the Khud

◦◦ Feroze's Long Night

Feroze and Zohra and Moustapha arrived home just as the late-afternoon call to prayer was sounding. Feroze quickly did his ritual washing, took his prayer mat out, and went through the motions, but when he had finished, his heart was not in the peaceful state it should have been.

"You had to be so stupid to go and get in a fight!" Feroze started with his voice low, but before he knew it, he was yelling. "Have you no sense? What will everyone say? Yusuf Baig is already telling me his friends don't want their daughter to marry you after all."

"Good!" Moustapha stared daggers into his uncle's eyes.

"What do you mean, good!"

"I mean, I wasn't going to marry her, so what does it matter?"

Feroze felt as if his head was filled with too much blood, and his heart was beating far too hard in his chest. "You'll do what you're told to do."

"That's where you're wrong," said Moustapha. "You think I'm just going to stay here my whole life, cutting out gym uniforms, you're completely wrong."

"The life of a *darzi* isn't enough? You're too good for this life?"

"Please, please, don't fight," Zohra pleaded. "We've already had enough trouble! Come, eat!"

"I'm not hungry!" said Moustapha.

"I'm not, either!"

"You haven't eaten since morning," cried Zohra to Feroze. "I beg you, just eat something."

"I can't eat in this state," said Feroze.

"Walk a little bit then," said Zohra. "Walk until your head clears. Then come back. Moustapha, you go somewhere else. And come back when you're prepared to be polite to your uncle."

Moustapha said, "Prepared to be polite? That will be a long time from now!"

"Leave this room," yelled Feroze.

"Gladly," said Moustapha.

When Moustapha was gone, Feroze was still trembling. He said to Zohra, "That boy has brought disgrace upon us."

Zohra said, "He is young, he makes mistakes. This happens. He will come back and beg your forgiveness, I'm sure of that."

"I won't forgive him!" said Feroze. "I'm going to take the air."

"Yes, go, that's a good idea," said Zohra.

He set off toward the Upper Bazaar. The desired state of calm did not come to him; he kept walking, past the little Tibetan stores and tobacco and *paan* shops. He passed from the Upper Bazaar to the main road leading to the Far Oaks School, growing more and more tired. The light was fading. He stood, looking out over the mountains, exhausted, now more sad than angry, and decided to turn around.

The Far Oaks School was well behind him, the Upper Bazaar still ahead. He came to a stretch of road that had washed out repeatedly in the monsoon. There was still no parapet. Where is the government? Feroze thought crossly. Weren't they supposed to maintain the road? British government, Hindu government, kings, this democracy arrangement—if there was one thing they were all supposed to do, it was to maintain the roads.

Suddenly he heard hoofbeats, first muffled, then loud and close. He stepped back toward the retaining wall just in time to see Sandra Stuart-Smith, fifty feet ahead, jump aside to miss the oncoming runaway horse. She escaped the galloping hoofs, but he saw that she had dropped her handbag. Once the horse was gone, Feroze looked over the *khud* and saw the handbag caught on a scrubby bush growing out of the hillside. Then he saw Sandra peer over the side and, one hand against the hill, edge down on a rough path. The back of her cardigan caught on a bush, but eventually she recovered the bag. She was resting on a ledge when a pile of stones and mud, disturbed by the horse, slid down, blocking the path, and left her trapped.

"Missahib," he called. "Missahib!"

She looked up, a flash of relief crossing her face. Below her, the mountainside dropped off in a jagged knife edge. Feroze could hear, way below, a stream gushing.

Best to run back to the school, Feroze thought, and find Bernard sahib, with his hooks and ropes. But Sandra was yelling something to him.

"Feroze Ali Khan, can you pull me up?"

In the failing light, Feroze could still see part of the path. If he could get most of the way down, he could take off his coat and hold one sleeve; she could grab the other one and scramble back to the road. He sidled carefully down the path, stood at the top of the rock pile, and called to Sandra: "Missahib! Take! I will pull." She nodded, and he threw down his coat, hanging on to one sleeve.

The moment Feroze started tugging to pull Sandra up, the rocks and earth slid again. Now nothing was holding firm; Sandra was yelling, Feroze was sliding, and Sandra was tugging on the coat with all her might. There was a ripping sound and Feroze fell back suddenly, with one sleeve in his hand. Next, he saw Sandra falling into a little cavity in the mountainside. With a sudden burst of strength, he pushed himself over the rubble and collapsed next to her. There he sat, trembling from the effort. He was still holding the sleeve to his coat, and he saw the rest of the coat in the dirt.

"Are you all right?" said Sandra.

He looked out toward the ravine, now almost completely in the dark, and to the side, where the pile of rocks was still shifting and sliding. "All right" didn't describe the situation very well. Yet . . . "I am all right," said Feroze. *"Inshallah."* He put the coat on, and then the single sleeve.

Sandra brushed the dirt off her dress and her legs and thought for a while.

"I have a flashlight in my bag," she said. "We could signal."

She aimed the flashlight toward the town. "My dad taught me some Morse code once. For help, you do three shorts and three longs and three shorts, or the other way around. I can never remember. I'll just do both."

Across the ravine, lights were going on in the Upper Bazaar and the Central Bazaar. A tall structure on one building stuck out above the rest, the lookout tower to the Jolly Grant House. The sundown call to prayer echoed, faint and quavering on the wind.

Sandra's flashlight, not strong to begin with, lasted for only a few minutes before going out. "I have a pocket mirror that might work," she said. But it didn't seem to flash enough light over to the town, and she put it back in her bag.

"I hope someone rescues us soon," said Sandra. "I have medicine I have to take. Otherwise I get seizures."

"What is that, missahib?"

She grimaced. "Shaking." She rolled her eyes back in her head.

"Ah," said Feroze. "The falling sickness."

"Yes," she said.

Feroze thought this over. Some said seizures were the work of the devil, others a sign of divine favor. Some even said the Prophet (praise be upon him) also had seizures, during which he had visions, although others said that was a lie. In any case, Feroze hoped that Sandra would not have a seizure while they were sitting in a small cavity in the mountainside.

"Not to worry, missahib," Feroze said. "I know that kind of sickness. It will pass."

Time passed, the clock tower chiming each hour from the Central Bazaar. Feroze and Sandra Stuart-Smith sat next to each other, shivering, saying nothing. Would it be better to talk or not to talk, Feroze asked himself. He had never been trapped on a hillside with anyone before, let alone with a girl whose life was, except for her clothes, a complete unknown to him. What should one say? What in her life would be at all similar to his own? Family, perhaps? He finally asked, "Missahib's parents are in Delhi?"

"My father's supposed to be," said Sandra. "He left here. He should be in Delhi by now."

"And missahib's mother?"

To Feroze's distress, the girl started to weep. Her mother is dead, he thought. I have asked the wrong question, and now she is weeping.

"Missahib's mother has—gone to heaven?"

"No, she's not dead," said Sandra. "She's back in the States."

"In America," said Feroze.

"Yes. My parents are getting divorced. It's final next month."

"Oh," Feroze said slowly. "I'm sorry, missahib."

He sighed heavily. He had heard that there was a lot of divorce in the West; it went with the immorality, the alcohol, the cinema.

Sandra stopped suddenly, as if she had just remembered that she had resolved *not* to cry. "Oh, it's just the way things are. My mother ran off with someone else. And my father will probably marry his secretary." She gave a bitter little laugh. "So then they'll all be happy. You'd think grown-ups would act like grown-ups. Hah."

"Sometimes people act correctly, and sometimes they do not," said Feroze.

Sandra reached into her handbag, broke a chocolate bar in

two, and handed one half to Feroze. He hesitated, then took it. "*Shukriya.*"

The chocolate was a moment of sweetness in his mouth, and it briefly damped down the hunger pangs.

There was another long silence. Feroze racked his brain for something more to say. Finally he asked, "Do you like this place, missahib? I mean, this *town*. This *country*."

Sandra took a while to answer. "It's all right, I guess. I mean, the mountains are pretty. If you like mountains."

"School is good, no?"

"No," said Sandra, "I don't like this school. I'd rather go back to my old school."

Feroze's mind strayed briefly to his own school days, sitting in a row chanting verses from the Qur'an by memory, and hoping the teacher wouldn't slap him across the head if he forgot one. Did the teachers whack this girl in the head? That would not be good for her seizures.

"The teachers in your school are not kind?" Feroze thought of his customers Miss Orley and Mr. Bernard. They both seemed very kind indeed.

"Oh yes, some of them," said Sandra. "Some aren't. Some are dumb. Really stupid."

Shocked by this disrespect for one's elders, Feroze decided to change the subject.

"Missahib has brothers and sisters?"

"Two little brothers. They're really brats, but they can be pretty funny."

She shifted her weight in the dark and asked, "Do you have any children?"

"My nephew," said Feroze.

"That's all?"

"I had a daughter . . ." He never spoke of Rania. But why not, here on this ledge, to this unhappy girl? "She ran away. To be in films."

"Really? Wow!" Sandra's voice went up, and Feroze regretted that he had said anything. The girl hadn't understood at all.

"No wow. Bad thing, missahib," said Feroze. "Very bad. We arranged her marriage; everything was ready; then she disappeared. Our whole family was dishonored." He cringed at the memory of the scandal.

"But maybe she'll get famous and rich and then everyone will say, Oh, you're so lucky. Your daughter will take care of you in your old age."

Feroze gave an almost noiseless snort.

The temperature had dropped, and Sandra made a sniffling sound.

"Don't be sad, missahib," Feroze said.

"I'm not sad. I'm *cold*." Even under normal circumstances, her dress was not warm enough for the season, nor were her stockings and delicate leather pumps. He took off his coat. "Here, take."

"No, no," she said. "Then you'll be cold."

"Take, missahib."

She put the coat around her shoulders.

"Thank you," she said. "*Shukriya*. Feroze Ali Khan, do you think anyone's ever going to find us?"

"Of course, missahib! They're out looking right now. Everyone will be looking."

"I'm going to shout," she said.

She tried to stand up, but the little cavity in the hillside was not big enough. She leaned out and yelled, at the top of her voice, "Help!" She screamed again, louder and higher, but her cries were drowned out by the wind. Finally, she gave up.

"Feroze Ali Khan, why are you so calm? Aren't you afraid?"

Why was he so calm? He looked up and saw the stars coming out, saw tiny wisps of cloud floating by.

"Feroze," Sandra said, "*are* you afraid?"

He drew a deep breath.

"No, Sandra missahib."

No, he was not. Tonight he was on a small ledge, talking to another human being. That's what human life was: a brief stay on a narrow ledge before a plunge down the precipice into the unknown. All you could do was share your thoughts with the person sitting next to you, whoever that might be. What good was fear, thought Feroze. Fear, as his friend Yusuf Baig was always saying, was a result of inadequate faith—and did it ever change anything?

There followed a long silence, while Feroze looked up at the full family of stars now dancing in the sky. A new topic of conversation occurred to him.

"Missahib has ridden on a ship?"

"Oh, yes." Her voice was full of enthusiasm.

"Good? You liked it?"

"I loved it." The girl's voice sparkled with enthusiasm. "There was this big dining room with huge menus in leather covers, and white tablecloths and sparkling clean crystal and lots of different forks and butter curled into little balls and good French bread. And you could walk on the deck and play shuffleboard and go to movies. Just like being in a little town at sea. Actually, there was more to do than in *this* town."

Feroze could make no sense of the flood of details. But one thing was clear: Miss Sandra Stuart-Smith liked ships. He continued.

"Missahib has ridden on a plane?"

That, too, brought a gush of information.

"Yes, planes are fun, too," said Sandra. "I like getting a new Pan Am bag and all those little goodies they stuff into it. Like fold-up slippers and a sleeping mask. It's fun to open up the little packages and see what's in there."

Again the details were very mysterious, but the tone of voice was clear. Planes were a pleasure.

"And train travel?" he asked.

"They're okay," said Sandra. "It's fun to look out the window. People wave to you."

In peacetime, Feroze thought, that is quite possible. In peacetime, trains would not be full of dismembered and bloodstained corpses. Perhaps—maybe he could actually go on a train and enjoy it. Or a ship, or an airplane. He could make the hajj, and be called "Hajji," just like his friend Yusuf Baig.

Now Sandra was asking *him* questions again, which felt strange but only fair.

"Do you like being a *darzi*?"

Feroze thought of his workshop and of the sound of sewing machines humming and of the feeling of the needle as it slipped through the cloth.

"Yes, it pleases me," he said.

"Why?"

"It is my work," said Feroze. "It was my father's. And his father's. My family has been stitching for five hundred years. We stitched for the Emperor Shah Jehan. And then for the British sahibs and memsahibs. And now for young American sahibs and missahibs."

Feroze could almost hear Sandra's mind working on something. "Feroze Ali Khan. Here's something I want to know about India. Did you have an arranged marriage?"

"Yes and no."

"What do you mean, yes and no?"

"The first time," Feroze said, "my parents chose. Then that wife died. The second time, I chose."

"Aha," said Sandra.

Now she seemed to be getting up the courage to ask something else. "So . . . you . . . do you love your wife?" There was curiosity in her voice but an edge, too, Feroze thought, a bitterness. He was grateful for the darkness as he felt the blood rush to his face.

"My wife . . . is a good woman. Very strong and intelligent."

Sandra persisted. "I just want to know: do you really love her?"

Feroze took a deep breath. There was nothing to do but tell the truth to this curious missahib sitting next to him in the dark. "She is . . . she is the air I breathe."

Sandra's voice caught. "I hope someone says that about me someday." He heard a sniff, and he realized she was wiping away tears. "I thought that was how my mother and father felt about each other. But I guess not." She put her head down on her knees and hugged her legs to her chest.

After a while, Sandra slid down and curled up, and Feroze

realized that she was asleep. His coat had slipped off her, so he arranged it around her shoulders. He wrapped the single sleeve around his neck, like a muffler. It is too cold for me to ever sleep, he thought, but near dawn, he dozed off.

Feroze had only slept an hour or so when he heard Sandra stirring.

"I'm awake," she said. "But I feel really strange. I think I'm going to . . ."

The next minute, she was having the seizure she had warned Feroze about. Feroze had told her not to worry, but in reality he had never seen such a thing, only heard about it secondhand. He noticed that her head was banging against the side of the hillside, and he shifted her as best as he could. The shaking seemed to last a very long time, but at the end, Feroze supposed it had been less than a minute, and then Sandra lay still.

A few minutes later, she opened her eyes. "Damn," she said. "I'm sorry."

"No need to be sorry, missahib."

Between the tears of the night before and the grit dislodged from the hill, her face was streaked with dirt.

After the bitterly cold night, the sun pouring in from the east brought welcome warmth to Feroze's cramped body. He found he could half stand, his head emerging from the small cave. For several minutes, he shouted at the top of his lungs, his calls mixing with the cawing of the crows. There was no answer.

"Missahib?" he said. "Miss Sandra? Where is that mirror? Let us try again."

She reached into her handbag and handed it to him. Almost automatically, he glanced at himself; he was shocked by the old man with the grayish-brown face he saw. Quickly, he tipped the mirror away, then starting flicking it to catch the sun's reflection. Short-short-short, long-long-long, short-short-short, or the other way around; either way would do, he thought as he flashed a call for help from Miss Sandra Stuart-Smith and himself, Feroze Ali Khan.

·⌀ *Flashing Lights*

The alarm clock shrilled, shocking Jana into consciousness. She felt battered. The overnight in the jail had been long, cold, and uncomfortable, and then, after she and Moustapha had been released, the search for Mr. Ganguly had been exhausting. Armed with flashlights, Lal Bahadur Pun, Tilku, Munar, and she had circled the square, the Municipal Garden, and the grounds of the Victoria Hotel. They'd gone up and down the side roads and out into the woods, calling. But to no avail.

She pulled on her workaday clothes and went down to the salon. The empty bird mansion looked desolate and accusing. She went over to the window seat, but somehow the sun seemed too bright for her; in fact, there was something glittering on the hillside that hurt her eyes. She turned her back on the view.

"Jana mem, eat something." Mary was there, with a scrambled egg and a pot of tea.

"I'm not hungry," Jana said.

"One bite." What Mary used to say to the children.

One bite led to the next, and after the egg and two cups of tea, Jana admitted that she felt more willing to face the world.

"Memsahib?" It was Tilku, a look of determination having replaced his usual high-wattage smile.

"Yes, Tilku."

"Today, we look some more. Right?"

She drew a deep breath. If they found Mr. Ganguly . . . she was afraid that at best they would find a small dead body, although even that was unlikely. A vulture would have carried it off, or a dog, or even a rat. She shuddered at the thought.

"*I* will look," Tilku said firmly.

"Both of us will," said Jana.

Jana walked slowly through the town, peering up at the eaves and balconies, into the alleyways. Tilku ran ahead, into shops, tell-

ing everyone to keep their eye open for the famous parrot, telling people how the bird had made Bandhu Sharma's son talk,
telling them they would have especially good luck for a long
time if they happened to find the bird. He and Jana went to the
mosque and asked the muezzin if he'd seen a parrot in the
tower; to the temple, where they asked the temple priest if he'd
heard, above the tinkling of the bells, the screech of a bird. The
rickshaw pullers said they would keep on the lookout, and so did
the Tibetan peddlers, and the Nepali charcoal carriers.

"He loves the birdbath in the Municipal Garden," Jana said.

They turned in at the gate, and found Mr. Powell walking his
dogs, binoculars in hand. On hearing the problem, he scanned
the trees in the park, then shook his head. A flock of parrots
took off from the trees, as if the foliage itself had suddenly risen
and flown away.

"Like looking for a needle in a haystack, isn't it," said Jana.

"Don't despair," Mr. Powell said.

But she felt very despairing as she and Tilku went back to the
house.

As soon as they had gotten back to the Jolly Grant House, Mary
hit Jana with another piece of news.

"Feroze Ali Khan is missing! Moustapha and the cousins have
been out looking for him since dawn."

Moments later, Kenneth Stuart-Smith arrived, his shirt crum-
pled and a dark stubble on his face.

"Have they found her?" he asked.

"Her?" said Jana.

"Sandra."

"Oh *no.*" *Another* missing person?

"I was at an official function last night, and at about ten
o'clock, the embassy sent someone to find me. The school had
called to say Sandra wasn't in the dorm. Thank God the call got
through; you can't always count on that! Anyway, I was on the
road an hour later. I'm on my way to the school now. But I

thought I should stop and see if *you* have any idea where she might be."

"No," said Jana slowly. "I really can't imagine." She thought of the times she'd seen Sandra in town, out of bounds and breaking the school rules. Could the girl have taken a taxi to Dehra Dun and run away by train? Or—could she have fallen over the *khud*, maybe not even very far away from here?

"Let's go up into the tower," Jana said.

In the tower, Kenneth Stuart-Smith put his eye to the telescope.

"We used to look out here during the war. The idea that the Japanese would get all the way up here was far-fetched, but we kept watch every day even so."

He stepped away from the telescope.

Jana said, "Do you see something funny on the side of the hill in between the town and the school?"

He looked back into the eyepiece. "There is a glinting . . . wait . . . it's actually a message, I think. And there's a man sort of sitting with his knees up."

He stepped aside to let Jana look.

"It's Feroze Ali Khan . . ." she said. "And I see another pair of legs sticking out, too. Those little shoes . . . they look like the ones Sandra wears."

Kenneth Stuart-Smith set off at a run toward the school, leaving Jana to go across to Royal Tailors and tell them that Feroze had been found.

In the Golden Rain Tree

⚘ *Tilku to the Rescue*

When Jana got back, Tilku was in the courtyard, desperate to continue the search. They set off again, this time covering the Upper Bazaar and the villas of Maharajah's Hill. Again their calls brought no familiar answering cries of "Namasté" or "Salaam." They returned to the Central Bazaar, shaking their heads at the questioning looks from Mr. Joshi and Abinath and Muktinanda.

"One more time to the Municipal Garden," Tilku said.

"All right."

Inside the park gate, Jana caught a glimpse of a burly man in khaki, flanked by a little woman in a pale yellow sari and a little boy pulling forward. She tensed. Bandhu Sharma was the last person in this town she wanted to see. But Tilku ran forward, calling out to them. The trio turned, and Raju ran up to Tilku.

"We're looking for the parrot," Raju said, loudly and clearly.

"Raju," called Manju, "come back here."

But the two boys were already skirting the ironwork fence surrounding the gardens, calling into the trees. Jana, now face-to-face with Bandhu and Manju, said, with a great effort to keep her voice neutral, "Good afternoon, Commissioner, Mrs. Sharma." Bandhu gave a nod and an equally noncommittal "Good afternoon," but Manju dropped to touch Jana's feet.

"No, no," said Jana, lifting Manju quickly by the shoulders. "No need . . ."

"But my boy is now talking . . ."

"Because he decided to. Because he wanted to."

From the other side of the park, there was suddenly a cry. Raju and Tilku were standing under the spreading branches of the golden rain tree, pointing upward. Tilku started to climb, and Raju followed him. Bandhu headed toward them at a sprint, Jana and Manju rushing after him.

"Come down!" Raju called, his head cocked to the branches above.

"*Tota sahib!*" called Tilku. "Mr. Ganguly!"

There was Mr. Ganguly, higher than he'd ever flown before, flapping an occasional despairing flap, and utterly stuck, like a kitten needing to be rescued.

Jana joined in, calling, "Come down," but the bird did not budge.

"I'm going farther," said Tilku, and he heaved himself up to the next level of branches, and then to the next. When he was one level away from Mr. Ganguly, he stood upright on a branch and edged over, holding on to the branch above.

"*Tota sahib*, crawl onto my arm. Come onto my shoulder." Tilku's voice was calm, soothing. "Don't worry. We'll get down out of the tree."

Jana felt her heart speeding as she looked up and saw the branch Tilku was standing on bounce up and down. Maybe it's a good thing that the child hasn't gained the weight I've been trying to put on him, she thought.

"Come on, *tota sahib*!" Raju, too, was calling, imitating Tilku's calm voice.

"Now all be quiet," Tilku called softly.

A noisy crowd had gathered at the base of the tree, but Jana and Manju and even Bandhu shushed them. Mr. Ganguly edged forward on the branch, stepped onto Tilku's thin wrist, and made his way down Tilku's arm to his shoulder. The crowd kept silent as Tilku carefully edged across the branch and lowered himself down the tree, Raju scrambling to get down ahead of him. When they were within a few feet of the ground, Raju tumbled into Bandhu's open arms, Mr. Ganguly flew to Jana's shoulder, and the crowd burst into cheers. Tilku, once on the ground, gave a leap of triumph, yelling, "Mr. Ganguly zindabad!"

And the parrot answered, "Tilku *ki-jai*! Tilku *ki-jai*!"

And Raju, too, echoed, "Tilku *ki-jai*!"

·❧ *Just Paper*

Mr. Ganguly seemed little the worse for his adventure, but Jana was exhausted for the next two days. Bandhu's eviction notice was still sitting on top of the manuscript of old Ian's tunes, and the move-out deadline was now only ten days away. An image flitted through Jana's mind of uniformed men marching in to deposit them all on the street.

What could they do? Barricade themselves inside and station Lal Bahadur Pun at the gate to keep out all comers with a wall of sound? Appeal to some higher-up governmental authority? But to whom? Where? In Dehra Dun? Delhi?

Distractedly, she shuffled the deck of Hindu gods, turned down half a dozen on the salon table, and said to Mr. Ganguly, "Pick a card, please."

Lakshmi, goddess of wealth.

"Some wealth would be nice, certainly," she said. "I wonder if the card is telling me to just pay a bundle of baksheesh to Bandhu and be done with it. Let's try the tarot cards. Pick one of these," she told Mr. Ganguly.

"Aha. The Hanged Man." A young man hanging upside down. Well, things were definitely in suspension. When she turned the card upside down, the fellow appeared to be dancing. It's all point of view, she thought.

She studied her palm and got no answer there. She'd had no

dreams for several nights. The fact was, she just *didn't know* what was going to happen or what to do.

She had put her head down on the table, discouraged, when Mary came with the account books.

"What is this, Jana mem? Feeling pulled down again? Everything is better now."

"Except we've still got this—" Jana held up the eviction notice.

"Just paper!" Mary said. "What can paper do to you? I say tear it up. Just keep living, Jana mem. Put the music on the page. Everything will be all right, I promise."

"But we don't even know for sure that the dam has been canceled."

"Tilku says it has."

"*Tilku?*"

"Yes, Jana mem. Remember—he plays in the park every day with Raju, who can now repeat things he hears. And Tilku eavesdrops every day outside the police station."

"Aha," said Jana.

"Just do your work, Jana mem. Everything will be all right."

When Mary had left, Jana held the eviction notice in her hands for a moment, deciding. What difference would it make whether she ripped it up? Nonetheless, she tore it in two, and then in two again, and put the pieces in Mr. Ganguly's cage.

"Have some fun," she said, and Mr. Ganguly went to work, shredding with abandon.

Hamara Nagar in the News

◦ƒ The Philosopher-Tailor

Rambir was in the salon, red-eyed and rumpled but triumphant.

"I stayed up all night writing the story," he said to Jana. "And then copying it onto one of those forms to send the telegram! So by now, the *Times of India* should already have it. And All India Radio, too. Finally we're going to put this town on the map."

"*Jai Hind! Jai Hind!*" squawked Mr. Ganguly, beating the air with his wings.

Jana felt that if she had any wings, she would flap hers, too. "What did you put in the story?"

"I made it a people-to-people story. Mostly about Feroze. The philosopher-tailor! I wrote about how he tried to rescue the young girl, and how they were both trapped on the mountainside all night, and how they made conversation to the best of their ability."

"Rambir, you did really well. Bravo."

"Really, I haven't felt so alive since my student days, when I would stay up all night to get the campus newspaper out on time. Of course, I never felt like *this* in the morning during those days."

"Well, you have all day to sleep."

"Alas!" said Rambir. "I'm *way* behind on the paper. And the press has developed this little hiccup where it doesn't print, and then all of a sudden spits out the pages faster than we can catch them."

"Oh dear," Jana said. "Why don't I send Tilku to help you? He can catch the pages as they fall. And then he can deliver them, too."

Two days later, Rambir dropped by again, triumphantly waving a long telegram.

"Look at this! All India Radio is sending a reporter to tape Feroze reading from his notebook! They'll play the readings right after the news and just before the Urdu ghazals. And the reporter is the wife of the Ministry of Cultural Development! And a friend of Nehru's daughter. I think we're really on the map now. We have friends in high places!"

✑ Mr. Ganguly Zindabad!

Mary's pockmarks seemed to have receded, or maybe it was that her bright new orange sari and the brilliant yellow zinnias tucked behind her ear simply outshone them. With a broad smile, she held out a copy of the *Hindustan Times*.

"Jana mem! Look!"

Jana picked up the paper. " 'Pundits Debate Parrot Story,' " she read. " 'Zoologists and psychologists are arguing about how much the famous parrot of Hamara Nagar actually understands of his own speech.' "

She looked up. "Maybe they should debate about how much humans understand of *their* own speech."

"The *Hindustan Times* felt left out since they didn't get the philosopher-tailor story firsthand," said Mary. "So they sent a reporter to see what was going on in town. He learned about the demonstration for Mr. Ganguly! So the next day he went and interviewed Bandhu. Bandhu gave him this song and dance about how he took the parrot into custody for its own protection, because he was afraid it was being mistreated."

"Mistreated!" Jana Bibi spluttered.

"Yes, he gave them a long story about how he had always been an animal lover. Also that he and his wife are especially fond of birds, especially parrots."

After a pause to let the irony sink in, Mary continued: "The reporter asked Bandhu if there was significance in the parrot coming to this very town. Bandhu said yes, this town is very good, very special! Manju and Raju were also there and the reporter coaxed them, Come, say a few words. Raju said, 'Mr. Ganguly zindabad!' Then Bandhu said, 'You see? A miracle! And, by the way, please to give a scholarship to Raju to the best school in the country!'

"And here is the last thing. I saw Manju in the bazaar. She doesn't look pulled down anymore! Wearing lipstick and all."

"Confiscated from Abinath's Apothecary," said Jana. "At least Bandhu gave the loot to his own wife. That's progress, anyway."

⁓ A Run on the Emporium

"You'll wear your fortune-telling costume, right, Mrs. Laird?" Ramachandran had refused Mary's tea but settled in the bay window seat.

"Don't worry," Jana said, "I'll be in full regalia."

"Might we have the lecture here?" Ramachandran asked. "In the emporium, we would barely have enough room for the ladies, let alone any chairs."

It was going to be a challenge to provide seating for the ladies of the American Women's Club, who were coming up from Delhi in a chartered bus. Perhaps, Jana thought, the Victoria would have some chairs they could borrow? She dispatched Tilku with a note to Mr. Dass.

The day before the lecture, a dozen of the Victoria Hotel's men, each with two straight chairs strapped on his back, arrived at the salon. Lal Bahadur Pun directed the unloading, and soon there were four tidy rows of chairs arranged, in between the birdcage and the statue of Saint Francis of Assisi.

"It's a tight squeeze," said Jana. "But I think the ladies will be comfortable."

At noon on the day of the American Women's Club visit, Jana heard the Victoria Hotel rickshaws rolling by. Going out to the gate with Mary, she watched the ladies alight and go into Kwality for lunch.

A short woman who looked like an older—but not very much older—version of Roo Wiley led the way. She wore a bright red suit with black velvet trim and red-and-black high heels and had a corsage of white carnations pinned to her lapel. Another lady appeared to be an only slightly older version yet—Roo's grandmother, thought Jana. Even from a distance, both women's pearls looked expensive.

The other ladies were a complete miscellany. Some wore dresses, others pedal pushers; some had expensive-looking jewelry, others plastic clip-on earrings in the shape of flowers or hearts. In any case, their voices rang out, and their smiles were broad. Their handbags were oversized and, said Mary, "full of money."

"Let us hope that is the case," said Jana.

They went back inside and checked the flowers, straightened the pictures, and let Mr. Ganguly out of his cage and onto Jana's shoulder. While the ladies were still at lunch, Ramachandran came in, clutching a sheaf of notes.

"I haven't done something like this since my BHU days. I was in dramatics there, and I always got stage fright. I can feel the butterflies in my stomach right now." He made fluttering gestures with his fingers and gave a coordinating waggle of his head.

"Come now," Jana said soothingly, "if Padma's astrologer said the day was propitious, it is propitious. All will go well. And you look splendid!"

Ramachandran beamed across his round face. He had on a new silk *dhoti* tied with some South Indian twists and flourishes, and a new silk shirt embroidered with tiny flowers, all dazzling white.

Rambir arrived next, notebook and pencil in hand. "Another news story in the making. This one will go straight to the *Illustrated Weekly of India*."

"Namaskar! Welcome, cherished American guests!" Ramachandran managed to sound both formal and friendly as he addressed the ladies assembled in the borrowed chairs.

"Hello! Namasté! Salaam! *Bonjour!*" Mr. Ganguly bowed from his perch.

"How *adorable*," the ladies said.

Ramachandran looked miffed at being upstaged, but he recovered his composure and his smile. "Ladies! It is a great honor to have you here. I wish to thank Mrs. Wiley, who has brought her distinguished friends . . . and her distinguished mother, too, who is making a tour around the world and a special visit here. It just shows you that American ladies retain their youthful energy. The world is their oyster!"

This brought identical startled smiles from Roo Wiley's mother and grandmother.

"Now," said Ramachandran, "with your kind permission, I'm going to tell you what a person's treasures say about them.

"They say you have a sense of place—of history—of style. That you are not mass-produced, any more than each individual human being is mass-produced. Your treasures are the proof of your journey along life's highways and byways! Souvenirs, of course. But they are more than souvenirs. Sometimes they assist you in creating a persona. Take my friend Mrs. William Laird, sitting in the back row. She is now known to this town, and to

many in India, and even in the world, as Jana Bibi, the inspirer
of excellent fortunes. Mrs. Laird decorated her salon with art-
works from Ramachandran's Treasure Emporium. Each artifact
carried with it the ethos and spirit of its previous owners, so that
within Mrs. Laird's salon is gathered multifarious points of view
and multitudinous influences. The wit and wisdom of the ages!
Mrs. Laird, do rise and take a bow."

Jana rose, and the ladies of the American Women's Club
applauded heartily.

"Jana Bibi zindabad," crowed Mr. Ganguly.

Then Ramachandran talked and talked. He went into Mughal
history, existential philosophy, socialism, and the influence of
African art on Picasso. Jana had a sudden flash of insight. Ramachandran was making up for all the years he would rather have
been a university professor. He was in heaven. The American
ladies' eyes, however, were beginning to look vacant. One actually fell asleep, surprising the others and waking herself with a
start when she gave a barking little snore.

Throughout, Jana felt that Roo Wiley's grandmother was
staring at her intently. Jana looked down at her clothes. Was the
Jana Bibi costume too stagy? she wondered. Had she gone too
far?

While Ramachandran was talking, Roo Wiley's grandmother
took paper and pencil out of her handbag, scribbled a note, and
passed it to Jana. As unobtrusively as possible, Jana opened it and
read, "Where did you get your emerald necklace?" Jana mouthed,
"Ramachandran's," and Roo Wiley's grandmother's perfectly
groomed eyebrows shot up.

The audience having been completely subdued with facts,
theories, and poetic visions, Ramachandran wrapped up his talk.
"And if you have questions, ladies," he added, "I invite you to
come up and talk to me, and then we will proceed to the emporium."

An earnest woman dressed in a sari, looking as odd as most
American women did that way, cornered Ramachandran to ask

him about Rajput miniatures, and a knot of women formed around the proud, if somewhat exhausted speaker.

Meanwhile, Roo Wiley's grandmother was at Jana's elbow. "I'm Pearl Goldsmith," she said. "Would you mind coming over to the window? I'd like to hold those stones up to the light."

They went over to the full light of the bay window, and Jana took off the necklace. Mrs. Goldsmith extracted a small magnifying glass from her handbag and examined the stones.

"You said you got it at Ramachandran's Treasure Emporium? I didn't realize they sold jewelry."

"Oh, it was in a box of old costume jewelry in the back room. Things Ramachandran had been meaning to sort through but hadn't gotten around to yet. He gave it to me, actually, for my fortune-telling attire."

"Well, I must say that was good luck! I can't speak too loudly; it might cause a stampede among these jewelry-collecting ladies."

"Oh?"

The woman whispered. "That big green stone is not glass. It's an emerald."

"It couldn't possibly be a real emerald," said Jana Bibi. "I remember my mother saying most emeralds have a lot of flaws and many are pale and not very pretty. This one looks too dark and green to be real. It doesn't have *enough* flaws."

"Inclusions," corrected the woman. "Honey, I know my emeralds. I've studied them all over the world. That emerald was probably found way across the world in Colombia, in the seventeenth century, mined by Indians with Spanish overseers standing with whips in their hands. Then it would have taken a long journey around the whole continent of South America and across the Atlantic to Spain, where it could have traded hands several times. The Mughal emperors were good customers of the Spaniards."

Jana stared at the woman, who gave the necklace back and put her jeweler's loupe into her purse. "The rough emerald was probably cut and polished here in India, maybe in Agra or Jaipur.

If you don't believe me, you could have its chemical composition analyzed. But I know whereof I speak."

Jana's head was spinning. I'd better look at the rest of that jewelry, she thought. The red paste could be rubies and the blue paste sapphires.

"Then," Mrs. Goldsmith continued, "when the Mughal empire fell, in 1857, jewels started finding their way back to Europe. Paris, London, Edinburgh, Madrid . . . Some got into the crown jewels of European countries . . . but some disappeared. Perhaps your emerald has been back and forth a couple of times. Perhaps it was worn by Queen Mary when she came for the Delhi Durbar of 1911, to be crowned empress of India. I've heard rumors of gems that were stolen from her during that time and never recovered. You could well have one of those."

"Queen Mary—well, when she was still princess—*did* visit Hamara Nagar and stay at the Victoria Hotel," Jana said. "Maybe she had a dinner ring or a brooch or pendant. . . . And the emerald might have been stolen right out of her room at the Victoria."

"Perhaps it wasn't even stolen," said Mrs. Goldsmith. "Maybe she sold it. Or gave it to someone as a reward for doing a good deed. I wouldn't leave it lying around."

Despite Mrs. Goldsmith's attempt to whisper, in ten minutes every woman in the American Women's Club had learned the story of the emerald that had been hiding in a box of costume jewelry in the back room at Ramachandran's. In a flash, they were out the door and heading up the street, urgently buzzing to one another: "If he had jewelry, perhaps other things in his shop are worth a lot of money." "The furniture." "The books." "The statues."

Ramachandran, Rambir, and Jana rushed after them. By the time they were in the Treasure Emporium, it was in an uproar, Aunt Putli gaping and Asha and Bimla utterly bewildered, as the ladies swept from room to room.

One lady headed straight for the Rare Book Corner and examined the frontispiece of every single book. "Oh my God!"

she gasped. "This is an autographed copy of Rudyard Kipling's *Kim*. 'To my friend Cecil Rhodes, with all best wishes!'"

"Madam, madam . . ." said Ramachandran.

"Mr. Ramachandran, I will give you a thousand dollars for this book," said the woman.

Meanwhile, the noise level rose and rose, like a hurricane. "Look at the inscription on this walking stick: Colonel George Everest! A letter from Edwina Mountbatten to Jawaharlal Nehru, and Nehru's report card from Harrow! A silver cigarette case inscribed *Mohammed Ali Jinnah*!"

Ramachandran sank into a chair, one hand pressed against his chest. Dazed, he watched Aunt Putli and Asha and Bimla collect the cash and wrap the purchases in newspaper. Jana and Rambir stared at each other, not knowing what to do. After a while, Rambir shouted at the top of his lungs, "The emporium is closed until further notice! Please vacate! Please leave in an orderly fashion!"

But he could not even be heard over the hubbub. Finally, Jana grabbed a Tibetan gong that had somehow not yet been discovered and thumped on it as hard as she could with its padded wooden mallet. The ladies of the American Women's Club staggered off under armloads of treasures. The cash box of the emporium was bursting. The shelves and tabletops were empty, only a few scraps of string and newspaper left on the floor.

"This *is* a story," said the wide-eyed Rambir. "I will write it up in the PTT office and send it off before they close." And he disappeared out the door.

"Are you all right?" Jana asked Ramachandran, who was slumped in a chair.

"I don't know," he said. "All those old things I never even looked at very carefully. Some of them had been in here forever. To think, I've been babbling about ethos and personality and what not—and all the while, there were objects worth a fortune in honest-to-God rupees. To tell the truth, Mrs. Laird, I don't know whether to laugh or cry."

"Don't cry, Mr. Ramachandran, please don't," said Jana.

"You'll be able to pay . . ." She was going to say "your debts," remembering what Mrs. Paniwalla had confided, but caught herself from being that rude. Besides, Mrs. Paniwalla had probably been full of bluff and nonsense. Instead, she said, "You'll be able to restock in no time. Or renovate your house. Or perhaps both!"

Ramachandran brightened, and he yelled at the minions to start sweeping the floor. "Mrs. Laird, we may just have had more good luck than we can easily absorb. But too much good luck is hardly cause for complaint. On, I say, on we go! To a brighter tomorrow!"

A Postmark

A khaki-clad employee of the PTT arrived at the salon and called, "Is anyone there? Telegram for Laird memsahib."

It was the first telegram Jana had received since arriving in Hamara Nagar. Getting a telegram never bodes well, she thought, remembering the telegrams people had received during the two world wars. Holding her breath, she opened the envelope and unfolded the cable.

It was from Jack. With characteristic thrift, he had composed a tight story. "Family letters contained postmark first commercial airline flight Allahabad to Naini 1911. Collector interested. Minimum two thousand pounds. Letter follows."

Two thousand pounds. Enough to live on for a long time at the Jolly Grant House, to buy big sacks of rice for the household, to pay Mary's wages and keep Tilku in *Bata* tennis shoes. Jana felt dizzy with relief. She was going to be saved from herself, from her bad habit of not paying attention to money. She'd never served the goddess Lakshmi, but now, with charming randomness, Lakshmi seemed to have favored her.

A week later, the promised letter from Jack arrived.

Dear Mother,

Your moving to Hamara Nagar and making friends with the local merchant has indeed turned out to be a piece of colossal good fortune. I've read through the letters. Yours are absolutely charming. Now I understand more about your fairy-tale childhood of playing with maharajahs' children and watching emperors crowned and riding on elephants. I now realize that the shock of life in the mission must have been tremendous. You nursed Father through a horrific illness, and then served as his eyes for twelve more years. You buried Caroline and Fiona. Then you supported yourself—admittedly, in unorthodox ways—in Bombay. And now you set off for adventure at an age when other women are content to be sitting by the fire.

He still sees me as about ninety years old, Jana thought, but she smiled and read on.

An explanation of my telegram. The stamps on the envelopes weren't particularly rare, although my ten-year-old neighbor was delighted to add them to his collection. But there was a rare postmark. *Remember you wrote to Great-Grandfather Jolly about an air letter? It turns out that your letter was sent on February 18, 1911, on the world's first official aerial post, from Allahabad to Naini Junction. The flight was six miles long, a stunt to add excitement to the United Provinces Industrial and Agricultural Exhibition. There were 6,500 pieces of mail, which were then transferred to overland post.*

The fact that we have three *of those pieces—from members of the same family—and that the postmarks are nice and clear makes this quite a find in the philatelic world. I showed them to an expert, and he asked if he could tell the story to the BBC. I didn't think any harm would be done, so a radio reporter chap showed up and took a long interview with me. I told him about Hamara Nagar and Ramachandran's and all, and the story got aired the next day. It's also going to appear in*

Philatelic Weekly. *Please pardon the invasion of privacy, but I know that publicity is more what you're looking for, to put the town on the map. This should help.*

Your loving son,
Jack

On the Map

·ᴄ₰ *Stay of Execution*

Mary brought in the mail—one large manila envelope—and Jana slit it open and withdrew a stack of official-looking papers. The top sheet read:

Ruling: Occupation of Jolly Grant House.

This is to inform you that your papers and tax payments are in order and that you are authorized for another year to occupy the historic property of 108 Central Bazaar.

"Mary! We can stay in the house!"
Mary folded her arms smugly. "Am I not saying that?"
"Let's see what this next document says." Jana scanned it.

Ruling on Charge of Cruelty to Animals Against Mrs. William Laird, 108 Central Bazaar.

Re: One individual of Genus *Psittacula,* species *krameri,* subspecies *manillensis*.

Your case has received careful scrutiny. It has been decided that the individual creature referred to above has not been subjected to cruel or unusual treatment or punishment by its owner.

There were several signatures, stamps and counterstamps, dates, and stickers on both papers.

"Bandhu wrote all those different signatures himself," said Mary.

"But that's fine," Jana said. "What he's saying is, he's not going to harass us anymore. In his own odd way, he's made an apology."

"Better if he came and said sorry in person!" Mary exclaimed.

"Don't expect miracles," said Jana.

"Someone is knocking, Jana mem," said Mary. "I'll go to the door."

"Bother," muttered Jana. "I don't feel like telling any fortunes right this moment."

But it was Zohra, with a smug little smile on her face. She threw off her burqa and gave Jana a hug.

"Guess what, *didi*."

"What?"

Mr. Ganguly was already crowing and flapping. "*Mubarak ho! Congratulations!*"

Jana looked at the bird and then at Zohra.

"Yes?"

"Yes! And there are two of them. . . . The lady doctor heard two with her stethoscope."

"*Mubarak ho* indeed!" Jana said. "That makes up for lost time, doesn't it!"

"I know." Zohra chuckled. "Oh, *didi*, my husband is going around with a big smile on his face. And he is telling me, Don't fatigue yourself. We will hire one houseboy to peel the potatoes and such."

"Excellent," said Jana.

"Only one thing." Zohra's smile faded. "He is still angry at Moustapha. Maybe not purely angry—deep down, maybe he's just very sad, so he feels even angrier. That boy has not come home yet. And my husband says he can't come home. He won't let him in. And I tell him, Don't shut him out." Zohra shook her head slowly. "What will happen, *didi*? Honor—pride—these things will keep them apart when really they are fond . . . when really they love each other."

Jana sighed. "Too often that's true."

"Well," said Zohra, "well, if Moustapha comes here, tell him his uncle wants to speak to him."

Jana nodded. Feroze might deny that he wished to speak to Moustapha, but of course it was true.

Moustapha's Future

"Moustapha! Moustapha zindabad!" Mr. Ganguly was going into ecstatic 360-degree turns on his perch.

"Moustapha, where on earth have you been?"

The last time she'd seen Moustapha had been in Bandhu's lockup. Then his face had been bruised and streaked with dirt, his clothes torn and dirty. Now he was transformed, his hair cut and his beard trimmed; he looked handsome—even distinguished—in a high-collared coat and narrow trousers. This young man is going somewhere, she thought.

"Have you been home?"

He shook his head.

"Where have you been staying?"

"Friends."

What friends, she wondered. Moustapha was now holding out his arm to Mr. Ganguly, who climbed up to his shoulder and nuzzled his ear.

"Well, sit down," Jana said. "Tell me—what's going on?"

Moustapha sat down, started to speak, then stopped and looked out the window.

Jana broke the silence. "Are you all right?"

"I'm all right."

"You know Zohra's news."

"Of course!" said Moustapha. "Who doesn't? The entire neighborhood knows. You'd think my uncle had done something really miraculous."

"It's always miraculous," Jana said.

"Women are so sentimental."

"Did you come here to tell me your views on women?"

Moustapha took a breath. "I came to ask you for something."

"Yes?"

"For a loan. A hundred rupees. To get me to Bombay."

"And what will you do in Bombay?"

"I told you in the jail. I've got the address of Mr. Vincent D'Souza, who is the music director for Dreamistan Studios. He's the one who gave me his card at the talent show. I'm going to go for an audition."

Moustapha spoke with quiet confidence. Jana felt that she had seen a boy turn himself into a man, practically with a single decision.

"Don't worry—I'll pay you back very quickly."

"I'm not worried about repayment," she said.

Moustapha spoke passionately. "Mr. D'Souza says lots of people don't make it in Bombay. Everyone wants to be in films, people line up to be extras in the crowd scenes. . . . As for singers? He says that they're as plentiful as grains of rice. So I will have to work to stand out from the crowd."

"You will."

You know—" Moustapha paused. "We're taught from the earliest age *not* to stand out from the crowd. Don't be *prideful*. It's a sin, it's not Islamic . . . things like that."

"You can still develop your talents without being prideful," said Jana. "I have read that Mohammed Rafi is a quiet, humble gentleman. Do you intend to be that, too?"

"Humble," Moustapha said. "That's not one of my virtues. But I will try to do better." He adopted an exaggerated air of humility that made Jana laugh. "Do you think I can do it?"

"Be humble?"

"No, be a great playback singer."

"Of course! No doubt in my mind."

Moustapha's old mischievous smile came back. "Okay. You'll be hearing from me."

"From you and about you," said Jana. "But one thing. Before I give you the hundred rupees, I want you to make me a promise."

"Of course," said Moustapha quickly.

"I want you to go to your uncle and talk to him. Tell him where you're going, and why."

Moustapha shook his head vehemently. "He'll have a fit!"

"I don't think so," said Jana. "He wants the best for you. And if you'd seen his expression the night you sang . . ."

She saw a curious mix of emotions cross the proud and handsome face.

"After the concert, he was telling me . . . and Zohra . . . that yes, you *will* be the next Rafi sahib."

Moustapha stood up—struggling to contain tears, Jana thought. He put Mr. Ganguly gently back on his perch.

"Okay. I will do that. I will do that for you, because you asked me to. I cannot guarantee what my uncle will say in return. But I will go . . . and talk to him."

Treat Feroze gently and ask his forgiveness for any pain you have caused, Jana wanted to add. But then she told herself, Trust that Moustapha will say the right thing.

ꙮ Pride and Joy

"Yes, I will do the hajj with you next year," Feroze said. During the night on the ledge, he had resolved to do that, and he was not about to back down in his resolve.

Yusuf Baig stopped in his tracks. Why, he almost looks disappointed, thought Feroze. He has always assumed that I will not go to Mecca—or anywhere else, for that matter—even though he has made a great show of urging me to do so all these years.

"Yes, it will be very pleasant to travel with you, and to stay in Bombay with your relatives before we get on the boat." Feroze found himself saying this with conviction and energy and, he had to admit to himself, with delight at Yusuf Baig's astonishment.

"That's . . . that's very good, my friend, very good indeed," said Yusuf Baig. He stared at Feroze as if searching for another topic of conversation. "It must be very quiet in your shop these days. All your workers gone to Lahore for that wedding. That was very good of you to give them time off."

What he did not say was "especially with your nephew disappeared to who knows where." Feroze heard that anyway, but he brushed the thought aside. Instead, he said, "I must get back now and do some stitching. Miss Orley the teacher, she wants her new wool suit soon."

"Yes, yes, you are a hardworking man," said Yusuf Baig. "You are an inspiration to me. And to all."

Strange, Miss Sandra Stuart-Smith's father had said something like that about inspiration when he had come to Feroze's house to thank Feroze for saving his daughter. But I didn't save her, Feroze had said, I just sat there in the same place with her while we waited for someone else to come save us both. But you talked to her, said Stuart-Smith sahib, and kept her mind off her plight. Sandra's father was a man who knew what to say, Feroze had decided, and he had said it in perfect Urdu and with excellent high-class manners. A pity he had not taught the Urdu to his daughter, but that was the way of things. People did not always pass on everything they knew to the next generation.

"Well, I leave you here," said Yusuf Baig, "and return to my humble shop."

My! An expression of humility from Yusuf Baig! Feroze took his leave politely, unlocked the padlock to Royal Tailors, and slid up the wide metal door. The sunshine flooded in, showing some dust on the table-model sewing machine. Feroze found a cloth and wiped off both the table and the machine, then gave the machine a drop or two of oil.

It was later than he usually opened up, and the street was humming with midday commerce. Feroze had not yet put in a full day of work since spending the night on the ledge. The day after that night, he had slept the whole day long, awaking only when Zohra brought him soup and a vial of Abinath's special elixir of vitamins "from A to Zed." She also brought Abinath's special cream to rub on his knees and ankles and shoulders, and, determined to prevent him from catching cold or something worse, she wrapped a long cloth around his throat. With all these ministrations of the past two weeks, he was beginning to feel more normal, although his knees, rather more annoyingly than usual, were troubling him.

Now, determined to get to work, he went to the cupboard and took out the pieces he had cut for Miss Orley's suit. Very fine burgundy-colored wool, with a good-quality silk for the lining. Same as for her last suit, although this time she had given him some buttons that had come off a suit of her mother's. She'd been saving them for years and now, she said, they'd better use them before it was too late.

Settled at the table sewing machine, he was grateful that he did not have to sit on the floor. When his workers got old and could not sit comfortably on the floor themselves, perhaps he would indeed replace the old Singers with new table models. Moustapha was always telling him to do that. Moustapha! He forced the thought of that ingrate out of his mind. He was not going to worry about what that boy thought.

With his employees gone, Feroze realized that he did not have to turn the radio on, nor endure film talk. But now, just a few doors down, a radio was blaring from some other shop, and Feroze was forced to listen to "My Shoes Are Japanese." He tried to block it out of his ears and get on with the day's stitching.

This garment—like everything he did—was going to be up to the standard of Royal Tailors. Feroze would pink the seams very carefully and bind the buttonholes and put just the right amount of padding in the shoulders. He would do the finishing by hand, hem the skirt with small, small stitches that would be invisible from the outside.

The shop was quiet, a bubble of quiet in the noisy street. He had thought he would enjoy it this way. No cousins making their stupid jokes and singing their lewd songs. But it was also . . . so lonely! With Moustapha gone . . . No, he shut out that name again. Moustapha had broken Feroze's family with his rowdy behavior and his disrespect and his disappearance. Feroze would have a new family soon; he did not need the old one. Break and mend, break and mend, that was the cycle of his life. Many times his heart had broken; many times he had pulled himself together and rebuilt.

Break and mend. This happened even to Americans. He thought of Miss Sandra. Princess Grace, Zohra called her. Yes, perhaps she looked like a princess, but really, she was just a sad girl whose family was breaking apart. All of us have pain. A sudden thought came unbidden: perhaps his daughter, Rania, had pain, too. Perhaps—should he have forgiven her? Forgiveness was a virtue; it said so right there in the Qur'an. If Moustapha came back and asked for Feroze's pardon . . . No, that wouldn't happen anyway. Moustapha had too much of a young man's pride.

Feroze squinted at the tension dial on the sewing machine. His eyes were not so good anymore; maybe he would have to go to Sharp Eyes Vision and get some spectacles, as Moustapha had been telling him to do for ages. Feroze's irritation rose again. Why wasn't Moustapha here, with his sharp young eyes, to help Feroze now? If he were here, that would make so much sense. Moustapha was such a careful tailor. All this nonsense about wanting to go to Bombay! For Moustapha's own welfare, Feroze said angrily to himself, he should come back, ask my forgiveness, and stay. The boy will inherit such a well-established business from me.

Now another tune was coming from the radio down the street, and, with a sudden lump in his throat, Feroze recognized it as the song Moustapha sang about Bombay. He saw Moustapha in his white salwar kurta and red vest, in the spotlight of the Far Oaks stage. . . . *This song is for my uncle.* . . . And then Moustapha standing outside the auditorium after his performance, receiving congratulations from strangers.

Suppose the boy *did* go to Bombay and *did* become the next Mohammed Rafi. Wouldn't Feroze burst with pride to hear him on the radio? And more than his own pride—Feroze remembered Moustapha's eyes shining, the laughter spilling out of him after he sang his heart out. It is not just my pride that is at stake, Feroze found himself thinking. It is not just what *I* want. It is the boy's soul.

Get back to your stitching, he told himself, and he picked up the pieces to the jacket of Miss Orley's suit. Skirts are easy, but jackets are more important, he decided, and he would tackle the important thing before the easy thing.

He had sewn the darts, put on the collar, and attached the sleeves when he heard footsteps. He looked up and, momentarily blinded by the bright sunshine, could not see who was standing in the storefront. But the figure stepped forward into the room, and Feroze felt his heart flood with relief and with joy.

"*Salaam aleikum*, Uncle."

Jana Feels at Home

There were only a handful of other people having lunch in the Victoria Hotel. The government engineers were gone, as were the hangers-on from the Futurology Convention. The tourists who had come to see the postmonsoon glory of the hills had also left, leaving only a few parents visiting their children in boarding school.

"The old goat is pretty good today," said Kenneth Stuart-Smith as he attacked the mutton curry.

"It's disgusting," said Sandra. "So was the soup. Leftover

vegetables and mushy lentils. Dad, what did you put in the guidebook?"

"I put that their mulligatawny was authentic and their cuisine eclectic."

"Guidebook?" Jana asked.

"*The Globe-Trotter's Companion,*" said Kenneth.

"You—?"

"I've been doing some moonlighting," said Kenneth. "Writing up northern India for a new tourist guide—a competitor to Fodor's and the Michelin guide. The first edition should be out by the time the tourists come again next year.

"We're including places slightly off the beaten track," he explained, "so that people won't be tripping over other tourists. And including enough information so that you not only know where to eat but what to order when you get there. For example, go to the Why Not? for chili omelets, but to the Hot Spot for cauliflower *pakoras*. I think I gained twenty pounds getting that kind of information."

"Oh, good fun!" said Jana. "What else did you put in about the Victoria?"

"I said that the place was permeated with history. 'Rudyard Kipling and Princess Mary slept here. Not together, of course.'"

"Dad!" Sandra rolled her eyes. "Did you actually say that in the guidebook?"

"No, I didn't."

"And what did you say about Hamara Nagar?" asked Jana.

"I said to check out Jana Bibi's Excellent Fortunes if you wanted your future predicted by an avatar of Vishnu."

"You *did*?"

"I actually did. I said Mr. Ganguly had acquired quite a reputation locally and even nationally by getting a mute child to speak. Also that you would give the tourist a reading with charm and self-deprecating humor. So make certain you're charming and self-deprecating when someone comes in clutching a copy of *The Globe-Trotter's Companion* under his arm."

"All right, I'll do my best. Did you put Feroze in?"

"Of course. I called him the philosopher-tailor and said that he would give you wise saws as well as straight seams."

"Poor Feroze! The pressure is on now. People will be expecting pearls of wisdom to drop from his lips when he's taking their measurements. 'Waist: thirty; the youth of the body has gone but the youth of the spirit remains, is it not, madam?' "

Kenneth chuckled. "That's the price of fame. You people wanted to save the town, and you succeeded. Be careful what you ask for."

"Oh, how could we regret saving the town?"

"You couldn't. I guess it's more accurate to say, Be careful how you bill yourselves. People will demand that you live up to your advertising."

Jana turned to Sandra. "So, what did you decide to do? Will you be back next term?"

"No," said Sandra. "I'm not coming back. Dad's letting me go to the American International School in Delhi. But we'll come back on vacation when it gets so darn broiling down there."

They munched their way through the rest of the meal, and even Sandra said that the ginger soufflé was good. "Better than fish-eye tapioca at school, anyway! Dad, put the ginger soufflé in the book."

After dinner, they walked through the bazaar, which was still lit up for evening. At the Jolly Grant House, they paused on the threshold, and Sandra threw her arms around Jana.

"Good-bye."

Jana shook hands with Kenneth Stuart-Smith.

"Come visit us in Delhi," he said.

"That's kind of you." She looked at him, thinking, Perhaps I will.

"No really, do."

"I well may. Safe return," she said, and went into the house.

That evening she sat in the tower, thinking, How wonderful and peaceful it is to be at home. She watched the sun going down, dipping into the orange of the first stripe of the horizon and then falling deeper and disappearing into the browny mauve of the next layer. The trees and buildings she could see from the tower were black cutouts, shadow puppets against the evening display of dark and light.

Mr. Ganguly flapped his wings. She played him a few jigs on the violin, and he danced on his perch. But then her own music was drowned out by the strains of Lal Bahadur Pun practicing. He was sounding a retreat march—a march traditional for when the day's work was done and the troops returned to the barracks. She put down her fiddle and scratched Mr. Ganguly on the head.

"We're home, aren't we?" she asked.

"Good bird," he said.

GLOSSARY OF TERMS

Many of these words have alternate spellings.

Adab   a polite Urdu greeting

Allahu akbar   an Arabic phrase meaning "God is great" or "God is the greatest"

Almirah   a freestanding closet or wardrobe

Angrezi   English, British

anna   a coin worth one-sixteenth of a rupee

aré   an expression of surprise, dismay, or alarm

ayah   a nursemaid or lady's maid

baba   an affectionate term of address; also, a child

badmash   a villain or scoundrel

baksheesh   an offering of alms; a tip or bribe

bapré bap   an expression of surprise, dismay, alarm

bearer   waiter

begum   a Muslim lady of rank

Bharat Mata   the personification of Mother India

Binaca Geet Mala   a popular radio music show sponsored by Binaca toothpaste

biri   a small cigarette consisting of a twist of tobacco in a tobacco leaf

Birla   the name of a prominent and wealthy business family in India

chai   tea; does not imply tea with spices

chaprassi   an office messenger

charpoy   a wooden-framed bed or stringed cot

chokidar   a watchman

chota peg   a small alcoholic drink

darzi   a tailor

Devanagari   a script in which Hindi, Sanskrit, and other languages are written

dhobi   a laundry man

dhoti   a traditional men's garment consisting of a length of cloth wrapped around the waist and legs in various ways

didi   big sister

Divali   a Hindu festival of lights

djinn   a spirit that can inhabit animal and other forms

ekdum!   right now!

ghazal   a lyric poem on love or other themes, often set to music

Gurkha   a soldier of Nepalese origin in British or Indian armies

hajj   the pilgrimage to Mecca

hajji   one who has made the hajj

harmonium   a keyboard instrument whose sound is produced by hand- or foot-operated bellows; depending on its size, it can be positioned on a table or on the floor

hill station   a resort established in the mountains, at first for colonial rulers; later used for general tourism

Hindustan   India

huzoor   a deferential term of address; "Your Highness"

imam   a Muslim religious leader; one who leads prayers in a mosque

Inshallah an Arabic phrase meaning "If God wills it"

Jai Hind! Long live India! or Victory to India!

ji a suffix indicating respect; also, an expression of assent or inquiry

Jinnah, Mohammed Ali the first governor general of Pakistan

jungli uncivilized, rough; an uncouth person

kabariwalla a junk dealer

kameez a tunic, shirt, or dresslike garment

khud a precipice, cliff, or mountainside

Khuda hafiz an Urdu expression of parting meaning "God be with you"

ki-jai! hooray for! or victory to!

kismet fate, destiny

kukri a carved knife carried by Gurkha soldiers

kurta a loose collarless shirt

laddu a sweet ball-shaped confection

mali a gardener

malik a master, owner, or lord

Mangalore Ganesh a brand of *biri*

memsahib ma'am, Mrs.; may be shortened to *mem*, informally.

missahib miss

mochi a shoemaker

mofussil the provinces, rural areas, outlying districts

mony a mickle maks a muckle a Scottish expression meaning "Keep saving a little and you will have a lot"

mubarak ho! Congratulations!

namaskar Hello, Good day, or Good-bye

namasté Hello, Good day, or Good-bye

nawab a Muslim ruler, prince, governor, or nobleman

Nehru, Jawaharlal   the first prime minister of India

paan   a chew made of betel leaf wrapped around areca nuts and various spices and flavorings

pukka   good, genuine, solid, completed (literally, "cooked")

Ramadan   the ninth month of the Muslim calendar, during which daily fasting occurs

ram ram   a Hindu greeting

sadhu   a holy man or ascetic

sahib   sir, Mr., man of importance

sahiba   a lady, a term of reference or address meaning "your ladyship"

salaam   an Urdu greeting; hello or good-bye (literally, "peace")

salaam aleikum (also **w'aleikum salaam**)   peace to you

salwar   loose trousers, usually tapered and fitted at the ankle

shukriya   thank you

subedar-major   a senior rank for a Viceroy's commissioned officer in the Indian Army during British rule (similar to a non-commissioned officer elsewhere)

sweeper   a man or woman who cleans floors, drains bathrooms, etc., or sweeps streets and other outdoor places

Tata   name of a wealthy Parsi family preeminent in Indian industry and philanthropy

thik hai   okay; that's fine

veena   a plucked stringed instrument with a long neck, used in classical Indian music

wah   wow

wallah   a person associated with a particular trade, place, activity, or situation

zindabad!   long live!

ACKNOWLEDGMENTS

I wish to thank the people who made this book possible:

my agent, Suzanne Gluck, who I believe has magic powers;

my warm and wonderful editor, Marjorie Braman, who suggested making Jana Bibi the anchor of the series, and who has taught me so very, very much;

Joanna Levine at Henry Holt, who combines tact and competence with a keen editorial eye;

Bonnie Thompson, whose meticulous copyediting transformed the raw manuscript into something pukka;

my sister and patient first reader, Lee Woodman, whose unfailing loyalty never clouds her professional judgment; and

my generous friend Elizabeth Berg, who egged me on.

Thanks also to the many people—and other sentient beings—who gave me ideas and information:

Jerry Karr, who told stories while his parrot, Annie, figured out new ways to play tricks on human beings;

veterinarian Cindy Fulton, who answered lots of questions while *her* parrot, Cosmo, listened anxiously;

palmist Juliet Bell, who has things firmly in hand; and

tarot reader Tim Boyd, who read Jana Bibi's cards.

• • •

And I offer my appreciation to the beloved folks who keep me on an even keel:

My sister Jane Cohen, my cousin Nancy Schlosser, and my son, Ben Coonley.

I also add a note in grateful remembrance of my parents, Everett and Ruth Woodman, for giving me such a treasure trove of childhood memories.

Finally, Woodstock School friends, including Charlene Chitambar Connell, Ted Chitambar, and Phil Jones, have answered many questions over the years about such things as cricket magazines, the price of music lessons in 1960, and Himalayan trekking. Hank Lacy jokingly asked, "Are you going to have a Gurkha piper?" so Lal Bahadur Pun is for him.

etc.

extras...

essays...

etcetera

more author
About Betsy Woodman

more book
About *Jana Bibi's Excellent Fortunes*

. . . and more

Joanna Puza Photography

Betsy Woodman spent ten childhood years in India, studied in France, Zambia, and the United States, and now lives in her native New Hampshire. She has worked as a teacher, history book editor, survey researcher, and music director. She has contributed nonfiction pieces and several hundred book reviews to various publications, and was writer/editor for the award-winning radio documentary series, *Experiencing War*.

This is Betsy's debut novel and the first of a planned series to feature Jana and her parrot, Mr. Ganguly.

To contact the author, please visit her website: www.betsywoodman.com ■

There's always a story behind a story, and another one behind that. I grew up in India because my parents, Everett and Ruth Woodman, wanted to see the world. My father came from a small town in New Hampshire, my mother from a Boston suburb. In 1952, they set off for Madras (now Chennai), India, with their two little girls: me, age six, clutching a Raggedy Andy doll, and Lee, age four, who was in charge of Raggedy Ann. My dad was headed for a stint as a cultural affairs officer at the United States Information Service; my mother, who had trained as a ballet dancer, was seven months pregnant with my sister Jane. We would spend ten years in India, where my youngest sister, Deborah, would also be born.

When we were back in the States on home leave, people would ask, "Have you ever ridden on an elephant? Have you seen the Taj Mahal?" They assumed our lives were somewhat exotic.

They didn't know the half of it. Our lives *were* exotic, but my sisters and I didn't think of it that way at the time. For us, it was just ordinary existence. Completely normal to live next door to three young movie stars who were the rage of India, as we did in Madras, and to have my mother studying dance with their guru and performing with their troupe. Routine to vacation on houseboats in Kashmir, to have dancing bears, stilt walkers, and snake charmers perform for our birthday parties. Commonplace to have a household staff of seven—or eight? nine?—with extras signed on when there was a new baby or houseguests coming for a while. My best friend in Delhi at age ten was a Muslim princess, and for a while our next-door neighbors kept a tiger in the backyard, as a gift for Jacqueline Kennedy.

When we walked out the door, the pageant of India swirled by, day after day. Camels and bullock carts on the streets of the capital, cows with painted horns helping themselves to tomatoes in the marketplace, wandering holy men, a perennial fashion show of women in beautiful saris or swirling skirts and shawls, even the humblest decked out with earrings, necklaces, and armloads of bangles.

There were also the Indian holidays, religious and secular. To name only a few: Holi, when people gleefully smeared colored powder and squirted colored water on one another; Divali, when the nights rang with fireworks and houses were lit up with little clay lamps; Republic Day, with its awe-inspiring parade of soldiers, cavalry, tanks, elephants, and folk dancers.

The parade occurred not only on Republic Day, or from afar. It was right in our house, all the time. Hating the paranoia and parochialism of the Cold War, my dad had a simple approach to diplomacy. "Our job," he wrote home, "is to make friends. And what could be more fun!"

Make friends my parents did, with people of all ages, nationalities, and walks of life. Our "head bearer" (the majordomo of the household) kept track of how many dinner and lunch guests we had per annum; some years, counting repeat invitees, it totaled more than nine hundred. Our Christmas Day reception, held on the lawn in the bright December sun, became a Delhi institution—after the first year or two, my parents didn't even bother to issue invitations to it; people just knew, and they came.

Not only diplomats visited our house, although there were plenty of those—American, Iranian, German, Cam-

bodian, British, Dutch, Canadian. There were Sikh indus-
trialists, Japanese businessmen. An American dancer
came to pay his respects and ended up teaching at the
ballet school my mother had founded. A well-known
Indian painter would sit cross-legged on the terrace,
chugging whisky and spouting politics while he made
brilliant, swift sketches with our school pastels. A young
Indian academic always bubbled over with ideas; he
urged me to learn Sanskrit so that I could boast of being
"the only American teenage Sanskrit scholar." My parents' guests included filmmakers, airline pilots, teachers,
college presidents.

When the guests weren't there, the vendors were, and
they, too, were marvelously colorful. A favorite jeweler
came often to display loose gems on a cloth on the living
room floor; then he and my dad would sketch designs for
earrings and brooches on the backs of envelopes, for gifts
for my mom. Other merchants came with brass and cop-
per wares, magazines, embroidered tablecloths.

Life was endlessly rich and entertaining, and we over-
flowed with creative projects. "Little theatre begins here,"
said one local newspaper article, showing a picture of
Jane, at age eight, putting on a puppet show. We orga-
nized fairs with booths of games. Lee and I were always at
work writing, acting, and choreographing. We copro-
duced family newspapers, never lacking for stories with
all those people in the house.

We wrote plays, generally tales of crime and adventure. One of them we called "The Abduction of Brenda
Brussels." Another was based on Washington Irving's
"The Legend of Sleepy Hollow," and we staged it in the
neighbors' driveway so that we could build their pony
into the plot. Ichabod Crane was supposed to gallop
wildly away, but when the time came, the pony wouldn't
so much as trot, not even when goaded on by our yells of

"Hi-yo, Silver!" It plodded off, leaving us to rescue the climax with extradramatic acting.

The time came for high school, and I went off to Woodstock School, a coed missionary boarding school in the first range of the Himalayas. Here, too, there were new people to meet: American missionary kids of all different stripes, from the fundamentalist evangelicals to the relatively worldly Methodists; Nepalese aristocrats (who always seemed to be the backbone of the soccer team); kids from Thailand, Denmark, Taiwan . . .

Add to that the fascinations of the nearby town of Mussoorie, which, like Hamara Nagar in *Jana Bibi,* had three distinct bazaars, or shopping areas, full of textile and bangle shops, Tibetan jewelry peddlers, movie theaters and tea shops, and other ways for students to spend their allowances.

With all this wonderful material, I might have written *Jana Bibi* or some other book at an early age and lived happily ever after. It didn't exactly happen that way.

My family came back to the States, where I finished high school in New London, New Hampshire (oh, that first winter!), went to Smith College, married, taught French, studied and taught in Zambia for a year with my husband, and got a master's degree in anthropology from Brandeis University. Later, I raised my son, Ben (that was my practicum in primatology), and worked as a computer programmer.

From the mid-1970s on, I wrote hundreds of book reviews, mainly for *Kliatt* magazine, and the editors often assigned me books set in India. I'd go chat with them, and as I was leaving, they'd always say, "Oh, take whatever books you want from the pile we *aren't* reviewing." Free drugs for a book addict! I carried off bags and bags. Books by the South Indian writer R. K. Narayan; by Brits-in-India Rumer Godden and Paul Scott; by the gentle Anglo-Indian writer Ruskin Bond. Later, I also reviewed for *Publishers Weekly* and, much after that, for SoundCommentary .com.

It was after a trip back to India that I decided I had to get my own India experiences down on paper. I was lucky enough to join Sally Brady's writing group, which included Elizabeth Berg, Sebastian Junger, and other wonderful writers. On the first day, I thrust a three-hundred-page manuscript into Sally's hands. After reading it, she sat me down and fixed me with a kind but honest eye. "You can certainly write," she said. "But . . . there's no plot. There's no character development. And you also have a few problems with style." I had a lot to learn.

I also had some other things coming up, including a divorce and a move to New Hampshire. I settled into my new life, fact-checked history textbooks, did social surveys, studied the recorder, and joined a Scottish music society. I kept reading, writing, and reviewing, and books about India continued to fill up my shelves. I now also had another interest: Indian movies, increasingly available on DVD. When Netflix arrived, I could binge with impunity on the last sixty years of Indian filmmaking.

I liked watching the movies from the 1950s and '60s because the street scenes and the interiors were very much what I remembered. Instead of the enormous crowds, air pollution, street traffic, cell phones, television, and computers of modern India, these movies showed stubby-shaped Hindustan taxis and horse-drawn tongas, on streets that looked, by today's standards, practically empty.

I was also thrilled to rediscover songs I'd heard coming from radios in the bazaars as a kid: "Mera Joota Hai Japani" (My Shoes Are Japanese); "Chal Mere Ghode, Tik Tik Tik" (Go, My Horsey, Tik Tik Tik); "Hava Mein Udta

Jaaye, Mera Lal Dupatta" (Off It Goes in the Wind, My Red Scarf). Then I found clips of them on YouTube. It shows how long scraps of songs can stick in your head that all I had to do was pick up the phone and sing one line, and my sister Lee could instantly fill in with the next. People still sing these songs in India.

My interest in Indian film went hand in hand with a campaign to learn more Hindi, my knowledge of which had been embarrassingly scanty. There is a story about an American missionary who came back to the States after thirty years and was asked to give a prayer "in the language of the people you served." All he knew how to do in Hindi was count to twenty, so he did that with dramatic intonation and reverent pauses. When he had finished, someone at the back of the room cried out, *"Shabash!"* which means "Bravo!" I pictured something like that happening to me.

I now have an ever-growing passion for Hindi, with its onomatopoeia, shadings of politeness, and, as at least one textbook so winningly put it, "coloring verbs." (Lest anyone underestimate its importance, Hindi is also one of the five most widely spoken languages on earth.)

Not long ago, after several decades of collecting material, I ran out of excuses. So I wrote a book I intended to be the first of a boarding school series, possible audience unclear. But the real-life material wouldn't stay put on the page; the milieu changed, the town took on a character of its own, and adult characters crept into the plot. A Muslim tailor . . . his nephew who wanted to be a singer in the movies . . . the owner of a store called the Treasure Emporium . . . Then, one day, I tossed off ten pages about a fortune-teller of Scottish origin who had a talking parrot. Jana Bibi was born. ■

Jana Bibi is Scottish, not arbitrarily, and not only because I had been playing Scottish music when I conceived of her. I saw Jana (born Janet MacPherson) as coming from a long line of Scots who worked in India—even before the time of the British Empire. Scots were heavily represented in the civil service, the army, the professions, and as tea planters, missionaries, and businessmen in British imperial India. Scottish educators founded schools and colleges; Scottish architects designed monuments and public buildings. The Scottish cemetery in Kolkata has fifteen hundred graves.

Moreover, many Scottish men, especially in the eighteenth century, took up Indian dress, ate Indian food, and married Indian wives. William Dalrymple's stunning travel and history books, including *White Mughals,* tells about some of them. Flamboyant Scottish characters in India existed in real life, not just in fiction.

Jana is direct, pragmatic, and flexible and connects easily to people, no matter what their nationality or place on the social scale. She is at home in India, and she doesn't feel happy anywhere else. It's not surprising that she becomes an Indian citizen. At the wane of the British Empire, in newly independent countries all over the world, at least a few Brits "stayed on."

Jana's son, Jack Laird, in contrast, wants to keep the categories distinct and is working very hard to carve out a simple national identity for himself. His birth and early childhood in India and his father's American roots don't interest him at all. He goes at being Scottish with a vengeance—bagpipes, golf, and all. You can be sure that he attends formal social functions back in Glasgow in a kilt.

Lal Bahadur Pun, as a musician and a soldier, also represents a remnant of empire and, in his own musical way, is a world citizen. As for bagpipes as a weapon? John Master's memoir *Bugles and a Tiger* describes Gurkha pipers playing for British army officers before dinner with a sound like "an approaching squadron of jets." I think the monkeys in Jana Bibi's Jolly Grant House would indeed scamper before such an onslaught of sound. Indeed, I read a news story about how the Austrian capital of Vienna had a piper drive the rats out of its sewers in 2010.

"Mary Thomas" doesn't sound like an Indian name, but it is common enough among South Indian Christians. The "Madrassi ayah" (nursemaid) is a character found in Indian fiction and in real life; my family employed one in Madras and two in New Delhi. Two were lovely, but one was very bossy and spanked my sisters and me with an old slipper. (My mother didn't believe this until the ayah got into a fight with an ex-lover in our driveway and broke his arm.) In contrast, Mary Thomas is definitely not violent, but she does have a strong will. Though from a very low caste, she does not have the typical subservient and fatalistic attitude; she has rejected her "sweeper" past and learned to read and write, and also to cook. Working for foreigners has given her a good opportunity to escape her origins.

The contemplative Feroze Ali Khan is one of the most important characters in the book. In India, the *darzis,* or tailors, are very often Muslim, as was Faiz Mohammed, who sewed for my classmates and me at Woodstock School. Like Feroze, Faiz would jot down our measurements in a little notebook, and he would consult a Sears, Roebuck catalog for styles. Did he write his private thoughts in his notebook when he got home? It's not hard for me to imagine that he did. A vein of sentiment and philosophy runs deep in the Urdu-speaking people of India and Pakistan, even among the humble. In 1961, the Pakistani camel driver invited to the United States by Vice President Lyndon Johnson charmed everyone with his poetic statements. When Ramachandran, in *Jana Bibi*, says, "We're all poets and philosophers here," he means it.

Moustapha, as a character, is partly self-indulgence on my part . . . the beautiful young man with the golden voice who wants to be a singer in the movies. But lest he be dismissed as a cliché, I must point out that in real life, there are some famous examples of people in the Indian film industry who came from implausible backgrounds: a barber's son, a fruit merchant's son, a bus conductor . . . And Moustapha might indeed succeed in cinema. In the film industry, Muslims, a largely disadvantaged minority in India, work side by side with Hindus, Parsis, and Christians, and some have become megastars, including legendary playback singer Mohammed Rafi (1924–1980) and modern Bollywood giants Shah Rukh Khan and Aamir Khan.

Ramachandran and Rambir are high-caste Hindus (although not Brahmans). Although Ramachandran has kept more to traditional ways and dress than Rambir has, both have made unconventional choices by settling in Hamara Nagar. University graduates, entertaining conversationalists—they owe a little bit to my dad's friend who wanted me to be a teenage Sanskrit scholar.

Because I don't know any villains personally, Bandhu Sharma had to come out of my imagination, and also (perhaps this is not a surprising confession) out of Hindi movies. If his turnaround seems overly sentimental, my defense is that in plenty of Hindi movies, especially the old ones, bad guys have a change of heart, and gangsters weep when they disappoint their mothers.

For the Far Oaks students, I barely scratched the surface of my own boarding school experience.

Finally, Mr. Ganguly, Jana Bibi's parrot. In India, members of his tribe (*Psittacula krameri manillensis)* are everywhere; they swoop down like green clouds and have conferences in the trees. Good talkers, they were brought to Europe in the time of Alexander the Great, and are now favorite pets all over the world.

At the end of this book, we leave Jana in a tranquil state. However, I worry about Moustapha in Bombay, and about Ramachandran, with his growing family. Editor Rambir could easily work himself to exhaustion. Also, with a Cold War going on, could Kenneth Stuart-Smith be collecting more information than the merits of the local tea shops? Might Jana find romance? I'm eager to revisit Hamara Nagar for the next book, and confident that, no matter what, Mr. Ganguly will provide his candid avian opinions.

MAGIC CARPETS

Here are a few films that would have been shown in 1960 at a movie theater like Hamara Nagar's Bharat Mata. I like them for their engaging plots and zingy song-and-dance sequences, and for the ideals they express—redemption, reconciliation, hard work, and the search for justice.

Boot Polish (1954). Two orphans take to the streets, determined to earn their living without resorting to begging.

Do Aankhen Barah Haath (Two Eyes and Twelve Hands, 1957). A prison warden tries to rehabilitate six murderers on a remote country farm.

Jis Desh Mein Ganga Behti Hai (The Land Where the Ganges Flows, 1960). A simple trusting minstrel wanders into a gang of outlaws and falls in love with the leader's daughter.

Mother India (1957). A village woman struggles to surmount repeated catastrophes.

SOME MEMOIRS OF PEOPLE AND PLACES

These memoirs by Westerners may help explain why Jana Bibi considers India home. Stephen Alter's *All the Way to Heaven: An American Boyhood in the Himalayas* (New York, Henry Holt and Co., 1998) chronicles American missionary life in the hill station of Mussoorie in the mid-twentieth century. In *A Time to Dance, No Time to Weep* (New York, William Morrow, 1987) British author Rumer Godden describes, among other things, surviving in World War II India as (essentially) a single mother living on a shoestring. Norah Burke was the daughter of a British Forest Officer in the early twentieth century; her *Jungle Child* (New York, W. W. Norton & Company, Inc., 1955) recalls the enchantment of that experience.

As for evocation of place, R. K. Narayan's *My Days: A Memoir* (London, Penguin, 1989) is good background reading for his novels set in the fictional town of Malgudi. Ruskin Bond's *Landour Days: A Writer's Journal* (New Delhi, Penguin, 2002) takes us into the first range of the Himalayas. Narayan's terrain is South India, Bond's is in Jana Bibi's territory, but both writers pull me in and make me feel at home. ■

13

1. The idea of going on a pilgrimage comes up several times throughout the novel. Are there any parallels to be drawn between Jana's decision to live as a missionary or her decision to move into the Jolly Grant House and Feroze's pending pilgrimage to Mecca? What about Moustapha's journey to Bombay to pursue his musical career?

2. What role does Western society and culture play in this novel?

3. What purpose does Jack serve in this novel? What image does he project of life outside of India? Do you see Jana differently once Jack has been introduced in the story?

4. How does Jana's history help shape her as a person?

5. How does religion affect the characters' lives?

6. Compare the different images of family we see in this novel: Jana and her son; Jana and her adopted family (Tilku, Mary, etc.); Feroze, Moustapha, and Zohra; Police Chief Bandhu, Manju, and Raju; and Sandra and her father. More specifically, how do the parent-child relationships differ? What do they have in common?

7. What role does the Far Oaks School play in the daily life of the small town?

8. Between his conversations with Yusuf Baig and his diaries, the author gives us many chances to get to know Feroze. Does the Feroze we see with Yusuf Baig differ from the Feroze we see through his diary?

9. Music is everywhere in Hamara Nagar. Discuss its different functions throughout the novel.

10. Is there a moral to be taken from this novel?

11. Do you like the way the author ended this novel? Do you think Jana will ever leave India? Why or why not? What does the book have to say about nationality, belonging, and home? ■

Namaste
from
THE WOODMANS

Everett M. Woodman

For more on Betsy, Jana, and the whole gang, please visit
www.betsywoodman.com, where you'll find photos, notes
on the writing process, and much more, including news
about Jana Bibi's upcoming adventures!